Poseidon's
Scar

The sequel to Echo and the Sea

Matthew Phillion

Poseidon's Scar
Lost Continuity Press
Contact:
theindestructiblesbook@gmail.com
www.theindestructiblesbook.com
February 2019
Printed in the United States of America
© 2019 Matthew Phillion
First Edition: © Matthew Phillion / Lost Continuity Press
ISBN-13: 978-0-9979165-9-1
Cover Design by Sterling Arts and Design:
http://www.sterlingartsanddesign.com
"Echo Diving - Silhouette" art by Matthew Phillion

To Steph, the navigator
and
To Lucas — welcome aboard, little man

Acknowledgments

I'll be honest: I didn't know if there'd be a sequel to *Echo and the Sea*.

I knew I wanted to write one, for sure, but sometimes writing feels like it's done in a vacuum – you send a story out into the world and you're not sure anyone will find it, or if they do, whether or not they'll want more.

I worked the comic con circuit this past summer, though, and I was incredibly encouraged by the number of people who came up to me asking when the next adventure of Echo and her friends would happen. I didn't realize that people were waiting for the story to continue, and, because of them, I walked away from those conventions knowing I had a job to do – and knowing that there were people out there who cared about Echo and her crew and wanted to learn more.

I always have an idea for the next story when the previous one concludes, but I also always want to make sure that each tale has a true ending as well. But clearly, *Echo and the Sea* left a few things unfinished. It was time to get back to work.

I will say that almost everything about *Poseidon's Scar* surprised me. The enemies were not what I first envisioned, nor were all of the character arcs. New heroes emerged I didn't know existed until they first appeared on the page. I also found some connective tissue to the overarching "Indestructiverse" that more directly ties Echo's crew to the other heroes in the world she inhabits. I stumbled across mythological references I'd never heard of and took the characters places I never expected.

So my first thank-you goes out to those readers who approached me at the conventions this year to say you wanted more of Echo, Yuri, Artem, and Barnabas. You're the reason this book happened right now. Thank you for your inspiration.

I have to thank all the usual suspects who make these books possible as well. Editing props go out to Christine Geiger and Jay Kumar for saving me from myself over and over again from typos and grammatical errors and my inability to spell "dinghy" right. Thanks to Stephanie Buck for being a sounding board for not only the story but keeping me sane on the business side of writing as well, all the time, every day. Colin Carlton took time from his own writing work to offer awesome feedback on story and motivation, and Christian Sterling Hegg, as always, created yet another beautiful cover and let me harass him endlessly about imagery and color palettes.

And last but not least, thanks to my family, who puts up with the weird uncle who is always in superhero tee shirts and talking about worlds that don't exist. I appreciate that you bring me back to the real world so I don't get lost at sea.

Now then. Hope aboard the Endless with me and let's set sail. There's sea monsters to fight and strange lands to explore together.

Prologue: The hole in the bottom of the sea

The afanc had not felt pain in hundreds of years.

For centuries, the beast had been the undisputed king of the stretch of ocean it called home. Nothing threatened the afanc; smaller creatures fled in terror at the very hint of its presence. Once, perhaps three hundred years ago, another of its kind challenged the afanc for this territory, and the water became clouded with red as they fought a silent, elemental battle. But that was the last time this creature had felt anything resembling pain.

Until that were-shark sunk tooth and claw into the afanc's snout, rending and tearing, a feral, relentless fury that drove the afanc to flight.

This raw, ragged pain drove the afanc mad. And it felt something it had not experienced for as long as it could remember: fear.

After the battle with the were-shark, the great beast took shelter in the ravine that lacerated the ocean floor beneath its territory. The Atlanteans called this long, narrow wound Poseidon's Scar, but the afanc had no need for names. It was simply a place where it sometimes basked in the warmth created by lava flows below. It had certainly never reached the bottom. Nothing lived there. No prey, no mates. Nothing but emptiness, a great black void occasionally lit by slow-moving snakes of molten rock.

But now it was safe harbor, shelter from the mad thing that had turned the afanc's snout to meat.

The beast stayed in the ravine for several days, healing and waiting. It didn't understand, in its simple, ancient mind, that it remained out of fear. The afanc lacked the self-awareness for that. But the monster, bigger than a school bus, remained in hiding, soaking in the warmth from the lava, safe from prying eyes.

A few days later, it saw the bomb fall.

During the battle the Atlanteans had driven some sort of vessel into the seabed near the Scar. It lay there like the corpse of a metal whale, a sunken vessel never to be found. But the sands shift in this part of the ocean, and the vessel had disturbed the ground upon impact, unsettling the whole area. The metal frequently creaked and groaned as the dead submarine settled.

At a certain point, a cylindrical object rolled out.

The afanc had no point of reference for what this object might be. If any of the Atlanteans saw it they might have guessed, but this was a forgotten, hidden place, rarely frequented by them.

The current toyed with the cylinder, rocking it back and forth. Over the course of days, it moved closer, and closer, and closer to the edge of the Scar.

And eventually, it simply rolled over the edge, tumbling into the darkness below.

The afanc watched curiously, knowing whatever it was, the object was not food, but not believing it to be a threat, either. The beast was no stranger to falling debris. With the calm curiosity of a creature who had all the time in the world, the afanc observed as the cylinder plummeted, crashing against the stone edge of the Scar, disappearing into the darkness below, occasionally lit gently by the reddish glow of a lava stream.

None knew how deep Poseidon's Scar really was. Perhaps the cylinder might have fallen forever. Perhaps it would reach the center of the Earth.

But not this time. The cylinder—a surface to air missile, a

weapon of mankind—landed nose-first in a pool of lava. It sat there for a moment like a knife jabbed into a countertop.

And then it exploded.

The afanc began to flee at the first tremor of the explosion, afraid for the second time in such a short order. Stone split and fell from the Scar's walls. Bubbles of air escaped from below, pinned beneath the molten surface, rising to the surface filled with noxious poisons.

The afanc regained its composure, if such a beast could do so, and, feeling suddenly more curious than fearful, swam deeper to investigate.

The water where the explosion occurred was turbulent, tangy with a chemical taste the afanc had never experienced before. Something in the water burned the fresh wounds on the monster's face. It drifted ever deeper, feeling once more like the master of its own domain.

Then it saw the eyes looking up at it from below. Yellow eyes, many of them, blinking and glowing, watching and waiting.

Something deep in the ancient instincts of the afanc told the beast to swim away. Three times, three times fear entered the monster's heart after a millennium without. Old memories, thoughts that carried on through some inborn, genetic knowledge, screamed out at it.

Flee. Flee now.

The afanc turned to swim for open water.

It felt the first teeth bite into its tail, sharp, needle-like pain it tried to shrug off and ignore. But then more teeth, nipping and tearing at its fins, at its sides, the water growing red with the beast's blood and gummy with its own shredded flesh.

The afanc had ruled this stretch of water for centuries. But in that moment, its reign was over, its body given over to the sea, as all things are.

Chapter 1: New Tortuga

Echo didn't like to admit it, but she'd started to get attached to New Tortuga.

The pirate haven—built like an M.C. Escher drawing of a Mervyn Peake novel—had become a temporary home for Echo and her crew after the events in Atlantis. Well, she thought, not directly after. They'd spent some time on the open seas, looking for trouble and looking to stay out of it, mostly avoiding anyone involved with Atlantis or its near-war with the surface until things settled down. But after a period of aimless wandering on the high seas, they'd settled here, among the other freaks and rejects, to try to get their bearings and figure out where to go next.

She walked through the main marketplace, a net bag of fruit and breads casually looped around the prongs of her trident as she ate an apple with her free hand. The trident at this point was mostly for show, since it took only one incident in which Echo was accosted for the general populace of New Tortuga to know to leave her well enough alone. She'd thrown a cyclops—a literal cyclops, with one eye and a hands-y attitude—bodily over the edge of a rope bridge, screaming as he fell a hundred feet into the water below.

Still, she carried the trident everywhere. She amused herself with how casual she'd become with it. Today it was an implement for carrying groceries. Other times it was a percussion instrument as she walked and whistled. Regardless, the weapon felt like a part of her, now, as if she'd been training with it her whole life instead of just a few months with Artem.

Artem still worked Echo hard, trying to wake up further latent Atlantean abilities locked away in her mind, but he'd been distracted lately. She worried about the Amazonian. He'd lost his husband during a vicious attack on their home island, and while Artem had found the revenge he sought, Echo wasn't sure he'd found time to process his loss or to grieve.

I know I haven't, Echo thought, feeling guilty, as she often did, that her mother was not here to enjoy these adventures. She felt guiltier still that she found this life so much fun. I shouldn't have had to lose her to be this free, Echo thought. Maybe I haven't figured out how to mourn either.

She spotted Artem in the market, holding hands with a staggeringly beautiful man with pale blue skin and an elegant fin rising from the center of his head. Echo had no idea what kind of being the other man was, but she'd seen Artem with him before, and she wasn't sure of the right way to ask the question. She'd ask Barnabas next time she saw him, she thought, if the magician didn't distract her as he usually did. Barnabas was having his own issues with processing the battle below in Atlantis, and being easily distracted was one of them.

Echo finished her apple and watched Artem and his date part ways. Artem caught sight of her leaning against a post and grinned at her through his perfectly maintained dark beard, a curl of hair falling over his left eye.

"Hey, dude," Echo said as Artem reached her. "How's that going?"

Artem looked over his shoulder as the blue man disappeared into the crowd.

"It's fine," he said, unconvincingly.

"Artem, don't be offended by this, but I think you're having a

rebound," Echo said. "I mean, he seems very sweet and all, but…
You know what a rebound relationship is, yeah?"

"Is that when you are spending time with someone whom you
may genuinely like, but know they are mostly a distraction from the
sadness of a relationship you no longer have?" Artem said.

"That's… a pretty succinct definition of a rebound
relationship," Echo said.

"I know exactly what I'm doing, Echo," Artem said. "I'm not
fooling myself. But Yenn is nice, and he's very pleasant to look at
and to be around, and he makes me feel less alone and less sad, and
when we inevitably sail away from New Tortuga, I will only miss
him a very slight bit. I left my heart shattered in pieces on the
Island of Unwanted Things, and I have not yet put it back together
again. But I get lonely."

"I'm sorry," Echo said. "I just want to look out for you."

"I know," Artem said. "And I do appreciate it."

Echo nodded and brushed her hand through her seafoam-
colored Mohawk, grimacing as she realized her fingers were still a
little sticky from the apple she'd eaten.

"You're lonely, too," Artem said.

"Aren't we all?" Echo said. She began walking back to the
dinghy they'd rowed out from their ship, the *Endless*, where they'd
left Barnabas.

"I suppose we are," Artem said. He lifted her net bag from the
tip of the trident and withdrew an orange, which he began to peel
perfectly in one winding strip. Echo found herself watching the
process with scientific fascination. "I think we've been here too
long."

"Maybe we have," Echo said. "Is that your way of saying you're
ready to move on before you get attached?"

Artem gave her a sad, gentle smile.

"Maybe. But I also think you know what you want to do next,"
Artem said.

"Yeah," Echo said. "I guess we should tell our pet wizard it's
time to go."

***

Echo found Barnabas Coy below deck, alone, tinkering in his workshop. The room was covered in arcane implements, spell books and components, strange animal parts, contraptions, weapons, and baubles.

Barnabas was hunched over his desk, beads of sweat trailing alarmingly down his stubbly head. Echo walked up beside him to look at what he was working on.

Laid out in pieces on the table were the remnants of a flintlock pistol. He'd carried a similar one when they first met, but it was not a functioning gun. Instead, it acted as a sort of focus for his spells, able to unleash lethal mystical energies. He called it a wand shaped like a pistol, which went along with his entire look—tattooed and scarred, wearing an almost comical approximation of a classic pirate's garb, with striped pants and wide-topped boots, a long, loose coat over his shoulders.

Echo winced when she saw his still-bandaged hand. He'd lost his flintlock wand by channeling a spell through it. The spell had been too powerful for the focus to contain, and it had blown up in his hand, breaking several bones and leaving the hand bloody and temporarily maimed. He'd been healing up nicely, all things considered. But he kept his ring and little fingers bandaged together for support, and parts of his hand showed signs of shiny pink scars.

"I thought you weren't going to build another one of those," Echo said.

"Okay, so here's the thing," Barnabas said, looking up from his table, revealing a comical monocle over one eye acting as a magnifying glass, creating the look of one enormous eyeball staring at her. He noticed that she was about to laugh and removed it. "I really didn't intend to build another one, but it's just so effective, y'know? And if we're going to go into dangerous situations, I'd rather have a magical focus I know how to use rather than trying to learn something new."

"You could pick up an actual magic wand," Echo said. "I know I've seen them in this room before."

Barnabas pointed at a shelf. Echo walked over and picked up a smooth wooden case, cracking it open. Inside was, in fact, a wand, made of some sort of gleaming bone.

"That's one of them," Barnabas said. "I think I have three or four. I forget. I sort of... acquired them before we left the island."

"So why not use them?"

"Magic's a funny thing, Echo," Barnabas said, putting aside his work and standing up, stretching. When they'd first met, he seemed older, but she'd come to realize much of it was hard living. He was still young enough that she learned he had looked up to her mother in an almost parental way as well. Barnabas Coy had been hired by an Atlantean spy to watch over the family, and Echo's mother Meredith had been very kind to the struggling young magician and smuggler. He'd had a harder life than he let on, though, and carried those rough years in his eyes, hiding behind enchanted tattoos and a wild beard.

"Funny how?" Echo said.

"It's very personal. I've met wizards who only use a magic staff. Others who use wands. Others can't use a focus at all. I met one magician whose focus was a cat. A cat! She cast spells through her cat because she herself could not see, but she could share her cat's vision and use that bond to see the world."

"I think you should trade in your pistol for a cat," Echo said.

"I wish I could do that," he said. "But look, you know I hate actual firearms. It's just..."

"Why don't you put a trigger on a wand if that's what you need?"

"How did you know I need a trigger for my focus?" Barnabas said, honest surprise in his voice.

"It's a crutch," Echo said. "We all have crutches. I have crutches. You think I can't pick up on yours?"

Barnabas scratched his head.

"Remind me to never play cards with you," he said. "Anyway. You come down here to tell me I'm doing magic wrong, or is something on your mind?"

Echo inhaled deeply.

"I think we should go find Yuri," she blurted out.

"Absolutely," Barnabas said.

"What?" Echo said.

They'd left Yuri Rodriguez, her best friend before all of this happened, alone since the battle. He had fled the fight, either in fear or shame, Echo couldn't tell, after learning he'd contracted shark lycanthropy, transforming into a man/shark hybrid. That transformation had turned the tide of the battle not once but twice, and Echo would be forever grateful for that, but Yuri hadn't stayed around for her to tell him that, darting off into the sea without saying goodbye. The group together agreed to let Yuri have his privacy. Barnabas gave Yuri a magical artifact to help him find his way home, a compass that pointed to Echo. The magician suggested Yuri could decide for himself when he was ready to return. Echo had avoided pushing to search for Yuri as long as she could, and anticipated Barnabas refusing to violate Yuri's privacy.

"I really thought you'd say no," Echo said.

"Nope, absolutely not, I am not going to argue against this," Barnabas said. "I was wrong. Yuri may be a were-shark and therefore very powerful, but he's also an extremely naïve young man out there alone and I'm a terrible person for suggesting we don't go find him."

"Why didn't you say this earlier?" Echo said.

"Because I thought you agreed that he deserved his privacy and I didn't want to contradict you. Or myself. But I'm wrong. Let's go find Yuri. He's probably in the fetal position somewhere waiting for you to find him."

"You are a horrible man, Barnabas Coy."

"Who gave him the compass to find you?" Barnabas said.

"You did."

"And who may have maybe cast a spell on said compass so that

15

I know if Yuri's injured?"

"You what?" Echo said.

"I am totally low-key spying on your friend," Barnabas said. "Sorry."

"You really are a terrible person," Echo said.

"I know," Barnabas said. "I…"

Before he could finish, Echo grabbed him in a rib-cracking hug. Barnabas exhaled with a high-pitched, pained squeak.

"So, he's okay?" Echo said.

"I mean, he's Yuri," Barnabas said. "Okay is a relative term. He's unharmed, I know that."

"And do you know where he is?" Echo said.

"Right now? No," Barnabas said. "But I am your favorite sea wizard, Echo. Your favorite sea wizard can cast divining spells to do things like locate enchanted objects."

"Like his compass," Echo said.

"Like his compass," Barnabas repeated.

"I almost don't hate you right now," Echo said. "When can we leave?"

Barnabas gestured upstairs.

"Go talk to the ghosts," he said, referencing the spirits who crewed the *Endless*. We can leave whenever they say we're ready."

Echo darted for the stairs. Before leaving, she turned back to Barnabas.

"You're not really as awful as you pretend to be, are you?" Echo said.

"Oh, I'm awful," Barnabas said. "Just not all the time."

Chapter 2: Something to make me feel human

Yuri Rodriguez no longer needed glasses.

Of all the physiological changes he'd experienced since contracting shark lycanthropy, his improved vision was, perhaps, the one he found most off-putting. Sure, the other changes were scarier, transforming into a massive were-shark, breathing underwater, the fact that he was constantly hungry. But having perfect vision for the first time in his life made him uncomfortable.

He rose out of the water, transforming from shark man to human more easily than he did even just a few weeks ago. He still felt a strange dragging on his body when he moved from the ocean to the surface, as if his entire frame felt more at home beneath the waves.

Pulling an enormous tuna behind him with one hand, he reached into a protective pouch he kept at his side in both human and were-shark form and withdrew his glasses, placing them gently on his face. It was a useless act. He'd carefully removed the lenses a while back, wrapping them in soft cloth and storing them safely in case he ever needed them again. But the frames he kept, devoid of glass, an affectation rather than vision correction.

"I've seen a lot of strange habits among the changed ones, Yuri, but your need to keep those glasses is one of the funnier ones," the brute waiting for him on the shore said. The other man, wide-jawed, thick-necked, with a shock of white hair slicked back atop his head, was also a were-shark. Whitetip, as he called himself, was brother of Maw, the huge shark-man whose pack had infected Yuri during a frenzy, and he'd spent all this time helping Yuri acclimate to his life among the were-sharks. Whitetip, despite looking like a sea-faring gladiator, had maintained his sense of humanity better than most of his fellow lycanthropic sharks, and saw an opportunity in Yuri to help the younger man to not lose himself to this new, more bestial nature.

"They're something to make me feel human," Yuri said, hauling the tuna onto the shore and immediately beginning to prep it for dinner. He'd learned to cook from Whitetip, who, unlike many of his fellows, did not let his baser instincts dictate his diet. They cooked together, and talked about life as were-sharks, about the vastness of the ocean, about what Yuri could do to control the darker parts of his newfound nature.

"They do make you look smarter than the average were-shark," Whitetip said, running a scarred hand through his swath of bleached hair and drawing a knife to help Yuri clean the fish.

It was strange, Yuri thought, this whole relationship. Yuri lost his dad at sea when he young enough that his memory his father was more myth than a man. Some idealized hero he barely knew. His mother passed away early, too, but at least, afterward, Yuri had found family with Echo and her mother. Meredith had been very much a second mother to him in the end, and his grief for losing her was nearly as powerful as Echo's own. But this time with Whitetip—a gruff man, and hard, but also surprisingly understanding, and a teacher of understated ability—had been the first time in a very long time he felt a sense of fatherly affection from anyone. He hadn't needed it, but he had certainly appreciated it.

They prepared the tuna and ate it alongside a strange salad Whitetip made from seaweed and scavenged materials. Yuri hadn't had much inclination towards eating vegetables before becoming a were-shark, and even less so since, but Whitetip insisted—he said that doing things that went against their were-shark nature helped encourage the human side to stay in control.

Eat plants. Breathe air. Read poetry. Talk to people, Yuri, whatever you do, talk to people, Whitetip had told him during those first few days together. There was a temptation as a were-shark to give in to a baser nature, to be the silent, relentless predator their animal side was famous for being. A perfect hunter, silently stalking the depths… that was what they could be, what some were-sharks argued they should be. But they were also human. The shark within them would always remember what they were, Whitetip explained. The human side needed reminders. It needed anchors, else the hunter would swallow them whole.

"I suppose at some point I need to leave this island," Yuri said.

"That's up to you," Whitetip said, eating his seaweed salad with a ridiculously elegant pair of chopsticks he had salvaged from a sunken yacht, which were among the older were-shark's most prized possessions. "You don't have to leave here. But it's a big ocean, Yuri. And there is little out there you need to fear. You could go anywhere."

"You know the funny thing? Before all this, I was a homebody," Yuri said. "I never figured I'd leave my hometown. Work at the icehouse, marry a nice girl, have some kids who would go to the same school I went to…"

"Fate hates when you make plans," Whitetip said.

"I'm picking up on that," Yuri said. "I suppose at some point you'll get sick of me."

"I'll get tired of this spot," Whitetip said. "I'll be honest, kid. You're better conversation than most of our brethren. I wouldn't refuse the company if you wanted to travel together a while. It's my brother's fault you're out here anyway. We're practically family."

"Yeah," Yuri said. He looked out across the waves, the sky above turning a lavender-pink as the sun neared setting.

"You have family, though," Whitetip said.

"I shouldn't go to them until I know I'm not a threat," Yuri said. Whitetip had been teaching him ways to control his transformations, to keep the ferocious anger of the were-shark form under control, but he still felt as though he were at its mercy, that at the slightest provocation he could lose control and become a killing machine.

"Everything out here's a threat," Whitetip said. "If you wait until you think you're perfectly safe, you'll be alone a long, long time."

Yuri shrugged. The two men sat in silence for a while, eating as their nature demanded they do all the time.

A smell tickled the inside of Yuri's nose. An uncomfortably familiar scent. He turned to Whitetip, whose face had become a mask of concern. Brushing sand from his legs and butt, Yuri stood up to scan the horizon.

Something was in the water. Dark, shapeless. The waves pushed them closer to the beach. Whitetip stood up as well and together they walked to the edge of the shore, waves lapping over their ankles.

"What the hell is that?" Yuri said.

He moved to wade out into the water, but Whitetip put a hand on Yuri's shoulder.

"Patience," he said. "Let the tide bring it to us."

Minutes rolled by. It felt like hours. But as the sun began to touch the horizon in the west, the first of the objects washed up on shore.

It was a body.

Whitetip stomped out toward it until he was knee deep. Yuri joined him. As Yuri reached down to grab the body, another bumped his leg. Whitetip grabbed the first corpse by the collar and Yuri did the same with the second. They dragged the bodies to shore, but it was a pointless endeavor, the tide depositing a third on the sand without any help from either man.

Yuri rolled his corpse over, involuntarily sucking in a breath between his teeth.

"This is an Atlantean," Yuri said.

The body itself had been ravaged, pierced by sharp points and torn elsewhere to the point that it might be unrecognizable if Yuri didn't remember the stylistic appearance of Atlantean armor. This was a soldier, he knew. Glancing over at the body Whitetip had dragged ashore, he confirmed both corpses were dressed the same. The body Whitetip dredged up was legless below the knee.

"What did this?" Yuri asked.

"These wounds are from bites," Whitetip said. "Mostly. Look at the circular patterns."

Yuri could see it now. Among the injuries were crescent shapes where rows and rows of teeth had sunk into and rent the flesh.

"Do you know what could've done this?" Yuri asked.

"There's a lot of things in the sea," Whitetip said. "I can't say for sure I know what did it, but I could imagine a few dozen creatures that could have."

"To a squad of Atlantean warriors?" Yuri said.

Whitetip shrugged.

"There's a lot of teeth out there, kid," he said.

And then the third body moaned.

The two were-sharks looked at each other and, abandoning the corpses they'd dragged ashore, ran to the one that had washed up on its own.

Yuri turned the living Atlantean over onto his back. He didn't look any healthier than his peers. Covered in wounds, one eye completely gone, he seemed to drift back into consciousness as the two men tended to him.

"The scar," the warrior said, his voice raspy and weak.

"Oh man, sorry, buddy, you are definitely going to have some scars," Yuri said.

The Atlantean barely registered Yuri's words.

"They came... from the Scar," he continued. "So many... eyes... teeth... legion..."

Whitetip checked the Atlantean's armor, trying to find a way to get the dying man loose and assess the damage. His hands came away covered in blood. Yuri noticed an alarmingly heavy trail of blood running from the Atlantean's body into the ocean, the familiar metallic tang sticking with him.

"What did this to you?" Yuri said. He held the warrior's head to maintain eye contact. "What was it?"

"From below…" the Atlantean said, and Yuri watched the life go out of the man's eyes. Gone, like his companions. Yuri set him down gently on the sand and looked back out over the water. Other bodies floated there as well, unmoving, face down.

"I hate to say it, but someone should, like, warn Atlantis or something," Yuri said.

"I don't disagree," Whitetip said. "But the likes of you and I won't be welcome there. Can't exactly mail them a letter. Or ship a dead Atlantean soldier to their gates with a warning note."

Yuri grimaced, his heart simultaneously filling with anxiety and elation.

"I know who they'll listen to," he said. "I guess it's time to go home after all."

Chapter 3: Muireann

Muireann watched the sea unfold behind her, cold and merciless as the one who pursued her.

The ship she rode upon was destined for faraway shores, warmer than her homelands, more welcoming than those she was born upon. Gone, she knew would be the black waters of home. The thought of clear seas, welcoming as a bathwater, did not bring her comfort. Home was harsh, but it gave her strength, and she would miss the music of waves crashing upon rock, the dark stone rising along the coastline, the green of so much life everywhere she looked.

She placed her hand in her pocket and clutched her stolen cargo, smooth as a pearl and not much larger than a golf ball, warm to the touch, radiating life.

She stole it from a man who did not deserve it, and would never use it, but men like that did not take well to thieves, especially thieves who put them off their guard with a smile and a song.

I need it more than he does, Muireann thought to herself as she pulled a knit hat down tighter over her dark hair. It would have gone to waste with him.

Still, she thought, she might have felt a little guilty about stealing it if he hadn't decided to kill her for the affront to his pride.

The crew did not know exactly what to make of her, or why the captain allowed her onboard. If asked directly, the captain himself might have trouble explaining. Part of Muireann's magic was the ability to pass where she needed to be unchallenged, and to mystify those who needed mystifying. Hers was a subtle magic, the sort fairy tales were made of, not adventure stories.

She sang, and the wind was at their back. She sang and their fishing nets were full. She sang and sailors slept without nightmares, thinking of home, and those they left behind.

Who ever said it was bad luck to have one of my kind on their ship? Muireann thought. I'm a good luck charm is what I am.

But then the storm hit, something ferocious and malevolent, as if it had a sentience of its own. They drifted over waves the size of skyscrapers, great colossi devouring the horizon. They took on water. They nearly lost men to the sea, saved only because they were lashed to the ship. One man lost a finger. Another nearly lost an eye.

And they began to look at Muireann as if perhaps she was the cause of their misfortune.

They came to her at night, a mob of sailors, intent to throw her overboard, or worse. But the captain—stinking of bourbon, but fierce and commanding—called upon their decency and mocked their superstition. The men relented.

And the next day, the storm passed.

The navigator was astounded. He could not place them on a map. They'd been driven so far off course he had no bearing on where they found themselves, waiting for night to fall so he could plot their course using the ancient rules of the stars.

The sea drew calm. It was as though they sailed upon glass. The engines, by some miracle still functional, plugged along, but not knowing where they might be, they simply pushed their way south, hoping to find their way again.

Night fell again. The navigator looked to the stars. He laughed. It was not a joyful laughter, and bordered on hysteria.

"We're hundreds of miles off course," he said. "Hundreds. It's as if that storm picked us up and dumped us on an entirely different map. This shouldn't be possible."

Muireann sang. The sea sang back.

"You'll find land to the west," she said. "A day's journey. You can buy fuel there, and food."

"How do you know this?" the first mate asked.

Muireann shook her head, barely more than a twitch. She sensed a growing distrust among the sailors. The captain put a hand on her shoulder. He looked older than when they began, and very tired.

"They take credit cards on this land you're pointing us to?" he asked. He smiled at her. It was remarkably kind.

"I think so," she said, smiling back.

"You should go below deck," the captain said softly. His next words were almost a whisper. "Lock yourself in my cabin. Don't open the door for anyone. I'll sleep elsewhere tonight."

Muireann wanted to question why, but saw the look in the eyes of the other men. If they did not find land that day, if she sent them in the wrong direction, she sensed that not even the captain could protect her from what the crew in revolt would do.

"Thank you," she said. And she went below.

The captain's quarters were sparse and cramped, but more than the other men had. She locked the door behind her and sat cross-legged on his bed, singing to herself. She drew the sphere in her pocket out to admire it, its hazy golden glow illuminating the dimly lit chamber.

The latch on the door rustled once. An hour later, it rustled again. She could hear the men talking above her, their footfalls on the deck. She heard snippets of conversation, but nothing she could make out clearly.

And then she heard the screaming.

Bolting out of bed, she went to the door, but did not unlock it. Instead, she listened, her ear pressed to the door. The sailors were yelling in fear, crying out in pain. She heard the blood-freezing screech of a death rattle. Strange breathing, too, inhuman, wet and rasping, the sound of soggy footprints.

The door began to rattle violently.

Falling backward, Muireann looked for something to defend herself with. She found a wooden ax handle, bladeless, which she held up like a club. In the back of her mind, she tried to call up defensive magic, but her heart pounded too loudly, the fear in her chest making her sloppy and slow. She waited for the door to burst open, for some terrible thing to come charging through, but it never did. Eventually, the door grew silent, and so did the ship.

Blood began to run under the door, deep red, like wine. Muireann pulled herself back onto the bed so the blood would not touch her feet.

Hours went by. She did not move. She did not sing.

Eventually, sleep took her, the sort of terrified exhausted sleep that only fear inspires. She woke hours later, the smell of blood and worse in the air, but still the ship was silent.

She crossed the room and opened the door, her shoes sticky with congealing blood.

In the hallway, a dead sailor lay mangled. It had been his blood running under the door. He looked as though some animal had gone to work on him.

Muireann clutched the ax handle at the ready and moved on.

Up on the deck, she found a massacre. Every sailor on the vessel had been brutally murdered, ripped apart like dolls. The navigator's head rolled back and forth on the deck with the rocking of the waves, completely separated from his body.

She found the kind captain holding his guts together, his fingers clutching at his green knit sweater. At first, she thought he was staring at her, and she rushed to help, but she found only dead, blank eyes looking back at her. She gently closed them with her fingertips.

Muireann went to the prow of the ship, looking out across the water for any sign of what did this. The sea was empty, glittering beneath a rapidly setting sun. She sat down, cradled in the prow, and stared once again at the gleaming sphere she'd stolen.

"I don't know what to do," she said as the ship creaked and groaned, devoid of life in the middle of the vast blue sea.

Chapter 4: The old spymaster

Grimmin would never say it out loud, but he enjoyed things better when the twins were trying to usurp each other.

The old spy loitered in the back of the council chambers, listening, as he often did, to the Atlantean leadership bicker. He had spent a long time as the personal spymaster to Rhegis, one half of the ruling family of Atlantis. Rhegis had long followed his now deceased father's isolationist beliefs for Atlantis, keeping the kingdom unknown to the surface world.

That philosophy had very nearly ended in outright war with Rhegis' twin sister, Reina, who led a splinter group of Atlanteans who wanted war with humanity for the things they'd done to the ocean. Grimmin had to give Reina some credit—they all knew someone who had suffered from pollution-based illnesses, or had otherwise felt firsthand the destructive nature of humanity. But Grimmin was a soldier and strategist, and he knew the undersea kingdom was ill-prepared to go to war with the entire surface world, and he believed his prince was in the right.

This had almost killed both him and Rhegis in recent months, something Grimmin, still healing from wounds received during an assassination attempt on his own life, would not soon forget. If not for the intervention of Rhegis' secret daughter, Echo—who Reina had, in her most egregious error in judgment, attempted to use as a hostage to manipulate her brother—Atlantis would be at war with all of humanity right now.

Instead, again because of Echo, brother and sister were working, albeit mostly through arguing, to build a better future for their kingdom.

It was slow going, but at least they weren't trying to assassinate each other, Grimmin thought. He hadn't given up his role as spymaster, so he knew, or at least he hoped he still had the talent and contacts to know, that Reina wasn't plotting her brother's murder anymore.

If someone could kill me so I don't have to sit through another of these council meetings, though, I'd welcome the action, he thought.

"I don't miss these," the man sitting to Grimmin's left said. The spy smiled to the even older man, a former politician and ally to Rhegis named Brendis Kor. Kor came to the meetings as an advisor, but he took advantage of his advanced age to play the tired and restless card, and often came and went during the meetings to stretch his legs.

"I used to have moments wondering if I were perhaps morally bankrupt, given my career," Grimmin said. "But if I've learned anything, it's that spies have nothing on politicians."

The two old men stared at the bitter arguments around the council table, made up not just of brother and sister, but each sibling's political allies—some of whom Grimmin would have preferred to put behind bars for what they tried to do to Rhegis and Echo. But politics, he thought, is all about compromising with people you don't like. I prefer poisoned daggers, honestly.

He smirked as a woman put her hand on Rhegis' shoulder as if to calm him. She had the same pale green hair as Brendis Kor.

"Well, there is that, at least," Grimmin said.

Brendis grunted.

"Don't play coy with me, old man," Grimmin said. "You have been hoping your whole life that your daughter and my prince would realize they were meant for each other."

"I wish they realized it sooner so they might have enjoyed their lives together a bit more, is all," Brendis said. "I mean, love is love, and when you find it, you hold onto it, but..."

"Hard to schedule a wedding between infrastructure meetings," Grimmin said.

"You have children, you dastardly old spy?" Brendis said.

"Never got around to it, sir," Grimmin said.

Again, Brendis grunted.

"Can't say you made the wrong choice. You think you worry about the world as the spymaster? Try having a child," he said. "Worse, have a child in a world where political assassinations are a reality."

"I would have kept her safe," Grimmin said.

"I'm not saying you wouldn't have tried," Brendis said. "But I'm looking at an old man with a limp who almost lost his arm to an afanc."

Grimmin shrugged.

"Perils of duty," he said.

Out of the corner of his eye, Grimmin saw one of his men, a young Atlantean soldier in deep green armor, sidle into the room awkwardly, nervously scanning the attendees.

"Excuse me," Grimmin said. Brendis nodded politely to him and returned to the council table, a bit of hesitancy in his step.

Grimmin approached the soldier and pulled him aside.

"You look like you have news for me I don't want to hear," he said.

"Sir," the young soldier said, his eyes wide. "Our patrols found something you should be aware of."

"I'm head of spies, not head of the military," he said. "Why come to me first?"

"We found it out by Poseidon's Scar. Near the site of the... the battle," the soldier said.

The battle. No one had come up with a clever name for it yet— the fight for the soul of Atlantis, determined by a young woman who had never been allowed into the city before that day and a hodgepodge of allies the average Atlantean would have turned their nose up at. Stolen military hardware from the surface. A crisis averted.

And a place no one ever really wanted to go back to anymore. But still, Grimmin had his rangers patrol there, to keep an eye on the submarine buried at the bottom of the sea, to ensure no one got any ideas about starting the revolution anew.

"What did you find?" Grimmin said.

"An afanc," the young man said.

"Well, they're rare, but we know one considers Poseidon's Scar its territorial waters," Grimmin said. "Seeing one is disconcerting, but it's not unexpected."

"It was dead, sir," The soldier said.

"Having almost been eaten by one once, I will say I'm more comfortable with a dead afanc than a living one."

"Sir, it had been torn apart. Partially eaten."

"By carrion eaters, or something else?" Grimmin said.

"The marks were fresh, sir. The creature died an ugly death. And anything that can kill an afanc..." The soldier trailed off but looked as if he had more to say. Grimmin called him on it.

"What else, boy?" Grimmin said. "What haven't you told me yet?"

"One of our squads hasn't returned," the soldier said. "Rangers, sir. Even if they're deviating from their patrol, they leave word somehow. But all we found..."

Grimmin tried to hide his concern. He'd been spymaster for decades. He should be able to mask his emotions. But somehow, in that moment, he knew his men were dead before the boy said his next words.

"We found the corpse of one of their hippocampi," the soldier said, referring to the large seahorses the men rode on patrol. "It was marked up much the same way as the afanc."

"Did you bring the body back?" Grimmin said.

"Yes, sir," the soldier said.

"Eaten, you say."

"Yes, sir."

Grimmin sighed, looking over to the council table once again.

"Have it brought to the morgue and send someone to fetch Gilos Vos from the Academy," Grimmin said. "Tell him we have a specimen we need his help identifying."

"But we know it's a seahorse, sir."

"Not the horse, son. Whatever ate it."

Chapter 5: Ghost ships

Echo dreamed of home.

She grew up around the icehouse her mother owned, and memories of it—the clanking of machinery, the smell of chemicals, walking into the store room on a hot summer day and instantly being transported to another world—followed her like ghosts. I'll never be able to go back there, she thought. And she wasn't sure she wanted to, not with the life she had now. But the icehouse had been home, and it had been her livelihood, and, for better or for worse, it had been what she expected to be her life's work, as much as her mother hoped for bigger things for her.

But then her aunt, Reina, current co-ruler of Atlantis thanks to Echo's intervention, sent monsters to steal her away in the night. She wouldn't even know how to explain where she'd been for months to anyone back home. She wondered what the police thought—the house had burned to the ground during their escape, she knew, but no bodies would have been found. Echo, Yuri, and Meredith were, she assumed, missing persons still. Did they suspect them of arson, or murder? Did anyone care? Would anyone have taken over the icehouse business in her mother's absence?

I shouldn't worry about this, she thought. There's nothing I can do. I can't go home again. And that's fine.

Artem yelling for her shook her out of her reverie and sent her springing from the hammock in which she'd been lazing and running up to the deck. She found Artem halfway up to the crow's nest, Barnabas leaning against the rail near the bow. Both men were looking at something.

"What have we got—oh, what the hell is that?" Echo said.

They slowly approached a derelict craft that looked like a large, deep-sea fishing boat. It listed to one side a bit. Echo could see lights on, even in the daylight, but no movement.

"Is there anyone on board?" Echo asked.

Barnabas shook his head.

"I can't tell from here," he said. Then, to no one in particular, "Bring us in closer."

Echo sensed, then saw as they began to act, the restless spirits who crewed the *Endless*. They were a menagerie of lost souls, ghosts dressed in the garb they wore when they sailed the seas in life. Old-timey pirates worked alongside navy men and yachters in polos and deck shoes. Barnabas had explained when they first met that the *Endless* was a ghost ship in a literal sense, crewed by those who have lived by the sea and were not ready to move on to the afterlife yet. This haunted ship was a place for those travelers to remain here on Earth, on the ocean, where they were happiest. They were not trapped there, and often moved on. Some might crew the ship for a few days or weeks; others had been on it for a hundred years or more. They never spoke, but Echo had come to find their presence comforting. This was their ship, and they would keep it safe. The living were just passengers.

Good thing, Echo thought. None of us actually know how to sail this thing.

Ropes leapt off the deck and, by unseen hands, lashed themselves to the derelict vessel as the ships met side by side. Echo picked up her trident from where she'd, irresponsibly, she admitted, left it hours earlier and jumped to the other ship easily, her Atlantean strength propelling her through the air.

She landed on the other deck and immediately slipped, landing on her back.

Barnabas started clapping and yelled over that he gave her a 10 for the landing. Artem humorlessly asked if she was okay.

"I'm fine," Echo said, pushing herself into a sitting position. The black, rubberized deck was wet and sticky. Grossed out, she lifted her hand to see what slimy fish gut-based substance she'd put her hand in.

The palm of her hand was covered in dark red blood.

She popped to her feet and whirled the trident into a fighting pose.

"Guys! Get over here right now!" she yelled.

There was a heavy thump beside her as Artem dropped out of the air, somehow propelling himself off the mast in one leap. He looked at her cockily until he also slipped on the blood and fell on his backside. Barnabas carefully stepped from one ship to the other and, noticing the blood, daintily held his long coat up so it wouldn't drag through it.

"Seriously, guys, I don't know who you're trying to impress with the acrobatics. We're right alongside the ship," Barnabas said. "Holy hell, look at this place."

"We need to check for survivors," Echo said.

"Like hell we do," Barnabas said. Echo and Artem glared at him with an almost identical look. "Fine. We'll look."

It didn't take them long to find the first body, or what was left of it. By this point all three of them were used to horrific sights, but the brutality they saw in the first few victims was enough to turn Echo's stomach, and her companions didn't look any better. Artem drew both of his short swords, and Barnabas the sabre he carried.

"Where's your magic flintlock?" Echo said.

"Oh sure, now you want me to have my magic wand," he said. "It needs one or two more enchantments before it's ready. You're stuck with me as-is today, your highness, and I'm not any happier about it than you are."

"Can you cast a spell to detect... anything?" Artem said.

"Monsters? Survivors?"

Barnabas looked at the Amazonian man quizzically, then nodded.

"Where'd you learn about magic?" he said. Barnabas muttered a few arcane words, and a pale blue trail left his hand and darted down below deck.

"Oh good, let's go down into the dark bowels of the ship," Echo said.

Artem, without hesitation, followed the trail, taking point. Echo and Barnabas exchanged raised eyebrows.

"I can never tell if he's incredibly brave or possibly suicidal," Barnabas said.

Echo refused to respond and followed Artem downstairs.

The smell of blood and worse was stronger here, trapped without ventilation. They came across more bodies, claw marks on the wall, an older man leaning up against one corner where he had clearly made his last stand.

"Echo," Artem said, pointing down.

On the ground, they could see tracks. Human-sized, the footprints were clearly not human, with four toes, webbed feet, unnaturally wide at the ball of the foot. There were many tracks, but with the blood spatter and puddles of seawater, impossible to gauge an accurate number.

"Ever seen tracks like those before?" Echo said.

"Sure," Artem said. "A humanoid with webbed feet? I grew up on the Island of Unwanted Things. Half my friends had webbed feet or claws."

"So that's a no," Echo said.

Barnabas brushed past them, following the glittering blue trail. Artem looked vaguely offended.

"How often does he want to go first?" Artem said.

"My spell detected life, Artem," Barnabas said. Around the next corner, the trail ended at a barred door. The door itself was battered and cracked. Another human body, mangled and brutalized, lay on the ground just outside.

"So, by 'life,' do you mean, life in need of rescuing, or just, anything, like, living in general?" Echo said.

Barnabas held his sword out in front of him and called out.

"Hello? Is there anyone in there?"

There was no answer. The magician turned to Echo.

"There's someone in there," he said. "Friend or enemy, I can't be sure, but…"

"Something tried to get in there, and someone died stopping them," Echo said.

"We're here to help," Artem yelled. "It's safe to come out."

He turned back to Echo.

"It's safe, right? Are we in agreement that it's safe?"

Echo shrugged. Barnabas walked right up to the door, squeamishly stepping over the body, and knocked. Echo and Artem joined him.

"Okay, we're coming in!" Barnabas said. "We want to make sure you're all right, but if you don't want the door kicked in, you should probably open it!"

No answer again. Barnabas reared back and kicked the door.

It didn't move.

"Ow," he said. "Maybe you could, like, with the super strength, y'know?"

Echo repeated the kick and the door swung open.

Then they heard singing.

It was wonderful singing, Echo thought. She didn't understand that language, but that didn't seem to matter. It spoke of distant lands, of love lost, of places you know you can never return to. It made her heart hurt. She glanced at Artem and saw a single tear escape the corner of his eye. He let his swords lower toward the floor, lost in the music.

"Oh, no, no you don't," Barnabas said gruffly. "My mother was a sea nymph. Those song spells don't work on me, sorry."

The wizard waved a hand and the room flashed with a soft purple light for just a moment, and instantly, Echo felt her broken heart return to normal. Artem snapped out of his dreamlike state as well, lifting his swords once again.

"What was that?" Artem said.

Barnabas held up a hand for the warrior to be quiet. Sitting on a rickety cot, they saw a young woman with dark hair, a knit hat pulled down over her head. She had one hand protectively in her pocket, and the other was held at an awkward angle that Echo recognized was a gesture associated with spellcasting she'd seen Barnabas perform. The remnants of a failed spell fell from her palm like pollen.

"It's okay," Barnabas said. "I'm sorry for that, but I couldn't have you hypnotizing my friends. I hope you understand."

The woman nodded to Barnabas. Her irises a dark sea green. She stared at the magician intently.

"Your mother was a nereid," the woman said.

Barnabas smiled.

"Her name is Galatea," he said. "Do you know her?"

The woman shook her head.

"I'm not a nereid. I'm… something else," she said.

"What happened here?" Echo said.

The woman shook her head.

"I don't know," she said. "I was locked in here to keep me safe from the sailors, but…"

"Something else got the sailors first," Artem said.

"They're all dead?" the woman said.

"Seems so," Barnabas said. "Something terrible happened here."

Echo held out a hand to the dark-haired woman. She took it, and Echo helped her to her feet.

"Well, you can't stay here," Echo said. "Will you come with us?"

Artem shot Echo a questioning look. Echo ignored him.

"If you'll have me," the woman said. "You don't have to take me with you if…"

"You are more than welcome on my ship," Barnabas said.

Artem and Echo both gave him questioning looks. He knows

something about what she is, Echo thought. I suppose that's good enough for me.

"I'm Echo," she said.

"My name is Muireann," the woman said.

"Well, Muireann," Echo said. "Welcome aboard. Let's get you out of here."

Chapter 6: Autopsy

Gilos Vos was among the more ridiculous denizens of Atlantis. Grimmin fought the urge to shake his head as the jittery professor trampled his way into the morgue, a mop of bright purple hair curling off to one side like it was trying to escape his head.

"I have things to do, you know," he said, giving Grimmin the evil eye. "This better be important. My students need me."

"I'm sure they do," Grimmin said patiently. He gestured over to the stone slab where the remains of the seahorse were stretched out. "Right now, though, your kingdom needs you more."

"Oh look," Gilos said. "A seahorse carcass. There. I've properly identified it. Can I go now?"

"Gilos, I hate to play to your ego, because you don't need it, but you are the most knowledgeable zoologist in Atlantis," Grimmin said. "And we need you to look at that body and tell us who ate it."

Two of Grimmin's rangers were in the room as well, one, the young soldier who had found Grimmin in the council chambers, looking squeamish, while the other, a more grizzled veteran, simply watched Gilos Vos with a sort of bemused expression.

Gilos meandered closer, feigning disinterest, but leaned in cautiously for a closer look.

"Gods below, what did you do to this poor creature,

Grimmin?" Gilos said.

"This is what we're trying to find out," Grimmin said. "If anyone can identify a predator by bite marks in this city, it's you. What did this?"

The zoologist, invested now, took a monocle from within his robes and affixed it over his eye. He rolled up his sleeves and began to inspect the dead beast.

"My, my," he muttered. "Interesting."

The younger soldier turned to Grimmin with an expression filled with questions. The old spy waved him off.

"What do you say, Gilos?" Grimmin prompted.

The zoologist turned his attention on the spymaster, the one eye behind the monocle comically large and out of focus.

"First of all, this animal was not eaten," Gilos said.

"Sir?" the young soldier said.

"Those do look like teeth marks, professor," Grimmin said.

"Oh, these are teeth marks, or most of them are. But look at the wounds," Gilos said, gesturing. "They are ragged wounds, very clearly made by creatures with a large, circular bite radius, but they were not pulling the flesh away. These wounds were made to cause pain and injury, not for sustenance."

The young soldier blanched. Grimmin winced, thinking of the rangers who hadn't returned.

"Can you think of creatures who hunt like this? Who might… I don't know, bleed out their prey first?" he asked.

Gilos shook his head.

"Oh, there's any number of creatures whose jaws match this pattern," he said. "The teeth are clearly narrow and pointed, not serrated and triangular like a shark's, so that narrows it down. But as for not consuming its prey? I'm not sure. There are, of course, creatures who play with their food—you've seen an orca throw a sea lion around like a toy, I assume?"

Grimmin nodded his head. Even as a hardened warrior, he found that sort of hunting—which, he understood, was a learning exercise, not vindictive—to be unnerving. Just eat the damned thing, he found himself thinking the first time he'd seen it happening.

"So, you're saying the predators that did this were… toying with it?" he asked.

Gilos shrugged insolently. He lifted the body to examine the other side of the seahorse, but finding much the same, gently placed the remnants back down on the stone table.

"I can't tell you their motivations, Grimmin," he said. "This was an act of violence, but nature is violent. By nature. You know what I'm saying. I will say that this does not appear to be a hunger- or feeding-motivated attack. Either the creatures felt threatened, or they participate in acts of violence that are not hunting-related, which might indicate sentience, or might not. Again, I'd need more evidence to tell you which is the case."

"What about numbers?" Grimmin asked. "Can you tell how many creatures attacked the seahorse?"

Gilos twisted his mouth into a derisive sneer, then shrugged insolently.

"Have you looked at the body? There are hundreds of bites. It's partially decomposed. I mean I could hazard a guess and say…"

He looked at the body through his monocle again.

"Oh, at least… maybe, a dozen different sets of jaws, just eyeballing the various injuries, but I really don't know. I'd have to do a very extensive accounting of all the wounds, compare the dental structure, reconstruct the pieces of the body that are sloughing off… do you want me to do that? I can do that."

"I'd rather you didn't honestly," Grimmin said. "I feel like your time is better spent doing something else."

"Good, because I don't want to do that, at all," Gilos said.

Grimmin looked at the ravaged body of the seahorse one more time and sighed.

"Question," he said.

Gilos raised an impatient eyebrow at him.

"What do you know about the ecology of Poseidon's Scar?"

"You're kidding, right?" Gilos said.

"Strictly between us, that's where this attack happened," Grimmin said.

"Huh," Gilos said.

"You're uncharacteristically mum right now."

Gilos wrinkled his nose at the spymaster in an angry grimace.

"Nothing lives there, Grimmin," the professor said. "Creatures pass through, of course, as they do everywhere, but there's nothing there. It's a barren landscape. Little to no vegetation for fish to feed on, and without prey there, the predator population doesn't spend much time in the Scar either. It's a dead zone."

"That's what I thought," Grimmin said. "Maybe this was a school of... something passing through?"

"Possibly," Gilos said. "The other possibility is it's something from deep down in the ravine, but there'd need to be a good reason for anything down there to come back up to the shallower water."

"But it's possible," Grimmin said.

"I suppose it is. I've never been down inside the Scar before," Gilos said. "Have you?"

"Not yet," Grimmin said. "But I have a terrible feeling that might change very soon."

"Well, if you go, bring me back specimens," Gilos said.

Chapter 7: Water spirits

Barnabas instructed the ghosts to get their ship as far away from the derelict fishing vessel as possible, with Artem darting up to the crow's nest to watch for anyone, or anything, that might pursue them. *The Endless* headed southeast, powered by a fair wind and whatever mystical manipulations the spirits and Barnabas conjured up to move the craft along.

When they sensed they were a safe distance away, Echo called the two men over to her and together, they sat down on the deck with Muireann.

"So," Echo said. "That was a thing."

Muireann nodded to Echo, an unenthusiastic smile on her face.

"I mean, we've been in bad situations before. You're safe here with us. I promise. But that," Echo said. "That was intense."

"I'm sorry you saw that," Muireann said. "But I'm glad you found me. I don't know how long I would've stayed in that room."

Artem disappeared briefly, then returned with a metal pot and several cups. He handed one to Muireann and poured her a cup of coffee, then one for Echo, and one for himself. Barnabas eyed him expectantly, but the Amazon man did not offer the magician a cup. Barnabas went below deck and returned with a chipped mug of his own and helped himself, glaring at Artem as he poured.

"You have no idea what attacked the ship?" Artem said.

"No," the dark-haired woman said. "It was horrible. They came out of nowhere. I was already locked away, so I never got a look at them, as I said."

"And you were locked away to protect you... from the crew," Artem said.

"I was the only passenger, and we'd had a bit of bad luck with a storm," Muireann said. "I think they felt superstitious about it."

"Was anyone after you? The crew, I mean. Did you have any trouble?" Echo said.

"No," Muireann said. "Well, not really."

"Not really," Echo repeated.

"There's someone looking for me," Muireann said, meeting each of their eyes separately in turn. "But he wouldn't do that. He's not a monster. He just..."

"I don't want to pry," Echo said. "But we did take you onto our ship. If someone's after you, we need to be ready. If he's trouble we'll protect you, but we need to know what we're up against."

"Oh, no, we should pry," Barnabas said. He pulled a bottle of unlabeled booze out of his coat, poured some into his coffee, then offered it to Muireann. She seemed almost confused for a moment, then nodded, and Barnabas added a splash to hers.

"Barnabas," Echo said.

"What?" the magician said.

"What is that, and where did you get it?

"It's rum, and look at me," Barnabas said. "I'm a pirate magician. You'd be disappointed if I didn't have rum on this ship."

He waggled the bottle at Artem, who shook his head, then looked at Echo, then handed his cup to Barnabas.

"Artem?" Echo said.

"I can't get the smell of the blood on that ship out of my nose," he said. "So, yes. If there's someone after you, Muireann, we need to know who it is."

"And what you stole," Barnabas said.

"Barnabas!" Echo said, appalled. Artem's eyebrows shot up like arches.

"You took something they want back, didn't you?" Barnabas said. "Not whatever killed the crew of that ship. The person chasing you."

Echo began to protest, but Muireann spoke up first.

"Yes," she said. "He wasn't using it, but it seems like it's always the case that men most resent when you take from them things they don't need."

"Barnabas, now I feel like you know something the rest of us don't," Echo said.

He sat down cross-legged across from Muireann and sipped his spiked coffee.

"You're an ondine," he said.

"A what?" Echo said.

Muireann looked horrified for a moment, and then, strangely, she almost smiled.

"I haven't heard that word in so long," she said. "How did you know?"

"I wasn't pulling your chain when I said my mother was a nereid before," Barnabas said. "She taught me about all the ocean spirits and nymphs and mermaids. I knew what you were the minute you tried that charm spell on me."

"You are really not... I'm not sure the right way to say this. You're not pretty enough for me to have guessed your mother was a nymph," Muireann said.

"Wow," Echo said.

Artem began howling with laughter and had to walk away for a moment before he could pull himself back together.

Barnabas, oddly, didn't seem the least bit put off by it.

"It's the beard, isn't it?" he said.

"And the tattoos. And the scars. Also, you look really angry all the time," Muireann said.

"Nereids are angry a lot," Barnabas said.

"But they hide it better than you do," Muireann said.

Echo sipped her coffee and scratched at the stubble along her temple.

"I feel like I'm listening to a private joke I'm not in on," Echo said.

"You sort of are," Barnabas said. "So, Muireann… what did you steal?"

The ondine's mouth twisted up into a sheepish smile and then she reached into her pocket, drawing out a gleaming golden sphere.

"Oh, you didn't," Barnabas said.

"What is that?" Artem said.

"You took his soul?" Barnabas said.

"What?" Echo said, more loudly than she intended.

"It's not his soul!" Muireann said. "It's just… a fragment of his, y'know. Eternal life force."

"So just a fragment of his soul," Barnabas said.

"If you're going to be gauche about it," Muireann said.

"Souls are real?" Echo said.

"It's not a soul. It's a piece of his spirit."

"Wait, why did you steal a piece of his spirit?" Artem said. "And what do you mean he wasn't using it?"

Barnabas at this point was coughing from belly laughing.

"I thought that part about ondines was a myth," he said.

"It is a myth," Muireann said. She looked at Echo, seeing that she'd taken on a panicked expression. "The myths say that ondines don't have souls, and the only way to get one is to marry a human man, which, quite frankly, is sexist bullshit."

"I completely agree," Barnabas said.

"You shut up," Echo said to him. "So, what is that, then?"

"We do need to, um, we need to borrow some essence from mortal beings, though. Not their soul. Just something to sustain our magic. Sometimes it's given freely, but why should I have to go around asking for someone to give up a bit of their life force? So I… take it from bad people."

"So, you stole a bad guy's soul," Artem said.

"It's not a bloody soul, you plank," Muireann said.

Artem whipped his head to Echo.

"What did she call me?" he said, genuinely confused. "And seriously, you stole a man's life force and then ended up on a ship full of butchered sailors. Why are we helping you again?"

"The guy you took this life force from. He wouldn't do something like what happened on the ship?" Echo asked.

Muireann shook her head.

"He's a vicious bastard, but that," she said. "That was not done by human hands. You know that."

A silence fell over the group. Artem and Echo stared at each other expectantly for a moment, neither sure what to say or do.

It was Barnabas who finally broke the verbal stalemate.

"A nasty old crook on your tail we can handle," Barnabas said. "And I know what that is you stole. If he had it coming, I believe you. I don't know why, but I believe you. But that doesn't explain what happened on that ship."

Muireann closed her eyes for a moment, then met Echo's gaze.

"I have seen many strange things in my life," she said. "But I can tell you, with complete honesty, I have never been so afraid as I was on that ship. I don't know what killed those sailors, but I will hear their screams the rest of my life."

"Well then," Echo said. "I guess we better find out what it was."

"I can help with that," Barnabas said.

"I somehow knew you were going to say that," Artem said. "How do you plan to do that?"

"Magic," Barnabas said, grinning broadly. "Of course."

Chapter 8: The vast emptiness of it

There was so much Yuri struggled to adjust to in his new life, but the one thing he felt as though he'd never get over was that he had so little to fear now.

He hadn't been a man given to fear back home. He was a big dude. He hit his growth spurt early, so despite a gentle and easygoing nature, he had been left mostly alone by bullies and thugs. Yuri looked like trouble, even though he was the furthest thing to it, and he knew, and even resented that: people looked at him and saw trouble. He was profiled often, hassled occasionally, and often just simply avoided by those who were uncomfortable around his appearance.

But he'd lost his father to the sea, and the ocean scared him in ways both primal and logical. The ocean was predictably unpredictable, generous in its cruelty, and egalitarian with who it turned its wrath upon.

Yuri wasn't afraid of the water. He was afraid of the sea itself, the vast emptiness of it, the way it could swallow up the bodies of its victims so easily. And, of course, the way things lurked in its depths. Particularly in New England where Yuri grew up, the sea was dark and mysterious. It lacked the glasslike clarity of tropical waters.

Sure, deep blue sea. Yuri thought. More like an endless darkness.

And yet now, Yuri thought as he moved quickly through the ocean in his man-shark form, I've lived to become one of those things lurking in its depths. And worse, I'm one of the scariest creatures down here. Nothing challenges me. Most fear me. I've become the thing I feared.

But Yuri was still afraid.

The way the daylight broke through the water's surface in filtered streaks of golden light. The way shadows in the distance moved, obscured by water itself, ghostly and vague, their true size unknowable, their intentions even less so. The way sound carried here, whale songs drifting over miles and miles, rocks clattering like percussion instruments across the ocean floor. He could swim for hours or days without seeing another living thing, but they were there. The world around him was forever alive. He sensed creatures flee from him, an apex predator in their waters.

I never wanted to be terrifying, Yuri thought. It's the last thing I ever wanted. I've spent my whole life working to be just the opposite, and yet here, living creatures flee from the very sight of me.

What did I do so wrong that I became a monster? he wondered.

Yuri wanted to go home.

He felt his heart tighten in his chest at the thought. Meredith's kitchen. Breakfast with Echo. Working in the icehouse, the comforting ache of his muscles as he hauled huge blocks around with a pick.

He missed home so badly. He missed Meredith. He missed being ordinary.

Yuri felt the enchanted compass within the cuff he wore on his wrist pulsate. The compass knew where Echo was. The last person who remembered home for what it was, Yuri thought. I guess Echo is my home now, wherever she is.

Yuri let his eyes drift from side to side. Yes, he repeated in his head, the vast emptiness of it. The ocean, reaching out in all directions, the sort of unknowable distance that made his chest tighten and his heart hurt. Agoraphobia of the sea.

"You are the master of this place," Whitetip had explained to him. "I understand your hesitation, but you have nothing to fear from it. The ocean is your kingdom. Enjoy it. You don't have to be afraid anymore."

I'm afraid of being alone, Yuri thought, a flick of his were-shark tail propelling him faster toward wherever Echo was, the compass telling him clearly he was swimming the right path. I'm afraid of being alone in this vast, empty place.

He thought of the Atlantean bodies washed up on his shore. They believed they had nothing to fear either, Yuri thought. Above or below, the ocean punishes those who don't respect it. Maybe a little fear is what you need to survive down here.

I've spent too much time alone, Yuri thought. I'm stronger now. I'm braver.

But the ocean will devour you if you're alone.

He surged forward, a relentless, elemental power the tides had no control over. He followed the mystical beacon on his wrist.

And he let the ocean scare him, as it always did. Because Yuri knew he wouldn't be alone much longer. And that was all he needed to know.

Chapter 9: Scouting party

Grimmin took three men out to Poseidon's Scar, and with them a nagging feeling they'd never come back.

He left the young soldier—whose name, Fenn, Grimmin was embarrassed to admit he'd forgotten—back in the city with orders to tell Rhegis where they'd gone if they did not return in a day.

"But shouldn't we tell him... now?" Fenn had said, genuinely concerned.

"We needn't escalate this to royal intervention level until we know for sure we need it," Grimmin said. "Besides, I'm sure whatever ate that seahorse has moved on to other prey further away by now."

And that was absolutely a lie, Grimmin thought, reining in his own seahorse to look at the darkened expanse where the Scar lay. He'd brought along two veteran rangers and one of the magic wielders the Atlantean army considered a battlemage. Grimmin held up a hand, signaling for them to go no further. The seascape near Poseidon's Scar was a murky, empty space, bleary with heat from the lava below and filled with odd shadows cast from the molten rock's light.

"I think this is close enough," Grimmin said.

"I don't see anything, who knows what's down in the crevice," one of the rangers said.

"I believe this is why you brought me along," the magician said. Grimmin nodded.

"Don't suppose you've got some divination spells you could call up for us to take a look down that ravine from a distance," Grimmin said.

The magician nodded and rolled up his sleeves, producing a clear crystal sphere from one.

"I assume you want to see what I see," the magician said.

"If that's doable," Grimmin said.

The magician beckoned Grimmin over. He held the sphere with one hand, then put the tips of his fingers on the other splayed out on Grimmin's forehead.

"This will be disorienting," the mage said.

"Not my first divination spell," the old spymaster said. "I'm ready."

The sphere lit up and instantly Grimmin's vision went blank. Seconds later, it returned, but he did not see through his own eyes. Instead, he looked through the sphere itself like a camera. The sphere darted up out of the magician's hand and shot away, heading for the ravine.

It began to descend. The walls, unsurprisingly, were scarred by time, cracked in places, melted in others. It was clear some of the more ragged stone had been recently broken, too jagged to have been smoothed yet by the passage of time and tide. When he looked closely, Grimmin could make out pieces of shrapnel embedded in the wall.

"One of the bombs must've gone off," he said. His voice sounded far away, his words slurred.

"Focus," the magician said, his voice eerily close, as if he spoke right into Grimmin's ear. "Talking risks detaching you from the enchantment."

Grimmin nodded, unsure if the mage could see the gesture or not.

The sphere dove deeper, slowly and carefully scanning the walls of the ravine. They found nothing unexpected. Grimmin, like all Atlanteans, had never gone spelunking in the ravine, where the pressure was unbearable and the fluctuating temperature dangerous, but what they saw didn't deviate at all from his expectations. Just rock, some magma, a lot of shadows.

And then they found writing.

"Tell me that's not what I think it is," Grimmin said.

"It's language," the mage said. "I can't read it. Can you?"

"It's not an alphabet I've ever seen before," Grimmin said. "How deep down is this?"

"With the mystic nature of the orb, I'll be honest with you sir, it's hard to judge how far. The sphere travels very quickly," the magician said. "It's a few miles at least."

"So we've been ignoring an ancient, deep-sea society for entire generations because none of us bothered to look down a hole in the bottom of the sea," Grimmin said. "And we call ourselves a pinnacle of civilization."

The globe went even deeper, but the connection seemed to fade, slightly, whether due to lack of available light or the distance itself loosening the connection.

"I'm reaching the furthest extent of my spell, sir," the mage said. "We…"

The mage trailed off, and Grimmin saw exactly why. The sphere had settled over a depression in the trench wall, an enormous gash in the stone. It was littered with bones. Large bones.

And it was empty.

"Son, drop the spell," Grimmin said.

The spymaster's vision snapped back into his body. He felt weirdly disoriented and weightless for a moment, his eyes readjusting to place and time. He immediately tugged on the reins of his seahorse, turning it away from the trench and back toward Atlantis.

"Gentlemen, we're leaving. Now," he said.

He waited only long enough for the others to turn to leave before spurring his steed on. The two rangers rode on either side of the mage, who had clearly used up much of his own energy maintaining the divination spell. They guided his seahorse expertly, enabling the wizard to rest in the saddle.

"What did you see, sir?" one of the rangers asked.

"I'm more concerned about what we didn't see," Grimmin said.

"Sir, forgive me for saying so, but you look…"

"You can say it. I look scared," Grimmin said. "I didn't live this long by not listening to my fear instincts. And that back there, that scared me more than anything I've seen in a long, long time."

Gods damn the sibling rivalry that got them here, Grimmin thought. We've been looking at the demons on the surface for so long, we've forgotten monsters live down in the depths as well. We need to fix this. I hope it's not too late.

Chapter 10: The man with no soul

There was an ache in Anson Tessier's chest he could not ignore.

It's a broken heart, he joked bitterly. There was some merit to the jest, as bitter as it was. The pain felt vaguely vascular, for one, not a heart attack, but a similar sort of tightness in his chest. And the reason for it was a woman, though she certainly hadn't stolen his heart, metaphorically or literally.

No, she was just a thief, and she took something from him, and no one steals from Anson Tessier without consequence.

Normally, Tessier would send someone to fetch whatever might have been stolen. He had goons and bounty hunters aplenty in his pool of resources. They came in handy for the work he did, the work that had built an empire, through blood and corruption. But this, this felt personal. It felt different. It needed a direct hand for rectification. Anson Tessier would find this woman and take back what was his, and she'd look him in the eyes when he enacted his revenge.

A shooting pain arced across his chest, down to his fingertips. Tessier clutched the rail in front of him where he stood on the private sea craft, fighting back the urge to gasp.

"Sir?" one of the hired sailors said. Tessier grunted, steeling himself against the pain, and turned, composed.

"What is it?" he said.

"We're about to hit some serious weather," the sailor said. "Just wanted to give you a head's up in case you wanted to head inside. The captain said not to disturb you unless absolutely necessary, but we're going to be hitting some rough conditions. I mean, 'sweep you off the deck' type rough."

Tessier grunted again, but then softened his expression.

"I apologize. I'm just in a foul mood. Thank you for the warning. I'll head inside."

The sailor walked away, and Tessier followed soon after.

He went to his private room, a suite with a view on the starboard side. The ship was quite large, the best money could buy. Money Tessier had endless amounts of, more than he'd ever need in ten lifetimes. What Tessier valued more than money was control. And this woman had taken that control from him. No, not a woman, a creature, Tessier knew, something not quite human masquerading as a human woman. Tessier, like many who grow too wealthy to be satisfied with ordinary entertainment, had explored the unknown in his spare time, and he knew this world had a shadow world, an entire reality often unseen or unexplored by ordinary people. You could go your whole life without encountering that other layer of reality, without ever knowing that monsters exist. Perhaps you are better that way, Tessier thought.

But they do, and a monster stole some piece of me, and I will have it back, and more, Tessier thought. He poured himself a glass of wine and watched as clouds the color of rage surged toward them, rain so heavy he could see it approaching like a wall of water. The storm seemed to have a life of its own, a will. Maybe this was another monster, he thought. The wrath of some sea god, protecting the little trickster whole stole a part of me.

Tessier finished his wine, then crossed to the luxurious closet along the back of the suite. He removed the light suit he wore, hanging it up precisely, folding the shirt though he knew he would have it laundered before he wore it again. He pulled on more rough and tumble clothing, a waffled long-sleeved shirt and jeans, shoes with no-slip soles. He slipped a survival knife onto his belt and strapped a slim knife onto his forearm, pulling his sleeve back down over it. He thought about adding the pistol he had packed to the ensemble, but changed his mind. If he ended up out in the elements helping during the storm—he might be paying top dollar for this trip, but he knew his way around a vessel and would lend a hand if needed, wealthy patron or not—he didn't want to risk the weapon getting waterlogged and unusable.

The rain slammed into them like a solid object. Tessier could hear it pounding against the deck, the crew running around, a sense of urgency and panic in their voices. This was no ordinary storm. Maybe it really is a monster, Tessier thought.

Tessier made his way up to the bridge and stood in the back, out of the way. His presence caught the captain's attention, who seemed torn between his duties to the ship and acknowledging his employer's presence. Tessier waved him off. Outside, lightning arced across the sky like blue fireworks.

"Are we sure we're headed the right way?" a crewman asked, not realizing their benefactor was in the room.

Again, the captain looked to Tessier, but this time for an answer, not an acknowledgement.

"We're headed right for our target," Tessier said. Finally, the captain spoke.

"How can you be sure?" he said.

"Because in this case, my heart is a compass," Tessier said. "I know where the target is, and for better or for worse, we need to sail through the gauntlet to find her."

Chapter 11: You could have knocked

Echo dreamed of dark things roaming beneath the waves.

She hadn't had this sort of dream for months, not since her Atlantean powers began to surface. She found herself briefly seeing through the eyes of sea creatures, which occasionally felt magical and thrilling, but more often than not left her shaken, witnessing the casual brutality of nature through the eyes of predator and prey.

But tonight, she dreamed of a great shadow, a many-armed thing moving slowly in the depths. She could not make out its complete shape, and the size of it was hard to judge as well. She couldn't tell how close the vision was to the creature, and there was nothing in the murky depths to provide scale.

Things swarmed around it. She thought at first they were parasites, but they were too organized, too structured in their movements. They seemed to be an extension of its massive body.

What are you? she thought in her dream.

And then the colossus, whatever it was, turned its eyes toward her, a pair of burning orange orbs burning through the foggy salt water. She felt her blood turn cold, her stomach turn to acid; but there was no malice in its gaze. If anything, it seemed disinterested in her, as if it took her measure and, in an instant, deemed her utterly unworthy of its attention.

But the creatures that swarmed around it had other thoughts.

Those bright eyes turned away from her, the bulk of the creature moving away as if in slow motion. But the parasites began to move closer, charging at her like a swarm of wasps, and then she could hear the hissing and the sound of teeth grinding...

Echo woke up gasping for air, nearly knocking herself out of the hammock she slept in by taking a swing at the monsters in her dreams. Her mouth tasted like seawater, and her skin was covered in enough sweat to make her feel like she'd been swimming. Moonlight shone through the window in the cabin she'd taken to calling home. Great, she thought. Terrified, wide awake, and it's the middle of the night. I'll never get back to sleep now.

She closed her eyes and tried to relax, but every muscle fiber was tense, her skin crawling at the memory of those burning eyes looking up at her from the depths. So, was that a nightmare or a vision? she thought. Is that some rough beast slouching off to Bethlehem to be born? That thought, as morbid as it was, brought a smile to her face. Her mother would be proud to know she could still quote William Butler Yeats when she needed to. Meredith wanted more poetry in Echo's life, and she'd been particularly fond of Yeats. Having "Second Coming" spring to mind after a nightmare wasn't comforting, but remembering her mother always was.

She heard a thump on the deck above her and opened her eyes again. Both the boys had tendencies to wander at night, especially Barnabas who seemed to sleep not much more than four hours a night, and Artem had a tendency, like, Echo, to wake at odd hours and patrol the ship for no reason. She listened for the familiar graceful footfalls of Artem or the uneven gait of Barnabas, both of which she'd had plenty of time to grow accustomed to hearing in recent weeks.

She didn't recognize the footsteps. She did recognize the sound of water hitting the deck above however, as if someone had pulled themselves up out of the ocean.

Echo slid quietly from her hammock and picked up her trident.

She glanced at her armor neatly set aside on top of a cabinet, but decided she didn't have the time for it. Instead, she crept toward the stairs and listened.

Dragging footsteps. Heavy. Wet. Unfamiliar. A fierce smell of the ocean, not just the sea breeze but something deeper, more primal.

Was her dream a warning?

She made her way to the top of the stairs, waiting for her eyes to adjust. Standing in the dark was a thick-set figure, broad-shouldered, skin shifting from mottled gray to a more human tone. The visitor's body shook as it changed shape.

Echo readied to throw her trident, reaching back with perfect form like Artem had instructed her.

"You better have a damned good reason to be on my boat," she said.

"Y'know, I really thought about the first thing you'd say to me when we saw each other again, and that was definitely not on the list," a familiar voice said from the darkness.

Echo let her trident fall to the ground, clattering all the way back down the stairs. She ran across the deck and launched herself into the arms of the newcomer, throwing a bear hug around him.

"Yuri Rodriguez! I was looking for you!" she said, clutching her oldest friend tightly enough to break him. He hugged her back, picking her up off the deck and holding her so her feet dangled. "What are you doing sneaking on board in the middle of the night?"

"I was looking for you, too!" Yuri said. He set her down, but Echo held onto both of his hands as if to make sure he wouldn't disappear. "I didn't think I'd find you out here in the middle of nowhere in the dead of night. I figured I could, like, swim circles around your ship like a creeper until morning or climb on board and hope someone was awake."

"You could have knocked," Echo said.

"What, on the hull?" Yuri said. "That wouldn't have been creepy or anything."

"What the hell is going—oh, it's you," Barnabas said. Standing in an undignified combination of striped pirate pants and his long coat and nothing else, holding out a magic wand made out of driftwood like a pistol, the magician looked bleary-eyed but ready to defend his ship. Beside him, a sleepy and shirtless Artem, looking as always like he'd been sculpted of marble, let his sword arm drop to his side.

"Hello, Yuri," Artem said with a polite smile.

"Hey, dude," Yuri said. "Holy crap, Barnabas, you look like what would happen if someone startled a sleeping, bald Sirius Black."

Barnabas tucked the wand into the waistband of his pants and pointed at Yuri.

"I... do not get that cultural reference," he said. "But I assume it's an insult."

"Depends on who you ask, I guess," Yuri said.

"I'm allergic to banter," Artem said. "I'm going back to bed. Yuri, it will be a pleasure to hear stories of where you've been. In the morning, with coffee."

"Sorry for the rude awakening, Artem,'" Yuri said.

The Amazon waved him off.

"Morning. Coffee," he said, disappearing below deck.

"You okay? In one piece?" Barnabas said.

"More or less," Yuri said.

"Well then, I'll let you two catch up," Barnabas said, wrapping his coat around himself like a bathrobe. "Good to have you back on board, kid."

"Thanks, Barney," Yuri said.

"You get one freebie. Next time you do that I cast a spell and you wake up with termites in your pants."

"Got it," Yuri said as Barnabas went back below.

Echo grabbed Yuri by both shoulders and shook him affectionately.

"I missed you, you goofball," Echo said. "You know I wanted to look for you. I just thought you... needed time."

"I did," Yuri said. "But Echo… I saw something I think you should know about. Something about Atlantis."

Echo felt her shoulder slump involuntarily. She forced a smile.

"Well then," she said. "Let's put some coffee on and you can tell me about it. Are you here to stay?"

Yuri beamed at her, the joyful smile she'd grown up with and missed so much when he was gone.

"I think it's time I came home," he said.

Chapter 12: It's not our fault, but it's our fault

Echo and her crew had breakfast on the deck, sitting or standing in a semi-circle as Yuri retold everyone what he'd told Echo the night before, about the island, and Whitetip, and more importantly about the dead Atlanteans.

"Whom you didn't kill," Artem said.

"No," Yuri said. "Which I've explained multiple times."

"Just making sure," Artem said. "You did have some self-control issues last time we saw you."

"I really thought coming home to you guys would be a lot nicer," Yuri said.

"And they said it was something coming up from out of Poseidon's Scar? You're sure?" Echo said.

Yuri nodded, devouring some bacon Barnabas had brought up from the mess earlier.

"That's what they told me. Before, y'know. They expired," he said.

"Walk me through this one more time," Artem said. "Barnabas and I were elsewhere. What happened in the Scar?"

Echo, sitting cross-legged on the deck, leaned back on her hands.

"One of the submarines was headed closer to the surface to

launch an attack," Echo said. "While Yuri over there fought off a huge monster that might have been being manipulated by Reina's people, I… y'know. Punched the submarine until it sank."

"You punched the submarine into submission," Artem said.

"I punch really hard," Echo said.

"Why was all this happening?" the girl Echo had introduced to Yuri as Muireann said. Yuri eyeballed her, trying to figure out her angle. She certainly wasn't his replacement as the funny companion, that was clear from the conversation so far.

"We were stopping a war," Yuri said. "Typical superhero stuff."

"Long story," Echo said. "I guess the shortest way of explaining it is some Atlanteans thought it'd be a good idea to start a war with the surface world, stole a bunch of submarines, and then we came along and stopped them."

"By punching the submarines," Muireann said.

"When all you have is a hammer, every problem looks like a nail," Echo said.

"I'm going to start calling you Aqua-Hammer," Yuri said.

"Please don't," Echo said.

"So… something woke up in the Scar, then," Artem said. "The combat stirred it up."

"The Atlantean soldiers I met didn't say that specifically, but that has to be it, right? I mean you sort of deposited a nuclear submarine on the doorstep of Poseidon's scar," Yuri said.

"You?" Echo said.

"We?" Yuri responded. "I mean you want credit for punching the submarine."

"It really did seem like a good idea at the time," Echo said. She took a sip of coffee and rubbed her temple. "So, it's not our fault, but it's sort of our fault that something terrible is coming up out of the ravine and eating Atlanteans."

"Don't say what I think you're going to say," Barnabas said.

"We have to go tell Atlantis," Echo said.

"That is exactly what I was hoping you wouldn't say," Barnabas said. "They're an astronomically powerful undersea society. They don't need our help. They can totally handle this, Echo."

"Why don't you want to go help them?" Echo said, leaning forward.

Barnabas stood up, clearing his plate.

"Because in our direct experience, Atlantis is nothing but trouble," he said. "And worse, they don't appreciate it when people help them."

Artem laughed.

"This is about politeness?" he said.

"I'm just not fond of helping jackasses," Barnabas said.

"Will you help if we go?" Echo asked.

"Of course I will," Barnabas said. "I will just glare at everyone judgmentally when everything goes pear-shaped."

"We do keep you around for your overwhelming sense of maturity," Echo said.

"This is assuming they want to see any of us in Atlantis again. We might have done some good there, but half the ruling party did try to kill, well, all of us," Yuri said.

"Half the ruling party killed my husband," Artem said, his tone deathly cold.

No one spoke for a moment. Echo broke the silence.

"You don't have to come with us, Artem," Echo said. "You have every reason to not care what happens to Atlantis."

The Amazon shook his head.

"No, I'm not going to take out my rage at a handful of evil people on an entire city," he said. "We'll continue to do what we have done all along and fix the messes the Atlanteans create for themselves. Clearly this is our lot in life now. Just... keep me out of the room with your aunt, if you can."

"I will," Echo said.

Muireann raised her hand.

"I... So, I suppose I must ask—am I invited along with this? Will they let me into the city? Do you even want me along?"

Barnabas' face twisted into a pained expression.

"You are welcome to stay on the ship when we go," he said.

"I'm half-tempted to stay here myself, but unfortunately I'm the designated magic user in this group, so I might be stuck tagging along."

"I'd like to see Atlantis, if you'll let me join you," Muireann said.

Barnabas looked at Echo, who looked at Yuri, who looked at Artem.

"None of us actually want to go there," Yuri said. "I guess it'd be nice to have someone along who would actually, like, enjoy seeing it for the first time?"

"The other question is how we're getting there," Artem said.

"The ghost crew remembers roughly where the city is, so we can get to the waters above Atlantis," Barnabas said. "You still have the water-breathing earring, yeah?"

"Yes, but that's still a deep dive," Artem said. "Are Echo and Yuri going to drag the rest of us?"

"I can breathe underwater," Muireann said. "If that's helpful."

"That's a start," Artem said.

"How did you get there before?" Muireann asked.

"A giant jellyfish," Yuri said.

"Excuse me?" Muireann said.

"Oh, I'd forgotten about that," Barnabas said. "That was one of the most disconcerting journeys I've ever made in my entire life. Let's not do that again."

"I don't think it's an option," Echo said. "We set the jellyfish free, remember?"

"I think I can help with that," Muireann said.

"Please tell me ondines can't transform into giant jellyfish," Artem said.

"What's an ondine?" Yuri said.

"No, I can't transform into a giant jellyfish," Muireann said.

"Oh. She's an ondine," Yuri said. "Doesn't exactly clarify what an ondine is, but at least it gives me a point of reference for this conversation."

"I can summon a traveling sphere," Muireann said.

"A what now?" Yuri said.

"It's like a bubble that I can control," Muireann said. "I can summon one and we can ride it wherever we need to go."

Barnabas' entire demeanor changed. He leaned in curiously.

"Can you teach me that spell?"

Muireann shot him a mildly annoyed look.

"No," she said.

"Fair enough," Barnabas said. "Giant force field bubble. That'd work."

"Welcome to the team, I guess," Echo said. "Where we instantly put your special powers to work in mundane ways."

Muireann shrugged.

"You saved me from a ship full of dead sailors. This is the very least I can do to repay you."

"You saved her from what?" Yuri said.

Echo rubbed her temple again as if fighting off a growing headache.

"We have so much to catch you up on," she said. "Barnabas, want to tell the crew where we're headed?"

Barnabas saluted her and trotted off, talking to the invisible crew the way he always did, as though chatting with the deceased was something people do all the time.

"I guess I'm going home," Echo said.

Yuri gave her a sheepish smile.

"I'm sorry," he said. "This is sort of my fault."

"Nope," Echo said. "I think there is so much blame to go around on this we'll never get it sorted out."

Chapter 13: I don't really call it home

The ghost crew took them through the weird and winding pathways Barnabas was so fond of, where time and space on the open ocean bent and twisted, taking them to the waters above Atlantis far faster than they naturally should have been able to.

Echo watched Muireann's reaction to the journey, but the ondine seemed to not be the least bit put off by it. It's as if she's no stranger to the aquatic leylines they followed, Echo thought. She wasn't one hundred percent inclined to trust her, but it did lend credibility to her story about being a magic user herself.

The skies above Atlantis were gray and overcast when they arrived, but the air warm, almost welcoming. Different from the last time they were here, under brighter skies, but cooler temperatures.

Yuri leaned over the railing and looked straight down.

"I guess this is where we jump in," he said.

Artem and Barnabas watched Yuri expectantly. He noticed.

"What," Yuri said.

"Curious about your transformation," Artem said.

"I'm dying to see it," Barnabas said.

Yuri looked to Echo as if for help.

"I mean, you don't have to transform, I guess," Echo said.

"Muireann, how many people can fit in the bubble you're going to conjure?"

Muireann pursed her lips as if calculating.

"I mean, we could all fit, but it'll be tight," she said. "With four, we'd be a bit cramped, but alright."

"I'll swim down beside the bubble," Echo said. "Yuri, why don't you ride with everyone else?"

"I was really hoping to see you transform in a non-combat situation," Barnabas said.

"I'm self-conscious!" Yuri said. "And now I'm twice as self-conscious because you're being creepy about it!"

"All things being equal, not showing up at the doors of Atlantis with a were-shark in tow might be the better approach," Artem said.

Muireann approached the port side of the ship and uttered a quiet incantation. An incandescent bubble, like one made of soap, rose out of the water and floated before her. She stepped off the ship and dropped into the bubble, a bit ungracefully, and then beckoned for the others to follow.

"Okay," Barnabas said, preparing to jump in. His old flintlock pistol was holstered to his left thigh.

Echo caught his arm.

"I thought you were changing your mind about that," she said, pointing at the gun.

"Last time we were in Atlantis, I knocked over an entire prison," Barnabas said. "I feel like maybe it's in my best interest to be prepared to defend myself."

"We saved this city," Echo said. "I'm sure they're over the prison thing."

"Still, I didn't get this far in life by assuming the good nature of strangers," he said, then jumped off the boat and into the bubble to join Muireann.

Artem followed, dropping down with catlike grace. Yuri smiled to Echo as he prepared to join them.

"I missed you," he said.

"I missed you more, you goofball," Echo said.

"Think your family's going to be happy to see you?"

"Not a chance in hell," Echo said.

Yuri laughed and jumped clumsily into the bubble. Echo dove off the edge of the ship, and Muireann, her hands raised, gestured downward, the bubble following her commands.

Echo took lead, swimming—at a speed that, even after months of knowing the powers she possessed, still scared her a little bit—down into the depths. For a time, they were surrounded by deep blue nothingness on all sides, the light from the surface growing dimmer and dimmer. Eventually, Echo could make out the lights of Atlantis in the distance, the city looking as if someone had dropped a vast, glittering tiara on the ocean floor. She beckoned the bubble to follow her and darted forward.

They didn't get much closer, however, before they were intercepted by a pair of armored Atlantean guards, who darted up on the backs of giant seahorses to stop them.

"Halt," one said. Echo almost laughed at the quaintness of it. "Go no farther."

"It's her," the other guard said. "Princess. Welcome home."

Echo waved a hand casually at them, as if she did this all the time.

"I don't really call it home," she said. "And no need for titles, guys. I'm just Echo."

The guards looked at each other, then back at her.

"I honestly don't think I can bring myself to call you by your first name, Princess. Protocol and all that."

"What's your name?" Echo asked.

"Dranis. Ma'am."

"Oh no, I'm definitely not ma'am either," she said. "Princess is less painful than ma'am."

"I could maybe do... my lady?" Dranis said.

"We just keep digging ourselves deeper into an awkward social situation," Echo said. "How about we just avoid calling me anything?"

"I will try," Dranis said. His compatriot put a hand on his forehead and looked away as if ashamed of his partner. "I assume you wish to enter the city?"

"That was my hope, yeah," she said. "I have my team with me. The ones who helped during the... Y'know. The thing."

"We remember," the second guard said. "You should know—the common folk speak warmly of you all, even though most never met you. Your companions all left quite an impression for a..."

"For heroes," Dranis said, jumping in to save his partner from speaking.

"You were going to say something slanderous, weren't you?" Echo said. "And if you ma'am me I might cry."

"I was going to say surface dwellers," he said. "I'm sorry."

"That's... I mean that's an accurate description," Echo said.

"It's usually said as a slur," Dranis said, giving his partner a heavy dose of stink-eye.

"Well then don't say it to us again, I guess," Echo said. "Even though we do dwell, like, on the surface. Anyway, can we go in?"

"This way," Dranis said with a grand gesture toward the city.

They were led downward to the main gates, which Echo found somewhat hilarious given that it was possible to swim up and over the walls of Atlantis into the city proper. She'd asked her father about it briefly before they parted ways last, and he said it was a holdover from a city that had not always rested on the bottom of the sea. Much of the city was air-filled, either through powerful technology or equally powerful magic, but the walls themselves were nothing more than what they appeared to be, marking the edge of Atlantis in golden stone, carved with ancient, intricate reliefs of sea life and mythological figures.

I hate that I think this place is beautiful, Echo thought.

They were joined silently by an honor guard of sorts. Additional guards, some swimming and others riding seahorses or other exotic creatures, formed a vanguard around them as they approached the gates. The archway into Atlantis opened as they arrived, no message sent, no words spoken. The daughter of the co-ruler of

Atlantis apparently still warrants some pomp and circumstance, she thought uncomfortably. So much for making a quiet entrance.

The honor guard led them down a thoroughfare to a central building, massive and ornate, where Echo knew much of the government did its work. It broke into tall, coral-like spires, which were broken up by windows lit from within. Again, a set of doors opened without a signal, and the two guards who first found them let Echo and her team inside.

Within, they found themselves in an underwater foyer, terminating in a set of steps that led up to an air-filled zone.

Dranis bowed.

"This is where we leave you, Princess," he said.

"We talked about the princess thing, Dranis," she said.

The guard smiled broadly.

"Well, we're within earshot of people who would get mad at me for breaking protocol," he said. "I apologize, and I leave you to their care."

"Stay safe out there, Dranis," Echo said. "Bad things are afoot. Or a-swim. Or whatever the Atlantean euphemism is for that."

"Understood," he said, backing away.

Echo made her way up the stairs and stepped from the water. Behind her, the bubble containing her friends followed, inching close to the landing. She glanced back and saw all four of the passengers watching her expectantly, unsure whether they should step out of the bubble.

When Echo turned forward, she saw why.

A royal escort awaited her, guards in gold and green armor, tridents in hand and swords at their hips. Standing amongst them, beaming at her proudly behind his elegant, curly beard, was her father, Rhegis. King of Atlantis. Or, Echo corrected, whatever you call someone who shares rule of a place with his sister.

A complicated mix of resentment, annoyance, joy, and pride wrestled in her chest as she looked upon her father for the first time in months. She wanted to be angry with him, desperately wanted to not forgive him for everything that happened before, but her dad was smiling at her like she was the center of his universe, and Echo couldn't help but smile back. Somehow, this made her even angrier than she already was.

She turned to her friends and made an exaggerated "get out of there" gesture with both arms. Artem stepped from the bubble smoothly; Barnabas with a bit of a process, seemingly catching his coattails on the force field; and Yuri almost face-planted as he moved from bubble to platform. Muireann calmly exited as well, and with her leaving, the bubble winked out of existence.

"I missed you, Echo," Rhegis said.

"I… right," Echo said. "I guess the king doesn't usually just meet guests at the door regularly."

"Not regularly, no," Rhegis said. He turned a less high-voltage but still warm expression on her friends. "Welcome back, all of you. I see you have a new companion?"

Muireann bowed her head politely.

"I'm called Muireann, your grace," she said. Echo spotted Artem and Barnabas swap a confused look at how easily Muireann slipped into a proper courtly tone.

"Well, Muireann, welcome to Atlantis. Any traveling companion of my daughter is free to walk these halls," Rhegis said. He returned his attention to Echo. "I'd ask what brings you here unexpectedly, but I suspect whatever it is, this isn't a simple social call."

"Yeah, um," Echo said. "Yuri found something, and, ah, can we talk? We should talk. Maybe not in the hallway."

Rhegis nodded.

"I suspected as much. A room is being prepared. We'll get you fed and you can tell us what you and your friends have found."

Chapter 14: A collection of facts

I don't know about everyone else, Yuri thought, struggling to fit his broad frame into an Atlantean-style chair, but I am ridiculously uncomfortable.

They'd been led to a large open room, lined with windows on one side overlooking the city. Inside, several people already waited, some of whom looked vaguely familiar, people they might have come across when they first came to Atlantis the last time.

A large table dominated the room. A wide variety of food had been laid out, little of which Yuri could identify, let alone get up the courage to eat. He watched as Artem eyed different fruit-like objects, picked one up to examine it, and then gingerly ripped it open and began to eat it. Echo watched which items her father chose and copied him. Barnabas ignored all the food and went right for a carafe of something dark and unpleasant-looking.

Yuri took a guess at cubed fish he thought looked a bit like sushi he'd had before, popping it into his mouth and swallowed without chewing. Yup, definitely some sort of sushi fish, he thought. I wish I liked sushi.

"Yuri," Rhegis said, sitting down at the head of the table. The other Atlanteans followed Rhegis' gaze. Yuri felt his skin grow hot. "I understand you found some of our soldiers."

"I did," he said. "They washed ashore. I went to Echo before coming here because I thought it would be better if you heard it from her."

"Your entrance into the city was probably more pleasant because of that decision. I understand your hesitation. Can you tell us where you left the bodies?" Rhegis said. "We want to send people to retrieve them for proper funerals."

"Yeah. Yeah, of course," Yuri said. "I can explain where."

Rhegis thanked him as the door to the chamber opened, interrupting. In strode Reina, Rhegis' sister and Echo's aunt. They all had reasons to hate her, but Yuri stole a glance specifically at Artem. It had been Reina's assassin who killed Artem's husband. *I should hate her too*, Yuri thought. It was that same assassin who hired the were-sharks to attack the Island of Unwanted Things, where Yuri contracted lycanthropy from a bite. Maybe a few months ago he would have hated her, but after all the time he'd spent learning from Whitetip—who, Yuri hoped, would not run afoul of the Atlanteans when they came to retrieve the bodies— he'd come to see the value in his ability to transform as well. The experience of changing haunted him, and he was still more than a little afraid of himself when he was not in human form, but there were worse fates.

He didn't lose the person he loved the most in the world.

Artem watched Reina with a burning gaze, but said nothing, ropey forearms folded across his armored chest.

"Well, this is awkward," Reina said, sitting down close to, but not directly beside, her brother, and not particularly close to her niece, either.

"Yuri, Echo told me you said the Atlantean soldier you spoke with before he expired said whatever attacked them came from 'the Scar?'" Rhegis said, ignoring his sister.

I know we're at the bottom of the ocean, but this room just got cold, Yuri thought.

"Yeah, that's what he told me," Yuri said. "I'm sorry I don't have more information. He was barely hanging on when I found him and... I don't think I could have saved him.

"Nobody's blaming you for that," Rhegis said. "If whatever killed him took out his entire squad, it's fortunate he made it away to warn anyone at all. And, unfortunately, we have some mounting evidence that this was not an isolated incident."

As he said this, the doors opened again. Yuri recognized one of the men entering as the old spymaster they'd met when they snuck into Atlantis that first time. He looked harried.

"Keeping things from me again, brother? I thought we were finished with cloak and dagger nonsense," Reina said.

"This is new information that came to Grimmin's attention very recently. We didn't want to worry anyone without further investigation," Rhegis said. He gestured for Grimmin to sit down, but the old spy made an awkward motion with his hands as if to say he'd prefer to stand.

"I only just informed his grace today," Grimmin said. "Our patrols found a dead afanc and the ruined corpse of one of our seahorses, most likely the mount of one of the men who washed up on the surface."

"Today," Reina said. "And how long have you known?"

Grimmin looked to Rhegis, who nodded.

"No more than forty-eight hours, your grace," Grimmin said. "Long enough for an autopsy on the seahorse, and to send out a scouting party to follow up."

"We can't rule this city equally if you keep things from me, brother," Reina said.

"I'm sure you have pockets full of secrets you're not sharing with me, Reina," Rhegis said. "And given what Grimmin discovered, I'd beg you to leave the petty infighting alone this time."

"Petty infighting? Don't project onto me, Rhegis. You're the one whose spymaster is running scouting missions no one else knows about."

"How about we hear what Grimmin found so we're not all sitting around the table in suspense like a bunch of idiots?" Echo

said.

Rhegis looked mortified, Reina scandalized, Grimmin like he was fighting back an inappropriate smile.

Barnabas burst out laughing.

"Okay, right then," Grimmin said. "Let me just fill everyone in."

He described the mystical exploration of Poseidon's Scar, the depth they went to, and the empty, massive nest they'd found deep below. All infighting went quiet as he spoke. For all their squabbling, Yuri could tell that the council and the ruling siblings put their differences aside when there was a clear and present danger to their home.

Yuri raised his hand.

"You said a dead afanc?" he said. He felt all eyes in the room turn on him. Catching Reina staring, he gave her his most awkward smile.

"I… so I fought an afanc last time," he said. "Like, hard. That thing wasn't dying easy."

"This boy fought an afanc?" one of the councilors Yuri couldn't identify said.

"This boy's more than he appears," Rhegis said. "Everyone in my daughter's cadre is."

"Yeah, I got infected with were-shark lycanthropy while trying to keep the queen from killing my friends," Yuri said, then held up a hand apologetically. "Water under the bridge, though, no hard feelings. We're cool. But like, you know were-sharks, right? We're pretty much indestructible, and I bloodied the afanc's nose pretty bad, but he was still alive and kicking when I left."

"When my men found him, he was shredded into bait," Grimmin said.

"Well, that's terrifying," Echo said. "That's like finding out someone chewed up a school bus."

"So, let me make sure I understand this," Reina said. "We have a dead giant sea predator, a number of our men murdered, and a giant empty nest deep in Poseidon's Scar. Do we have any evidence all these things are connected? I'm not disagreeing, necessarily—I'm just trying to take a larger view now that we have the pieces on the table."

"Yuri," Rhegis said. "I hate to ask such a... grim question, but how were our men injured when you found them?"

Yuri's stomach turned into a pool of acid remembering the sight.

"They were ripped up pretty badly," he said. "Lots of, well, they looked like bite marks."

"Half-moons, roughly this wide?" Grimmin said, holding his hands apart about a foot and a half.

"I mean, it was hard to tell," Yuri said. "But yeah, they were half-circle bites, like that. And lots of pointed puncture marks. Not the triangular style you'd…. um, see a shark make."

Grimmin looked to Rhegis, who frowned, and then turned to his sister, as if having a silent conversation.

"Oh, no," Echo said. She put a hand on Artem's shoulder since he'd sat closest to her. "The bodies on the ship."

"What bodies on what ship?" Yuri said.

"You came across more corpses?" Grimmin said.

Echo threw her hands up, frustrated.

"I didn't even connect everything," Echo said. "We found a derelict ship on our way here."

"Half-moon bites," Artem muttered. "Gods, how did we not notice that until now?"

"We didn't know about the dead creatures here," Echo said. "And we hadn't reconnected with Yuri yet so…"

"Were there no survivors?" Rhegis said.

Muireann stood up.

"Sir, I was on the ship, but locked away when the attack happened. Something climbed aboard the vessel and murdered everyone on board. They might have killed me too if the captain hadn't locked me in a cabin for my own protection."

"From the attackers?" Rhegis said.

Muireann wrinkled her nose.

"From the crew, to be fair, your grace," she said.

Reina exhaled heavily, but not in a judgmental way—Yuri caught himself staring at the expression on her face, which seemed almost empathetic to Muireann's story.

"What concerns me, if I may," Grimmin said, taking the floor. "We have several attacks now that seem to indicate a swarm of some sort. The bodies I've seen almost look like something you'd expect from piranhas, except the bodies weren't consumed, just violated with bites. But that nest I saw through the scrying spell... something big lived there."

"How big?" Echo said.

"I... I can't really say. Why do you ask?" Grimmin said. "Do you know something?"

"I had a vision. Again. By the way, do Atlanteans have visions all the time or is this the whole human/Atlantean DNA thing acting up again?" Echo said.

"Visions are not common," Reina said. "But some of us have them. What did you see?"

"You say that like you're not mocking me, Aunt Reina," Echo said.

"That's because some of us have visions, niece Echo," Reina said, a slight curve of a smile forming in the corner of her mouth. "You saw something?"

"I couldn't make it out clearly, but it was big, and... I want to say it was lumbering through the water. Not swimming, really. More like plodding along, you know?" Echo said. "And it looked at me, with these big orange eyes, and then I woke up. That's all I saw."

The room went quiet for a moment. Finally, it was Reina who broke the silence.

"We need to look up the history of Poseidon's Scar," Reina said. "There must be something in the ancient archives about it."

"It might be the best place to start," Rhegis said.

"You have a library down here?" Echo said.

"Of course we do," Rhegis and Reina said simultaneously, both sounding equally offended.

"How do you have a library... under water?" Echo said.

"Magic, darling," Reina said. "Not that we haven't had a few flooding incidents."

Again, Barnabas laughed in appropriately loudly. Reina shot him the dirtiest look Yuri had ever seen.

"Oh, yes, laugh about that, magician," the regent said. "After all, our last library flood was a direct result of someone damaging our prison, causing foundation cracks across a tenth of the city."

"Oh," Barnabas said. "Sorry about that. Um, need some help looking through the archives? I'm a bit of a speed reader."

Chapter 15: The Library of Atlantis

For the first time in a very long time Barnabas Coy had to pretend he wasn't excited about something.

Given his history and life choices, he found enthusiasm hard to come by. He envied people who found simple joy in looking forward to the little things in life. He wasn't a joyless person, exactly. He just rarely showed it. He learned the hard way how often the world will disappoint you.

But as Reina led them graciously into the Library of Atlantis, Barnabas—pirate, wizard, seeker of secrets—saw a room full of things worth knowing, and he instantly wanted to know them all. Stacks of books rose several stories high, long, elegant archways connecting catwalks and landings. Between the shelves and racks, artifacts—some clear of purpose and others inscrutable—broke up the endless tomes to offer visual mysteries. The room was relatively empty, with just a scattering of Atlanteans making their way among the higher stacks. The room, he noted, was bone dry. He could smell the enchantments built into the room protecting it from the moisture of the ocean.

"I could legitimately spend five years here and never leave," he muttered under his breath. Echo smirked at him.

"I wouldn't have pegged you for a bookworm," she said.

"Every magician is a bookworm," he said. "Books are where all the things worth knowing are."

"This is what it takes to get poetry out of you," Echo said. "I'm good with that."

For once, Barnabas withstood the barbs and had nothing with which to retort. It was taking all his willpower to not dart off and just start opening books at random to see what they contained. He did, however, drift a bit to the side behind the group so he could scan the shelves, surreptitiously pulling a pair of small, simple glasses from within his pirate coat.

Artem caught the sleight of hand.

"Oh," Artem said, staring.

"Are you going to make fun of me, too?" Barnabas said.

"No, you just... The glasses suit you, oddly enough. They look nice on you."

"I really can't tell if you're making fun of me," Barnabas said.

"Just take the compliment before it gets any more awkward," Artem said.

"Deal," Barnabas said.

"Hey, you wear glasses now?" Yuri said. Barnabas groaned. Yuri held out his hand for a high-five. "Glasses bros!"

"We're not glasses bros," Barnabas said. "These are enchanted glasses. They let me read languages I can't otherwise speak."

"Some might consider that cheating," said an Atlantean woman she had never met before. Her hair was a soft shade of purple with a silver streak along the part. "Though personally, anything that assists in the gaining of knowledge I approve of."

"Echo and company, let me introduce you to our head librarian, Lady Sawya," Reina said. She introduced them in turn. "Princess Echo, my brother's daughter. Her companions, Artem of New Scythia, the smuggler Barnabas Coy, and Yuri of..."

"Massachusetts," Yuri said. "Grand Poobah of the North Shore."

"I know you're lying to me, but I really can't be bothered to argue," Reina said. Sawya had affixed her eyes on Barnabas.

"You," she said. "You're the one who flooded the prison."

"Y'know, that really wasn't my fault," he said. Sawya appeared unconvinced.

"We're here in search of information about Poseidon's Scar," Echo chimed in. Sawya gave Echo her full attention.

"I can honestly say I can't remember the last time anyone asked about that particular topic," Sawya said.

She led them up a walkway to an area above, somewhat cut off from the rest of the collection. She examined the spines of several books, then withdrew a map case. Reina held out a hand, and Sawya handed the case to her.

"Do you know what created the Scar?" Echo asked as Reina carefully opened the map case and gingerly rolled out the map inside on a nearby table.

"I don't know if you'll find your answer here," Sawya said. "Poseidon's Scar predates Atlantis. It was, as far as I know, here when we arrived."

Reina beckoned the group over to view the map.

"It's as I suspected. Atlantean cartographers have mapped out the surface of the Scar very well, but none have done significant exploration of its depth," she said.

"Any particular reason why?" Yuri asked.

"Because we thought nothing was out there," Grimmin said, entering the library and the conversation unexpectedly. He walked up the stairway to join them. "A dark, hot pit in the middle of the ocean where nothing could live. Our engineers considered looking at ways to use the thermal energy for something, but turned to other means of powering Atlantis instead. It was just a geological graveyard."

"All this time, and nobody ever wondered what was down there," Artem said.

Reina chimed in, rising from where she'd hunched over the map.

"Atlantis considers itself the caretaker of the entire ocean," she said. Noticing a frown on Echo's face, she continued. "Whether or not you believe we've failed at that task, the truth remains we have people and forces watching over the seven seas, from the poles to the Equator and back again. Were some of our scholars curious about this gash in the earth in our own backyard? Of course. But we had wars to fight and monsters to manage and, as you've seen, our own internal struggles. We had a surface world hell bent on killing us all. And in fairness, nothing ever came out of that ravine, not in a thousand years."

Barnabas scanned the nearby shelves, not sure what, exactly, he was looking for, hoping for a gut instinct to grab him.

"What about mythology?" Barnabas said.

"What now?" Echo said.

"We're talking about expeditions, or history, or geology, or whatever," Barnabas said. "But places like Poseidon's Scar, they usually have a story behind them. Myth is often used to explain away the unknown. And myth is right here in the name."

He turned away from the books to look at the room and saw half the room making awkward faces of disbelief.

"What?" he said.

"There's a fairly strong belief that Poseidon is not a myth among some Atlanteans," Grimmin said.

"Do you honestly believe the Greek pantheon is real?" Barnabas said.

"There's a fairly strong *belief* that Poseidon is real among *some* Atlanteans," Grimmin repeated, this time putting strong emphasis on very specific words. Clearly Grimmin didn't believe it himself, but knew when to be polite.

Echo, however, had no such compulsion.

"Look, back where Yuri and I grew up, almost everyone in this room is a myth, so I know the line is a little blurry, but that's a heck of a line of yarn to pull on," Echo said. "If Poseidon is real, doesn't that mean all the rest of it is real?"

The room went dead silent for a moment. Then Reina started laughing.

"I like you more and more the longer I know you, niece," she

said.

Echo gave her aunt a raised-eyebrow side-eye look but kept whatever thoughts she had running through her head at that moment to herself.

"The sleazy one has a point, though," Reina said. "Perhaps we're looking in the wrong place. There might very well be information we can glean from myth that doesn't exist in textbooks."

Echo turned to Sawya.

"Do you have that sort of information here?" she said.

The librarian frowned deeply.

"We have some, but the Greek pantheon, despite a certain love of Poseidon among some of the population here, isn't our deepest collection. And I know I've never encountered something along those lines. Another library more inclined to track the complete picture of that pantheon might be a better bet."

"Where should we go?" Echo said. "My friends and I will travel wherever you need us to."

She pointed at Barnabas as if he were about to speak.

"Don't contradict me," Echo said. "This is important."

"Hey," Barnabas said, putting his hands up defensively. "I like books. I'm not arguing."

"The closest library I can think of where you might find answers is…" Sawya began, but Artem cut her off.

"New Scythia," he said, folding his arms across his chest.

"Where?" Yuri said.

"Oh," Echo said. "But can you… can we…?"

"You're the son of an Amazon," Reina said. "Oh, this took a fascinating turn."

"Oh!" Yuri said. "Oh, oh no. Are you even allowed to go home?"

Artem shrugged noncommittally.

"Frankly, I don't know that they'd allow any of us in," he said. "I was sent away, but for something this important they may allow me to visit. You two I can almost promise they won't let in."

He pointed to Barnabas and Yuri. Barnabas shrugged in an almost mirror image of Artem's gesture.

"I've been banned from better places," he said.

"What if I send Echo as our representative, from the royal family of Atlantis?" Reina said. "We have sent emissaries before, with honor guards."

"They may let us dock. I can't promise anything after that," Artem said. "If you explain what we're doing and our role in the previous conflict, that would help. The Amazons honor heroes and heroic sacrifice. They may look more positively on us for that."

"Your father and I will have something drawn up and a message sent," Reina said.

Echo placed a hand on Artem's shoulder.

"You don't have to do this, you know," Echo said. "I can go alone."

"No," Artem said. "Part of me is afraid they'll bar me at the gates. But part of me is more afraid they won't. And you know I don't like being afraid. I'll go with you."

Barnabas, in a last attempt to dial down the disdain he felt from the librarian, leaned over conspiratorially to Sawya.

"Is there anything we can check out of their library for you? Maybe pocket some rare edition you don't have access to?"

"What a terrible thing to say," Sawya responded, almost smiling. "But if you could tell me all about what you see in their collection, I might dislike you slightly less when you get back."

Chapter 16: An ideal I may never be able to reach

Echo's group was provided with rooms in the castle, despite protests that they'd be happy to return to their ship to sleep.

"Humor me and give me one day knowing my daughter is safe under my roof," Rhegis insisted. But in the end, they all agreed that sleeping in a real bed would be a nice change of pace. They were fed an embarrassingly nice meal and most made their way to their individual rooms, leaving Echo to talk with her father alone.

Artem closed the door behind him and wandered anxiously around the sumptuous room he'd been provided. One entire wall was translucent, providing a view of the city below. A huge bed dominated the center of the room, and someone had left out a kit to polish his armor, and to sharpen his swords, as well as soft garments he assumed were some sort of pajamas.

I should hate this city, he thought to himself. He'd been able to restrain his emotions earlier around Reina, but she was, in the end, the reason Merrick died. She'd cost Artem the love of his life. And saving the city had almost killed all of them, several times over. Atlantis doesn't deserve the things we've done for it, Artem thought.

I'm not a vindictive man, he thought. But this place should

bring out the worst in me, and yet here I am, willing to do it all again.

He unclasped the elegant armored breastplate he wore, emblazoned with the eagle crest of the Amazons. A male breastplate, he thought, marveling again that it existed at all, or that Barnabas had found it among the discarded treasures of the Island of Unwanted Things and had given it to him. Someone, somewhere in time had been like him, a son of the Amazons. I am not unique, he thought. I am not alone.

No, I'm alone, he corrected. More than one person has worked hard to make that the case. Whoever owned this breastplate is long dead, and was just as alone as I am.

A knock came at his door. Artem waited a moment, then opened it. Echo stood outside. She'd changed from her own armor into a loose gown, borrowed from somewhere here much like the pajamas left for him. He held the door open for her and she entered.

"Room with a view," she said.

"I think every room here has a view," Artem said. He sat down at a tidy writing desk and spun the chair around to watch Echo, who found a spot on the corner of his bed.

"So," Echo said. "Going home."

"Not home," Artem corrected. "But the place I was born, yes."

"You don't have to, if you don't want to," Echo said. "I can go on my own. I get the impression if I'm designated as an emissary, they'll at least let me plead the case for Atlantis without turning me away."

Artem inhaled deeply, then turned to the watery world outside. Schools of fish darted around the way flocks of birds would on the surface. It's so alien and yet so mundane at the same time, he thought.

"I have to admit to you, Echo, I'm morbidly curious about going home," he said. "I really do wonder what they'll do."

"You weren't exiled, right?" Echo said. "You were…"

"Given away for my own safety, they say, but I think I just

made everyone too uncomfortable," Artem said. "I was an aberration. The older I got, the more I might be distrusted. The Amazons are, even I'll admit, better than the average society, but I was such a strange thing to them, they couldn't help but be unsettled by me."

He absent-mindedly released the tie keeping his hair in a coiled knot at the back of his scalp, letting his dark hair fall almost to his shoulders. He tugged at it, brushing out the tangles.

"The assassin talked about how the Amazons threw their sons off cliffs. Do you remember that?" he asked. Echo nodded. "That was true, once upon a time. In a time when everyone was less civilized, Amazon or otherwise. I wasn't discarded like garbage. The Island of Unwanted Things is not a rubbish bin. It's a place for people who have no place, and they teach those Unwanted Things how to survive at all costs. It was the best thing my mother could do for me. What else might she have done? Give me to your world?"

Echo grimaced.

"No," she said. "I don't think you'd like my world. Sometimes I don't like my world."

"So there," Artem said. "My mother made sure that I would survive. Without her and her people, yes, but she didn't pitch me off a cliff. She didn't put me in a reed basket and set me adrift. She gave me to good people."

"But still," Echo said.

"But still, my mother gave me away," Artem said. "It's a hard thing to forgive."

"And now you have a reason to go home," Echo said.

"You know something? I'm a bit envious of Barnabas," Artem said. "His story isn't much different from mine. Born in a place where he was not wanted and was not safe, given away to people who gave him a fighting chance, but still, abandoned."

"You two do bicker like brothers, you know," Echo said.

Artem gave her a pained smile.

"I know," he said. "But Barnabas knows his mother. He goes to her. She welcomes him."

"You weren't with us the first time we visited her," Echo said. "That whole island didn't want him there. I could feel it. The other nymphs were wound up by the very presence of him. I mean those mermaids almost killed Yuri, too."

"And here's the odd thing," Artem said. "The place Barnabas was born would have been a source of perpetual risk to him. Every day, some supernatural creature would have wanted to spill his blood. And he's almost clever enough that he would have survived, or at least would have after learning all he did on the Island of Unwanted Things. But it would have been exhausting. You can't live that way."

"No," Echo said. "But the Amazons aren't like that, right?"

"My life would not have been under constant threat," Artem said. "I simply would not have been looked upon as a real person. I was a reminder of a mistake. Barnabas was given away for his physical safety. I was given away for..."

"Shame," Echo said.

Artem held his hands out at his sides.

"Maybe. Or maybe someone would have tried to goad me into a fight and put an end to me. I'm not the easiest person to get along with. It wouldn't have been hard."

"But now you're grown," Echo said. "And everyone we've ever met says you're the greatest swordsman they've ever seen."

"None of them have seen Amazons fight," Artem said. "I'm chasing an ideal I may never be able to reach."

Echo squinted at him.

"Are you really sure you want to go back there?" she said.

"I absolutely do not want to go back there," Artem said. "But I know in my heart I need to."

Chapter 17: Weird little town

Simon Yee had no idea what he was getting himself into when he moved to Fogarty's Folly. It was a quiet town built around an old fishing village that had expanded into a hideaway where bluebloods with old New England money mixed with suburban social climbers with aspirations of wealth. Woven throughout Fogarty's Folly were the townies, the folks who were born here, working the sea or managing any of the quaint, rustic businesses that dotted the downtown and hooked tourists in during the summer.

Simon Yee moved here because it was a beautiful place, the old seaside buildings blended into the hilly, rocky coastline that gave the town its name, aging farmhouses refurbished by the wealthy into high-end single-family abodes that seemed to rise up throughout the tree-lush hills. From the water, it looked like a bit of a fairytale town, and it was easy to fall in love with.

Simon moved to Massachusetts from the West Coast, and he very much wanted to live on the ocean as he had back home, though New England waters were an entirely different creation than Californian. He moved here to help open a new office for his work, a government gig for a department that had very nearly been shut down years ago and only recently been refurbished.

It was a weird gig, and folks involved often called it the Department of What? Because the work was so hard to explain to laypeople, but Simon enjoyed the weird work.

Downtown Boston housing prices were insane, so he expanded his search, and found Fogarty's Folly, where a ferry ran into the city every day, meaning he could have the ocean breeze in his lungs as he commuted in, already logged into his laptop, rather than sitting in gridlock traffic. He'd had enough sitting in traffic in California to last a lifetime.

All in all, the move was good for him, though he hadn't quite figured out to make friends here yet. So, in the evenings, after work, he'd haunt the quaint downtown of Fogarty's Folly, having a drink at a local pub, grabbing dinner at the roast beef place that looked like it hadn't changed its décor in sixty years, and getting some soft-serve ice cream from a little shop, shaped like a giant plastic sundae, down by the beach. Simon was fit—part of the job requirements, really—but if this kept up, he'd be bursting through his shirts soon.

On this particular evening, he'd picked up fish and chips from the local seafood takeout place and was debating whether or not to carry it home or find a spot to sit down and eat it. The sky, near sunset, was a peculiar combination of deep, almost purple-blue clouds above, a hazy yellow along the horizon. It didn't feel natural, but it did look pretty. Simon found a bench, pulled the Styrofoam container from its greasy brown bag, dug out the cheap plastic utensils they'd given him, and decided to dine alone by the water. The sky was a bit creepy, but the temperature was pleasant. The smell of rain was on the air, but it was a nice night, overall.

As he finished, he started thinking about getting a coffee at the Ishmael's Donuts on the way home. Ishmael's stood out here in Fogarty's Folly because it was a national chain. The town seemed hell-bent on preventing chains from opening here. Clearly the local government had put some severe restrictions on how the building would look, because it lacked a lot of the signature exterior designs the chain used, offering an almost cute variation using old-fashioned wood signage that fit in better with Fogarty's Folly's historic vibe.

Before he got there, though, Simon saw something out of the corner of his eye that caught his attention, one lone figure at the end of the peer, staring out at the ocean. He thought he recognized the man, and started toward him, confirming that it was, in fact, one of the locals Simon had conversed with a bunch of times. Jeb Sykes was an odd character, well-known around town, but not for the right reasons. He bounced between jobs: bar back, manual labor unloading fishing boats, sometimes just panhandling outside the coffee shop. He was nice enough, and folks in town wanted to help him out, either by throwing him some work when they could or some spare change when they couldn't. Simon had talked to him pretty often and found him interesting in the way he seemed to be something of a survivor.

"How's it going, Jeb?" Simon said, strolling up the peer to join him.

Jeb Sykes said nothing in return. Simon slowed his pace, wondering if something was wrong. Jeb never appeared to have a substance problem, but you never knew with folks, and maybe something had changed. Jeb lived a hard life, and Simon would certainly understand if he'd fallen to drink or drugs.

"Jeb? It's Simon. Simon Yee. You okay, buddy?" Simon said. His job training kicked in immediately as he freed his hands from his pockets, kept his gait loose and ready to move.

"He has awoken, finally," Jeb said in a creepy, almost whispered tone.

Simon stopped walking.

"What's that, buddy?"

"Long have we waited," Jeb Sykes said. "Long have we built. Long has he slumbered. But he comes this way."

"Who's this you're talking about now?" Simon said.

Jeb turned around slowly. His eyes were bloodshot, his hair stiff and sticking up in all directions. His clothes looked unwashed, but that was sort of standard for the man.

"You," Jeb said, smiling a sickly smile. "Have you accepted the Old One into your heart?"

"I'm going to need a little more context than that," Simon said. He briefly regretted leaving his gear at home, but a stun baton felt like it might be overkill in this situation.

"He is awake, and he comes to his children!" Jeb Sykes said. "Can't you hear it? All I hear is his footsteps. Coming this way. We need to be ready!"

Jeb Sykes broke into a run, and Simon jumped back, unsure if he was about to be attacked. But instead he watched as Jeb darted off into the distance, yelling "Be ready!" at the top of his lungs, past Ishmael's and up into the hills beyond. The wealthy residents are going to love that, Simon thought. At least Jeb was a known figure in town. The local cops would go easy on him. Maybe he just got into something he shouldn't have ingested.

Not for the first time, Simon found his eye caught by a simple, blocky building that was nearly central to the downtown. Perfectly square, he'd never seen anyone coming or going from it, but had been told it was a lodge, like a local version of a Masonic temple. Apparently, it was a traditional hangout for local figures, like the town counsel, the police chief, small business owners.

Simon had been downtown almost every night since moving to Fogarty's Folly, and not once had he seen the lights on. Really, there was only one place to see light emanating from the building at all, the elegant stained glass windows surrounding the front door, depicting ocean scenes. Otherwise the structure was windowless, with odd symbols etched on to the outside, again, not unlike some Masonic temples he'd seen in other towns.

Tonight, though, he could see light through those windows, and from the roof as well, as if filtered through skylights.

Simon looked back over his shoulder, out to sea, at that strange, two-toned sky. This weird little town just got weirder, he thought. He wondered, with no small amount of anxiety, if he was going to have to call this in to the home office or not.

Chapter 18: Do I look like a Disney princess?

The next morning—at least it felt like morning to Echo, though day and night this far beneath the surface was hard to determine—they gathered once again in the council chambers. Her father and aunt were both waiting for Echo and her crew, along with Grimmin and a few other familiar faces, including the woman, Kara Kor, who had helped them sneak into the city on their first visit. Echo noticed, somewhat uncomfortably, that Kara stood noticeably close to her father's side.

I'll have to ask him about that little situation later, she thought.

"So, you're headed to New Scythia on our behalf," Rhegis said.

"Apparently," Echo said. "Think you can fend off the vicious, man-eating mystery monsters until we get back?"

"I think we can make do," Rhegis said. "Before you go, though, we have a few things for you."

"Presents," Yuri said. "You know what I miss? Presents. We don't do presents anymore. Too much fighting for our survival going on for tchotchkes."

Someone—an ornately dressed servant, whose role was unclear to Echo—stepped forward with an oversized seashell, like an oyster's. She presented it to Rhegis, who lifted it open.

"You'll be our representative," Rhegis said. "And while you're my daughter, we felt like you needed something a little more obvious to show your role here in Atlantis. This was to be yours regardless, but now seems like the appropriate time to give it to you."

He drew from the shell a crown of thin, elegantly worked gold, inlaid with pearl and other, more exotic gems Echo couldn't identify. It swooped up dramatically, like a wave, and yet somehow wasn't ostentatious. It conveyed royalty, but not excess, as pretty as it was. She hated it instantly.

"I'm not wearing a tiara," Echo said. "Look at me. Do I look like a Disney princess?"

"Maybe not a princess, but if I take my glasses off, you kind of look like someone drew a mashup of Pocahontas and Princess Kida," Yuri said.

"I have no idea who either of those people are," Rhegis said, smirking ever so slightly at Yuri's quip.

"I've been to the mainland and I have no idea who either of those people are," Barnabas said. "I think Yuri and Echo just had a surface-dweller bonding moment."

Echo stared at Yuri like he'd just belched in public.

"What?" Yuri said. "I meant that as a compliment."

"Since we're speaking of compliments," Rhegis said. "The rest of you will also be representing us and…"

"We're a hot mess," Yuri said.

"Speak for yourself," Artem said.

Muireann, who had been utterly silent so far, leaned in to Echo. "What about me?" she whispered.

"Just listen," Echo said. "Don't worry."

Grimmin walked up to Yuri with clothing draped over his forearm.

"You, Yuri Rodriguez, are a disaster," Grimmin said.

"Been told that my whole life."

"You are wearing clothes that clearly haven't been washed in weeks, and have visible blood stains," Grimmin said.

"Y'know, I've been meaning to try to bleach those out," Yuri

said.

Grimmin handed him the items in his hand.

"These are…" Grimmin began, but Yuri unfurled the clothes and held them up in front of him.

"These are balloon pants," Yuri said.

"They are loose-fitting garments favored by many of our outriders," Grimmin said. "And given your relatively new powers involve you nearly doubling in size, we thought perhaps pants that would fit you in both human and were-shark forms would be useful. There's a shirt as well that…"

Again, Yuri cut him off.

"This is a blouse," Yuri said. Echo disagreed—it looked more like a short bathrobe, cut like a tunic with a belt to hold it closed in the front with loose sleeves. Not flattering, Echo thought, but the Atlanteans had thought his transformation through more than anyone else had.

"Yuri, you're literally wearing blood-stained pajamas and a tank top that is stretched out to within an inch of its life," Echo said. "Just take the nice clothes."

Yuri eyed Grimmin suspiciously.

"Thanks, I guess," he said.

Rhegis took stock of Artem in his unusual, Amazonian-made armor.

"You, I assume, are content with your gear?" he asked. "If not, we can happily provide you with Atlantean armor."

"No, I'm curious to see their reaction, sir," Artem said, rapping his knuckles on the breastplate. "But thank you for the offer."

Rhegis held out a hand to Muireann. She took it.

"You we know nothing about," he said. "You wear surface garb, which I'm sure is fine, but it might be less conspicuous if you had more traditional Atlantean clothes, at least when you first arrive among the Amazons."

"If you think so," Muireann said.

Rhegis gestured over his shoulder and two servants, one male and one female, stepped forward.

"You don't seem the type to wear armor, but my allies here have a few items you can take with you," he said. The servants led Muireann over to a small table a few steps away. Echo watched as the ondine chose a deep blue top, form-fitting and long-sleeved, built to breathe in and out of the water. She found a pair of leggings in a silvery green and a sarong in the pale blue of tropical water, and added a pale headscarf, which Echo had learned the Atlanteans often favored on the surface, as unused to the beating sun as they were.

Rhegis and Barnabas had an almost resigned stare down. The king shrugged.

"I'm not sure we have the capability to make you look respectable, wizard," he said.

"I completely understand and totally agree," he said. "Just call me your daughter's personal magician. You know everyone just assumes we mages are weird anyway."

"That's working on the assumption they even let you off the ship," Artem said.

Rhegis and Barnabas shrugged simultaneously and in such a similarly resigned fashion Echo almost screamed.

"Lastly," Rhegis said. "My sister has a few things for you."

Artem took an involuntary step back as Reina approached. Echo's aunt had a pale sphere in her hands, a little larger than a softball.

"This will let you speak with us here," Reina said. "It's an orb of sending. Just place your fingertips on the sphere like this."

Reina held the orb in her palm and touched all five fingertips to the surface with her other and the sphere lit up from within with a soft white light.

"One of our magicians will be alerted," Reina finished.

"Does this listen to us when it's not activated?" Echo asked.

Barnabas let out a snort.

"No, it does not," Reina said, sounding mildly offended. "We are able to reach out to you in the same manner from another orb, but you have to touch the sphere to activate it."

Echo shot a quick glance at Barnabas, who was watching her. He nodded very subtly as if to confirm Reina wasn't lying. Echo noticed Grimmin watch the exchange, but the old spy, whom Echo knew had no love for Reina either, just grinned slightly.

"Alright then," Echo said. "I guess we set sail for the land of the Amazons? Do we even know how to get there?"

"I can get us to the general area," Artem said. "It's hidden, of course, but I think between myself and Barnabas we can find the entrance."

"Our ship is crewed by ghosts," Barnabas said. "You'd be amazed at how badly deception magic and illusions work on ghosts. It's come in handy surprisingly often over the years."

Echo wrinkled her brow, making a mental note to ask him about that offhand comment later.

"Now all we need is a song," Echo said. "You ready, Muireann?"

"Of course," the ondine said, gently draping the gifted Atlantean clothes over her arm. "I am at your service, princess."

"Oh no, not you too," Echo said.

Muireann winked.

"Just trying to fit in," she said.

Chapter 19: Theories on transmutation

Even with Artem's memories, Barnabas' knowledge of the places where time twisted differently on the open ocean, and a crew that didn't need to sleep, they still needed a couple of days' travel to arrive at New Scythia. They spent their time idly, Yuri and Echo catching up, the former excited to talk about what he'd learned about being a were-shark. They all worked to get to know Muireann better, with the newcomer open about many things and extremely closed about others, particularly the man who pursued her.

Artem, as expected, was quiet. Barnabas waited until the second day to catch him alone.

"Not the reception you expected, huh?" Barnabas said casually as he found Artem by himself on the deck close to sundown.

"Please tell me you're not here to have a heart-to-heart," Artem said. He leaned against the railing casually.

"No," Barnabas said. "Not at all. I was just hoping I could pick your brain about their library."

Artem breathed a sigh of relief.

"That I can do," he said. "But I should warn you, it's pretty unlikely they'll let you in."

"I figured," Barnabas said. "But if you and Echo are there,

maybe I can help tell you what to look for."

"You're not the only one around here who's book smart," Artem said.

"Yeah, but I'm the one who has spent most of my life looking for hidden secrets in books," Barnabas said. "I might be able to point you in the right direction."

Artem shrugged.

"Fair enough," Artem said.

"Do they have a curator of some sort?" Barnabas said, tucking his hands in his pockets.

"Of course," Artem said. "They have a whole order. The Keepers of Athena. One of the old goddesses they revere."

"That's interesting," Barnabas said. "They never struck me as being particularly religious."

"They're not," Artem said. "Their aesthetics scream ancient Greece, but they're technologically advanced, not unlike Atlantis. Actually, they're quite a bit like Atlantis, except they're smart enough to avoid all the petty infighting."

"So, the Keepers of Athena are more like an academic order than a priesthood," Barnabas said.

"Exactly," Artem said. "It's more of an ideal than worship. For example, there are the Daughters of Artemis as well, the hunters and warriors. I'm named after her."

"Y'know, I always thought that, but I was afraid to offend you," Barnabas said.

"You? Worried about offending me?"

"I don't worry about offending most people," Barnabas said. "I very early on decided you are the type of person I have a limited number of times I can offend, so I pick my battles."

Artem almost smiled.

"Anyway," Barnabas said. "I'll give you a list of old tomes that might be useful, if they have them. A few writers and historians who are off the beaten path. I'm sure the Keepers will already know about them, but just in case."

"Fair enough," Artem said.

"I really hope they let me in," Barnabas said. "A magician in the library of the Amazons. That's a once in a lifetime opportunity."

"Yeah, keep talking like that and they are definitely not letting you in," Artem said.

"What if I use a spell to temporarily turn myself into a woman?" Barnabas said.

Artem stared at him in silence for a full minute.

"You're pulling my chain," he said.

"Seriously, I can do that," Barnabas said. "Spells that transform and transmute are classic arcane magic. It's really not that complicated a spell."

"It... just turns you into a woman," Artem said.

"No, it turns me into anything I want to be roughly the same size," Barnabas said. "I could look like you, for example. Or a giant sea turtle. An old man. A panther."

"And you've... done this before?" Artem said.

"Transformed myself? Of course. It's wickedly useful. Got me out of quite a few jams."

"Specifically, a woman," Artem said. "Specifically."

Barnabas smiled mischievously.

"This makes you really uncomfortable, doesn't it?"

"I'm just very happy in my own skin," Artem said. He inhaled sharply. "Was there a good reason for it? Turning into a woman?"

"Yes," Barnabas said. "Because I could. Wouldn't you? I wanted to see how the world treated me. Which, by the way— Echo's people? They're awful to women. Just for your information. I don't know how she didn't regularly knock someone's head from their shoulders."

Artem inhaled sharply again, squinted, sighed, shrugged his shoulders, and exhaled.

"You get more interesting every time I talk to you," he said.

"Thank you," Barnabas said.

"That wasn't really a compliment."

"It is if I take it as one."

"Look, it might work," Artem said. "But I'm no magician. I

don't know if they've got what do you call them, the things that..."

"Wards," Barnabas offered.

"Right, the things that protect against magic," Artem said. "Or if they'll just see right through it. But if you want to try..."

"It's less that I want to try and more that I want to see that bloody library," Barnabas said.

"Well if you try, I ask only one favor," Artem said.

"Sure," Barnabas said.

"Promise me you won't warn Yuri ahead of time," Artem said.

Barnabas' smile broadened.

"You, Artem, consistently surprise me," he said.

Chapter 20: New Scythia

On the morning of the third day, they spotted a series of rocky islands, more like stone spires, jutting up from the ocean ahead. Not large enough for habitation, they could see a few sparse birds nesting on the higher places.

The ship began to alter course to avoid them, but Artem called out.

"Go through," he said. "See that gap right there, between those spires? Straight through there."

Echo squinted out across the water.

"You sure?" she said.

"They're not real," Muireann said. "Look at the birds. They repeat."

Artem nodded. The others spotted it as well. The birds were on a sort of loop, landing, flying out, skimming the water, returning. It was a long and varied enough loop that you needed to look for, but once you spotted it, it was clearly unnatural.

"In the old days, they used fog clouds to hide the island," Artem said as they passed between the rocks. Behind them, the rocks disappeared. "Now the trick is to make the area simply look impassible. Modern technology will let you navigate fog, but a bunch of rocky islands? Not worth it, just go around."

"Is this all done with illusion magic?" Echo asked.

"Some magic, some technology," Artem said. "I don't know the specifics. They sent me away before I learned the inner workings."

The horizon flickered for a few seconds, like heat off pavement, and then changed. Before them, a staggering sight appeared: a massive island, lush and green at sea level, dotted with stone cliffs. Buildings decorated the island above the tree line, beautiful architecture drawing on a dozen or more cultures, a great castle-like structure in the center, tall and bold in gold-red stone. Tapestries, intricate and brightly colored but too far away to clearly read, billowed in the sea breeze from every window. Central to the island was a bay, where small, fast ships bobbed gently in the green-blue water.

A small craft approached. It looked, much like the *Endless*, like an older vessel, but moved against the wind, propelled by some unseen, quiet power.

"So I'm gonna just assume that's not a welcoming committee," Yuri said.

"Security," Artem said. He pointed off the starboard bow, then port. Two other outriders were headed their way as well. "Just behave and we'll be fine."

The first craft pulled up alongside them. Warriors waited at the ready, aiming bows and arrows Artem knew they could wield with more deadly accuracy than any firearm trained on all of them. They wore an interesting mix of armor, a mix of modern materials crafted to harken back to classic armor styles.

One, clearly in command, spoke, shouting over.

"I hope you have a very good reason for coming here," she said.

Artem almost laughed as Echo adjusted the crown on her head, its design obviously meant for someone with a full head of hair as it slipped and went slightly crooked against the bare skin of her temples. Princess with a mohawk, Artem thought.

"I am, um, Princess Echo of Atlantis. I've been sent by my father Rhegis and aunt Reina to seek your guidance on an, ah, on a matter of… okay there's a big dangerous thing happening and we were hoping we could look something up in your library," Echo said. "I'm really from Atlantis. I have a tiara and everything."

The commander, deeply tanned with a wild main of red hair and a spray of freckles, seemed dubious. Then she saw Artem.

"Where did you get that?" the commander said. Artem placed a hand on his breastplate, then made the traditional greeting of the Amazons, touching the tips of his index and middle fingers to his forehead.

"Hello, Areto," he said. "I don't think you'll remember me, but I am Artem. Son of Orithyia. I'd like to seek an audience with my mother, on behalf of the Atlanteans, if she'll see me."

The Amazons are nothing if not disciplined in situations like this, Artem thought. He watched as none of the archers moved or displayed visible signs of surprise, though he could tell—because he'd lived among them, and only for that reason—that they were caught off-guard by his presence. Areto, whom he'd known as a child, only a few years older than him but unmistakable with her mad corona of red hair, was surprisingly less composed. She stared him down for a few seconds that felt like an eternity.

"Artem was a little boy when he was sent away," Areto said. "How do I know you're him and not an imposter?"

"I think my mother will recognize me, even behind this beard," he said. "She might have given me away, but I'd like to think a mother will recognize her own child."

Areto frowned, then signaled to her soldiers. Several of the Amazon archers broke rank and stepped away, out of sight.

"You didn't answer my question," Areto said. "Where did you get that breastplate?"

"A friend found it on a man long dead," Artem said. "And thought it only fitting he give it to me."

Areto said nothing, eyeing the armor with more interest than she wanted to let on.

"How many aboard?"

"Five," Artem said. "Myself, the princess, her bodyguard, her mage, and an ondine we rescued at sea, from what we believe is related to the threat we seek answers regarding."

Areto nodded.

"Follow us. We'll allow you to dock," she said. "You'll be vetted before you are allowed to go ashore. And I'll have my archers watching you the whole time. Don't try anything unexpected. If you are who you say you are, you know how we treat intruders."

"Understood," Artem said.

The Amazonian ship moved forward, taking the lead, while the two outriders moved to flank on either side. Artem exhaled deeply, not realizing he'd been holding his breath the whole time.

"You okay?" Echo said.

"That crown looks ridiculous on you," Artem said, laughing anxiously. "I'm fine. Honestly. They're reasonable people in the end. We'll either get what we came for or be sent away. It's fine."

"I'm a bodyguard now?" Yuri said, looking down at his flowing clothes. "I look like I'm her butler in this outfit."

"I had to think fast," Artem said. "It wasn't likely they would let you accompany her if they knew you were what you are."

"Which is?"

"A newly minted lycanthrope and accidental adventurer," Artem said.

Yuri pursed his lips, nodding in resigned agreement.

"Not untrue," he said. "What about how our magician looks like a knockoff Jack Sparrow—who the hell are you?"

Yuri had turned to point a thumb at Barnabas only to find a slightly smaller, somewhat slimmer, and much more female version of the smuggler standing beside him.

"Hi," Barnabas said. His voice had been altered as well, keeping his accent but more befitting of the body and face he now wore.

"This is freaking me out," Yuri said. "Did you do this on purpose? Have you been a woman the whole time?"

"It's a spell, Yuri," Barnabas said, biting back a smile. "It's fine. It's temporary."

"No, it's not fine!" Yuri said. "First, you need to warn me before you do stuff like that, and second, why do you look like Natalie Portman in that movie where she shaved her head?"

"I have no idea who that is, and the spell just converts me into a feminine version of myself," Barnabas said. "I didn't think about the hair thing, that it would stay like this."

"Is this what you look like under that nasty beard?" Yuri said.

Barnabas shrugged.

"I just look like me, Yuri," Barnabas said. Even Artem found himself slightly put off by hearing the strange new voice speaking in Barnabas' accent.

"You actually look like your mother a bit," Echo said.

"I think you should keep it," Muireann said. "It suits you."

"You're doing this so they let you on the island, aren't you?" Yuri said.

Barnabas pointed at him.

"Got it in one," he said.

"I swear if I end up being the only one stuck on the boat because of this spell, I'm going to rat you out," Yuri said.

Artem turned to watch as New Scythia grew closer, its elegant, intimidating structure causing his heart to race.

"At this rate, I hope they let any of us off the boat," he said.

Echo put a hand gently on Artem's shoulder.

"Not the homecoming you were expecting?"

"It's hard to say what kind of homecoming I was expecting," he said. "When I never expected to return home at all."

Chapter 21: Mother

Echo could feel the tension radiating off Artem as they docked. Somehow his stoic demeanor betrayed even more tension than if he'd actually been panicking, as if it were obvious he was holding in his emotions.

She tried to lighten the mood by pointing out to him the looks on the faces on several Amazons as the ship, its ghost crew invisible to them, seemed to dock itself, ropes tying themselves into knots as the humans onboard casually watched. Artem almost cracked a nervous smile, but it came across pained.

Areto stomped down the docks to meet them, flanked by a half-dozen guards. Artem nodded to Echo, and together, they put on their best confidence-faking masks and approached the commander.

"Permission to come ashore?" Echo said.

Areto eyed the whole crew.

"Just the five of you?" she said.

"The ghosts will stay with the ship," Echo said.

Areto tilted her head as if to question her, but said nothing.

"Men are rarely allowed on the island," Areto said. "But if you truly are an emissary from Atlantis, that is one of the occasions we make an exception. Your bodyguard is unnecessary, but it's bad form to ask you to leave him behind. Please remind your leaders that we consider it a great sign of respect if they send all-female contingents on missions like this."

"I'll convey that," Echo said. "I should apologize. I travel in a very specialized troupe here and we didn't think ahead to consider that."

Areto shook her head.

"It's a small thing. We're big on tradition, but as I said—for Atlantis, we make exceptions when we can. Your magician should drop his spell though."

"What?" Barnabas said, his voice still disturbingly alien.

"We hide our entire island behind a massive illusion," Areto said. "Did you think none of us would notice you've cast a transformation spell on yourself?"

"I was trying to be respectful," Barnabas said.

"Well, masking your identity is a poor start to that," Areto said. "But please, feel free to remain on the ship if you'd rather not drop the illusion."

Begrudgingly, Barnabas let the spell drop, returning to his usual bald and bearded self. Several of the Amazon guards muttered.

"Barnabas Coy," Areto said.

"Uh-oh," Yuri said, sidling closer to Echo. "This isn't good."

"I have no idea who that is," Barnabas said. "Okay, no, that's a lie. I'm Barnabas Coy. Yes."

"Interesting company you keep, Princess Echo," Areto said.

"What did you do?" Echo asked Barnabas.

"What haven't I done?" Barnabas said. "As for how they know me, I have no idea."

"Your magician is a notorious smuggler and transporter of dubiously acquired enchanted items," Areto said. "Suffice it to say, Captain Coy, you will be watched very closely while you are here. I recommend you keep both hands in your pockets at all times."

"Sure, yeah," Barnabas said. "I can do that."

Areto gestured for the crew to disembark. The docks were cool with ocean air, slightly hidden in the shadow of the towering castle at this time of day. In fact, Echo thought, the whole island was cooler than she expected, less tropical and more like home.

As they stepped off, Areto stared Barnabas down until he literally put his hands in his coat pockets. Yuri and Muireann followed, the former looking distinctly uncomfortable, the latter full of wonder.

"Yeah, y'know, I'm less of a bodyguard and more of a confidante, I think," Yuri said. "This is so nerve-wracking. Maybe I should just stay with the ship."

"Think about it," Muireann. "How many men alive have seen this island? A dozen? Fewer? You're experiencing something almost no one ever does. Live a little, shark-man."

"Did you just call me out?" Yuri said.

Muireann smirked at him.

"You're braver than you want to admit," she said. "You should own that."

"You definitely just called me out."

Areto moved to stand beside Artem. He froze, adopting a stiff, formal pose.

"Your mother will see you now," she said. "Follow me."

***

They were escorted—not roughly, but not exactly welcomingly—away from the docks and up toward the grand castle central to the island. Areto guided them toward a large, square structure just outside the castle itself, barred by massive doors simultaneously reinforced and decorated with wrought iron woven into the shape of leaves and trees. The doors opened without a command, revealing a large courtyard, lined on either side by more Amazons, all wearing the same blended modern and classic armor.

The courtyard was open-aired, with small tree-laced gardens in each corner, high walls of golden stonework rising around them with the smooth simplicity of master craftsmanship. It feels like a receiving hall, Echo thought. No, different from that. This is a safe place to hold court without allowing them into the castle proper, a space where a guest who might turn out to not have the best of intentions could be trapped, barricaded in, and swiftly dispensed with by two dozen highly trained Amazon fighters.

They put us in a kill box and call it a receiving room, Echo thought. This is how a culture stays unharmed for centuries. The right blend of practicality, ruthlessness and paranoia.

A woman in far more ornate armor waited for them on the other side of the courtyard. Her armor, similar in cut as that of the standard warriors, gleamed in the sun, burnished gold with silver highlights, the Amazonian eagle, less prominent on the standard armor, carefully sculpted in bright metal. She wore an old style Grecian helmet, gold with a bright red crest, which she removed as they approached, revealing hair so dark it seemed to absorb the light as it fell past her shoulders. Her eyes were a pale sea green, the left marred slightly by a perfectly straight scar running through her eyebrow and down her cheek. She had a sword at her hip, also adorned with the Amazonian eagle, upon which she casually rested her hand. Beside her, two honor guards, their armor less ornate but still more impressive than the others, stood stoically, not removing their helmets.

The woman exhaled sharply, gritted her teeth, and, Echo was shocked to see, looked to be on the verge of tears.

"Hello, mother," Artem said coldly.

"My son," the woman said. She lost all decorum and walked to them too quickly, grabbing Artem's hands in her own.

Echo scanned the gathered troops. They seemed simultaneously confused and ill at ease, but no one spoke, and certainly none moved to stop her.

Artem looked at the woman he called mother with an almost blank expression, his eyes studying her the way Echo had seen him study his enemies, looking for weaknesses and flaws. Echo saw none of that analytical behavior in Artem's mother in return. No, what Echo saw there, instead, broke her heart in a way only possibly for someone who had lost her own mother not long ago—a fight against tears, a jaw gritted to hold back a sob.

She loves him so much, Echo knew instantly. How could she send him away if this is how she felt?

But Echo could feel the eyes on them now. Somehow, all of this broke a powerful protocol. But this was her son, Echo thought. This is an advanced society, she'd been told. How do they judge someone for loving her child?

Artem, though, said nothing. He simply watched. Echo felt a sharp twist in her stomach, fear and pity and empathy. She spoke.

"You must be Orithyia," she said, struggling for words.

Artem's mother turned to her as if seeing her for the first time. Echo smiled as warmly and as casually as she could muster.

"Yes," she said, flashing Echo a quick, unconscious smile. Then Orithyia, as if remembering the eyes upon her, shook her head slightly and stood up straighter. "General Orithyia, high commander of the armies of New Scythia and the Sword of her Majesties, Queens Marpesia and Lampedo. They granted me leave to greet you all. You must be Princess Echo."

Echo could hear the pain in Orithyia's voice, the tremor she hid with formality. Echo held out her hand, and the general took it. Echo put her left hand over Orithyia's warmly.

"Please just call me Echo," she said. "I'm new to this princess thing, and it makes me feel silly. We're here to ask for your help, and it is… General, it is my honor to meet you."

Orithyia beamed a genuine smile at Echo, then glanced over her shoulder at her son. Echo took a moment to look to her other companions: Yuri looked terrified; Muireann simply taking everything in; but Barnabas watched Echo with blatant admiration. Well done, he said without uttering a sound. Well done.

"Echo," Orithyia said. "You are the reason I am looking at my son for the first time in twenty years. For that, I will name you however you please. Please, welcome to New Scythia. I want to hear your story, and discover if we can help you in your quest."

Echo watched as Artem's brow knitted together, pain and confusion on the swordsman's face.

But holding his mother's hand, remembering her own, she'd be damned if she wouldn't try to fix that somehow.

Chapter 22: The Queens of the Amazons

Not for the first time in his life, Yuri felt like an imposter.

He walked beside Echo as confidently as he could, but that wasn't saying much. Being here, surrounded by professional warriors, lying about his role, hiding his powers, he had this sinking feeling he could, at any moment, be thrown unceremoniously off the island without warning. Worse, he could feel that anxiety funneling into the strength of the shark in his heart, demanding he transform and fight. The shark was powered by what Yuri wanted to call it pure id, but that wasn't right. To call it "id" implied it was mindless want. It was fueled, rather, by a relentless desire to survive. And it sensed when he was afraid, and demanded he do something to change that.

He had a million questions for Echo, and maybe twice as many for Artem, but the former had a look of near-panic on her face as well as she tried to figure out exactly how to pretend she knew how to be Atlantean royalty, and Artem seemed green around the edges, as if he were fighting off waves of nausea. Barnabas kept falling behind, once even evoking a jab of a sword to his backside to keep him moving.

"It'll be fine, you know," Muireann said in her lilting accent. The woman was so quiet the past few days Yuri almost forgot she was there. "We're where we're supposed to be."

"I think according to tradition, we are exactly where the Amazons don't want strangers," Yuri said. "But I appreciate your optimistic outlook."

The guards funneled them through another ornate set of doors, opening into a cathedral-like room with a high, domed ceiling painted a gentle greenish blue. Directly across from the doors, set several feet up on a dais, stood a pair of matching thrones.

Only one was occupied, by a striking woman wearing a traditional metal breastplate over flowing robes of office. She sat calmly there, her white hair a corona of tight curls. Standing beside her, unarmored but wearing a sword on each hip, was another Amazon, her hair pulled back into a short nub of a ponytail.

The standing Amazon took a step back, giving her companion room to stand. Together, they descended from the dais to meet the group, the white-haired woman taking lead.

"Look at this menagerie," she said. "I'd bet on no more than one or two of you truly originating from Atlantis."

"You'd be right," Echo said. "I really am the daughter of King Rhegis of Atlantis, but my mother is human. From the surface. And these are my friends and companions, not Atlantean military."

The white-haired Amazon smiled.

"Honesty is appreciated here, Princess Echo of Atlantis," she said. "My name is Marpesia, and I share leadership of New Scythia with my sister, Lampedo. I understand your father and aunt currently share rule of Atlantis in a similar fashion."

"Are you the real Marpesia and Lampedo?" Muireann asked. The queen eyed the ondine suspiciously.

"I am real," she said. "I'm curious what you mean."

"There were sisters of the same names in Roman times who were said to co-rule the Amazons," Muireann said. "They called themselves the daughters of Ares."

Lampedo, the younger of the two, grinned.

"They told us you brought a bodyguard and a magician, but failed to mention you had a historian with you as well," she said.

117

"We were each named for those Amazon leaders, as you'll find many of the Amazons are named after our heroes and queens. It was a coincidence we went on to rule."

Muireann winked at Echo.

"I read a lot," she said.

"I am so glad we picked her up," Barnabas said, sounding almost in awe.

"Do siblings often rule together?" Echo said. "I… well, it's not the most efficient thing happening in Atlantis right now."

"We rarely share rule at all, with a sibling or a spouse," Marpesia said. "But Lampedo and I very much complete each other's flaws and see each other's blind spots, and so we lead together. I don't imagine it works so well with others."

"Well, it's sort of a work in progress back home," Echo said sheepishly.

Yuri noticed that Lampedo in particular kept returning her gaze to Artem, allowing a stealthy glance at Orithyia, who had grown quiet once they entered the chamber. For just a split second he caught a knowing look between the two women, almost like a silent argument, and he averted his eyes as if knowing he'd caught something private he shouldn't have seen.

"Who else have you brought before us then, your grace?" Marpesia said, offering the honorarium almost playfully, which brought a smile to Echo's face. She introduced them all in turn.

"This is my oldest friend and protector, Yuri. Our history buff is a new member of our crew, the ondine, Muireann. This is…"

Marpesia stopped her before she could introduce Barnabas.

"That scoundrel we know already," she said.

"You'd think I was some sort of crime lord the way I'm treated around here," Barnabas said.

"And of course, this one," Marpesia said, looking to Artem. Again, Yuri spotted a silent exchange, this time between Lampedo and Marpesia, the two queens wordlessly hashing out a disagreement. The older sister took Artem's hand. "We should talk before you leave, you and I."

Artem nodded, but said nothing. Immediately, Marpesia returned her attention to Echo.

"So, you've come to us for help," she said.

"For knowledge. During the recent, um, incident in Atlantis..."

"Your civil war," Lampedo said.

"Yeah, that thing," Echo said. "We made a bit of noise on the ocean floor and we think we woke something up. Something old. And we were hoping perhaps we could ask your Keepers of Athena if they know anything of Poseidon's Scar."

"I think that's not an unreasonable request. I'm sure Atlantis would return the favor if ever the Keepers sought knowledge your people might have in their possession."

"I am a big fan of information sharing," Echo said. "Having, y'know, been an actual secret kept from a lot of people myself, I'm not a fan of locking information away."

Marpesia raised an amused eyebrow.

"In that case, I insist we sit down to dinner first and you tell us that story," she said. "Consider that the fee for use of our library."

"How my dad hid me away on the surface? I love telling that story," Echo said. Yuri couldn't tell if she were being sarcastic or enthusiastic. Possibly both. "That sounds like a fair trade."

"Very well, then," Marpesia said. "Orithyia, why don't you take them to the library to see the Keepers. We'll continue this conversation after you've done your exploring, and hopefully have found your answers."

Chapter 23: The Keepers of Athena

The library of New Scythia was something to behold.

Protected within the island's central castle, the structure was a round, domed space, elegantly lit in such a way that it seemed to allow no shadow. The walls were white marble, and each had been carefully carved with floor-to-ceiling recesses for books.

Barnabas scanned floor to ceiling, all the way to the dome. Not a single empty shelf. Centuries of books, every shape and size, an endless supply of knowledge.

He kept his promise and stuffed his hands in his pockets, though not before the placed the small, simple spectacles on his face, enabling him to read every language. He thought they might make him look a little more distinguished, too, but the look on the face of the first Keeper they encountered as Orithyia led them into the library removed any hope of that.

Despite the unhappy look she gave him, she welcomed the others warmly.

"General," she said. "I was warned we had guests. Been some time since we've had anyone from the outside in the library."

"This seems to be a good reason to break the rules," Orithyia said. "Atlantis has informed us something... emerged from Poseidon's Scar and they hope we might have some information that could help them."

The Keeper, who introduced herself as Sister Clio, sighed in such a way that Barnabas detected a note of judgment.

"The greatest civilization beneath the ocean, and they still can't keep their history in order," Clio said.

"Hey, I didn't grow up there," Echo said. "I have nothing to do with their education system."

Clio guided them to an area on the lowest level, where several other Keepers, who had either been instructed ahead of time or had simply overheard the conversation, were already gathering books for them to look through.

"Poseidon's Scar," Clio said. "You know that pre-dates Atlantis and our own history."

"I didn't know that," Echo said.

"The name is relatively recent as well," Clio said, thumbing through one book, then another. "Well, recent in the past few millennia. It had another name before that."

"Something's maw, right?" Barnabas said.

The librarian tilted her head at him curiously.

"The Maw of the Old One," she said. "Where did you hear that?"

Barnabas considered throwing out a sarcastic answer, but, more because he wanted to get the Keeper on his good side than be polite, answered straight.

"I used to run a smuggling route that connected with some tribes of fish-men. You know the types, the ones who seemed to hit a stage of evolution and hit a dead end?"

"Wow, Barnabas," Yuri muttered.

"No, I'm not being mean here, Yuri," Barnabas said. "They stopped at the stone age, live apart from the world, haven't changed technologically in thousands of years. No science, no magic, no art, really. Just survival."

"Still came out harsh, dude," Yuri said.

Barnabas shrugged dismissively.

"Anyway. I dealt with them a bit in my travels, and when we

talked trade routes and maps, they referred to Poseidon's Scar as the Maw, sometimes the Mouth. They didn't seem afraid of it, though. They thought it was holy. I just figured it was fish-men being superstitious."

"The Mouth," Yuri said. "As in a Hellmouth? Like in *Buffy*?"

"Again, I have no point of reference for what you're talking about," Barnabas said.

"Will you get on with it, Barnabas?" Artem said, his voice tight enough it could cut through metal.

"That's all I heard about it," Barnabas said. "I didn't think anything of it, as I said. Old tribes like that have their own names for everything. It wasn't unusual."

"It is interesting that they considered it sacred ground, though," Clio said.

"Why would others call it Poseidon's Scar, though?" Muireann asked.

Clio slid a book across the table to Echo, who thumbed through it gently.

"Like everything, the prevailing religious beliefs at the time flavored the language," Clio thought. "It looks like a great wound in the floor of the ocean. Myths and stories rose up about a great battle between Poseidon and some older, less rational god, whom Poseidon locked away, swallowing him up in his gullet."

"But that implies Poseidon is real," Echo said.

"Pick any mythos or pantheon and you'll find real-world places named after their exploits," Clio said. "Much of it is just fantasy."

"But with some truth to it," Barnabas said.

"Exactly," Clio said. "That book in front of you details a great battle between some dark beast and the lord of the sea. It's very poetic. Quite entertaining. And most likely a work of fiction."

Clio slid another book across the table. Barnabas tried to pick it up, but Artem intervened.

"That one talks about a being some thought was a god," Clio said. "And according to what few stories are written about him, he certainly believed it himself."

Artem squinted at the book.

"What language is this?" he said.

Barnabas deftly removed the book from his hands and began to read.

"Korthos of Aramaias," he said. "The Truthbringer, the Dragon's Son. This guy loved to rack up the melodramatic titles, huh?"

"He's a bit of a Herculean figure from a mythology almost no one remembers," Clio said. "We barely know of it ourselves, as it was gone long before the Amazons became a people, and there was little written about it to begin with. But the strange thing is, we know an immortal being named Korthos existed, though his whereabouts, if he still lives, are a mystery."

"Immortals," Yuri said.

"I'm a sea spirit. We're in the land of Amazons. He's a magician," Muireann said. "I don't see how an immortal hero is such a strange thing to believe in."

"Hero is giving him more credit than he is perhaps due," Clio said. "But with all the information we have here, this is strangely the most credible, because of our evidence that Korthos existed. He fought a great monster, one so powerful it thought itself godlike."

"So, two arrogant beefcakes who think they're gods duking it out at the bottom of the sea," Echo said.

"Korthos wasn't alone, of course. He traveled with mighty companions, some of whom fell in battle. And the monster was not alone either. Worshiped as a god, the creature had a massive, powerful cult of amphibious beings at his side."

"Did those beings have really sharp teeth?" Yuri asked.

Clio rolled her eyes at Yuri and then returned her focus to Echo.

"We do know that during the battle, Korthos used two mighty devices to bind the creature," she said. "Some sort of javelin or spear called the Needle of the Moon and a magical focus called the Eye of Dreams."

123

"Magical focus?" Yuri asked.

"Like my gun," Barnabas said.

"Please never say that again," Yuri said.

"I hate you," Barnabas said. "But seriously. It's something that helps a spellcaster intensify and focus their spells."

"What did these things do?" Echo asked, ignoring the banter.

"The Needle, according to the story, enabled Korthos and his companions to weaken this monster, and the Eye put him to sleep," Clio said.

"I'm going to work on the assumption that he didn't put these weapons in a nice, safe, convenient location after the battle," Yuri said.

"He lost them," Clio said. "The stories say that Korthos was a mighty warrior, but also something of an idiot."

"So, we just need to find two ancient artifacts that may or may not exist to defeat a creature that may or may not believe it's a deity," Echo said. "No problem. Just an average day for us."

"I don't suppose any of these books might give a clue as to where these things might have ended up?" Barnabas said.

Clio smiled.

"Oddly enough, Amazonian historians did find out where the Eye ended up," Clio said.

"Conveniently available, being used as a paperweight in a museum with low security somewhere, right?" Yuri said.

Clio gave him a half-hearted but still somewhat judgmental look.

"It is in the possession of the yacuruna," she said. "In their Eastern-most city, at the mouth of the Amazon River."

"Coincidence? The name thing?" Yuri said.

"I don't understand," Clio said.

"Never mind," Yuri said softly.

Muireann and Barnabas both let out heavy sighs, turned to each other in surprise, started to speak at the same time, and then stopped. Barnabas gestured for Muireann to continue.

"The cities of the yacuruna are fascinating. I've always wanted to see one," she said. "Not many people return from them though."

"Not many people go to them anymore," Barnabas said. "Like much of the magic in the world these days, they're dying out."

"So perhaps more of a diplomatic mission than a fight for the Eye," Artem said.

Orithyia spoke up, sounding concerned.

"You're just going to set sail for the city and hope for the best?" she said.

"It's what we do," Artem said. "It's worked for us so far."

"There's something that might be worth mentioning," Muireann said, turning to Barnabas for guidance.

"Be my guest," he said. "I don't want to be the one to tell them."

"Oh, no," Echo said. "What is it?"

"The cities of the yacuruna are, um, upside down," Muireann said.

No one spoke for a long series of seconds, as if the conversation stopped so that everyone in the room could ponder the logistics of an upside-down city. Yuri broke the silence, speaking solemnly to Orithyia.

"Please tell me you have motion sickness pills we can borrow," Yuri said.

Chapter 24: What we do for love

Echo found herself wandering the Amazon palace late that evening, full from dinner, fighting off waves of anxiety, as she always did lately. Her thoughts revolved around what was to come, with upside-down cities, river gods, mythic artifacts for binding old gods.

I worked in an icehouse a few months back, she thought. How do I feel too old for this already? I feel like my heart's been racing non-stop for months.

She could hear Barnabas and Muireann downstairs, talking with several Amazon cartographers about the best way to find the yacuruna. Neither the magician nor the ondine could sail a ship to save their lives, but Barnabas had proven a strongly effective navigator through his connection with the ley lines, and Muireann had a supernatural sense for direction on the open water. Echo felt mostly useless in the conversation and left it to the experts, seeking quiet away from everyone else.

There were few lanterns on the floor she wandered onto, most of the light filtering in through massive windows along one wall. She walked up to those windows and found that they were part of a set of tall, unlocked doors, leading out to a stone balcony overlooking the sea. She pushed a door open and was hit by a gust of sea air, refreshing, cool in darkness, slightly damp. She inhaled deeply and stared out over the water, looking for the *Endless* moored somewhere below.

"You're all such interesting beings," Orithyia said, emerging from the darkness and startling Echo, joining her at the stone balcony overlooking the harbor. "A collection of creatures never meant to exist."

"I don't know why I'm not insulted by that, but I'm not," Echo said.

Orithyia looked over her shoulder into the castle, her expression teetering on judgmental.

"Your father is Atlantean," she said. "What do you think of them?"

"I think they've built something wondrous and most of the time they don't know what to do with it," Echo said.

Orithyia studied her face, suddenly focused.

"He sent you away," she said. Not a question.

"Sent might be the wrong word," Echo said. "But he abandoned my mother, or seemed to. There was always someone watching over us. The last of whom was Barnabas, who my father hired when he was very young. But I didn't know it. As far as I knew, my father never existed. It was just my mother and me."

"I didn't... throw him away, you know," Orithyia said.

"He thinks you did," Echo said.

"I don't blame him. I always knew where he was, or I did until he left with you," Orithyia said. "I wasn't going to hand my child over to strangers. We've always known of that place. It calls itself the Island of Unwanted Things, but by all the gods, it is filled with such wonders."

"I know," Echo said.

"It's a place where you send beautiful things the world wants to destroy," Orithyia said. "We think we're so advanced here. And we are. We are. I've seen the mundane world, and we are not them. Neither is Atlantis. But we are not without our flaws. No one is."

Echo said nothing, just listened.

"I know the myths. That we throw our boys into the sea. That's a complete fabrication. We don't have boys anymore. We haven't for centuries. We don't need them. We don't throw babies off cliffs. That's barbaric."

"How did Artem happen, then?" Echo asked.

Orithyia slipped, a sly smile crossing her mouth.

"I fell in love with a stupid man," Orithyia said. "Oh gods, was he a stupid, lovely, impetuous idiot. Now *he* almost found himself thrown off a cliff. I bargained for his life, for the chance to set him loose on the open sea with a small boat and some food so they wouldn't kill him, to protect the island. He would have deserved it. He was here to rob us."

"But you fell in love with him," Echo said.

"I know you're young, but surely you've fallen for an idiot who didn't deserve your affection," Orithyia said. "We're mortal. It's our job to fall in love with the wrong people."

Echo felt something twinge in her chest, a strange realization she'd never had before. Her life in the icehouse, her adventures, her youth. I don't think I've ever fallen for anyone, she thought. It was just never something she needed. Never something that happened. I suppose it just happens for most people, she thought. You run into someone who doesn't deserve your affections. But standing here, looking over the hidden island of the Amazons, Echo realized for the first time she'd never really fallen for anyone. And it had never bothered her before. She had too much else to do to fall in love.

Good, she thought. What a waste of time, anyway.

Why do I suddenly feel so lonely?

She caught Orithyia watching her, the older woman smiling sympathetically.

"You just had a profound thought," she said.

"It's not important," Echo said, forcing that loneliness down into a place where she could process it later. "You regret sending Artem away, don't you?"

"I have never loved anyone as much as I love my son," Orithyia said. "But look at this place. As beautiful as it is, as peaceful, as advanced, there was no place for him here. I didn't want him to grow up as a footnote. That's all he would have been here. A note on a ledger, a passage in our history books, about the Amazon general who was derelict in her duties and fell in love with a thief. I gave him to the Island of Unwanted Things not because he was unwanted, but because I wanted so much more for him."

"He's a hero, y'know," Echo said. "He saved Atlantis. He saved me. He's the greatest swordsman anyone's ever seen. And he's lost so much, and has a big broken heart he doesn't know what to do with, which makes him kind of an ass sometimes, but we all know why. And I think everything he does leads back to you. I think he misses his mother."

"But Echo, all those things he became... they happened because I got him off this island. Where he could be something more," Orithyia said. She exhaled, the breath catching in her throat sharply.

The two women leaned against the rail, listening to the waves crash against the shore below. Without facing Orithyia, Echo spoke.

"I guess I'm a hero now," she said. "And I've got these powers, and apparently I'm a princess, and it's my job to save the seven seas or something stupid like that. But when all this was happening, I lost my mom. And ma'am, let me tell you, if you asked me honestly, I'd give it all up to have her back. Artem doesn't have to make that choice. He could have both. But that's on both of you to make that happen."

The waves continued to crash rhythmically below. Orithyia said nothing for a long while.

"You're smarter than the others Atlantis has sent to our door," she said.

"Maybe because they sent me away," she said. "Maybe because of my mother."

Echo pushed herself away from the railing.

"We set sail in the morning," she said. "I assume we'll be back, because your son will be with us, and saving the world is what he does. Maybe think about what you'd like to say to him when we return."

She walked inside the castle, leaving Orithyia alone, the ocean swaying beneath her like a song.

Chapter 25: Blood in the water

Anson Tessier stood on the deck of his rented ship, watching
bodies bob in the water below.

Money buys a remarkable amount, he thought. They'd passed
through that brutal storm and nearly lost several men, washed
overboard by hundred-foot swells. The ship was designed to
withstand terrible conditions, but we were never meant to master
the sea. Any man who thinks we might control the ocean is a fool.
We can only survive it. But money bought a ship that could
withstand the worst of what the ocean could throw at them, and
money made the men onboard stupid with greed, willing to risk
their lives for cash.

They exited the storm and found themselves alive, exhausted, in
still water that smelled of death.

The captain, a burly Englishman with a beard that seemed to
grow directly down his neck into his shirt, thought they had
stumbled across a capsized ship, a large fishing vessel caught in the
same storm. He pointed with the cigarette between his fingers to a
wrecked ship, tipped on its side and lazily drifting on the current, a
sizable hole punched in its hull.

"That storm was a killer," the captain said. Tessier nodded,
pretending to agree, but Tessier saw something the captain either

did not, or was steadfastly ignoring. There were gouges on the bottom of that ship, deep wounds like claw marks. Something big had capsized that ship from below.

The bodies in the water were savaged as well. If you turned a blind eye to them, it was almost impossible to ignore, and the crew worked hard to do just that. Tessier had no such compulsion though. He stared and studied from the deck while the crew made a perfunctory search for survivors. It seemed unlikely, given the damage, the smell, the silence. What a silence, Tessier thought. Just the rocking of the waves, the occasional creak of metal from the ship. Even the seabirds seemed content to leave these corpses alone.

He thought about bringing a body aboard to examine, but that might give too much away to the crew.

"Who do you report this to, if at all?" Tessier asked. "We're in international waters."

The captain gave a half-hearted shrug.

"No survivors, no salvage to speak of," he said. "If we can spot an identifying feature on the ship to notify its country of origin, we could reach out, but I thought we were to keep this excursion as quiet as possible."

"That's true," Tessier said.

"Then I suppose we leave it for the next ship to call it in," the captain said. "Not like these guys are in need of rescuing. Wouldn't be the first folks lost at sea."

"Commendably cutthroat, Captain Bonner," Tessier said.

Bonner shrugged again.

"You didn't hire us for our moral compass," he said. "So... any idea where the target we're chasing is from here?"

Anson Tessier inhaled deeply, waiting for the familiar, sharp twinge in his chest. A supernatural homing beacon, his pain telling him where the girl had gone, where she hid.

"East," he said. "And south. We should look at the charts."

The captain agreed, both men happy to step away from a sea full of corpses. Captain Bonner called up a digital navigational chart on a table with a large, expensive screen embedded in the top. Tessier indicated where his unnatural senses told him Muireann would be.

"I assume that's more of a general idea," the captain said.

"Why do you say that?"

"That's just empty ocean," the captain said. "Not that it's dangerous or anything, but there's just... nothing out there. Do you think she's just hiding out on a ship? You won't find any land there."

"It's possible she's simply on the run on another vessel, yes," Tessier said. The captain tried to hide a look of doubt on his face but did so poorly. Tessier ignored it.

"Would love to know what trick you're using to track this person," Bonner said. "You can't just be relying on hunches."

"I have my ways," Tessier said. "Believe me, my sense of where she's gone is painfully accurate."

The captain reviewed the map one more time, then sighed.

"Well, if we're headed that way, I have to suggest we stop and refuel," he said. "This ship can go a long time between stops, but that storm beat the hell out of us. I'd like to dock, restock, make any repairs we need to make before heading out to the middle of nowhere."

Tessier grimaced.

"She's moving remarkably fast. I don't want to lose her," he said.

"We sink or get stranded, you're really going to lose her," the captain said. "Where could she be going, anyway? If she's out there, she's not trying to disappear in some foreign country, right?"

"Find a stop that will delay us as little as possible," Tessier said.

"That was my intention," Bonner said. "I don't want to slow you down, sir. I just want to make sure we can get home again. Figured that was something we both want."

Tessier nodded and stepped away from the table.

"I need to check on a few things in my room," Tessier said. "I'll be back shortly."

"Of course," the captain said.

Tessier began heading for his room, his heart tightening in his chest. The moment he was alone in the hallway, he clutched the wall, fighting a sharp, blinding pain. His physician had told him these were not heart attacks, these bouts of pain, but could offer no explanation. But Tessier knew what they were. He needed the piece of himself she'd stolen back soon, he thought as his vision went gray for a moment.

There were moments when he wanted to forgive her, to simply take back what she'd stolen, remembering the way she'd looked at him before she learned what he really did to make all this money, before she knew who he really was. But in these moments, gasping for air, feeling for all the world like he was dying on his feet, he knew there'd be no forgiveness.

This was not a retrieval mission. This was revenge. She crossed him because she knew the evil he did, and Anson Tessier had every intention of proving her right when he took back what was his.

Chapter 26: Why are you here

The *Endless* set sail the next morning with little fanfare. Orithyia
and Areto led a small honor guard, or possibly security detail
depending on perspective, to see Echo and her crew to their ship,
the docks shrouded in fog too dense for work to have begun for
the day.

"We leave under cover of darkness as usual," Echo said, mostly
to herself, so quietly only Muireann really heard her.

The ondine watched each crew member in turn, reading their
body language as they departed. Echo seemed determined but
tired, as always, as if dragging a great weight behind her. Yuri was
visibly relieved to be leaving the island, the were-shark having been
in a constant state of self-conscious anxiety during the visit.
Barnabas' eyes wandered the architecture, taking everything in like
a man who knew he'd never see this place again. And Artem was
stony and emotionless, barely making eye contact with the
Amazons, avoiding his mother entirely.

Muireann watched Orithyia's response to his behavior. I don't
know this woman, the ondine thought. I don't know any of these
people, really. But I know pain when I see it, and that is a mother
living with great regret.

The boarded their ship one at a time, Echo stopping to speak to the Amazon general and commander.

"We'll be back with the Eye soon," she said.

"I hope so," Orithyia said. "Be safe, and be swift."

"We're usually one of those," Yuri said almost reflexively as he climbed onto the ship.

"We'll do our best," Echo said. She saw Muireann watching and waited for the ondine to board before her. Muireann complied.

"Okay, everyone. Take us out to sea," she said to the empty air, which quickly swirled with phantom sailors ready to be on their way. "Barnabas will tell you where we need to go."

Without a single living person lifting a finger, the *Endless* gently left the dock, through the fog, and out into the open ocean.

Artem slipped up to his frequent perch in the crow's nest. Echo wearily found a spot in the prow and sat down. Yuri wordlessly joined her. Muireann watched as Barnabas headed up to the quarter deck alone and followed him.

The magician leaned against the wheel for a while, not so much steering as feeling the movement of the ship as the ghosts safely sailed them out beyond the Amazonian illusory terrain. Once the magical environmental effects were behind them, Barnabas opened a wooden chest that had been somehow fastened or nailed to the deck and withdrew a piece of chalk. He began drawing arcane symbols on the wood, muttering to himself—no, not himself, Muireann corrected. He was talking to the spirits, telling the ghosts where they needed to go, which faerie lanes they needed to find to cross great distances faster.

She observed the process for a while, surprised at its simplicity. Muireann knew instinctually how to find those mystical pathways on the ocean, but she'd never seen them written out so others could understand them.

"It looks like art," she said.

Barnabas smiled up at her, wiping the leftover chalk on his pants.

"Magic is art," he said. "My mother thinks it's science, but she's a diviner, an alchemist. Her magic frequently requires mathematical precision. Mine's more improvisational."

"Your mother, the nereid," Muireann said.

Barnabas nodded, tossing the chalk back into the wooden chest, avoiding stepping on the magical symbols he'd drawn on the deck.

"It sort of makes us alike, you and I," Muireann said. "That your mother is a nymph."

"I don't know about that," Barnabas said. "Please don't take that as an insult. I just think the things you've been through and the things I've been through probably don't overlap much."

Muireann observed his face, the way he hid behind the beard and ink and scars, the false way he carried himself.

"I can't figure you out," she said.

Barnabas raised an eyebrow curiously.

"Really," he said. "Interesting statement coming from a mystery woman we picked up on a ship full of dead sailors."

Muireann shrugged her shoulders and looked down at the deck below where Echo and Yuri sat, then up at the crow's nest where Artem pensively watched the horizon.

"Them I understand," she said, ignoring Barnabas' sarcasm. "Echo might not like it, but she feels responsible for her people. She takes action to protect them, or at least to protect the world from the harm her people seem so capable of causing."

"Yeah, I wouldn't say she's happy about that, but it's the state of her," Barnabas said.

"And the were-shark. Even in just a few days I can tell that his own interests matter less than what he needs to do to be by her side. Whatever danger she's running toward, he'll be there."

"Should have met him a few months back," Barnabas said. "Wouldn't have pictured him running toward danger voluntarily."

Muireann turned her eyes toward the crow's nest.

"Artem feels conflicted. Like heroism comes naturally to him, but also that he's trying to prove something."

"Doesn't take a psychoanalyst to figure that one out."

"But there's something else there, isn't there?" she asked. "He lost someone recently, am I right?"

Barnabas winced visibly at her words.

"That's a longer story," he said. "But this whole endeavor started out as revenge for him, and I think it turned into a purpose. Whether that's healthy or not is beyond me, but the world's better for having someone like him decide to dedicate himself to saving it."

"And then there's you," Muireann said. She stared at Barnabas, who tried to match her gaze, but turned away.

"Oh, no you don't," he said. "Don't try to magic a magician, lady. I can spot a spell when I see one."

"That wasn't a spell. It was, well, what I do," she said. "I read people, and everything I read about you says you shouldn't be here."

"That's because I'm good at what *I* do," he said.

"You have no reason to tell me," Muireann said. "But I'm curious, and I hope you would. Why are you with this crew? What do you gain from it?"

"Money and fame and fortune, kid."

"You're so much better at lying when you put effort into it," Muireann said.

Barnabas sighed, looking at each of his crew one at a time.

"I don't believe in anything," he said. "Or I didn't, before. I was a mercenary and a scoundrel and I liked it. But I was hired for a few years to look out for Echo and her mother, and I was there, watching over this family from a distance, making sure they were safe. Except nothing ever came for them. Nothing ever threatened them. They were so wondrously mundane, you understand? Echo's special. Her mother lived an unusual life. Yuri's become something bigger. But when I was just a young idiot sent to spy on them for some bigshot in Atlantis? They were just regular people."

Muireann listened, not interrupting. Barnabas' tone felt unexpectedly confessional. He made no eye contact, looking mostly at his feet, at the deck.

"But I failed them. Maybe I couldn't have succeeded. The things that happened—they were more than anyone anticipated. I wasn't enough to stop it alone. But that doesn't matter. What matters is I failed them, and Echo's mother died, and Echo and Yuri lost their normal lives, and they didn't deserve that, and you know what else? I lost the normal life I had watching over them. I knew Meredith. She'd offer me coffee sometimes when she'd catch me. You see, she'd always had a protector, from the time Echo was born onward. We all got caught at some point. I was just the last one she spotted. But she knew why we were there, and she was kind to me in ways people were rarely, if ever, kind to me."

Barnabas rubbed his palm across his stubble-covered head absently. He pointed at Artem.

"And that poor bastard. That's my fault too, you know. Not maliciously. I was trying to protect Echo, and that's how Artem lost the man he cared most about in this world. Blame's a funny thing—it's almost never direct. I'm the first step in the blame, but there's those who committed the acts of violence I couldn't stop, there's those who wanted those acts of violence to happen, there's the stupid drama at the very core of it all that caused it all in the first place. There's so much blame to go around," Barnabas said. "I don't stay out of guilt."

Muireann lifted one eyebrow slightly. Barnabas caught the gesture.

"It's okay, doubt the truth in that. But when Artem was on that revenge dirge, when Echo wanted to avenge her mother… I had my own reasons, y'know? You can't make things right. You can't fix what's happened. But you can contribute to what happens next," Barnabas said. "Did you cast a spell on me? Why am I telling you all of this?"

"Because I'm not them," Muireann said. "Because I wasn't there."

Barnabas closed his eyes for a moment, clearly struggling with words and thoughts. He swallowed hard, then spoke.

"So, no, I don't have an Atlantis or a tribe of Amazons to fight for," he said. "I only have them. And I don't believe in anything anymore. But I'll be the instrument they need to help make what happens next better than it could be. That's why I'm here. What about you, Muireann the ondine? Why are you here?"

Muireann smiled softly and joined Barnabas where he stood against the railing on the quarter deck. She took a deep breath, felt the wind rushing through her dark hair.

"Because you're the ones who found me," she said. "And I think that means something."

"By way of things to believe in, we're not a good bet," Barnabas said.

"I think you're wrong," Muireann said. "And I'm willing to stay long enough for you to prove it."

Chapter 27: Seeing the world through a blurred window

No matter how many times we do this, Echo thought, I'm never going to like it.

Yuri once referred to their ability to travel through places where time and distance worked differently as the equivalent of "fast travel" in a video game. It worked, really, because it was a weird, but useful, time-saving method. They weren't teleporting across the globe, but Barnabas and the ghost crew of the *Endless* could navigate these weird, warped faerie pathways safely to turn days of travel into hours, weeks into days. Yuri told Echo numerous times he wanted to ask Barnabas if the Bermuda Triangle worked like this, but never remembered to bring it up.

Useful, helpful, but also terrifying to cross hundreds of miles of ocean in a sort of mystical fast-forward state. If time weren't such a limited commodity in their current mission, Echo would have preferred to sail the normal way. I'm seeing the world through a blurry window, she thought, always wondering what sights had passed by unnoticed.

This time, the journey took them to the mouth of the Amazon River, which, Echo had to admit, looked nothing like she expected. She said so.

"I should've known the Amazon wouldn't just empty into the ocean," she said. She felt annoyingly ignorant not realizing that there would be a whole ecosystem at the mouth of the river. That she was caught off-guard there was an entire estuary there called the Marajó várzea. To her untrained eye, it looked far more like a series of large islands and canals than the mouth of a mighty river visible from space.

"I am so confused," Yuri said beside her.

"Oh, what, you didn't know this is what the mouth of the Amazon River looked like?" Echo said.

"Like you knew."

"I totally knew."

"You're lying."

"I am totally lying," she said.

Artem, climbing down from the crow's next, hit the deck cursing.

"I know this is something we should have asked before we left, but," Artem said, "how the hell are we supposed to find an underwater city here?"

"I'm assuming that's a rhetorical question," Yuri said.

"We didn't think this through," Echo said. "At all. We're idiots."

"We're not idiots," Yuri said. "We've never thought anything through all the way and look at us. We're fine."

"We can't search the entire Amazon," Artem said, a note of desperation, almost panic, rising in his voice. "We can't! Why did we think we could do this?"

"Because we've literally waltzed into every other adventure we've ever had with zero forethought and it's always worked out fine," Yuri said.

"I'm not a crier, but I honestly feel like I'm going to cry," Echo said.

"I do too," Artem said. "My gods, we really are idiots."

"I forgot how big this place is," Barnabas said, joining them on the deck. Muireann followed directly behind him, and Echo caught herself eyeing the pair suspiciously and not knowing why. Something about the mystery woman and the smuggler becoming cozy raised an alarm in the back of her mind.

"You've been here before?" Artem said.

"Oh, sure," Barnabas said. "Sort of."

"What do you mean, sort of?" Echo said.

"Long story," the magician said.

"No, no you don't," Echo said. "You don't get to 'long story' this one."

"I mean I've been here, in the estuary," Barnabas said. "I've only been up river by astral projection, so I'm not sure it counts."

"We nearly died together, as a team, and I still hate you with every fiber of my being," Yuri said.

Barnabas ignored him, walked up to the railing, and whistled.

"Man, this place is huge," he said.

"Have you been here before?" Echo asked Muireann.

The ondine shook her head.

"I've never been to the Americas at all," she said. "This is all new to me."

"We're screwed," Yuri said.

Barnabas held up his hands in a calming motion.

"Now, come on, gang. You have me," he said.

"It is a daily struggle, Barnabas, a daily struggle, to not cut your throat when you sleep," Artem said.

"Love you too," Barnabas said. "I'm telling you, don't worry about it."

"Finding an underwater city in one of the biggest rivers in the world?" Echo said. "I'm worried. I'm worrying right now. This is my worrying face."

"You guys need to stop thinking so literally," Barnabas said. "This is magic, right? Does magic ever make sense? Let me answer that for you. No, magic never makes sense. You're on a ship manned by ghosts. Roll with it."

"Less snark, more explanation please," Echo said.

"First of all, while you were all sleeping or chatting up the residents of New Scythia, I was talking with Clio, the Athena-worshipping librarian, which was not a particularly easy task, mind you, because someone has said some terrible things about me to her and she has decided she hates me," Barnabas said.

Yuri, Echo and Artem all exchanged looks back and forth as if to assess or attribute blame.

"Wasn't me," Yuri said.

"Whatever," Barnabas said. "But despite the fact she hates me, or possibly because she likes all of you, she gave me some information on these yacuruna beings we're looking for."

"Gods, I hate when you're useful," Artem said. "It makes hating you just slightly more difficult."

"Maybe the Cliff Notes version," Echo said.

"I have no idea what that means," Barnabas said.

"Please, please, tell us what she told you already," Echo said.

Barnabas nodded, ignoring everyone's building frustration.

"First of all, the yacuruna build their cities in the mouths of rivers, not the rivers themselves. And if we're looking for their biggest city…"

"It's here somewhere," Muireann said. "This is where the Amazon ends, correct?"

"Biggest city, most likely location would be here," Artem said. "But what if it's in a different city?"

"Then we sail up river and try again," Barnabas said.

"Okay, stupid question, but can we sail… sail, specifically, up river? Like, can you sail against the flow of a river?" Yuri said. Everyone except Muireann looked at him in shock.

"Did your time apart from us include lessons on seamanship?" Barnabas said. "Last time we were together you didn't know the difference between a boat and a ship."

"It's basic physics, you nitwit," Yuri said. "How much wind needs to be at our backs to push us up the river?"

Barnabas lifted a finger, pointed at Yuri as if to correct him, then dropped his hand to his side.

"Y'know, you're actually right," he said. "But we'll be fine. *The*

Endless looks like a sailing vessel, but it's propelled through more arcane means. The sails are honestly mostly for show."

"You're just mentioning this now?" Artem said.

"Nobody ever asked," Barnabas said.

"Guys! Focus!" Echo said. "So, we're probably not far from the yacuruna city. How do we find it? How do we get there?"

"Easiest way would be to get a yacuruna's attention," Barnabas said. "Best case scenario, plead our case, convince them to help."

"Worst case scenario?" Artem said.

"The yacuruna have a tradition of abducting beautiful people," Barnabas said. "We could, y'know, put out a trap, I guess."

"That is the stupidest thing you've ever said," Echo said.

"I do not volunteer," Yuri said.

"I said they abduct beautiful people," Barnabas said.

"I hate you," Yuri said.

"Hey, I wouldn't put myself on the volunteer list either," Barnabas said. "We need to be honest with ourselves and each other, Yuri. We're not pretty."

"I volunteer," Muireann said.

All four of her crewmates said "no" simultaneously.

"I'm almost afraid to ask if this has something to with my looks," the ondine said.

"It's not your fight," Echo said, her tone apologetic. "I didn't mean to insult you. I just don't want you risking your life for us."

Muireann shrugged.

"I can't drown. I'm not human. Barnabas told me a bit about what Clio said—the yacuruna eventually transform their captives into yacuruna themselves. I'm already a water spirit. I have to assume that means I'm immune to the transformation."

"I hate that she has a point," Artem said.

"Regardless, we have options," Barnabas said. "And in the end, they're not a violent type of spirit. The yacuruna are known as healers."

"Healers who kidnap people," Yuri said.

"Everyone has flaws," Barnabas said.

Echo clapped her hands.

"Okay, aside from bait, what are our other options?" she said.

"It's believed they can transform into the creatures of the Amazon," Barnabas said. "Clio's research said they prefer to explore in the form of the pink dolphin. Alternately, they are sometimes seen riding giant crocodiles."

"I hate everything about this," Yuri said.

"Y'know what? Fine. Let's just try it," Echo said. "Where do we start?"

Chapter 28: Splitting up always works so well

The *Endless* dropped anchor in a canal enabling Echo and her friends to take a dinghy to shore. The enormity of this place overwhelmed Echo's senses in a way the deep ocean hadn't. The explosiveness of life here, the vegetation, the almost deafening sound of it all, it was breathtaking.

It also had a certain raggedness to it, too, which Echo knew had to do with humanity's damage, dirty water from uncontrolled agriculture and worse. Everywhere we go, we poison the world, she thought. No wonder my Atlantean relatives wanted to wipe humanity from the face of the Earth.

When they reached land, Yuri and Artem dragged the boat onto the sand, both men grimacing at the heat.

"Let's make this a short trip," Yuri said. "This is miserable."

"How are we going to play this?" Artem said matter-of-factly. "We can't seriously be planning on just walking up river in the hopes we find these yacuruna."

"I had a thought," Muireann said. She had shed her heavier sweater and the knit hat she'd worn most of the time since they found her, tying her jet-black hair back in a rough ponytail. The dark sleeveless Atlantean top she'd taken to wearing beneath the sweater revealed swirling blue-green tattoos down both arms, almost like scales. Echo caught Barnabas eyeing the tattoos, but she could tell it wasn't lascivious—his own ink contained spells and magic wards, and Echo knew the magician was looking for clues to their new companion's own mystical abilities.

"Go on," Artem said. "I've got nothing to add. Curious what you think."

"Well," Muireann said. "As a… mythical creature myself, I will tell you that I'd never approach a group like ours. I want to encounter a human alone."

"That is so reassuring," Yuri said.

"No, she's got a point," Barnabas said. "The stories about yacuruna indicate they usually abduct people they find isolated so no one sees the kidnapping."

"Because splitting up always works so well," Artem said.

"On the upside, I think we're all pretty capable of defending ourselves," Echo said. "My only question is if one of us is approached by the yacuruna, how do we let the others know?"

"I can help with that," Barnabas said. "It's an easy spell. If one of us is in danger or distress, we'll each feel a slight tug in their direction, like an alarm."

"Magic motion sensor," Yuri said. Barnabas shrugged but didn't argue.

"All right then," Echo said. "We split up, I guess?"

"I could take the dinghy up river a bit," Barnabas said. "Kind of act as an outrider from the water."

"Also, you're not pretty, so they're not going to steal you," Yuri said.

"Speaking of not pretty, what are you going to do?" Barnabas said.

"Oh, for the love of… will you two knock it off already?" Artem said. "This joke is getting old."

"So is Barnabas," Yuri said. Barnabas shot him a dirty look, but Yuri stuck his tongue out at him, taunting.

"You could be our scout underwater," Barnabas said.

"What now?" Yuri said.

"Transform into your shark-man form and swim up river," Barnabas said. "I'll watch from above, you from below."

"I hate to say it, but that's not a bad idea," Echo said. "Can you breathe fresh water when you're a shark though?"

Yuri opened his mouth to speak, stopped, started again, stopped, then threw his arms up in the air.

"I have no idea," he said. "This is not something I ever had to think about before."

"What kind of shark do you transform into?" Muireann said, her tone completely serious. While Barnabas, and to a lesser extent Artem, both looked ready to begin a new round of teasing, Muireann's earnestness felt simultaneously out of place, and also a pleasant change of pace.

"I don't know," Yuri said. "I'm a shark. I'm big, I have a shark head. I mean I know I'm a pretty normal shark, since I have the, like, the triangle type head. I'm not a hammerhead or something weird."

"That narrows it down so much," Artem said. Then, more seriously: "I remember the attack on the island… that swarm of were-sharks varied significantly. You could've been bitten by any number of types of sharks."

"I don't even know how it works, the water breathing," Yuri said. "Does it matter, what species of shark I transform into?"

"If you're a bull shark you should be able to breathe fresh water," Echo said. The whole group looked at her like she'd begun reciting Shakespeare from memory. "What? I read a lot of books about sharks as a kid. I was a surfer. It was research."

"So, I guess we hope you're either a bull shark or that were-sharks in general can do fresh water," Barnabas said.

"How do we find out?" Yuri said.

Artem threw Yuri in the river using some sort of martial arts leverage technique Yuri had no chance of preventing.

He landed with a splash and disappeared beneath the murky water.

His friends waited.

"I think I should go get him," Echo said.

"Wait," Muireann said.

They watched as Yuri, now in his bulky shark-man form, rose out of the water like a river monster. His jet-black eyes scanned the group as water poured off his snout, his wide, toothy grin gleaming white and deadly.

The were-shark spoke. His voice was broken, gravelly, the sound of running water and crashing waves.

"I can breathe river water," Yuri said in a voice that was barely his own, the words partially mangled by those sharp, triangular teeth.

"Good to know," Barnabas said, sounding vaguely sheepish.

"I wasn't a horrible person before I met all of you," Artem said. "I'll take point."

The Amazon put a hand on the hilt of each of the swords on his belt and began walking up river. Yuri nonchalantly turned around and dove, surprisingly gracefully, back beneath the water.

Echo and Muireann shared a beleaguered glance.

"I'm just working on the assumption this is how they always are," Muireann said.

"Most of the time, yeah," Echo said. "You want water's edge, or a little further into the forest?"

Muireann gestured at herself.

"Water is sort of my thing. If you don't mind," she said, peering over her shoulder at the water as Barnabas awkwardly dragged the dinghy back into the river.

"Sounds good," Echo said. "Be safe."

The ondine smiled and strode to the very edge of the river, singing softly to herself.

"Yup," Echo said to herself. "This is a terrible plan."

Chapter 29: Shark meets crocodile

Yuri was loath to admit it, but he'd genuinely started to enjoy the grace and strength his shark-man form offered.

Like right now, for instance. He swam up river against a powerful current with ease, barely noticing the river pushing him toward the sea. And the water itself was not particularly clear, murky with silt and vegetation, but his shark senses were almost supernatural. He didn't need his eyes to tell him his depth, or how close he was to the shore, or if there were fish swimming near him. It was almost a sort of swimming extra-sensory perception, and it made him feel safe, he realized. Not strong. Safe. He didn't feel dangerous. This form enabled him to be without fear.

I'm not afraid, and that alone makes it almost worth it, he thought. I never realized how afraid I was my whole life. It's like a chain removed from my heart that I never knew existed.

I was afraid the whole time after the were-sharks killed Meredith, he thought. Afraid on the Island of Unwanted Things. Afraid on the island of nymphs, afraid when the mermaid tried to drown me. How did I get this far being afraid all the time? Yuri asked himself. Yes, transforming into a were-shark was terrifying. It nearly killed him, literally. It came with a level of body horror he didn't think truly existed.

But now?

All the waters of the world are mine.

My mother spent my entire life trying to save me from drowning, Yuri thought. Everything she did was meant to keep me safe from the sea. But in the end, I passed through fire and blood, and came out the other side… well, a monster, of sorts. But the monster you want on your side.

I think I'm happy, Yuri thought, somewhat surprised at the idea. Am I allowed to be happy? Are were-sharks ever happy? I don't remember ever meeting one in a particularly good mood. Even Whitetip, my tutor, was sort of always vaguely melancholy. I don't think sharks have a happy status.

And that was the moment he swam full-speed into a giant log.

Something Whitetip had warned Yuri about, but still caught him off-guard, was the bane of were-sharks: they had an obscene amount of nerves in their snout. Just like their ordinary shark counterparts, punching a were-shark in the nose was a good way to put him on the defensive, and Yuri was not swimming slowly when he struck the log face-first at full speed. His vision flashed white with pain, his brain flaring with panic, his whole body jerking back involuntarily. He swore out loud underwater, which was an ineffective endeavor as nothing but bubbles drifted out of his mouth.

Okay, he thought, maybe the shark senses aren't quite infallible. I'll work on that.

Then the huge log moved.

Oh, great, Yuri thought. Nothing is ever simple, is it?

He turned toward the surface to get a better look at the now-twisting log, clearly not a fallen tree, and found himself face to face with a black-scaled crocodile at least twenty feet long. Its golden eyes burned into him not with anger, but with an almost human level of annoyance, as if it were as irritated to see him as he was to see it.

And then the crocodile clamped a set of jaws onto Yuri's torso.

Yuri felt himself dragged swiftly below the water again, pushed down into the silt, the crocodile twisting as if trying to break his neck. For better or for worse, the were-shark form was difficult to damage, though Yuri was unhappy to see some of his own blood dirtying the river water as the crocodile sank its teeth into his flesh.

The initial shock of the attack wearing off, Yuri resigned himself to a fight. I really didn't want to do this today, he thought. With a palpable sense of distaste, he sank his wide, toothy jaws into the nearest part of the crocodile's body.

The crocodile's reaction was, of course, exactly as expected.

The beast rolled again, its jaws clenching harder onto Yuri rather than loosening in shock. Yuri, now legitimately in agony, did the same, biting back and adding his clawed fingers to his attack, dragging them across the black scales, drawing dark reptilian blood. He threw a knee once, twice, into the softer underside of the crocodile, and now the creature began to let go, its jaw slackening just enough for Yuri to get a powerful hand in between himself and the teeth and start to push.

Now the crocodile was on the defensive, thrashing and snapping, finally releasing Yuri entirely. Everything about the beast's actions told him it wasn't used to prey that put up a fight— a croc this big, Yuri thought, probably had no natural enemies other than humanity to worry about. He swam backward, trying to get his bearings, still not quite sure in the murky waters which way was up. He went toward the light, trying to put some space between himself and the crocodile.

The river around him swelled, and Yuri knew immediately he wasn't alone. He dodged to the left, spiraling out of the way as the enormous reptile darted past, shockingly fast for such a massive creature. Yuri dove deeper, away from the air, assuming the crocodile would need to return to the surface to breathe, hoping this might buy him some time.

Buy time for what? Yuri asked himself. And do I really want to try to kill this thing? What if it's just defending its territory? What if this is the crocodile the river beings we're looking for ride? Didn't Barnabas say something about black crocodiles?

Yuri's internal conversation lasted just long enough for him to stop paying attention. The crocodile clamped back down on him with breathtaking swiftness and began to rocket toward the surface once again.

I should have stayed on my island, Yuri thought. No good ever comes from hanging out with this crew.

Together, the crocodile and were-shark shot out of the river, Yuri still held tight in the croc's jaws, the great river beast rising so that more than half of its entire length was airborne. Yuri slashed and clawed, unable to get his teeth close enough to the crocodile to do any damage.

And then he realized what the creature had in mind.

"Oh, come on," Yuri said, his words slurred by the wide jaws and pointed teeth of his shark form.

And then the crocodile, with almost comedic grace, threw the were-shark in a rainbow-like arc away from the river and into the forest.

Chapter 30: The pink dolphin

Echo skirted the edge of the river as best she could, realizing, as Artem faded into the tree line, how long it had been since she was really and truly alone.

Not that she had ever had much time alone. She lived with her mother, she worked with Yuri, there was a constant flurry of people in her life long before the Atlantis troubles happened, and since then, they'd barely had a moment to rest. Artem and Barnabas were constant fixtures. During their downtime, they were on New Tortuga, which was a bustling beehive of people.

I miss surfing, she thought. Maybe when this is all over, I'll be able to surf again.

But that thought led her to remember home, the tall flames as she watched her house burn to the ground from the deck of the *Endless*, her life, really, burning to the ground as well. She'd left her surfboard there, of course, alongside all normalcy. I still don't know if I can even go home, she thought, not for the first time. Have Yuri and I been declared dead? Did anyone ever look for us? Do they still? Or were we, like so many people, just swallowed up by the chaotic strength of the sea, ghosts on the waves never to be seen again?

But still, here I am, she thought, in this wondrous place. A place that is not wondrous because it's hidden, or magical, or out of some myth. I'm walking alongside the Amazon River. Fearlessly, because that is the gift my father gave me, unbreakable skin, a warrior's instincts. Golden sunlight weaved its way through the canopy and dappled her skin. The sound of animals, of birds and insects and a million other creatures she couldn't identify, was almost deafening. This place just exists, Echo thought. This mighty waterway splitting a continent in two.

Humanity's ruining this place too, though, she thought. Her mind flashed to the room in Atlantis where all the sick and dying were hidden, the ones suffering from illnesses born from human poisons in the ocean. Maybe I don't want to go home. Maybe after seeing all this, there's nothing for me there anymore.

She caught a flicker of something out of the corner of her eye, movement on the water. She darted skillfully forward, moving deftly through brush and root. Maybe it was just Yuri surfacing for a moment, she thought. But then she saw it again, an arching body, baby-pink and perfectly smooth, playfully making its way up river. A long snout broke the surface again, large, round eyes, an unmistakable face.

"I swear I thought calling them 'pink dolphins' was a semantics thing," Echo said to herself. The dolphin made eye contact then dove below the again. Echo looked to her left and right but saw no sign of Artem or Muireann. She scanned the river and spotted Barnabas in the skiff, but he was too far away for her to catch his eye.

Carefully, Echo put her feet into the water, preparing to swim out. This is stupid, she thought. That's probably just a legitimate, normal, Amazon river dolphin. Just because they say the yacuruna can become pink dolphins doesn't mean all pink dolphins are yacuruna.

"It can't possibly be this easy," Echo said.

"That depends on what you're trying to accomplish," a new voice said.

Echo whipped around to see a newcomer standing not fifteen

feet from her. The person was androgynous, willowy and tall, with sun-reddened skin and dark hair that fell like a waterfall down their back. They wore a thin Henley shirt, clinging to their skin with moisture, and pants made of a light, pale fabric, also indicating they'd been donned while the wearer was still wet. The newcomer was barefoot and wore only a single adornment, a bracelet of wood and bone on their left hand.

"Oh. Hi," Echo said.

"I want to congratulate you and your people on being incredibly subtle," the newcomer said. "I'm being sarcastic, of course. You're just slightly below loggers for avoiding attention."

"We were actually hoping to… are you the yacuruna?" Echo said.

"I am *a* yacuruna," the being said. "Although it's been so long since I've seen another of my kind, I may very well be the only yacuruna. I hope that's not the case, but here where the river ends, I am alone."

"That's terrible," Echo said.

The yacuruna shrugged.

"I hope my people are more plentiful deeper into the continent," they said. "Where they can be hidden. There's too much traffic here. Too much mankind meddles in. Too much destruction, though that is mankind's specialty."

Echo approached slowly, finding herself strangely at ease around this elegant person watching her with sharp, dark eyes.

"I think we figured there'd be a fight," Echo said. "There's always a fight. You don't seem like you want to fight."

"You have the look of an Atlantean," they said. "And all of you, except that girl over there, have a human shadow on you. It doesn't surprise me you expected a fight. Atlanteans and humans, all they do is fight and destroy."

The yacuruna pointed past Echo's shoulder, who turned to see Muireann just walking into view amongst the brush.

"We're all, well, we're not all human. I don't think any of us is just a run of the mill human anymore," Echo said.

"Quite the menagerie you've brought to my river," the yacuruna said. "No, I don't want to fight. I don't even want to steal you away, which I'm sure you thought I'd do. That's what the old stories say."

"Okay, yeah, that we expected," Echo said.

The yacuruna shook their head balefully.

"We never took anyone who wanted to go home," they said. "That was our rule. We took those who wanted to join us beneath the river. Only the willing."

"But the legends say otherwise," Echo said, sitting down on a large root shaped like a bench.

"Humans always make monsters of that which they do not understand," they said.

Echo nodded, feeling very tired.

"Echo!" Artem said, startling her. The Amazon charged out of the forest, drawing his swords. "Back away from him! You don't know—"

Before Artem could finish speaking, he was cut off as a giant snake, its body as thick as a bodybuilder's thigh, sprang out of the underbrush, tackling him. Echo watched in horror as the serpent coiled itself around Artem and gently rested him on the forest floor.

"Uh-oh," Echo said.

"Speaking of making monsters of that which you do not understand," the yacuruna said.

"Echo, help! What's going on!" Artem said, struggling against the snake's hold.

"I think we're cool, Artem."

"I'm tied up on the ground by a giant snake, Echo. This is not, as you say, cool," Artem said.

"Could you let my friend go?" Echo said.

"If your friend promises not to try to take my head off with his swords," the yacuruna said. They regarded Artem with a kind expression. "Sorry about my companion. He is there to protect me from threats, and you seemed somewhat threatening."

"Echo?" Artem said.

"Please let him go," she said.

The yacuruna waved a hand at the serpent, who released Artem, though not as quickly as the Amazon would have liked.

Muireann, seeing all this happen, approached much more peacefully, her hands stuffed in her pockets.

"I take it you found them," she said.

Artem struggled to his feet, righting his armor and sheathing his swords, but not without a resentful look on his face.

"I might have overreacted," he said. "I've been having a bad week."

"I'm used to people assuming the worst," the yacuruna said. "That's why I have my protectors."

"Protectors, plural?" Artem said.

The yacuruna nodded.

"Okay, no more violence," Echo said. "We're here because you have something we need. Or your people have something we need. A magical object to lock away a dangerous creature."

The yacuruna smiled warmly.

"Oh, why didn't you start with that instead of all this nonsense?" they said. "But then, I should have known. The only thing that brings Amazonians and Atlanteans and ocean spirits and shapeshifters together is a world-ending disaster. The minute I saw you all arrive together, I should have known something terrible was afoot."

"Believe it or not, we're actually friends," Artem said. "I mean, our people are all terrible to each other, but this group... we actually like each other. Well, mostly. The magician paddling around out on the river like an idiot right now is questionable."

The yacuruna smirked.

"Never trust a magician completely," they said. "Like the shaman of old. We used to help them, sometimes. But a wizard, even with the best of intentions, will always have a second or third layer to every plan."

"Sounds like our magician," Echo said. "But... you'll help us?"

The yacuruna laughed, a soft, huffing noise accompanying a radiant smile.

"You'll have to come to my city to get what you need," they said. "But that's easily done."

"Okay, so how do we…" Echo started to say. Then she heard a loud, wet thump, a roar that might have also been a cry for help, and then looked up to see a shadow shaped like a man-shark flying through the air like a ragdoll. "Oh, Yuri."

The yacuruna beamed that same radiant smile at Artem.

"Protectors, plural," they said. "It looks like your shark friend has met my crocodile."

Echo sighed and turned to Artem.

"I'll go get him," Artem said, resigned. "I'll be right back."

Chapter 31: It's a cult

Simon Yee was a professional weirdness investigator. He knew weird when he saw it. Weird was, in fact, his job. And he knew, beyond a shadow of a doubt, that things in Fogarty's Folly had gotten very, very weird.

Sure, Jeb Sykes rambling like a madman had felt out of place, but one guy going off the rails is one guy going off the rails. But in the days since, the whole town had taken on a kind of just-on-the-edge-of-cracking energy.

Well, not all of it. The new folks, like himself, seemed unchanged, and, frankly, somewhat put upon by the behavior of the Fogarty's Folly lifers. Stores had begun keeping weird hours. The townies hadn't always been particularly friendly to new residents, but they'd adopted an even stranger attitude, seemingly ignoring them rather than showing obvious annoyance, as if the new folks—with their hybrid cars and their long commutes—were barely even there, just objects to walk around in the street. The lifers puttered through the streets as if on a mission, eyes distant, faces somehow both rapturous and anxious.

The temple, which Simon sat looking at from his spot in Ishmael's Coffee across the street, had become a beehive of activity. If Simon was being honest with himself, this had become a stakeout. He curiously observed the comings and goings at the temple all day: local politicians, the chief of police, business owners, priests, other staples of the town, all of whom passed each other as they arrived and left without a word. None seemed particularly rushed, either, but focused, almost cartoonishly so.

"You look like you're on a stakeout," a woman said. Simon snapped out of his reverie and looked up. The manager of the Ishmael's branch, a thirty-something woman with a mop of curly hair and a quick smile, stood over him, hands on her hips.

"I don't…" Simon started to say, but she cut him off, sitting down at his booth with him.

"Look, you can deny it all you want, but you are casing that building over there. And you know what? I don't blame you," she said. "Clarissa, by the way. I'm the manager."

"Do you usually accuse your customers of spying on the neighbors?" Simon said. "Not that I'm admitting to spying or anything."

"You're staring at that weird temple," she said. "Honestly, I've worked across the street from it for two years now and I have never seen anything even remotely normal happen over there."

"I've never seen anything happen there at all," Simon said. "I'm pretty new to town."

"I could tell you weren't local. You don't have that wide-eyed, fishy stare the townies have," Clarissa said.

"Fishy?"

"Look at them," Clarissa said.

Simon turned back to the street and checked out the passersby and found that Clarissa wasn't exaggerating—the locals did have a certain wide-eyed, round-faced look. Not obvious, not over the top, but if you watched for it, there it was. A Fogarty's Folly face.

"Well, now I'll never unsee that," Simon said.

"I noticed it after my first few weeks on the job," Clarissa said. "I'm not local. Moved here to help open the branch, figured it was a good excuse to live by the water for a bit. But you see the same faces every day, you start noticing patterns, similarities."

"You think it's just genetics?" Simon said. "Small towns like this tend to have a lot of families who intermarry. Might just be a dominant feature or something."

"Maybe," Clarissa said, shrugging. "Maybe it's something in the tap water."

"Do you drink the water?"

"Up until this conversation I did," Clarissa said. "Rethinking that position."

Together, they stared at the temple. Another group of people left, several business owners and a town council member.

"I've got to find out what's going on in there," Simon said. "I don't even know what it is. Is it like the Masons? The Elks?"

Clarissa leaned in conspiratorially.

"That I can help you with," she said. "Okay, so when I first got here, I asked about it, and everyone in town passes it off as a community center. As you say, like the Elks. People giving back to the town, a sort of mock exclusivity that pretends it's a secret society for fun. But dude, it's a cult."

"Seriously?"

"No joke. Some of my staff are local teenagers, and like any kids being forced to join anything with their parents, they usually want nothing to do with the temple, right? Nobody wants to go to the local community center to volunteer at fifteen, they want to hang with their friends. But a few weeks later? Total change of personality. They're in it."

"What do you mean, total change of personality?" Simon said.

"Well first off, most of them quit. They get jobs with someone who's in the group. The local businesses, with owners who are lifelong residents, they hire all the local kids. I'm actually relieved this town is starting to attract the upper middle class folks from out of town now so I can hire those kids," Clarissa said. "I still hire townie teenagers when I can because it gets you points with the community, who hate that a chain coffee shop is here in the first place, but seriously, I've never had a kid stay on after they start going to the temple."

"Okay, so it's a closed circuit," Simon said. "But that doesn't scream cult to me. That screams, well, favoritism, maybe. Insular behavior."

"Oh, it gets worse," Clarissa said. "They don't talk about it openly, but you can catch snippets of it sometimes. There's a sort of religion involved. They hold ceremonies a few times a year. They keep it really quiet, but there's this talk of rising again—I figured it was like the Rapture, right? Except it's totally not. They mean something rising again... from the ocean."

Simon raised an eyebrow.

"Are you sure they're not just LARPing a Lovecraft game?"

"I'm telling you... I didn't get your name."

"Simon."

"I'm telling you, Simon, if what's going on over there is a game, the people playing it don't think so," Clarissa said. "I even asked if I could join as a local business manager, y'know, maybe sponsor a little league team or something. You would've thought I said something scandalous."

Simon sipped his coffee, grimacing as it had faded from lukewarm to below room temperature.

"I'll refresh that on the house," Clarissa said. Simon waved her off.

"Okay, look, all these anecdotes are interesting, but I need more to go on," Simon said.

"So, you *are* staking the place out," Clarissa said.

"Fine, yes, I am," Simon said.

"Are you a cop? A private eye?" Clarissa said.

"I am something so much weirder than both of those, but that's a story for later," Simon said. "I need something actionable. Is it possible to get inside the temple?"

"Are you willing to break in?" Clarissa said, barely concealing the hope in her voice.

"That would be a bad idea," Simon said.

"I was really hoping you'd break in," Clarissa said. "Although I don't know how you'd do that with no windows."

"Yeah, about that—who builds a concrete block of a building with no windows?" Simon said. "That's got to be some sort of safety violation. Anyway. No breaking and entering."

"Well, one of my regulars told me the temple folks are setting something up on Pickman's Beach," Clarissa said.

"Define 'something.' And maybe 'setting up.'"

Clarissa shrugged.

"I don't know. Just telling you what I know."

"Pickman's is the private beach down on the south side of town, yeah?" Simon said.

"Yup."

"So, I'll have to trespass on a private beach to get there," Simon said.

"That, my weird not-a-cop friend, I can help you with," Clarissa said. "Guess whose apartment building has a walking trail next to it that state law says has to allow access to the shore?"

Simon leaned in and pointed at Clarissa.

"I have this feeling either we're going to be best friends, or you're setting me up to get murdered," Simon said.

"So, I'm going to take that as a yes to coming by later to spy on Pickman's Beach?"

Simon sighed and threw back the rest of his cold coffee.

"It's a yes," he said. "What time should I come by?"

Chapter 32: The upside-down city

Artem had seen a lot of strange things in his life. He'd been to the bottom of the sea, fought monsters, lived among myths and legends.

But nothing prepared him for the city of the yacuruna.

The strange, androgynous being led them beneath the Amazon, smiling radiantly when the group told the yacuruna every one of them could breathe underwater.

"This river is a little different than the oceans you are used to," they said, and before Yuri could get a snide "I know" out, the yacuruna disappeared beneath the brownish river water. The others followed, Artem momentarily disoriented and uncomfortable, so much time having passed between the last time he had to use the magical earring he wore.

Instantly, the world made no sense.

He dove beneath the waves, expecting darkness, expecting confusion, but he did not expect anything like what he saw underwater—the riverbed seemed to expand, an inverted sky, disappearing into impossible depths. He immediately felt an animalistic panic set in, his mind trying to wrap itself around the impossible while his body fought against the belief it might drown.

He felt a strong, slender hand on his upper arm, and found

Echo there waiting. She took his hand in hers, and, without pride or embarrassment, let her guide him into the abyss beneath the river. I know my strengths, and I know hers, he thought. The wise man takes the hand when offered; the fool drowns.

Beside them, Yuri had transformed into his were-shark form, allowing Barnabas, in an accidental but not inappropriate approximation of a lamprey, to latch on for a ride as well. Muireann drifted on the currents as though she were born there, a fluid, elegant, effortless grace to her movements as she swam behind the yacuruna. Months ago, Artem might have been frustrated at feeling momentarily weak or out of his own control, but now, after fighting beside these strange people, he felt comfort knowing they watched out for him beneath the waves the way he watched out for them above.

Echo pulling him along also allowed Artem a chance to study their surroundings. The riverbed teamed with life along the edges, plant matter and fish, the glitter of daylight. And the deep emptiness they swam toward did not turn to dark the way such a space on the sea floor would—it seemed to glow with a light of its own, or to draw the daylight into it like warmth, a pale light made green by the living matter all around them.

As they dove deeper, Artem felt the strange sensation of gravity reversing. He no longer felt as if they were diving down, but rather floating up, drawn toward a surface that was not there. Artem felt a hint of vertigo the deeper they traveled, his internal senses telling him the opposite of what his eyes did. This feels a little bit like going mad, he thought.

And then he saw the upside-down city and truly questioned his sanity.

The city seemed to rest on the bottom of the river, but at an impossible depth, but also inverted, flipped so that spires of buildings were pointing downward into the blurry haze of the sky that was not the sky beyond. There were two skies, like in a mirror, and the effect was dizzying. It cast an alien shadow on the horizon, dark fingers of stone and wood reaching out to grasp at ghosts.

Artem felt Echo's hand tighten around his, shocked at the magnificent image before them.

The yacuruna guided them closer, swimming parallel to the floor of the river—both floors, Artem realized; the river mirrored itself, as above, so below. The being darted through the water with the flexible grace of sea lion. From the murky depths, a shape merged, enormous with a wedge-shaped head, and the yacuruna reached out to take hold of this new creature, another massive black crocodile, and together they guided the companions into the upside-down city.

The yacuruna effortlessly placed their feet against the street, the disorienting gravity of this place not impacting them at all. As Artem looked around at the city to try to orient himself—to try, in essence, to pretend up is down, to walk on the "ground" of this inverted place—he saw just how beautiful this city was. I need to take this in, he thought. I need to absorb this. I am amongst the impossible. I want to understand what this means.

Soon they were close enough to touch the first of the city's spires, and Artem saw, shockingly, that the buildings were made of pure crystal. Only vaguely opaque in some parts, pristinely clear in others, the upside-down city felt as if it were made entirely of glass. Beautiful, brittle, waiting for the wrong touch to master it, or to destroy it.

The yacuruna watched as the group awkwardly gathered around. Echo drifted, her demeanor calm but her eyes betraying confusion and discomfort. Muireann easily followed the river spirit's lead and placed her feet on the ground to stand upside down, soles of her feet aimed toward the surface of the water from which they'd come. Barnabas tried to stand as well, but kept slipping and drifting upright again. Yuri clearly gave up completely and floated with his back to the ground, completely upside-down in the eyes of the yacuruna.

The river spirit gestured for the group to follow them inside, and they complied. The beauty of the building once again struck Artem—walls made of pearl, floors and ceilings designed with

168

hand-crafted fish scales. He saw hammocks made from the feathers of birds the colors of which seemed impossibly vibrant. They were not alone, either—turtles the size of chairs walked around with meditative calm, and serpents like the one that trapped Artem on the surface had free rein of the place, though they kept a respectful, almost suspicious distance. Not a one seemed at all bothered by the upside-down nature of this place. Artem wondered if they ever left, or even if they were born to this life and knew no other.

Once inside the crystal building, the inversion of gravity fully took effect. Muireann, Echo, and Artem—with Echo's help—managed to stay on their feet. Barnabas tipped and fell like a drunk in the street, struggling to get back onto his feet. Yuri just flopped on the ground like a shark on a boat, laying there until he transformed.

"I feel like I'm going to vomit," he said.

"Perhaps your friend should just stay here, for now," the yacuruna said, and then, before their eyes, the spirit transformed. Gone was the androgynous beauty, replaced by a creature covered in fur from head to toe, a wide, inscrutable, but inhuman face looking back at the group.

"Your true face," Echo said.

"I have many true faces. This face is no less true than the one I wore above. Faces are meant for convenience, not truth," the yacuruna said.

"But this is the face you wear at home," Muireann said. "That means something."

The yacuruna smiled at her.

"Said well by someone who wears many faces herself," they said.

"Many faces?" Yuri said, trying to stand up but falling over again.

"We can talk about that later," Barnabas said. He was on his feet now, but had his eyes closed, and even wrapped a bandana from his coat around his eyes to remain balanced.

"Spirit," Artem said, interrupting. "You know why we're here."

"I suspected," the yacuruna said. "The rivers and the seas don't talk to each other the ways you might expect. We have different magic. We are siblings who have moved to different villages, who no longer speak, simply because our paths never cross. But even the rivers have heard that something has awoken, a malignance that spreads even here."

The yacuruna pointed at a corner of the room, where a corpse, brutally killed but tidily laid to rest, waited in eternal repose. It was a short creature, thick bodied but not stocky, with spindly limbs, large feet and hands, webbed fingers tipped with sharp claws. It had a fishlike head with a wide, crescent mouth. Artem immediately thought of the shapes of the bites on the seahorse body they'd seen.

"It's one of them," Echo said, noticing the same details.

"I don't know what you mean by that," the yacuruna said. "But it was an unwelcome invader in my lands, a straggler from a larger school, left behind and gluttonously ravaging the creatures I call friends. It had to be put down. Swiftly and painlessly, of course. We yacuruna are healers, not killers, despite what the legends sometimes say."

Artem took a step forward, but the moment he strode away from Echo, who had been quietly assisting his balance, Artem felt the room sway.

"Spirit, we were told you might have an object. Something that might help us bind this menace, to stop it from hurting anyone else," Echo said. Her voice was tight and strained. Artem could see the stress of this inverted place weighing on her. But then Muireann walked up to Echo, placed a hand on her shoulder, and leaned in, whispering something into her ear. Artem watched as Echo's body loosened, her eyes cleared, and a soft smile crossed her lips.

"Thank you," Echo said.

"Muireann, I'd hate to trouble you, but…" Artem said. Muireann moved softly to his side as well and repeated the gesture. He could not understand the words she whispered in his ears, but the felt like a cool bath, his skin rippling with a calm comfort. He stood at his full height and felt a strength return to his limbs he hadn't known was gone.

"What is that?" he asked.

"You have a true water spirit in your midst," the yacuruna said, watching Muireann with a bemused wonder. "A healer, like me. And a trickster, also like me. You remind me of a woman I stole away once, when I was very young. She had no place on the surface and did not know, before I found her, that there are worlds without end if you look for them. She became a mermaid and protected the river for many years."

"I'm not a mermaid," Muireann said. "But I'm glad I remind you of someone you miss."

The yacuruna looked around the empty, palatial room, their wide, inhuman face sad and lost.

"I miss a great many people these days," they said. "But you didn't come here to keep an old river spirit company. You came here something else."

"A weapon," Artem said.

"That's where you're wrong, warrior," the yacuruna said. "We did not accept a weapon in our midst. We are healers, as I said. You'll find no weapons of war here."

"If I'm this nauseous for no reason I'm going to be so mad," Yuri said, his voice distant and uncomfortable.

"It's a focus," Barnabas said. "Or a holy object. Right?"

"Close enough," the yacuruna said. They shuffled over to a wooden chest, obviously worn down by the sea, its clunky, aged look standing out from the surreal luxury of this place. The yacuruna unlatched the crate and opened it. A warm, orange-gold light seeped out.

Barnabas removed the bandana from his eyes, and Muireann quickly darted over to cast her spell on him as well. She cast a baleful look in Yuri's general direction, but he'd flopped down so far away he was barely part of the conversation anymore. Barnabas more solidly on his feet, watched the yacuruna hoist an object from the crate with a greedy interest that made Artem uncomfortable.

"This is the Eye of Dreams," the river spirit said. Resting gently in their hands was a sphere, perhaps the size of a cantaloupe, a glowing cat's eye of amber-colored stone, split down the middle with a dark vertical shadow in its core. The yacuruna looked at Barnabas, then Echo, then handed the Eye gently to Muireann.

"This is what we were sent to recover," Echo said.

"And this is what we were told to keep safe should this day ever come," the yacuruna said. "I'm just glad one of us was still here to give it to you. We have no stake in the battle for the oceans, but the world belongs to all of us, river and sea, stream and gulf. The heroes of yesteryear came to us because we had nothing to gain by holding it."

"Is there something to gain by holding it?" Barnabas said.

The yacuruna pointed at the magician in a scolding manner.

"All magic grants a boon, and all magic has a cost," they said. "You, little wizard, are more than aware of that. I can smell it in your blood."

Barnabas went very quiet, taking a respectful step back from the spirit.

"Do you know who has the other tool that was used to bind this threat before?" Echo said. "We were told we'd need the Needle and the Eye."

The yacuruna shrugged.

"I'm afraid I have no answers for you there," they said. "We took what was given to us, and kept it safe, and hoped no one would ever need it again."

"I'm sorry that we bring the bad news that your hope was not met," Echo said.

The yacuruna waved her off impatiently.

"No good comes from hoping. It comes from doing. And I sense you have much doing left in all of you," they said.

"Spirit," Muireann said. "I have a question, if I may be bold."

"The bold shall inherit the world," the spirit said. "Ask away."

"What happens to this city if you're gone?" she said. "I know that may sound disrespectful, or morbid, but you are all alone here, and this place is a wonder. It gives me such fear to think it could…"

"Be abandoned forever?" the yacuruna said. "Little ondine, I will find a successor. I will find several. My days are spent searching for someone the surface does not want, who does not want the surface in return. Someone who will become a yacuruna and keep our stories alive. That is the only job I have left."

"All the beautiful things in this world are disappearing," Muireann said.

The yacuruna favored her with a sad, mournful smile.

"All the more reason to make sure we preserve them," they said.

Artem watched in surprise as Barnabas put a gentle hand on Muireann's shoulder. I suppose she's speaking about them, Artem thought. But also about Echo's people, and about Yuri's newfound tribe. I saw the cracks in the walls of New Scythia, Artem thought. Time comes for us all. Even my people. I don't want to live in a world without wonder, as much as those wonders make me angry sometimes.

"Is there anything we can do for you, spirit, in return for keeping the Eye safe?" Artem said.

The yacuruna paused, thinking, pursing their lips. Then they spoke.

"You know how magic works," they said. "Tell people of the yacuruna. Talk about the cities of crystal, hidden in the reflections of the surface world. Myth only ceases to exist when the last minds forget us. That goes for all of you. Be not forgotten, and help others to not forget. That's all I ask."

"We'll tell the world your story," Echo said. "May your search for others like you be successful."

"May your fight be successful as well," the yacuruna said. "I sense my search will be far easier than the war you have ahead of you. Be strong. Be brave."

They turned to both Muireann and Barnabas, tilting their head,

"And you know my name," they said. "If one of you should fall, call on me. If I can, I will lend you the healing magics of my people."

"That's very generous of you," Barnabas said.

"I don't offer it often," the yacuruna said. "But you've convinced me of your cause. Now get your poor sick friend out of my house. You have a world to save, little menagerie."

Chapter 33: Slouching toward Bethlehem

The leviathan walked, and it dreamed.

All around it, minions looked to the creature like a god as they swarmed around it like parasites. The creature walked on trunk-like legs, like a human's but malformed, too thick and squat, ending in flat, webbed feet tipped with black claws. Its sagging belly, heavy with the sloth of a thousand years of slumber, wobbled lazily, the weight of it like an island unto itself.

Too many eyes dotted its face, an uneven, unbalanced number, red irises encasing golden pupils of different sizes, more like blisters than eyes. They blinked at different times, seemingly at random, ensuring that at no point would the eyes all be closed at once. Whether that eternal alertness made a difference to the creature was impossible to tell. If it saw everything, it gave no indication it cared. A beard of tentacles hung inert around its mouth, drifting on the current like fronds of seaweed.

The great beast stopped for nothing, never pausing its relentless, heavy stride. It neither ate nor slept, and paid no mind to passing creatures or ships, as though the matters of the world around it made no difference to it at all.

Its minions were not so passive. They devoured anything living that crossed their path without pity. Schools of fish, great creatures of the deep, ships full of human beings, nothing escaped their hunger. They left nothing living in their wake, blood only briefly staining the water before drifting way into the deep blue.

The ancient being did not need to rest. It had rested already for hundreds of years. Slumber was a thing of the past now. But it did dream. It dreamed of the voices of those who would call it a god, singing in temples along a distant shore. It heard the cries of those who have waited for it to awaken again for generations upon generations. Its minions, as stupid and feral as they were, could feel the building excitement, the orgiastic thrill of each footstep, closer and closer to its final destination.

The old one could feel the places in its flesh where it had been wounded before. Scars deeply healed over, imperfections in blackened muscle, places where its body no longer moved the way it once did. Would a god live with scars of battle? Perhaps not. But it mattered little to those who awaited the being's return. It would find its worshippers, and they would feed their master, make him fat and strong on the living of the surface world, and then this monster would level anything that stood in its way.

Before the great slumber, it had cults across the world. Temples half-submerged in dark places, where those who sought the creature's favor would lay gifts for it, where they would sing its name and ask for its favor. Words meant nothing to this elemental being, though. It read intent, and feeling; it sensed want, rage, desire. But its concerns were for something else, some forgotten place, memories of a world that does not exist anymore.

Like any immortal thing, the creature had almost no thought toward the mortal world, beyond what the world could give it, how it could be used. And now, the creature hungered for something that could not be eaten. It wanted not for flesh the way its minions chewed their way across the Atlantic Ocean. Its hunger was something else, something profound, and dark. One might call it evil, if morality meant anything to undying beings of might like this one.

It continued its slouching gait across the sea, toward those who would die in its name, never knowing how little it cared for them. It wanted to return to its place in this world, an undying titan, feared and revered, wordless and inscrutable.

Its worshippers awaited. It would not disappoint them.

Chapter 34: You stole from who?

The journey back to the *Endless* was relatively incident-free, which, Barnabas noted, was becoming an increasingly infrequent occurrence.

The yacuruna had been shockingly generous. They surrendered the Eye to Echo's group easily and without argument, when Barnabas had expected a fight. They even explained a bit about its magic, which Yuri and Artem visibly tuned out while Echo strained to understand. Barnabas had exchanged a knowing nod to Muireann, who clearly understood everything the yacuruna had said about the orb, the words and gestures that would need to be performed to awaken it, to "open" the Eye, so to speak.

We'll have to compare notes, Barnabas thought, still not quite sure what to make of the ondine's abilities. She seemed to be entirely instinctual in her magic—everything she did stemmed from the innate abilities that came from being an ondine, where Barnabas, though possessing a natural inclination toward magic because of his mother's heritage, had to bungle his way through spell books, old scrolls, and dangerous practice attempts to get it right. He was almost jealous of her, and at the same time proud of what he'd accomplished with so little worthwhile instruction.

The serpent had taught him a bit, he thought, back on the

Island of Unwanted Things. I can't take all the credit. I did have a
malevolent, almost-immortal snake handing me spell books since I
was a kid. Still, it was hard to understand things like the somatic
gestures many spells required when your teacher didn't have limbs.

He and Artem rowed the dinghy out to the *Endless* together,
Muireann sitting at the end of the little boat quietly, looking back at
the river wistfully. Both Yuri and Echo had chosen to swim back
on their own, and Barnabas could make out the streak in the water
where Echo darted ahead, leaping onto the deck without missing a
beat. Yuri, moving less like a rocket and more like the shark he
resembled, left almost no trail in the water, which Barnabas found
unsettling. For someone who, in human form, was a walking
disaster of clumsiness, it felt exceedingly unnatural to watch the
boy move like a true predator in the water. It caused a level of
dissonance Barnabas didn't particularly like.

They reached the ship and found Echo staring off into the
distance, her arms folded defensively. Barnabas left Artem and Yuri
to haul the dinghy back onboard and joined Echo on the deck.

"What are we looking... oh, that's interesting," Barnabas said.

"They're headed right for us," Echo said.

The path the new ship took left little question where it was
headed, its prow aimed directly at the *Endless*. It was a gorgeous
vessel, Barnabas thought, though a little too modern for his tastes,
a massive yacht, state of the art, stark white in all the right places,
chrome in the others, though it had clearly seen better days. There
was visible damage, possibly from a storm or rough seas, that he
could make out even from a distance.

A man stood on the prow, his body language imperious,
defiant.

"We know him?" Echo asked.

"I don't," Barnabas said.

The others joined them, watching the incoming vessel.

"I do," Muireann said softly.

Echo turned to her.

"What do you mean, you do?" Echo said.

Barnabas took that as a cue. He called out to his ship's ghost crew to get ready to leave. To the untrained eye, there was no way an ancient vessel like the *Endless* could outrun something like the yacht headed toward them, but if they could get a little bit of distance between them, the ghost ship could disappear along one of the ocean's faerie trails and escape. But they needed to get moving first.

Artem caught Barnabas' eye. The magician nodded to him, and the Amazon loosened his swords, rolling his shoulders to stretch for a fight.

"This is trouble, isn't it?" Yuri said, once again in his human form.

"I don't know," Echo said. "Is it trouble?"

"That's the man I stole from," Muireann said.

"The man whose… soul you stole?" Echo said, her voice hard, no nonsense.

Muireann looked to Barnabas for help. Barnabas shrugged.

"I thought you said you stole a bit of his life force," Artem said.

"Soul, life force, it's all the same," Barnabas said.

"That was not what you said earlier," Artem said.

"Magic is always open to interpretation," Barnabas said. "More art than science, y'know?"

"He wasn't using it," Muireann said. "And he doesn't deserve to have it back."

She had an edge to her voice they hadn't heard before. *She's ready to fight,* Barnabas thought. *I didn't think she had it in her. Now I'm curious about how this goes.*

"I'm going to need some clarity about what you mean by he wasn't using it," Echo said.

"I'm just working on the assumption that you mean that literally, and not that he wasn't particularly good at music, or very spiritual, or something like that," Yuri said.

"He had chosen to remove it from his own body," Muireann said. "For terrible purposes. And I needed it. So, I figured, if he was just going to throw it away…"

"Wait, you literally stole a guy's soul?" Yuri said. "Like that thing in your pocket his actual soul?"

"There's no literal when it comes to souls," Muireann said.

"That doesn't reassure me," Yuri said.

"You said he's a bad person," Echo said. "But he's somehow tracked us all the way to the Amazon, and he really doesn't look afraid of us. What are we talking about when you said bad person?"

"Anyone who surrenders their soul willingly is bad news," Barnabas said, drawing the flintlock pistol from his belt and examining it, hoping the last few mystical repairs he'd performed on it would work. "Even I wouldn't do that and I'm a terrible person."

"Well, you've got a wizard, a warrior, a were-shark, and the future queen of Atlantis on this boat with you," Yuri said.

"Ship," Barnabas corrected. "I thought we were past you getting that wrong."

"Ship," Yuri said. "I think we got this."

By now, the yacht was within shouting distance. The man, Muireann's pursuer, was dressed in expensive clothes designed to look casual and careworn, his blond hair in an expensive cut, clearly grown out from a few weeks at sea. He had movie star features, piercing blue eyes, a confident stance—clearly, he's not afraid of us, Barnabas thought—and wore a knife on his belt but appeared otherwise unarmed.

"Nice ship," he yelled over. American accent tinged with a British affectation. "I can't tell if it's an antique or just made to look like one."

"Nice ship yourself," Echo yelled back. "Looks expensive."

"All ships are expensive," the man said. "The cost of doing business on the sea. My name is Anson Tessier. You have something of mine, and you have the person who took it from me. Give me both and we can all get on with our day."

Echo glanced over at Muireann sternly, then back to Tessier.

"We can maybe talk about your stolen property," Echo said. "But we're not turning over the woman. No offense, but I don't think anyone who pursued a thief thousands of miles to confront them in person will just demand an apology."

Artem sidled up beside Barnabas.

"His crew looks unarmed. And frankly, confused," Artem said. "I don't think they're a threat. I honestly don't know what he thinks he can threaten us with to make us turn her over."

"Echo?" Barnabas said.

"I heard you, Artem," Echo said softly. Then she yelled back at Tessier. "Well, I appreciate that you asked nicely. But you're not getting her. No package deal. If you're not interested in bargaining over the stolen object only, whatever it is, I think we're done here."

"I'm usually a very reasonable person," Tessier said. "But I do always get what I want. I was hoping this wouldn't turn to violence."

"I find myself wishing things didn't turn to violence almost every day," Echo said. "And yet it just keeps happening. Unfortunately, that means we're all pretty good at violence."

"I'll take that as your final answer, then," Tessier said.

"Barnabas?" Echo said.

"Got it," he said. He shouted out an order to the ghost crew to get moving.

Nothing happened.

The ghosts all stood stock still, barely visible in the tropical daylight, staring straight at Tessier, as if awaiting his command.

"Oh," Barnabas said. "Oh, come on. You stole a soul from a necromancer?"

"A what?" Yuri said.

"Interesting ship," Tessier said. "I didn't notice the hauntings right away. I think I'll have to keep it."

"He's a bloody necromancer," Barnabas said, trying to fight the panic rising in his voice. "We're fighting someone who can control the dead and we're on a ship crewed by ghosts. I can't actually come up with a worse possible situation right now."

His eyes darted to Tessier, looking for any tells of how he was controlling the ghosts. No telltale mystical energies, no bone fetishes on his wrist or neck… but there, his right hand gripped like a claw, clenched tightly in an unnatural position. It wasn't a spellcasting trick Barnabas had seen before, but he knew a mystical gesture when he saw one. And Tessier wasn't releasing that hand gesture.

"He's concentrating on a spell," Barnabas said. "This isn't an innate ability. This guy's just a magician like me, we can work with this—what was he selling his soul for, Muireann?"

"There was some sort of bargain involved," she said. "I don't know with what."

"With what, or with who?" Yuri said.

"Same difference," Muireann and Barnabas said simultaneously.

"What do we do, guys?" Echo said.

"So, you're not going anywhere," Tessier said. "I can set your ship on fire right now if I'd like, but I think I want to keep it. So why don't you all just jump overboard and leave the little nymph for me? You don't have to die here."

"We need to break his hold on the ghosts," Barnabas said.

"And how do we do that?" Artem said.

"Hit him with something."

"He's a little far away for that," Artem said.

"I'll do it," Yuri said.

"What?" Echo said.

"I'm fast, I'm strong, and I regenerate if he hurts me," Yuri said. "Distract him for a minute and I'll run over."

"I should do this," Echo said.

Yuri smirked at her.

"C'mon, you haven't seen me in action since I got my powers under control," he said. "Let me show off a bit."

Echo grinned at him, then her smile faded.

"If we break free and start running, Yuri, I'm not leaving you behind again."

"You also haven't seen how flippin' fast I am when I shark out," Yuri said. "You get moving and I'll catch up. Trust me, I don't want to get left behind any more than you want to leave me. I just got you back. I'm not ditching myself without a fight."

"Okay," Echo said. "We just need a distraction."

"I'm not a man accustomed to waiting," Tessier shouted. "I do love your ship, but I will burn it to cinders if you don't disembark. You have ten seconds—"

"Screw it," Barnabas said and fired his pistol directly at the yacht.

The gun went off with a sound that, rather than a bang of gunpowder, was more akin to a thunderclap. A bolt of electricity burst forth from the barrel, arcing across the water to strike the side of the yacht. It splashed against the hull, creating a spider web of lightning across the front half of the ship. The men onboard cried out in panic as the lights flickered and dimmed. The blast left a blackened, melted burn mark on the hull, high enough to not leave the yacht taking on water, but clearly leaving structural damage.

Somewhere in the chaos Barnabas unleashed, he heard the faint sound of a body splashing into the water and hoped that Yuri had enough time to make the leap without being seen.

"Well, don't say I didn't give you a better option," Tessier said. "Nice trick, by the way. I'll be keeping that magic gun after I kill you. Don't worry, I'll take good care of it."

Barnabas began calling up a deflective spell as he watched Tessier begin tracing the air in the loose, languid shapes of a fire spell with his free hand. I'm not cut out for a magician's duel, Barnabas thought. He caught sight of Echo picking up her trident, readying a throw, and wasn't sure if even she could hit a target at this distance with the weapon. But then he heard Muireann begin to sing.

On the yacht, pale blue motes of light appeared around Tessier's eyes. He cursed, the fire spell he was preparing lost as he waved a hand in front of his face, shaking off whatever distraction Muireann had attempted. He gritted his teeth and began chanting again.

And that was when Yuri, fully sharked out, began dragging

himself up the side of the yacht, his massive claws leaving heavy puncture marks as he stabbed handholds in with his fingers. It took only a few seconds for Yuri to haul himself onto the deck, at which point Barnabas heard real fear in the voices of the sailors on Tessier's ship. Yuri was, even for someone who had faced were-sharks before, a terrifying sight, a monstrosity of muscle and teeth. Tessier at first didn't seem to notice, but then whipped around just in time to see Yuri's hand lash out to batter him aside. The necromancer flopped to the ground, sliding across the deck and out of sight.

Barnabas checked on the ghosts, who seemed to be sluggishly shaking themselves out of Tessier's control. He could see resentment in their eyes, too—they might be long dead, but they knew when they were being manipulated, and they were willful enough spirits to have chosen to crew the *Endless* precisely because the ship allowed them the free will to choose their afterlife.

"Full sail, or whatever!" Barnabas said, for the millionth time telling himself he needed to buy a book on sailing. "Get us out of here!"

From the yacht, a gunshot rang out, and Yuri roared, more in surprise than pain. Barnabas could barely see what went on aboard the other ship, but it was hard to miss a crewman tossed bodily overboard and into the ocean, alive, but screaming.

The *Endless* picked up speed. Barnabas called out to Artem.

"Watch for Yuri," he yelled. "I need to get us out of here."

Barnabas ran to the front of the ship, remembering the arcane phrases he'd used to open the path that took them here. He wondered if the necromancer could do the same, but for now, there wasn't much of an alternative. He silently cheered when he saw the barely visible break in reality, a sliver of light on the water, that would take them to the twisted paths where the ocean moved differently.

The ship shivered, and Barnabas feared they'd been hit, but instead, Yuri pulled himself onto the deck, bleeding from a small wound on his shoulder but otherwise as healthy as a massive were-shark could look.

Barnabas pointed the direction to the ghost crew and took aim at the yacht with his flintlock one more time. Again, it let loose an echoing thunderclap, striking the ship. He watched as Tessier, clutching one arm that hung limp at his side, stagger to the rail, but the lights on the yacht flickered and went out again. I don't know if he can make that ship sail with magic, but all that modern technology just shorted out, Barnabas thought, watching the blue electricity dance across the yacht's skin. Tessier might be a powerful dark magician, but a broken ship is a broken ship if you don't have the right spellcraft to fix it.

The *Endless*, now moving at full speed, passed into the breach in reality, taking them to a distant route. Barnabas holstered his pistol and watched as Yuri transformed back into his human form, the bullet wound in his arm sealing up with an alarming ease.

Echo caught his arm.

"Will they follow?" she said.

"Probably," Barnabas said, looking at Muireann, who stood on the quarterdeck alone, looking back at where they'd come from. "I'll plot us a few more jumps like that to take him off our trail. Back to New Scythia, I assume."

"Unfortunately," Artem said, nodding at Muireann. "What about her?"

"She's our responsibility now," Echo said. "I'm not handing her over."

Barnabas sighed heavily.

"You know I don't like sticking my neck out for anyone," Barnabas said, ignoring the eye roll he inspired from Echo. "But the magic that guy's into… having his soul stolen is the least of what he deserves. That's the bad stuff. The worst. Poison."

"That settles it," Echo said. "Can you help us make sure we're ready to fight him the right way next time?"

"Yeah," Barnabas said. "I'll do what I can."

Chapter 35: You put him into soul overdraft

Echo waited until Barnabas had plotted an indirect course along the ley lines and they were well and truly moving before addressing what had happened. Muireann spent the first few hours staring off the back of the ship, waiting for this Tessier creep to show up again. When it seemed as though they'd at least temporarily lost him, the ondine went below deck. Barnabas, handing the helm over to the spirits of the ship, went below as well. Echo followed.

She wasn't sure if she'd find them together or apart, and was somewhat relieved to discover the latter. The last thing she needed was the two magicians onboard conspiring. Muireann hunkered down in a dark corner, eyes closed, meditating. Barnabas had left his cabin door open, and Echo walked in without announcing herself, catching him uncorking an unlabeled bottle of booze.

"Seriously?" she said.

"Judge me all you want," Barnabas said, drinking directly from the bottle. "We just outran a necromancer. I'm celebrating."

"You keep saying that word," Echo said. "I'd like an explanation. Muireann, could you come here please?"

The ondine rose immediately from her meditation as if she'd expected Echo to call her. Together, the trio sat down in Barnabas' cabin. Echo almost laughed when she spotted Yuri eavesdropping from the steps leading up just outside the cabin door, and then saw Artem's leg barely in view, the Amazon clearly trying to feign disinterest. Well, we should all hear this anyway, Echo thought.

"So, this is the man you stole from," Echo said to Muireann. The ondine nodded. "And you stole... his soul."

"A piece of it. He wasn't using it," Muireann said, repeating that same excuse she'd used before.

"You keep saying that like it makes any sense," Echo said.

"In a way, it does," Barnabas said.

Echo waved a hand at him impatiently to go on.

"Okay, crash course in magic," Barnabas said. "There's different kinds. People like me, who learn magic. We read books, we use mystical tools to focus our magic, we build a skill that we don't necessarily have innate in us. A lot of us have some natural gifts—I'm the son of a nereid, I'm inclined to magic by nature— but not the ability to just cast spells at will."

He gestured to Muireann with the same hand he held the bottle with.

"Then you've got natural talent, like our friend here. You're an ondine. Pure sea spirit. Magic's in your veins. You cast spells without thinking about it. It's a part of you from birth."

"That's right," Muireann said. "I'm surprised even with a human father you don't have more natural ability."

Barnabas shrugged.

"Learning magic came naturally to me, so maybe that's my genetics chipping in," he said. "I was a terrible student because I learned too easily."

"You two can talk shop later," Echo said. "I want to know more about what we're up against."

"After the learners and the naturals, you've got the people who bargain for magic," Barnabas said.

"Bargain?" Echo said.

"They make deals. They receive their powers in exchange for something."

"Like their soul," Echo said.

Barnabas gestured at Echo with the bottle.

"Got it in one," Barnabas said. "So, my question for you, Muireann, is: was this Tessier bloke not using his soul, or was he planning on selling it and you pilfered it from him?"

"It seemed like a tragic waste of a perfectly good chunk of eternal life force," Muireann said. "He was going to trade it away. I figured I needed one, and I didn't want to take it from a good person, so…"

"Can I interrupt?" Yuri said, leaning in awkwardly. The cabin was getting crowded.

"You live here, too," Echo said. "Also, you saved our lives. You have the floor."

"Who could he possibly have been planning to sell his soul to?" Yuri said.

"Oh, any manner of terrible things," Barnabas said. "Demons, devils, hell spawn, a lich, an ancient unfathomable evil."

"All of those things are real?" Yuri said.

"You, who can transform into a shark-man, sound surprised," Barnabas said.

"Sorry, were-sharks are easier to believe than demons." Yuri said.

"Eh, 'demons' is more of a catch-all term," Barnabas said. "Don't take that literally."

"I can't take it literally, because as of two minutes ago, in my world, demons didn't literally exist," Yuri said.

"Yuri, don't panic," Echo said.

"I'm not panicking. I'm questioning my entire belief system, but I'm not panicking," Yuri said. "Question two: If he still had his soul, did he not sell it yet? Where does he get his powers?"

"The soul is part of a long series of bargains," Muireann said. "Tessier's not stupid. Only stupid people sell their souls immediately. He's bargained for money, and power, and access to dark magic. The soul is the cherry he is dangling before whatever vile thing or things he's made deals with. And as I said, this is only a piece of his. He's likely been doling out bits and pieces of his life force his entire life. This is just the last part."

"You stole the remaining balance of his soul," Yuri said. "You put him into soul overdraft."

"And you made it impossible for him to pay the man." Barnabas said.

"What happens if you can't pay a demon what you owe him?" Echo said.

"Bad things," Barnabas and Muireann said at the same time.

"For the record, I was just getting used to being the heir of Atlantis and believing all the weird stuff we've seen in the past few months actually exists," Echo said. "My best friend is a were-shark. It's taken some time to let that settle into my reality. I was not prepared to deal with bargains with demons on top of all that."

"You need a minute?" Barnabas said.

Echo ignored him.

"So Tessier doesn't get what you stole from him back, and like, demonic leg breakers come and take it out on him?" Echo said.

"He'll wish they only broke legs," Barnabas said.

"I'm failing to see how this is a bad thing," Yuri said. "Sounds like he has it coming to him."

Echo turned to Muireann.

"What do you need it for?" Echo said. "Can't you just give it back?"

Muireann stared at her, but said nothing.

"How much time do you have left, kid?" Barnabas said, apropos of nothing.

Muireann moved the dead-eyed stare from Echo to Barnabas. Then she turned her eyes to the floor, defeated.

"A few years," she said.

"Before what?" Echo said.

Muireann remained silent. Echo whipped around to Barnabas.

"Tell me," she said.

"Ondines don't live forever, the way my mother does," he said. "I don't think we explained before clearly—I know we said they need to borrow that life force from someone, but it's not just for

190

their magic. They need that life force—usually given freely—to live, or they fade away like dreams."

"What do you mean? How is it given freely?" Echo said.

"It's stupid," Muireann said.

"Try me," Echo said

"Out of love," Muireann said. "And Echo, I'm tired of this myth I'm forced to be a part of. I don't want some poor clod to fall in love with me and give me some of his eternal life force. I'd rather take it from terrible men instead."

Echo bobbed her head with an impressed expression on her face.

"I can totally respect that," Echo said. "So we should just assume this horrible man is chasing us until we deal with him."

"Until I deal with him," Muireann said. "I'm sorry I dragged you into this. This isn't your fight. You don't need to help me."

"You're part of our crew now," Echo said. "We take care of each other. So shut up and let us help."

Muireann appeared simultaneously both relieved and offended, settling on an uncomfortable, if grateful, smile.

"But in the meantime, we need to basically stop Godzilla from destroying thousands of people. So let's see if we can't avoid this Tessier guy long enough to deal with the giant sea monster first. Then him."

"I can live with that," Muireann said. "Thank you."

"Hey, why don't you come topside with me," Yuri said. "You look like you need some air."

Muireann placed a hand on Yuri's shoulder and the two headed up to the deck. Echo heard them talking to Artem in muffled tones.

"How are we going to fix this, Barnabas?" Echo said.

"I'm working on something," Barnabas said.

"Other than that bottle?"

"I said I'm working on something," he repeated. "Have I ever let you down?"

Echo twisted to get a better view of him, her eyebrows knitting together in curious surprise.

"Weirdly, no you haven't," Echo said. "You're shockingly reliable for a scoundrel."

"Don't tell anyone," Barnabas said. "It's bad for my reputation."

Chapter 36: First contact

The *Endless* arrived just outside the illusory protections of New Scythia like a ghost, drifting out of the cloudy reality-warping effects of ley line travel like a half-forgotten memory.

What they found, what they saw, caused Artem's heart to beat so hard he felt it hammer against the inside of his armor.

Fresh blood stained the deep blue waters outside his homeland. Broken ships as well. Several of the Amazonian attack skiffs they'd seen running security earlier were shattered like eggs. And bodies in the ocean, some of whom were not even remotely human. Creatures, half-man, half-fish, malformed and covered in scales of black or green or a pinkish color reminiscent of rotting meat. There were human bodies too, Amazon warriors clearly identified by their armor, though far, far fewer in number. It had been a bloody battle, Artem saw, but judging by the corpses, his people had been victorious, if bloodied.

Not all the ships had been destroyed. One of the skiffs approached rapidly, a familiar figure on the foredeck, clutching her arm at her side.

"You missed the party," Areto said. Her red hair was plastered to the side of her head, redder still from the blood of a recent wound. Her right arm hung limp, a vicious bite at the shoulder, bad enough to shred the lightweight armor she wore.

"What happened?" Artem said. Echo stepped up beside him while Yuri and Barnabas checked the water around them for survivors.

"They arrived like a swarm of locusts," Areto said. She commanded her crew to haul the body of one of their fallen comrades from the ocean. "I don't think they were looking for us. It was a mindless storm of hungry teeth. The illusions around our island didn't matter—they were just passing through, killing whatever was in their way, and we were most certainly in their way."

Yuri flipped one of the monsters with a boat hook. Its black eyes stared lifelessly up at them, its wide mouth, filled with razor-sharp teeth, familiar to everyone.

"Hi there," Yuri said. "Isn't this a handsome guy."

"These can't possibly be the creatures we're trying to stop," Echo said. "They can't be ranging this far already."

"They're damned fast," Areto said. "It's terrifying, to be honest, and I'm not afraid of much. But when you see something that looks like that, with those teeth."

"How many did we… did you lose?" Artem said.

"Too many," Areto said. "But we drove them off. They don't seem to be warriors. They're predators. And even a nasty predator will back off if it thinks the prey isn't worth the trouble."

Areto cast her eyes out over the blood water. Her body slumped, exhaustion and sadness crashing into her.

"I can't remember the last time we fought like this," she said. "It's been so long. We weren't ready. No, no, we were ready. We're fighters. We were ready. But for this? How do you prepare for this?"

"Areto," Artem said. "Is my mother okay?"

The guard captain nodded.

"General Orithyia is uninjured," she said, her tone professional. "Though she's distraught about our losses. We haven't had an Amazon slain in combat in decades."

"Are they gone?" Yuri said. "Or do you think they'll come back?"

"We think they've been driven off," Areto said. "As far as we can tell. They seemed to be migrating. They arrived in a great swarm, all headed in the same direction. They left as such."

"Fits with what we've seen, I think," Echo said. "Pass through, destroy what's in their path, carry on."

"Only this time they met with more resistance than they're used to," Yuri said.

"Damned right," Areto said, mustering a smirk despite the pain. "Were you successful?"

Echo nodded to Barnabas, who drew the Eye of Dreams from his coat.

"One relic down, one to go," he said.

"Then we'll have someone escort you in," Areto said. "Maybe our librarian friends have found that other item for you."

***

Artem was relieved—and again, surprised at his own reaction, that he felt any sympathy at all—to see the walls of New Scythia had held. The creatures had clearly made it to the docks, and a battle had left the coast of New Scythia bloody and battered, but the city itself appeared relatively unharmed. *The Endless* docked and the crew disembarked as Areto, her wounds and exhaustion catching up to her, accompanied them slowly to the main gates.

Word had arrived ahead of them. Orithyia waited just behind the gates, her armor bloody, a long spear resting casually against her shoulder while she held her helm, of a coppery Grecian design with subtle hints of high-tech additions hidden within, tucked under one arm. She handed her spear to a guard flanking her and, to Artem's surprise, placed an affectionate hand on his shoulder.

"When I saw the damage these creatures did to our army, I worried what would happen if your small group encountered them," she said. "I feared we'd…"

"It's fine, mother," Artem said coldly. "We saw no signs of them in our travels. No need to worry about us."

Orithyia seemed taken aback for a moment, then switched into a more harder tone as well.

"I assume if you've returned you were successful," she said.

"We found the Eye," Echo said. "It was easier to acquire than expected. The guardian was willing to surrender it to us willingly."

"Thank the gods for small favors, then," Orithyia said.

"What about the Needle of the Moon?" Barnabas said.

As Barnabas spoke, Artem studied the silent Muireann, standing beside Barnabas, taking in the chaos with her deep green eyes. She'd been quiet since the fight with Tessier, and now, with the smell of blood on the air once again, she seemed even more withdrawn. Artem wondered at what point she'd become a liability. One of our crew, though, he thought. Liability or not, she's with us.

"The Keepers of Athena had some luck before the attack. Follow me," Orithyia said. She motioned to her guards to seal the gate and started walking toward the library, beckoning for Artem and the others to follow. "I want to hear about your encounter in the Amazon, but I don't think we have the time for storytelling."

"No," Echo said. "I don't think we do."

Amazons stepped aside quickly as they saw Orithyia approach, the combination of respect for the general and distrust of the outsiders who followed her pushing them away. The path they took this time was different, along the outside of the central castle, up along a winding, outdoor staircase that led to a high balcony outside the library. Orithyia entered without knocking.

"Clio!" she called. "Our adventurers have returned."

The Keeper of Athena emerged from the stacks, setting aside an ancient, leather-bound tome. She wore a put-upon expression and was dressed, somewhat incongruously for the library, for war in a metal breastplate with a longsword at her hip.

"Hands in your pockets, wizard," she said, pointing directly at Barnabas, who complied immediately.

"We recovered the Eye," Echo said. "Please tell me the Needle will be just as easy to find."

Clio waved her hand at an empty table nearby. Yuri pulled out a chair for Orithyia, who looked at the younger man with an expression of confused shock before sitting down with an exhausted sigh, the battle's toll on her suddenly very clear. She smiled at Yuri warmly. Echo looked at her own chair, then to Yuri, then back at her chair.

"What?" Yuri said. Echo pulled her own chair out and sat down, eyes twinkling with a hint of amusement. The others sat at the table as well, except for Artem, who chose to lean against a nearby column while he listened.

"So, this god-like figure from the stories, Korthos of Aramaias," Clio began. "He's an idiot."

"This doesn't sound encouraging," Yuri said.

"It's not," Clio said. "I told you before he has a sort of Herculean mythology behind him, and if you've read of Hercules, you know he wasn't the brightest light in the night sky either."

"And yet somehow Korthos was able to stop this ancient threat the last time it emerged," Echo said.

"With help," Clio said. "He did not use the Eye of Dreams himself, but rather had a spellcaster, a wizard from Atlantis, who assisted him. That explains why your people seem somehow directly involved, but don't have clear history of it. Adventurers don't often leave clear notes of what they've done, and their deeds are left up to storytellers rather than historians."

"And why was this Atlantean wizard not mentioned before?" Barnabas said.

"From the books I've skimmed, it's quite possibly because Korthos was a braggart who over-spoke his own role in the battle," Clio said, rubbing her eyes. "He was certainly there. And he wielded the needle, which is either a very large sword, like a claymore, or possibly a spear of some kind. Translations are mutable things and the language is very old."

"But it's most likely a weapon, whatever shape it takes," Echo

said.

"So it would seem," Clio said. "Which this idiot of an immortal dropped somewhere in the chasm where he and his companions defeated the ancient creature."

"Dropped it," Echo said.

"He was an idiot," Clio said. "The battle was over, and he didn't particularly like the weapon, so he just… left it there."

"I feel so much better about myself as a hero right now," Yuri said.

"To clarify," Artem said. "He dropped it where the creature was laid to rest."

"Yes," Clio said.

"So, we have to go back to that bloody chasm in the ocean floor," Artem said.

"You could choose not to," Clio said. "Take your chances with one relic, see how it goes. I'm not telling you what to do."

"The librarian is sassy," Yuri said. "She's sassing you."

"Shut up, Yuri," Echo said, sighing heavily. "Time, guys. We're short on time. We can move around pretty quickly because of Barnabas and what he knows of the ley lines, but we don't know how fast this great beast is shuffling toward whatever he's shuffling toward, and now we have to go back to Atlantis and head down into Poseidon's Scar to find this weapon?"

"There's a bright side," Yuri said.

The whole table turned and waited for him to finish.

"We know the creature's not in Poseidon's Scar, right? So it's really just a fetch mission," Yuri said. "Right?"

"He's not wrong," Barnabas said.

"Unless not all the creatures went with the ancient thing," Muireann said, chiming in for the first time. "Maybe they left guards behind."

"I'm so glad you waited to speak until you had something really depressing to add to the conversation, Muireann," Yuri said.

"Look," Orithyia said. "We weathered this battle. Others can as well. The important thing is the mission. When was the last time any of you slept?"

"I think I took a nap three days ago," Echo said.

"Stay here for the night. Get some rest. We'll come up with a plan in the morning," the general said. "And if you give us the night, maybe we can come up with some other ways to help you."

"I thought the outside world was of no interest to the Amazons," Artem said.

"We've seen the face of this threat," Orithyia said. "Now is no time to sit behind our illusions and stone walls."

Artem and Echo locked eyes. Echo nodded. Artem saw the shadows beneath her eyes. They really had been on the run for days. Wherever they went from here, danger would follow. Artem returned her nod.

"We'll rest for the night," Echo said. "A few hours, at least. But I won't let these things hurt anyone else if I can help it. The longer we stay here, the more people die."

Chapter 37: The gods hate women

Echo's crew were put up in a set of rooms high in the central palace, a floor clearly intended for guests and dignitaries. The rooms were simple, but more than comfortable and divine compared to berthing on a boat, but also eerily quiet. Few guards made their rounds on this floor, and the crew was left pretty much to their own devices, high enough above the city that they could barely hear the minimal activity on the streets below.

Barnabas waited until he suspected most of the others were asleep and found his way to Muireann's room. He knocked lightly, not wanting to wake her if she had already turned in. The door opened, one deep sea-green eye peering out at him.

"Oh, hell," she said, but opened the door the rest of the way and gestured to invite him in. She closed the door behind him as he entered.

"I'd ask if I were interrupting anything, but I don't know that any of us have anything to interrupt tonight," he said.

"I'm afraid to ask why you're here," Muireann said. "But mostly because I think I know."

Barnabas stuffed his hands in his pockets and faced her.

"We have to talk about your friend the necromancer," he said. "You and I. Magician to magician. We need a plan for the next time we see him. And we will see him again, won't we?"

"Aye," Muireann said. "One little fight isn't enough to scare him off."

"One little fight we barely got away from," Barnabas said, rocking on his heels.

"Oh, sit down, would you now," Muireann said. "You standing there makes me anxious."

Barnabas found a backless stool with a surprisingly ornate cushion and sat. Muireann scooted onto the bed to sit cross-legged facing him. She seemed remarkably ordinary, Barnabas thought, for everything she's been through. Echo wanders around in Atlantean battle gear, and Artem has an Amazonian breastplate and a pair of swords he takes everywhere. Yuri's face might still look like a carefree young man, but he carried himself like he'd been through hell, and dressed to be able to transform at a moment's notice. And I know what I look like, Barnabas thought, almost laughing at his ridiculous outfit. But Muireann, with her dark hair restrained only occasionally by a knit cap, her stolen sailor's sweater of forest green, so long it made the leggings and sarong she's taken from Atlantis look mundane, she could be anyone, anywhere.

Except you know her kind, Barnabas thought, and you can see it in her. She's not some girl off the farm. There's ancient knowledge behind her eyes. Magic crackles across her skin. Not unlike yourself, he thought. It suits her better.

"You're almost out of time, aren't you?" Barnabas said.

"You're like me. You know that magic isn't what it used to be," she said. "It takes more effort."

"It does," Barnabas said. "You're short on time."

"I can't lose this," Muireann said, gesturing to her hand where the little globe of golden stolen life energy appeared as if from nowhere. "I don't know how long I'll last without it."

"Why steal it, really? Don't just say because he's a bastard. We know that," Barnabas said. "I have to ask. You know I have to ask. I'm no stranger to ondines. I know this isn't the way things usually work."

Muireann sighed angrily and turned to face the large window dominating the back wall of the room, facing out over the sea.

"Do you believe in the gods, Barnabas Coy?" she said.

"Not really," Barnabas said. "I believe in a lot. I could believe in some immortal higher power. I have trouble believing anything as fallible as a god is in charge of things though."

"I think they're real," Muireann said. "And I think they hate women."

Barnabas nodded. He didn't disagree. He'd seen enough throughout his life to find no reason to argue with that sentiment, not even a little.

"Ondines. Nymphs. Sirens. Harpies. Medusa," she said. "Everywhere you look, the gods made women into something to be afraid of. Something that steals your soul, or takes your life, or turns you to stone. What did we ever do to deserve all this? Every mistake a woman makes in mythology, she doesn't just pay for it, she is cursed for all of eternity for it. It's women who steal men away, who steal their souls. Your mother is a nymph, yes?"

"A nereid," Barnabas said.

"How much blame is placed at their feet? I know the place the nereids went to hide. The mermaids hide there, too."

"They do," Barnabas said.

"Poor creatures. Every sailor who doesn't return home, they're blamed for it," Muireann said. "Women are monsters. Men get to be heroes. Even you, with your faux scoundrel airs, even you get to be a hero."

"I'll have you know I have full scoundrel credentials," he said. "I'm certified."

"My arse," she said. "I've seen you risk your life like it means nothing to you over and over again since we met. All the heroes are men. Even here, on this island full of amazing women, they're hiding, because the world will have none of it from them; the world doesn't want them, because they aren't what the gods decree a good and just hero should be. But at least they're not bogeymen. Nobody ever said an Amazon would rise up out of the river and steal your son away."

Barnabas stayed silent, letting Muireann unfold her story. She inhaled, uncrossing and re-crossing her legs impatiently.

"I don't want to be the creature who seduced a man to steal his soul. I don't want to be someone who takes from someone unsuspecting. I don't want to create a victim. I wanted something else. So I stole from men who were terrible. Terrible to women, to other men, to the world. If I am going to be a monster by nature, then I want to be an avenging spirit. And if that helps me to live a little longer, then..."

"Then so much the better," Barnabas said.

Muireann turned the palms of her hands up in a gesture of agreement.

"This wasn't the first bad man you stole from, then," Barnabas said.

"I only took a fragment of his soul," Muireann said. "That's a funny thing, you see. Awful people, the currency of their life is worth less. They are sustained by forces other than life. So I had to siphon a bit here and there. I had to cobble together my prize. When I met Tessier, he'd put much of himself into a phylactery of sorts. I hit the jackpot. I had to take it."

"How do you think we should handle him?" Barnabas said. "Kill him?"

Muireann shrugged.

"You'd do that?" Barnabas said. "I have no problem killing a man like Tessier, if he's all you say he is, and I'm inclined to believe you after watching what he did to my ship. But killing a man is quite a thing."

"I know."

The two words hung in the room for a moment. Barnabas watched the muscle in her jaw dance as she clenched her teeth, eyes defiant but distant. Yeah, Barnabas thought. She knows.

"Can I ask why?" Barnabas said. "I don't need to know how you know. But I'm curious why."

"I have been alone in the world a long time, Barnabas Coy,"

Muireann said. "We do what we must. I imagine you've experienced much the same."

"Unfortunately," Barnabas said.

He studied her expression, then, tried to gauge her fury, trying to understand where he wanted to go from here. She really is just one of us, he thought. Driftwood from some forgotten wreckage, defiantly daring me to judge her and seeing without really trying just how balanced our ledgers are.

"Aren't we a bloody pair?" she said, almost laughing. "Admit it, you're at least mildly intrigued at the thought of fighting a necromancer."

"Wasn't on my list of things I wanted to do in this life," Barnabas said. "But hey. Could be fun."

Muireann took off her cap and held it in both hands.

"That river spirit. The yacuruna. They're like me. Wasn't that strange?"

"Everything about the yacuruna was strange."

"No," Muireann said. "They are a ghost story, someone who steals husbands and daughters away to never be seen again. But that's not it, is it? They take the ones who don't want to go home. They give lost souls purpose. They are a force of beauty and good in this world, hidden away in their upside-down cities, and mankind is terrified of them. Because they don't conform with expectations. Because they're the other."

"And in the end, mankind turns to them for help when they need it," Barnabas said. "For healing. For restoration."

"Nobody does that to ondines," Muireann said. "Anyone ever come to you to restore them?"

"Someone once came to me to protect the things they loved most in the world," Barnabas said, a sharp pain digging into his chest. "I failed that task pretty spectacularly."

"And that's how you ended up here," Muireann said. "Playing hero."

"Sort of."

"See, Barnabas Coy," Muireann said. "In the gods' eyes, even men who fail can become heroes. All I want is the same for me and mine."

She looked once again at the glowing orb with Tessier's life force within it.

"And time enough to get there," she said.

"I can't make you a hero," Barnabas said. "But I think we can make sure you have the time to get there on your own."

The ondine smiled at him, an honest and profoundly sad smile Barnabas felt infinitely familiar. The gods don't exist, he thought. But if they did, they'd have a hell of a sense of humor sticking us together.

Chapter 38: Separate directions

The crew gathered in a small dining area in the castle, where a table of simple foods had been prepared and left waiting for them. Orithyia was already there, listlessly nibbling on a piece of fruit.

My mother looks like she's crawling out of her skin, Artem noted as he entered the room behind Echo and Yuri. He could hear Barnabas and Muireann chatting in the hallway behind him.

Artem made eye contact with his mother, but Orithyia simply smiled weakly and sat down at one end of the long table that dominated the room. Artem picked up an apple and bit into it, barely tasting the fruit.

As soon as Barnabas and Muireann arrived—their simultaneous appearance caused Echo to shoot Artem a raised eyebrow of curiosity—Echo began to speak.

"We have to go back to Poseidon's Scar," she said.

"For the Needle," Artem said. *Mystical weapons to fight some mythical monster. Why can't we just fight something that dies when you stab it?* he thought. Artem was not a simple man, but he liked simple solutions, and magic made everything it touched more complicated.

"This is going to eat up a lot of time," Echo said.

"Our scouts believe the great beast will make landfall in a few days," Orithyia said. "They're keeping their distance and reporting back, but it's hard to miss the destruction the creature leaves in its wake."

"We need to get eyes on it," Artem said.

"We need to warn whoever lives wherever the thing is stomping toward," Yuri said. "We can't just work in the assumption we're gonna get there in time, right? We could give them a chance to evacuate."

"So we split up," Artem said.

"Only got one ship," Barnabas said.

"You'll have two," a new voice said. Queen Marpesia and Queen Lampedo arrived arm in arm, the elder sister leading the way, speaking. "Take one of our fastest."

"Thank you," Echo said.

"It's the least we can do to help," Marpesia said.

"Well, if we're going to go back to Poseidon's Scar and then catch up with this monster, that means the *Endless* is making that trip," Barnabas said. "No offense to the quality of your ship or crew, your majesties, but traveling the faerie lanes is hard enough with a supernatural crew who knows the routes. I'm not sure I could guide a crew that hasn't done it before. Not safely, and not without risking getting lost."

Marpesia tilted her head, acknowledging the magician's logic, but said nothing.

"And I'll have to be the one to go down into the Scar," Echo said. "I'm the only one who can. Even with that magic earring that lets you breathe underwater, Artem, I'm not sure you can withstand the pressures at that depth, and only Yuri and I possess the natural swimming abilities to dive that deep."

"I could probably go with you," Yuri said.

"Are you sure you'd be able to survive at that depth?" Echo said. "Even the Atlanteans said I was abnormally suited to survive the trench."

"I'd be willing to try, but I don't know," Yuri said.

"You can survive the pressure of the trench, but you're looking for—do we even know exactly what the Needle is?" Artem said.

"It's a bladed weapon," Orithyia said. "According to the Keepers of Athena. It's hard to tell if it's a sword or some sort of halberd or scythe, but it's a hand-held weapon, used to draw this creature's blood."

"And you're going to find a sword at the bottom of a trench, in the dark. Alone," Artem said.

Barnabas swiped a pastry off the table, bit into it, made a face, and set the pastry back down.

"Divination magic," Barnabas said. "There are spells that can find objects, especially powerful objects with a magical nature."

"So you get to go into the Scar, Barnabas?" Echo said.

The magician shrugged.

"Nereid blood runs through my veins," he said. "I'm pretty sure I won't die. Exactly. Possibly crippled? But hey, who wants to live forever. I'll go."

"Or send me," Muireann said. The room turned to face her as she spoke for the first time. "I'm a full-blooded ondine. A water spirit. Depth, temperature… water is water to me. I'm fine."

"And you know magic," Barnabas said.

"I do," the ondine said.

"You see, if I were a petty man, I'd feel like you were gunning for my job, but if you want to go into the undersea trench of death, that's all you, Muireann. I can teach you the spells I'm thinking of, too. They're not hard to learn. Unless you're Yuri."

"Really. End of the world coming up, and you're throwing low blows about my competence? Today?" Yuri said.

"I do it out of love," Barnabas said.

"Okay," Echo said. "I guess that settles that. But…"

Artem didn't need to work hard to see what had to happen next. It wasn't the destiny he envisioned for himself, but, he thought, there are worse things.

"I'll go after the monster," Artem said. "Someone has to be there. I'm useless at the trench. I'll do this, Echo."

"I'll go with you, dude," Yuri said.

Artem whipped his head around to stare at Yuri, shocked.

"What?" Yuri said.

"No," Artem said, legitimately angry. "This is a suicide mission, Yuri. I will not have your blood on my hands."

Yuri sighed heavily, stuffing his hands into pockets that appeared too small for his thick hands.

"I know I don't look like much now," Yuri said. "But guys, I'm… you remember the were-sharks who were after us. I'm really hard to kill. I'm walking hell and teeth when I transform. Bring me along, Artem, and I'll bet you my life savings I take out more of those fish-men than you do before we lose."

Artem smiled and slapped a hand on Yuri's oversized shoulder. Laughing, he took Yuri's face in both hands and pressed their foreheads together.

"I am so bloody proud of you, Yuri Rodriguez," Artem said. "There's the warrior I knew you had in you. By the gods, I am so proud to see you like this."

"Let's not get carried away," Yuri said. "I still feel almost scared enough to pee my pants."

"Fear is part of being a warrior, Yuri," Artem told him. "If you ever lose that fear, you know you've gone mad."

"Then I am still one hundred percent, totally, absolutely sane," Yuri said.

Barnabas threw a piece of orange peel at the other men, bouncing it off Yuri's back.

"As much as I want to come with you two lunatics, I need to go with the *Endless* if we're going to get to Poseidon's Scar and then catch up to you in time," Barnabas said.

"Then we have our teams," Echo said. "I hate this. I hate splitting up. I hate sending you two away."

"Hey, we're only fighting crazy fish guys with super sharp teeth," Yuri said. "You're going to be looking for a needle in a haystack in the ocean's belly button."

"Calling Poseidon's Scar the ocean's belly button is being awfully generous, Yuri," Echo said.

"I'm trying to be less impolite around royalty," Yuri said.

Queen Marpesia cleared her throat. She smiled proudly at all of them.

"Assuming the spirits on your ship will be sufficient, we'll send a good crew to go with you, Artem," she said.

"We don't want you putting your people at risk any more than you already have," Echo said. "Maybe we can ask some of the ghosts to go with him?"

"Doesn't work that way," Barnabas said. "The Endless is a spiritual anchor. They belong with the ship itself. It's a unique place where their spirits are safe."

"Princess of Atlantis, we've been sending people we love to die since the Amazons first set foot on this Earth," Lampedo said. "We are no strangers to sacrifice."

"You don't have to send anyone you love," Artem said. "You're sending me. The Amazons don't need to shed any more of their own blood."

Lampedo sized him up just then. Artem felt her eyes boring through him, taking his measure. Her mouth twitched, but whether in disgust or amusement or pride, he could not tell.

"Queen Lampedo," Artem said. "I was born for this. Let me win this fight for you. You don't have to send anyone else."

"I think we do, young man," Marpesia said. "Unless you and your courageous shark friend can sail a ship together alone."

Orithyia rose swiftly to her feet just then, her symbolic general's helmet under her arm, she walked boldly up in front of her queens and knelt on one knee before them, lifting her helmet up high, as one might a sacrifice.

"My queens," Orithyia said. "I volunteer for this mission as well. I've failed you more than once. I have dishonored my role as your general. I wish to step down as high commander, and I ask this for a chance to redeem myself to you."

She turned to look at Artem then. He saw tears glistening in his eyes, but not falling.

"And I have failed my son," she said. "To let him do this alone is a dishonor I cannot bear."

Marpesia took the helmet from Orithyia and studied it. She showed it to her sister, calmly.

"Do you remember when you wore this helm?" Marpesia said.

"I do," Lampedo said.

"And how often did you fail, when you were our high commander?"

Lampedo inhaled sharply. She placed the tips of her fingers on the helmet.

"I was high commander in peace time," she said. "I had no opportunity to fail. I never knew my weaknesses, because I wasn't tested."

"Our high commander has been tested many times," Marpesia said.

"And she has risen to the occasion almost every time," Lampedo said. "And she has learned from the times she did not. Which is all you can ask of someone as they face adversity."

Marpesia handed the helmet back to Orithyia.

"Rise, general," Marpesia said. "We reject your resignation. But we grant your request. Choose a crew. Be brave, be victorious."

"I would go with you if I could," Lampedo said.

"She's serious, you know," Marpesia said.

"I know," Orithyia said, the faintest hint of a smile on her face. She turned to her son.

"Artem," she said. "I've failed you most of all. So I ask and do not demand. Will you have me on your ship this one time?"

Artem did not consider himself an emotional man. He did not aspire to be one. But standing here, his mother, helm in hand, pleading for forgiveness, he felt a spark in his chest, of rage and regret, of longing, of loss. A million words flooded his mind, begging to lash out, to reach out, to forgive and ask for forgiveness. His mouth twitched with indecision. He wanted to say yes. He wanted to apologize. He wanted to demand an apology. He wanted to remain silent, filled with anger and sorrow.

"Gather your crew," he said instead. And without uttering

another word, he turned and left the room.

Chapter 39: Raise the dead

Anson Tessier leaned against the railing of his yacht's prow, watching the crew work as his impatience and disgust grew.

Mortals, he thought. Ordinary, mundane, flesh-and-blood mortal sailors. When he set out on this fool's journey, he assumed he would need only deal with Muireann herself, which he believed was well within his abilities to do alone.

A magician, a were-shark, and two others who appeared more than capable in a fight, though. Alone, none of these newcomers worried him, but together they would be a problem. And while he had no doubt some of the men on this crew knew how to hold themselves in a bar fight or brawl, they weren't warriors. They were ordinary men, used to ordinary lives.

Not facing a magician with a gun that could short-circuit their entire vessel.

The captain appeared from below deck and strode toward Tessier, wiping his hands on a dirty rag.

"Whatever that guy did, he fried a lot of our gear," the captain said. "We can fix some of it, but a lot of the damage is unrepairable, at least out here. We need to get replacement parts for the stuff that was completely destroyed."

"Can the ship sail, captain?" Tessier said.

"The side of the ship is scorched to hell, but it doesn't look like the hull was breached," the captain said, sidling up beside Tessier. "Our instruments are a mess, but we're an experienced crew. The technology makes it all easier, but we can get us to port with what we've got the old-fashioned way. Don't worry about that."

"And how soon will you be ready to continue our pursuit?"

The captain winced, examining the grease under his nails a moment before answering.

"Sir, we're in no shape for that," he said. "We're within sight of land, and I think we can find a port nearby where we can dock for repairs, but this ship is in no condition to be traipsing across the seven seas right now."

"I thought this was a world-class ship with a world-class crew," Tessier said, keeping as much of the anger out of his voice as he could manage.

"It is," the captain said, tension rising in his own voice. "But you failed to mention we might be engaging in any sort of combat on this trip. And you definitely didn't tell us the people you were following were monsters who could shoot electricity at us."

"Are you saying you're afraid, captain?"

"I'm saying we're not a combat-ready vessel, sir," the captain said. "We're sailors, not mercenaries. This ship is not outfitted for combat. It's a glorified luxury yacht and frankly I was willing to take your money and take you all over the world, wherever you wanted to go, right up to the moment you put my men's lives at risk. You want to void the contract, fine. We'll take you to court for expenses, we can do that, but I'm not putting my men in the sort of danger you're looking for."

"You didn't strike me as a coward, captain," Tessier said

"I'm not afraid of a scrap," the captain said. "Hell, I've dealt with pirates, corrupt coast guard officials, I've seen my share of trouble. But what we just saw? That's above our pay grade, sir. Respectfully, don't ask me to put my crew's lives in danger. The ocean is lethal enough as it is."

The two men stared each other down for a long, hard second.

Tessier shrugged noncommittally.

"Fine," he said. "I've asked you to go beyond the scope of the contract. You're mortal men, after all."

"Thank you, sir," the captain said. "When we put into port I can help you find the type of crew you're looking for. Or I can take you home. Your choice."

Tessier waved a hand dismissively and turned away to look at the empty water where Muireann's ship had once been. A cold fury burned in his guts. A ghost ship, he thought. She rode upon a ghost ship. An undead crew would never tire. They'd never question orders. They'd never be afraid.

I need a ghost ship, he thought.

A cruel smile grew across his face, and he returned his attention to the captain.

"Thank you for this conversation, captain," Tessier said. "It has been most enlightening."

"Sorry to speak so forcefully, sir," the captain said. "I really do believe the client is always right. But it's not just my life at risk out here. This crew, they have families."

"Of course," Tessier said. He held out a hand. The captain took it and they shook. A pale, reddish gray light lit up between their palms.

The captain looked at Tessier in shock.

"I'm sorry, captain. A living crew has become a liability," Tessier said. "I'm afraid I need something a little more pliant."

The captain opened his mouth to speak, but no words came out. He staggered, knees buckling, and then fell face-first onto the deck.

Tessier waved a hand across the width of the ship in front of him. He could hear the soft thumping as bodies collapsed, lifeless. In the blink of an eye, Tessier was alone on this ship.

And then with another arcane gesture of his hand, the dead began to rise. Without a question, without missing a beat, each corpse went back to doing exactly what it was doing before, preparing the ship to sale. Their eyes were vacant and cloudy white.

Their movements were slightly jerky, just a little off, and they kept their heads bowed in a subservient manner. The captain made no eye contact as he shuffled off to the bridge.

"That's better," Tessier said, smiling wickedly. "That's much better."

Chapter 40: Return to the Scar

The *Endless* arrived in the waters above Atlantis and Poseidon's Scar as deep storm clouds began to threaten overhead. Echo heard Barnabas ordering the ship's ghost crew, directing them to bring the ship as close to directly above the Scar as he could remember.

Nearby, Echo saw Muireann practicing the detection spell Barnabas has taught her to guide them to the Needle. Barnabas admitted, without shame, that Muireann is inherently a stronger spellcaster than he is. His range of experiences, however, gave him access to a wider catalogue of spells he could understand and use. It took less than an hour for Barnabas to teach Muireann the divination spell, but the ondine, seemingly self-conscious and nervous about her role in the dive, practiced constantly throughout the journey.

Echo walked up to her, clothing draped over one arm.

"Hey," Echo said. "You still feeling up to this?"

"The monsters are gone, right?" Muireann said. "I'm not afraid. I'm more concerned that it will take us too long to find what we're looking for than I am about either of us getting hurt."

"I'll be ready for a fight in case any of the fish-men stayed behind," Echo said. "And there were dangerous things living around the trench before. You should be aware of that, just in case.

217

The afanc lived here before these creatures killed it, and without the afanc as the top predator in the area, other things may have moved in."

"We'll be fine," Muireann said, offering a smile.

It rarely touches her eyes, Echo thought, studying that smile. Muireann is as haunted as the rest of us. No wonder we took her on board. We're all running from ghosts.

"Anyway," Echo said. "I know you're a sea spirit and all that, but I thought even you could use better clothes to go deep sea diving than a skirt and wool sweater."

She held out the clothes in her hand, revealing a spare pair of Atlantean-made armored leggings in bluish silver similar to the silver-green pair Echo herself wore, and a deep green cap-sleeved top, also of Atlantean make, with the look and feel of fine chainmail. Echo's people had gifted her with a chest of clothing and armor like this when she left, all designed to be worn in the water without weighing the wearer down. The Atlanteans had given the ondine the equivalent of a set of "street clothes" when last they were in city, but Echo wanted her protected as well as she was. The armored cloth was the strangest material Echo had ever encountered, not a wicking material, not a wetsuit, just a fabric that seemed to allow water to pass through it easily without trapping it, lightweight but warm. Incredibly durable, too, Echo had found, mostly through combat. It took quite a fight to rip the material despite the way it felt no stronger than thin, soft cotton in her hands.

Echo explained this to Muireann, where it came from, what it did.

"I can't take your things," Muireann said.

"I promise you, if I go home, the Atlanteans will just give me more," Echo said. "Something about being a princess who saved their kingdom or something. I won't take anything else, so they give me pants. It's okay, trust me. Plus we're about the same size. Should fit you fine."

Muireann let out a quick laugh at the comment about giving a princess pants and accepted the clothes from Echo, swapping her leggings for the armored pair, and turning her back to Echo to swap her knit sweater for the shirt.

"Look at us," Echo said. "Team Atlantis Pants, ready for duty."

"Do I get any armor to go with it?" Muireann said, noting Echo's scaled tunic and bracers.

"Oh! I... I'm sure we can get you something if you want."

"I'm kidding," Muireann said. "The armor would just get in the way. Honestly, Echo, that was just a joke."

"Okay, okay," Echo said. "I'm not used to... man, we really haven't had any time to talk like regular people, have we?"

"We've had a world to save and I'm being chased by a psychopath," Muireann said. "It's understandable."

"I'm sorry for that. It feels irresponsible of me."

"You're the leader," Muireann said. "Your job is to keep the rest of your crew safe. Sometimes that means not having time for niceties."

"Like learning your sense of humor," Echo said. "Well, tell you what, if we don't die saving the world, you and I sit down for coffee and trade life stories, yeah?"

Muireann smiled again, and this time, it brightened her whole face.

"I don't think any of you can really know how alone I had been before you found me," she said. "Thank you for everything."

"Well, don't thank me yet," Echo said. "We've recruited you to swim down into Poseidon's Scar. You may not want to be friends anymore after today."

The conversation was abruptly interrupted as Barnabas shouted for her from the foredeck.

"Echo!" the magician yelled. She looked up to see him pointing out at the water. Her anxiety spiking, she walked quickly to the rail to follow where he'd pointed. A wave of relief hit her when she spotted what had caught Barnabas' attention. Sitting in the water, astride one of those ridiculous, giant Atlantean seahorses, was Grimmin, the old spymaster who had helped them before.

Grimmin was flanked by a pair of Atlantean warriors, also on horseback.

"Good to see you, princess," Grimmin said. "Permission to come aboard for a moment?"

Echo sighed, half out of relief and half annoyed at the delay, but she reached down to the deck to scoop up a rope ladder and toss it overboard. Grimmin showed his age a bit, grunting as he hauled himself up out of the ocean.

"I really don't come up to the surface often enough," he said.

Barnabas trotted down from the foredeck to join them as Grimmin scanned the rest of the ship.

"You're missing a few," he said. "I hope…"

"They're fine. For now," Echo said. "They're scouting ahead, getting a look at where our monster is headed. What brought you to the surface, Grimmin?"

"My scouts saw you arrive," he said. "I… after our last meeting, you understand my concern. I wasn't sure if you were coming back to warn us or to tell us you'd won."

"Neither," Echo said. "We found out what we need to defeat the monster, but unfortunately, one of them is at the bottom of Poseidon's Scar."

"That is the worst news I've heard all day," Grimmin said. "The Scar is enormous, Echo."

"Yeah, I've been there. I remember."

"Is there anything we can do to help? I'll come with you if you need support. I'm old, but I can still put up a fight."

"The pressure of the trench is going to make a deep dive tough. This falls on me alone, I think, and Muireann here, who has… powers beyond that of a normal person, like me," Echo said. She put a hand on Grimmin's shoulder. "But thank you."

"How will you even know where to look?"

"With the right spell, I'm a living, breathing compass," Muireann said. "I'll guide her there."

"I do have one question for you," Echo said.

"Of course," Grimmin said.

"Do you know… have you ever heard of a weapon called the Needle of the Moon?"

Grimmin laughed, then caught himself.

"That's either a really good sign or a really bad one," Barnabas said.

"It's an old Atlantean story," Grimmin said. "I mean, it's one of many. All folklore talks about named weapons, yes? Even in Atlantis we've heard the story of the surface world's Excalibur, because sometimes it is said that the Lady of the Lake in that story was of Atlantean descent."

"She wasn't," Muireann said. "She was—"

She looked to Barnabas, who shrugged nonchalantly.

"Yeah, I know," he said.

"You know what?" Echo said.

"It's not relevant. No, I take that back, it's pretty irrelevant to this conversation. I might be related a little bit," Barnabas said.

"To the Lady of the Lake," Echo said.

"Like, distant, distant cousins, it's really not important," Barnabas said.

Echo raised her eyebrows and shook her head, returning her attention to Grimmin.

"So you've heard of it?" Echo said.

"Just in children's stories," Grimmin said. "And not regarding Atlantean mythology, specifically. It was just one of many named weapons you hear about in fairy tales."

"Well, we're supposed to find it. In the Scar," Echo said.

Grimmin tugged at his beard, then shrugged.

"At this point, I'll believe anything," he said. "A giant creature with an army of cannibal fish-men just climbed out of Poseidon's Scar. Mythical weapon, why not?"

"It would help immensely if we knew what it looked like," Echo said.

"Atlanteans aren't particularly invested in picture books," Grimmin said. "And honestly, it was a myth. Any image I might have seen of it would be a rumor at best, exaggerated at worst."

221

"All I want to know is what kind of weapon it was," Echo said. "Was it a sword? An axe? I imagine with the name Needle it must be pointy. I'm just curious what we're looking for down there so we have some vague idea what shape it is."

"Oh that, the stories talk about," Grimmin said. "It was a polearm. Like a spear, but the blade was wider, something you could swing like a sword. The stories said it was a long spear with a perfect blade on the tip, longer than a man's forearm, sharp enough to cut through time itself."

"Sword on a stick. Got it," Echo said. "Thank you."

"It was quite literally the very least I could do," Grimmin said. "Can I at least offer you a pair of horses to take you below?"

Echo exchanged a glance with Muireann, who smirked back at her.

"I think we'll be faster on our own, but thanks for the offer," Echo said.

Chapter 41: The Priesthood of the Fallen Star

Simon Yee showed up at Clarissa's house just after sunset. He'd chosen to wear a dark mock turtleneck sweater with dark coat over it light enough to hide the weapon he had stashed at the small of his back, dark jeans, and a pair of dark hiking boots. I look like what would happen if L.L. Bean opened a goth department, he thought, striding up to her door. He knocked politely.

Why do I feel like I'm going on a date? he thought. This is a terrible date idea. A stakeout date. A date-out. A stake-date.

Clarissa opened the door wearing dark jeans, a black hoodie, and black Converse All-Stars.

"Oh," she said, caught off-guard. "I'm underdressed. Am I underdressed? I feel underdressed."

"It's fine," Simon said, his own self-conscious anxiety building in response to hers. "This is just—this is what I wear to work. It's fine. I'm not dressed up. I promise."

Clarissa gave a conciliatory nod and stepped out into the night air, locking the door behind her.

"Good timing," she said. I could see lights on the beach from my window. Either the townie kids are having a hell of a bonfire, or something's going down."

Clarissa led Simon down a walkway that felt more like an alley than an access point, between two tall high-end condo buildings. It emptied out into a boardwalk along the beach. Fogarty's Folly was well-known for its coastline, but only certain areas offered a true beach-goer's experience to the public. The town jealously guarded its private beaches, requiring proof of residency to swim or sunbathe at most of the beaches along the coast. Simon had never encountered this part stretch of sand before, but that didn't surprise him. Much of the shore was private or hidden away.

Together, Simon and Clarissa dropped down from the boardwalk onto the sand, an undignified climb of eight or ten feet down the wooden walkway to avoid using the stairs where they might be more easily spotted. They stayed low as they darted along the edge of the beach, using the boardwalk for cover. Finally they could see the glow of a bonfire warming the area ahead of them.

"This is going to be so embarrassing if we just sneak up on some teenagers making out or something," Clarissa said.

They found a taller sand dune and clambered up, falling into a crawl near the top to stay out of sight. With almost comical care to stay out of sight, they peered over the top of the dune down to the beach below.

There was, in fact, a bonfire, but it was something more than that. All around the flames, men and women gathered, dressed in ridiculous robes, a noncommittal dark green with gold stitching that looked as if it had seen better days. A makeshift altar stood near the water, just a slab of driftwood on top of piled stones to form a flat surface. There were a few candles on the altar, but nothing special, a combination of half-used store-bought scented candles and cheap ones from a dollar store.

The whole thing looked like a cheap knock-off of a cultist ritual, makeshift and shoddy, a child's attempt at a dark religion. Except these were adults, some of whom, judging by their body language, were pillars of the Fogarty's Folly community, with knives on their knotted rope belts. This didn't feel like some fraternity prank anymore, Simon thought, turning his attention to the fire, which had been built with more care than a simple gathering on the beach would need.

The fire had been arranged with exquisite care, branches used to create a sort of cone to foster the flames, rocks of a material that looked completely out of place on the sand forming a circle around the fire.

In the center of the fire, Simon could see the distinct shape of a human being, unmoving as the flames curled around it.

Clarissa grabbed his arm and dug her nails into his flesh. Simon was honestly surprised at her restraint—screaming would have been a perfectly reasonable response. But he put a reassuring hand on hers.

"It's not a real person," he said. "Smell that?"

"Smell what?" Clarissa said.

"Just wood smoke. Burning people smells like... it smells like meat, Clarissa," Simon said. "If they burned a human being, we'd be able to smell it. That's just an effigy. See the hands?"

Simon pointed to the arms and hands of the human-shaped thing where each clearly ended in a bundle of branches or sticks instead of fingers, more like a scarecrow than a living thing.

"Why would they do this?" Clarissa asked. "What does it mean?"

"No idea," Simon said, then put a finger to his lips and indicated for her to listen with him. He tilted his head, trying to filter out voices from the waves and wind across the water.

"It's been generations, Sherman," a voice Simon recognized as Frank Buskin, the owner of the local grocery store, said. Sherman had to be Sherman O'Neill, the fire chief.

"It's okay if you can't sense it, Frank," Sherman said. "We've all lost some of our connection to the sea. None of us are pure anymore. We've mingled with the land dwellers for too long. Our senses are dulled."

"Screw you, Sherman," Frank said. "Now's not the time for your elitist 'my bloodline is more pure' garbage."

"I'm not trying to start a fight," Sherman said. "I'm just stating facts. And none of us are anywhere near as close to our lord as

Father Branson."

Sherman pointed to a portly, bow-legged lone figure near the alter. Father Branson was local priest whose denomination Simon had never been able to parse out. He dressed a bit like a Catholic cardinal, but called himself something else entirely, even claiming that his religion was almost extinct. Simon has avoided him as much as possible because of his weirdly superior attitude. And also the smell. The man always smelled like the pier.

"They're all flat-out cuckoo bananas," Clarissa said.

"Probably," Simon said. "But I don't think it's just that they're deranged or hallucinating. There's something else going on here."

"They are delusional, Simon."

"I'm not saying they're in their right minds, but I mean, look at all this," Simon said. "It's like something out of…"

He trailed off as all the cultists, at least a dozen, turned their attention as one to the sea.

"And now things get really weird," Simon said.

"Are you sure the thing in the fire isn't a real person?" Clarissa said.

"Yeah, I can see the shape of the branches and sticks they used," he said. "Looks like someone's lawn furniture had a bad day."

For the second time, Clarissa dug her nails into Simon's arm. He thought about making a joke about how he was going to look like a cat attacked him later but then he spotted what had caused Clarissa's second moment of panic.

Something was rising out of the sea. No, some things, plural. Humanoid, hunched, slim, skin shining in the moonlight not just from moisture but with the silvery sheen of scales.

They strode silently to the shore, toward the cultists.

"What the hell are those, Simon?" Clarissa said.

"I have no idea," Simon said, pulling out his phone. He'd stuck into a matte-black case intentionally, turned the screen brightness to its lowest possible setting, and made sure the flash was deactivated a dozen times before setting out tonight. Simon snapped a few quick photos before turning on the video feature.

"Welcome!" Father Branson said, splashing out into the surf to great the newcomers. "Our brothers in faith! The Priesthood of the Fallen Star has waited so long for you. The sacrifice awaits."

The creatures didn't speak. Instead, one shoved Branson off his feet into the surf. The others set upon him viciously. Simon couldn't make out the details between Branson's dark robes and the darker surf, but from the screams—and their sudden stop—as well as the horrific sounds of rending and tearing, it appeared Father Branson's life ended as a meal.

One of the scaled beasts, who had not partaken in eating the priest, pointed at the remaining cultists with a long, pointed finger.

"Prepare," it said in a gurgling voice. Then it pointed back out to sea. "Soon. Prepare. Ready."

The lead creature turned his back on the cultists and dove into the waves, disappearing. The others glared back angrily at the cultists, but left them be, also returning to the sea. Someone sobbed in the darkness.

Simon turned to Clarissa, who had gone sickly pale, covering her mouth with both hands.

"We need to get out of here," Simon said. "Come on. Quickly and quietly now. Okay?"

Clarissa nodded.

They made their way back exactly the way they'd come, struggling to move slowly and casually rather than run like the devil himself was at their heels.

They almost broke into a run as they returned to the street, instead ducking quickly into Clarissa's apartment building, pulling the foyer door tight behind them. Simon nudged Clarissa farther into the building until they couldn't be seen from the street.

"What were those things?" Clarissa said. "They killed that man! They ate him, Simon!"

"We shouldn't talk here," he said, eyeing the various first-floor apartment doors. Who knows who else is in on this in town, Simon thought. Anyone could be listening. Clarissa led them up to her apartment, where she slammed the door shut and bolted it.

"This is insane," she said.

"Yeah," he said.

"Why are you not reacting like you just saw the craziest thing you've ever seen in your life?" she said.

"Okay, that was a top ten," Simon said. "But I... look, I deal with weird things like this all the time. It's my job."

"Homicidal fish people and creepy beach cultists are your job?" Clarissa said, incredulous. "I will never complain about dealing with people who are picky about their lattes ever again."

Simon exhaled heavily. This is not what I wanted to do when I volunteered to open this field office, he thought.

"I have to call this in," Simon said. "You should stay here."

"The hell I should, I'm a block from the crazypants beach party," Clarissa said. "How can I stay here?"

"I think the one thing we don't want to do is let them know we saw what happened," Simon said. "But it sounded like things are going to get worse. I just meant you shouldn't go back on the street tonight."

"Oh. Oh no, no I'm not going back out outside tonight. Are you? You're not going back out there, are you?"

Simon sidled up to the window, which faced the water, and, without moving the curtains, tried to peer outside. He couldn't see the bonfire from here.

"I think I need to call this in," he said. "But maybe I should wait until daybreak to get back to my house."

"Call it in where?" Clarissa said. "Your job is... sea monster prevention?"

"Not exclusively," Simon said. "I work for the Department of What."

"The Department of Who?"

"The Department of... never mind. Yeah, bizarrely, this sort of thing kind of falls under my job responsibilities. Though I didn't move here thinking I'd be bringing my work home with me."

"Well, I think you're right to stay off the streets," Clarissa said.

"The morning commuters will give me cover to get back," Simon said. "Walking around this time of night will make me a target."

"This might sound weird, but you can stay here, y'know."

"Thanks," Simon said.

"Well, I'm not sleeping," Clarissa said. "I just watched the local priest get eaten by a fish-man."

"Me either," Simon said. "Do you have any coffee?"

"I'm the manager of an Ishmael's," Clarissa said. "All I have is coffee."

Chapter 42: Wisdom from the mouths of were-sharks

Yuri couldn't quite get comfortable on the Amazonian ship.

It wasn't the ship itself, although compared to the *Endless*, which was not a big ship to begin with, the Amazonian craft was cramped. It was narrow, like a blade, built for speed and combat. An attack ship, Yuri thought, almost laughing at the idea. But everything about the Amazons was a strange combination of anachronistic technology and modern flair. He'd had a few days to look at the armor the Amazon warriors who accompanied them wore, and while at a distance it looked like ancient armor or something you'd see in a period film, up close he could see the materials were modern, more like military body armor than a breastplate a hero of the Trojan War would wear. They avoided guns, but the bows they carried glittered up close with improvements on classic designs, and their arrows were made of a lightweight metal Yuri couldn't identify.

This wasn't an ancient culture unprepared for the real world, he knew. They honored tradition in how they built everything they touched, but they were more than ready for what waited for them outside New Scythia.

But the ship still made him uncomfortable. He knew why, too.

It had been too long since he'd transformed and been beneath the waves. The shark inside him called out to hunt. It made Yuri uncomfortable. Not the desire itself, but by how much his conscious mind wanted it, too. He'd become so accustomed to the solitude of deep water in his time apart from Echo and the others. Before his transformation, Yuri had been a little bit afraid of the ocean and very much afraid of himself, never comfortable in his own skin, always haunted by a sense of being out of place.

Somehow, this monster he had become gave him a sense of purpose and place. It felt like home.

And right now, it really wanted to go for a swim.

He found Artem near the prow, watching the horizon. That was what Artem did, apparently, Yuri thought. He watched the horizon looking like a movie star, his hair blowing in the breeze. Yuri wandered up to stand beside him.

"I was thinking about going for a swim," Yuri said.

"Business or pleasure?" Artem said. Artem had been wound tighter than Yuri had ever seen him on this trip. Bad enough to be surrounded by Amazons who seemed to quietly, but actively, resent him. But avoiding his own mother on a ship this size was nearly impossible. That part made Yuri particularly uncomfortable. He'd lost two mothers of his own, after all. Seeing someone struggle to reconcile, or not reconcile, with his own mother twisted a knife in Yuri's heart.

"I gotta let..." Yuri thumped his chest. "...the big guy out for a bit. Thought I might kill two birds with one stone, dive in and have a look around."

"Makes sense," Artem said, his tone quiet, but friendly. "You should do that. You won't have any trouble keeping up with the ship I assume."

"I'm so fast as a shark, man," Yuri said. "And as a shark-man. Heh. C'mon, Artem, that was at least a little bit funny."

Artem cracked a smile.

"A very little bit funny. I'll grant you that," Artem said.

"Hey, so, when was the last time you slept?" Yuri said.

"You say that like I can actually remember," Artem said. "Eh. It's been a while. I feel fine."

"I know you're the professional warrior and all, but maybe getting some sleep before the big fight might be beneficial, yeah?"

"Parenting me now, Yuri?" Artem said.

"Hey, dude, I just don't want the most dangerous man alive grumpy because of sleep deprivation is all," Yuri said.

Artem shook his head in disbelief and rubbed his eyes.

"Okay. Okay, fine, you win," Artem said. "Go for your swim and I'll try to sleep for a few hours. Don't get lost, and wake me if you see anything."

"You got it," Yuri said. Artem headed below deck, leaving Yuri in the prow of the boat alone. He looked over the rail, then looked to the starboard side, trying to figure out the most dignified way to jump ship without looking like a fool.

"At least he talks to you," a new voice said behind Yuri. He turned to see Orithyia walking toward him in full armor.

"Well, y'know. Artem and I have been through some stuff. We're buds," Yuri said. "And by buds, I mean he really doesn't talk to anyone much. He's not, y'know, a talker."

"He talks to me least of all, but it's good to know he's not talkative by nature," Orithyia said.

"He's… I don't know," Yuri said. "I think maybe he was happier before. When I first met him, he was happy. He was in love."

"Really," Orithyia said. Yuri picked up on a shift in her tone—no malice to it at all, but a hunger, a desire for any scrap of knowledge about her son she could acquire.

"I shouldn't be telling stories that are his to tell," Yuri said.

"I understand," Orithyia said.

"But… I don't know. He introduced me to the instructor who tried to teach me how to fight."

"Tried?"

"I'm a terrible student," Yuri said. "And he smiled then. But then Merrick was killed and, well. I mean we've all lost a lot recently. But I think Merrick changed him."

"Loss does that," Orithyia said. "We're never the same afterward."

Yuri studied the Amazon's face, trying to get a read on her. And what he found there surprised him. This was a general of a mythical army, the warrior-mother of someone he respected more than almost anyone else in the world, but what he found in her eyes was a profound loneliness. Yuri took a deep breath and spoke.

"So I lost my father when I was young," he said. "He was a fisherman. Lost at sea. You'd think in the modern world that wouldn't happen, right? But it does. Because the sea's still dangerous. It's what, three quarters of the planet? Of course it's dangerous. It should be dangerous."

Orithyia watched him intently, saying nothing.

"And then my mom died when I was a teenager. Cancer," he said. "You wouldn't put the two side by side, the ocean and cancer, but they're these two unstoppable forces, right? They're inevitable, and relentless, and we'll never fully understand either of them, and they take things from us. And... I guess the ocean I can forgive. It took my father, but the ocean gave my father a fighting chance. If you're brave and strong, the ocean will let you win. I can respect that. I miss my dad, but the ocean was where he lived his life. I think honor's a stupid concept, it makes people do stupid things, but dying doing what you'd spent your life doing makes a depressing sort of sense to me. But cancer. There's no honor to it. It cheats. It doesn't respect you. So yeah, I lost my dad, and then I lost my mom."

"I'm sorry," Orithyia said, a soft empathy to her tone.

"But then I went to live with Echo and her mother, right?" Yuri said. "And it was okay. More than okay. Not everybody gets to land somewhere they'll be loved. Somewhere that lets them stay close to where they were born. Meredith, Echo's mom, she gave me a chance to still be me. She was my mom's friend, you see, and she promised to look after me, and she did."

He cleared his throat, surprised at the way the words caught in his mouth.

"But then one night monsters like me—I mean literally like me, were-sharks—showed up for Echo and Meredith, and they killed her. They infected me with this… power later, and I've come to understand it, even use it, but at the time, they were just another unstoppable, unforgiving, senseless force taking away a person I loved," Yuri said. "So yeah. Anyway. I've had three parents, and I loved three parents, and they all loved me back, and they're all gone."

"You've had a hard life," Orithyia said.

"I haven't. Not compared to most. And I'm not saying all this to make you pity me. I think I'm saying it because I see you trying and I think whatever mistakes you've made, trying is important. Even if Artem doesn't know it yet, I see what you're doing. Someone should say it. So I'm saying it."

"I don't think he cares."

"At this point, you're sort of an abstract concept to him," Yuri said. "It's easy to be mad at an abstract concept. It's harder to be mad at a real person."

"Do you have any suggestions as to how I might make myself human to him?" Orithyia said. "I know that sounds flippant, but honestly—you know him better than I do now. I haven't seen him in almost twenty years. I don't know what he needs to hear from me."

"Tell him your story," Yuri said. "We're all just stories in the end after all. Tell him yours. Maybe he'll tell you his. Now if you'll excuse me, I've got a were-shark in my head demanding I go for a swim, so I should do that before I start chewing through the hull."

"Of course."

Yuri pulled off his loose-fitting top and prepared to jump off the deck into the ocean. He could feel the fierce beating heart of the shark in his chest, ready to be unleashed.

"Yuri," Orithyia said. "Thank you for your kindness."

"Lotta people have been kind to me my whole life," Yuri said. "Just doing what I can to pay it back."

Chapter 43: A hole in the world

Grimmin offered to deliver a message to Echo's father for her before he left to tell the Atlantean council about the latest developments. Echo said no, not sure what she'd say to her father at this point. He was still mostly a stranger to her, after all, despite their best effort to get to know each other during those few days in Atlantis.

No, she thought, I take that back. It wasn't our best effort. It was a bit of effort. A try. But not our best.

Grimmin did give Echo something useful, however—a thin chain she could attach to her trident and then to her belt in case she dropped her weapon in the trench. It was a fairly common accessory for Atlantean warriors, but one she hadn't had before, so the old spymaster gave her his own. She tried to turn it down, but he waved her off.

"I can get another. This is more useful to you today," he said.

And not for the first time she realized she was more comfortable around an aging spy than her own father, that the spy had been kinder to her in many ways, but she filed that information away for another day, watching as Grimmin and his guards dove beneath the water on their seahorses to return to Atlantis.

"Are you ready to go?" Muireann said, joining Echo on the

deck.

"No reason to wait any longer," she said. Barnabas also joined them, hands in his pockets.

"I'll keep the engine running, metaphorically," he said. "All you have to do is find a stick at the bottom of a giant underwater ravine, and then we'll be ready to run off and save the world, right?"

"Easy peasy," Echo said. "Muireann?"

The ondine nodded, then began to speak the words to the divining spell. A whorl of white light drifted around her hands, which she lifted in front of her face. With her right hand, she placed her index and middle fingers on her closed eyes. Withdrawing her hand, she opened her eyes, which were now pupil-less and glowed with the same soft white energy of the spell.

She peered over the edge of the ship and smiled.

"It worked," she said, smiling. The grin looked eerie beneath her glowing eyes.

"Did you know the spell would do that?" Echo said to Barnabas.

"Yeah, of course," he said.

"Didn't think to warn us about the creepy glowing eyes part?"

"Where's the fun in that?" Barnabas said.

Echo's shoulders slumped. She put a reassuring hand on Muireann's arm.

"Here we go, then," she said, and together, they dove into the water.

Poseidon's Scar was little more than a shadow at first, a darkness at the bottom of the ocean. But they moved quickly, Echo swimming with powerful grace, Muireann with an effortlessness that belied her water spirit heritage. Her whole appearance changed below the water, Echo noted—she still looked like herself, the same features, the same face, but her skin turned a ghostly bluish white, her hair no longer jet black but a deep, deep blue, the hint of a subtle pattern across her skin, like the dappled surface of water beneath the sun.

The ocean grew colder around them as they dove deeper. The last time Echo entered the Scar it was to prevent a war, the area filled with fighters ready to kill her, the sound of the submarine's great engines clanking, the squeal of its breaking metal hull deafening. Now the war zone was a vacant lot, a ghost town, haunted by the spirits of those who died here.

Beside her, Muireann absorbed the emptiness, her eyes gleaming in the darkness like twin lanterns. Together, they dove deeper, the opening to Poseidon's Scar like a dark, cavernous mouth on the sea floor.

The temperature began to rise. Echo hadn't noticed this before, but it would make sense—they knew volcanic activity occurred deep down in the Scar, so heat would naturally make its way in the direction of the surface here. She tried to judge the size of the Scar, but she did not have the mathematics to put it into words. Was it as wide as a football field? Wider? The ravine was enormous, and long enough that it faded into blurry obscurity in either direction.

She did notice one detail, though. New tears in the earth and stone at the mouth of the ravine, drag marks that looked terrifyingly, but unmistakably, like something had dug its way out from here. She tried to judge the size of those claws, swimming closer to use her own height to judge. Nearly as wide as she was tall, many times longer than her full height, whatever creature those fingers and claws were attached to, it must be vast. Tall as a building. A moving mountain of flesh.

Muireann stared into the darkness. Echo watched her as she scanned back and forth like a searchlight, like a lighthouse. She pointed, then, once again making arcane gestures with her hands, touched the tip of one finger to her lips, then to her ears. She repeated the same gestures and touched Echo's mouth and ears as well.

"Can you hear me?" Muireann said.

"Loud and clear," Echo said. "That's a handy spell."

"Easier than trying to communicate through sign languages or gurgling through the water," Muireann said. "I can't see the

Needle, but I can sense it. It's below us, of course. Distant, but not unreachable, I think. Should we keep going?"

"After you," Echo said, hefting her trident. "You watch for our prize, and I'll keep an eye out for trouble."

Their descent slowed as they traversed deeper into the Scar. Something about the trench itself seemed to want to push them away, to force them back up and out. It almost felt aware, or intelligent, she thought. Malevolent. Something doesn't want us here.

But that would be mad, she thought. It's just nature. The rising water pressure. The fact that our biology does not belong here. We're meant to float. We're going against nature.

As they descended, the darkness began to grow deeper, heavier, until with alarming suddenness the world around them became all but lightless. A sliver of vague blue light could still be seen above, but for Echo, the only light she could see nearby came from Muireann's glowing eyes. The ondine reached out and took her hand, leading the way ever further into the depths.

It didn't take long, though, before a very different kind of light began to filter up from below. Reddish and angry, this new light came with a heat Echo knew had to be from the lava flows that existed here. The pressure of the dive didn't bother her, but she worried if getting too close to the superheated rock would boil her alive. Impenetrable skin is one thing, but she didn't know for sure whether that also meant she wouldn't cook from the inside.

It was at this depth, though, that Muireann stopped their rapid descent and began to move lengthwise, scanning every which way in the ravine with her glowing eyes. Her head darted around, left to right, up and down, almost like an avian hunter sensing its prey. Tugging Echo along, Muireann led them to a darker patch of the ravine, a deeply shadowed section hidden from the light of the lava below.

As they swam closer, Echo could make out shapes in the shadow—not just a shadow, in fact, but a cave, a break in the side of the trench. The ground of this cave was littered with something that made Echo want to scream.

Eggs. Hundreds upon hundreds of eggs.

Tall, nearly waist-high, the eggs were plastered to the floor of the cave, thicker end downward, held in place with some sort of mucus. Most had hatched, leaving fleshy, leathery shells behind, membranous remains drifting like curtains in the current. Others remained unhatched, maybe one in ten, but something told Echo they were stillborn. Something about the surface of those eggs, some undefinable characteristic, hinted at lifelessness and emptiness.

Is this where the fish-men came from? She wondered. Did they just hatch here, like any other creature of the sea? How long were they here gestating before awakening? Or have they always been here, generation after generation, waiting for a reason to return to the light?

Echo locked eyes with Muireann, but both women remained silent. Something about this hatchery felt as much like a graveyard as a nursery, and to speak felt dangerous, disrespectful, profane.

Still, Muireann led them ever deeper. Now a new light source appeared, replacing the red glow of the lava. The walls were covered with a glowing slime that gave off a pale green tint. The glow felt alien and uncomfortable. It instantly caused the pressure in Echo's head to throb.

The ocean had always felt like another world to Echo, an alien environment where she did not fully belong. But this place felt even more so. She felt like an intruder. Unwelcome. Unwanted. There was a hum in the air that gave her a headache so bad that her eyeballs throbbed.

"It's nearby," Muireann said.

Echo nodded, squinting at the pounding in her head. She felt a growing sense of unease here, as if they were being watched. She gripped her trident tightly, releasing Muireann's hand now that the walls themselves gave off enough light to see by. At one point she swung around, believing she'd spotted one of the fish-men—and she had, dead, decaying against a sloping rock, its eyes hollowed out by time and rot.

The whole cavern felt older than it should, Echo thought. She didn't know why she knew that. She was no spelunker or expert diver. But something in this place felt ancient, out of time, dizzyingly so.

"Echo," Muireann said. Echo snapped out of her reverie and followed the ondine's gaze where she pointed to the stone below.

There, just a few dozen meters away, a single, perfect white line broke the darkness.

Echo swam closer, and soon that white line took shape. A long haft, white, like bone, flawless and smooth, ending in a gleaming blade the color of moonlight, a single, flat edge ending in a razor-perfect, diamond-shaped point at the end. The haft, she could see now as she drew closer, had swirls of silver and gray in it like marble. A metal cap protected the butt of the spear, and more metallic piping decorated the grip and the blade itself. It was a beautiful weapon, if a weapon of war could ever be beautiful, and looked as though it might never have been held by mortal hands.

Echo darted forward to retrieve it. Muireann drifted behind, scanning the room for anything out of place. But this cavern had become a boneyard, Echo thought. Nothing lived here now. It seemed strange that anything ever had.

She slung her own trident into a slim holster on her back, careful to not become entangled in the chain Grimmin had given her, and picked up the Needle of the Moon. It felt cool to the touch, but not uncomfortably so, and hummed with an energy that felt almost alive in her hands.

She smiled and looked back to Muireann to congratulate her. But instead, she found Muireann staring directly ahead, just past Echo's shoulder.

Echo spun around, holding the Needle at the ready, but found nothing to fight. Instead, she saw a pulsating slash of darkness at the back of the cave. It hummed with a loud, throbbing white noise, overpowering but empty at the same time. In the center of the break in the cavern, a deep purple, nearly black, shadowy slash of energy, almost like an absence of light, emanated in a slowly moving whirlpool. It did not feel as though it were physically pulling them in, like a vortex; rather, it seemed to call to Echo, asking her to join in becoming nothing.

"This is a hole in the world," Muireann said.

"What do we do?" Echo said. The gash in the cave, she could see clearly now, did not lead deeper into the stone. It seemed instead to open into a visible emptiness, like the night sky, endless, bottomless. I swear I can see stars through there, she thought.

"We need to go," Muireann said.

Echo tried to swim away, but she felt an urge, almost a command, to throw the spear into the pulsating slash in reality. It wants this weapon, Echo knew instantly. It knows this is dangerous. She could feel a malevolent wanting; centuries, millennia with the object of its desire sitting on the ocean floor, just out of reach. Whatever that is, it knows what this weapon is worth.

"Muireann, we're leaving," Echo said.

"Yes. Yes, we are," the ondine said.

And she began to sing.

Echo thought at first this was some sort of trick, that Muireann had betrayed her, or that the dark intelligence they stood face to face with had taken over Muireann's mind. But then Echo felt the weight of that intelligence, the commanding wordless voice, become drowned out by Muireann's song. She's using her song magic as a shield, Echo realized. Muireann was creating a barrier between them and the voice beyond the veil. Echo grabbed Muireann's hand once again. They held tight, so tight it hurt the bones in Echo's hand, and turned from that endless darkness. They swam for their lives.

The world went blurry as they rushed for the surface. The light of Muireann's spell, the glow of her eyes, went dim and disappeared. Echo kept her own gaze on that break in the surface, the pale blue sliver of hope above them. The ondine was nearly weightless in her grasp, but kept pace with her, meter after deadly meter.

Echo didn't remember breathing the entire way. Only the pounding of her heart in her ears, the death grip she held on the Needle, the reassuring presence of Muireann's hand in hers.

Finally they crested the ridge of the ravine, into the deep blue of the sea above. Echo could see the silhouette of their ship above them and swam for her life. In the back of her mind she could hear a deep roar, almost a scream, of rage, of frustration, of loss. It called to her. I need daylight, she thought, I need air, I need to get away from this terrible place.

The women burst from the water together, a cacophony of gasping breath and splashing limbs. Before she could clear her eyes, she felt herself pulled quickly from the water, deposited on deck, Muireann immediately beside her. She thrashed about, tossing the Needle aside purely so she could hear it bang against the wood of the deck, proving it was real, that she had truly found it. She felt Muireann's hand on her shoulder, and then an arm around her. Her body shook. Something dropped over her shoulders, a blanket. Barnabas draped each of them in a blanket and then stormed to the edge of the boat and shouted the incoherent words to another spell. A purple-blue light flashed, and her breath returned to her. Barnabas fell to one knee, shook his head, and dragged himself back to his feet and to their side. He picked up the Needle of the Moon and held it in his hands curiously.

"What did you two wake up down there?" he said, finally.

"Something that never sleeps," Muireann said.

"We got it, though," Echo said, taking the spear back from Barnabas. "Totally worth it."

She shot Barnabas a smile, who scratched at his beard and grinned back.

"Let's hope so," he said.

Chapter 44: The going rate for a soul

Barnabas watched Echo and Muireann dive beneath the waves and stood vigil over their descent for roughly five minutes. He waited in eerie silence as long as he could, waiting for signs of distress or a struggle, keeping an eye out for whatever oversized predators might have replaced the afanc in the area.

Nothing happened. He stuffed his hands in his pockets, looked around at the ghost crew of the *Endless* as if they were silently judging him, whistled an old Irish folk song, then a slightly off-color sailing ditty.

Then he ran down to his cabin and rummaged through one of his drawers until he found a crystal ball the size of a grapefruit, wrapped safely in a velvet bag.

He smooshed the bag into a pile and set the crystal ball down gently on top of it. With a quick spell, he ran his fingertips across the surface and activated the crystal, which lit up gently with warm golden light within.

"Lady Grey, are you available?" he said.

A few seconds passed before a tired, and more than a little annoyed, voice replied from within.

"I do have a phone, Barnabas Coy," the woman's voice said, a posh accent taking the edge off the clear annoyance in her tone.

"You don't have to use magic to contact me every time."

"Well," Barnabas said, sitting down at his desk and hunching conspiratorially over the globe. "I'm in the middle of the bloody ocean so cell phone reception is rubbish. I thought this would offer a clearer signal."

The woman's face came into view, as elegant as the voice it belonged with, her eyes glittering from within with deep golden flames.

"Well, you have me, in any event," the Lady Natasha Grey said. "I assume this means you want something."

"What, I can't just make a social call, check in, see how my friend is doing?"

"We are not friends, I don't have friends and neither do you, and you never call unless you want something. So are you buying or selling?"

"I'm actually just, okay, to be honest, I'm just looking for a price check," Barnabas said.

"Oh gods above and below. Don't you have access to eBay out there?"

"No, and I don't think this particular item is available on eBay," Barnabas said.

"You wouldn't believe the arcane relics I find online," Natasha said. "I mean working deals with immortals and demons is very rewarding, but when you can find a well-worn copy of the Necronomicon from a used bookseller in Australia, why deal with a hell lord? Thirty-five dollars Australian. The Necronomicon."

"Not the version with real human skin," Barnabas said.

"Oh no, not that one. That one is so vulgar. Human flesh leather is for posers and plebeians."

"I know, right?" Barnabas said. "Which one did you get?"

"The illuminated manuscript. You know, the limited edition from those blind monks in the sixteenth century."

"I never understood how blind monks made an illuminated manuscript," Barnabas said.

"Because hand-copying the Necronomicon is what struck them

blind, you idiot," Natasha said. "I thought everyone knew. How did you not know that? Have I taught you nothing? How did someone with your critical thinking skills ever learn basic spellcraft?"

"Just lucky, I guess," Barnabas said.

"Enough shop talk," Natasha said. "I have people to corrupt and demons to swindle. Or the other way around. What are you trying to sell, darling? I'll quote you a fair price."

"Actually, I'm wondering how much a soul goes for on the open market," Barnabas said. "To buy."

There was a long pause on the other end of the crystal ball.

"I didn't think you trucked with the darkest arts," the Lady said. "I don't know if I should be impressed or concerned."

"This is purely hypothetical. I'm wondering how hard it would be to buy one. Or a piece of one."

"Well, the price varies. Souls are like diamonds. They have different qualities we look for. Flaws can detract from their overall value. Size, cut, and clarity, so to speak," Natasha said. "I assume you're looking for a human soul? Other beings cost more, of course. Rarity. Humans are always giving their souls away. Idiots."

"Human, I guess," Barnabas said. "It's not for me. It's for a friend."

"Liar," Natasha said. "Well, I'll be honest, Barnabas Coy. The going rate for a soul is absolutely out of your price range."

"You don't know my price range."

"I know how much souls cost. Unless you've come into the sort of horrific materials that souls are usually traded for, you can't afford it. You're a scoundrel, Barnabas, but there is no scenario I can envision you getting yourself into that would lead you to have the trade you'd need to acquire a soul."

Barnabas wrinkled his nose, exhaled deeply, and rubbed his forehead.

"Should I be relieved about this?"

"If you don't need a soul, you should be very relieved about this," Natasha said. "I've been bargaining with the incomprehensible for longer than you can imagine, and all I know is, once you start trading in souls, you never go back. That's the end of the path, darling. A shadow will follow you until the end of your days."

"So you're saying I shouldn't buy a soul," Barnabas said.

"Coy, what in the seven heavens and nine hells could you possibly need a soul for?"

"I told you. For a friend."

"I have known some insufferable fools in my life, Barnabas, but you are a top-shelf nitwit."

"I always wanted to be the best at something," Barnabas said.

Again, the Lady let the air grow silent for a moment before speaking.

"Are you in trouble, Barnabas? I can get you out of it. It will cost you, but I am sure it will cost less than a soul."

"I'm not in trouble," Barnabas said. "Well, not this kind of trouble. I'm always in some trouble or another. But I'm okay."

"Good," Natasha said.

"Hey, Natasha?" Barnabas said

"Oh gods, what?" she said.

"How do souls work with creatures like me?" he said

"You mean part mortal, part something else?" Natasha said.

"Yeah," Barnabas said.

"Well, souls aren't an exact science. They aren't even real, in a way," she said. "They're a belief system, you could say. Some think of them as a fuel source. Others, a currency. But what they are is an anchor."

"To this world," Barnabas said.

"Exactly," Natasha said. "And I'll be honest. I don't know anyone else like you. I don't know how yours works. I could ask around, if you'd like."

"Sure," Barnabas said. "Sure, that'd be great. I can pay you for your time."

"No, you can't," Natasha said. "But I'll trade it for a favor down the line."

"Sounds fair," Barnabas said.

"Next time, use the phone, Barnabas. Looking at you through the fish-eye lens of a crystal ball is terrifying."

Barnabas nodded. The crystal went dark. He tucked it back into the velvet bag, then dropped it back into the drawer where he'd found it. Trotting back upstairs to the deck, he leaned against the main mast and waited. One of the ship's ghosts, an old peg-legged man in ragged pirate's gear, looked at him judgmentally.

"Don't you have a deck to swab or something?" Barnabas asked. The ghost shook his head and walked away, leaving Barnabas to wait with his thoughts.

He didn't wait long. Soon, he heard the sputtering splash of Echo and Muireann's return, and sprang to action, putting his conversation with the Lady Grey to the back of his mind.

Chapter 45: A man in irons

Artem heard his mother approach as she joined him below deck. He'd come here to be alone, sitting eyes closed in a straight-backed chair that had been nailed to the floor. At first it might appear he was meditating, or even sleeping, but Artem was simply exhausted of it all, tired of the people all around him, tired of the eternal battle for something none of them could ever have.

I don't want to talk right now, he thought, keeping his eyes closed. Please assume I'm sleeping. Don't talk. I can't talk with you right now.

"Artem," Orithyia said, and Artem opened his eyes, trying his best to hide his annoyance. "I'd like to talk, if you're willing."

"You have a captive audience, mother," Artem said. "Say what you will."

Orithyia found a seat nearby, then stood up again, then leaned against the wall. It was uncomfortable to watch her nervousness, Artem thought. She sent him away young, but even as a small child he remembered her never-ending self-control, the unshakable confidence. Had she not been his mother—and therefore, like all parents, vulnerable to the flaws and judgments all children see—she would have been a powerful role model. Instead he saw her behavior as a cold perfectionism, something he both strove toward and was afraid he would achieve himself.

But here, on this ship, she seemed shockingly human, terrifyingly imperfect, and for the first time in his life, Artem saw his mother as vulnerable.

She took a deep breath, and began to speak.

"I never told you about your father," she said.

"You did," Artem said. "Everyone did. No one let me forget my father was a thief who stole his way onto our sacred island. The only thing harder than being the only male on that island was being the child of a character of legendary and universal scorn."

"We don't believe the things a parent does should carry forward onto their children," Orithyia said. "But..."

"But it's one thing to believe something like that. It's another to practice it."

"We hold ourselves separate from humanity, Artem, but the Amazons are just as human as anyone else. We are prey to all the same mistakes and imperfections and prejudices as any other people."

"And I understand that, in theory," Artem said. "But this was my life we're talking about here. This is what made me."

"And that's why I sent you away," Orithyia said. "I don't know that I'll ever make you understand that, but I saw what being so alone was doing to you. I had to send you away. I was afraid of what you'd become if I didn't."

Artem felt a sharp pain in his chest. Rage or sadness or loneliness, he couldn't tell. Maybe all those emotions. More than anything, though, he remembered being alone. I know why I joined in with Echo and Barnabas and Yuri, Artem thought, watching his mother—the general of the forces of the Amazons, exactly who she was meant to be—watching him from across the cabin. I found the company of people who have no place in the world, because I never have.

"Even I'll admit you made the right decision," Artem said. "Sending me away. But I can't help believing it was insufficient to rectify your original mistake of having me in the first place."

249

Orithyia simply stared at him, unable to respond.

"That was petulant," Artem said, shaking his head at himself. "It's a difficult thing, believing your entire life was in error. No matter what you say, I know I was an anomaly that no one believed should happen. It's not easy to digest. I'm not unhappy, mother, despite what I say, or how I act. I have loved, I have loved so much, and I have done brave things, and I have been to remarkable places, and I've become something I am proud of. But every story has an origin, and mine is not pleasant."

Orithyia put a hand on his head, stroking his hair.

"You should know about your father," Orithyia said.

"What else is there to know?"

"The things the others won't talk about. The things I can't tell another soul on New Scythia. But I don't know what will happen tomorrow, and I've let this go too long. Every story has an origin, you say. Well, let me tell you ours. Yours and mine."

***

Once, Orithyia began, there was a man in irons.

He was a liar and thief, an insolent and terrible creature, and he had to be dealt with.

No. No, those are the things I tell myself because of what came after. The things I say to make myself feel better about it all, to convince myself what happened had to happen, that we had no choice, that it was simply the way things needed to end.

Yes, there was once a man in irons. But he was honest, and he took only knowledge, and that knowledge was not stolen but hard-earned. He was not insolent, but polite, even charming, though the conditions I met him in left the latter somewhat lacking.

He was a man in irons, locked beneath the castle in New Scythia, because he'd been caught scaling our walls. He had seen our city, and found our port, and for that he had to die. It was the way of things. It was our law.

But he was just a man, and when I went to interrogate him, he was afraid, and tired, and resigned to what was to come. I was not the first Amazon to speak with him. I was a captain then, not a general, and head of castle security, where he was caught, so my soldiers found him. And he had been handled roughly during his capture—we'd found a thief in our house, after all, and it did not feel unjust to make him aware of just how much danger he had brought upon himself—and he'd been thrown into chains and locked beneath the castle until we were done with him.

We couldn't execute him immediately, of course. We had to learn if anyone else knew of our island, if we should expect an invasion, or a war. He was not tortured, but he was left alone, for days and days, to think on what he'd done, to realize his mistake, to consider, to truly consider, how truthful he needed to be about the allies who may come to his rescue, or to seek to plunder our island.

But he came alone. He told me that. And I did not believe him at first. I told him as much, with words, and with my fist, when he smiled and told me no one knew where he was. But he never deviated from that line, he remained true to his claim, and no one came looking for him. No one ever came looking for him.

Because, it turned out, he'd told the truth.

We accused him of being a thief. Why wouldn't we? He came in the night, under cover of darkness. He scaled our walls like a burglar. Dressed in black. To a place he was not welcome, seeking an unlocked window. Of course, we thought he was a thief.

But he said he did not come to steal. He came only to prove that a myth was real.

He found a map.

We Amazons are relentless perfectionists. We had worked for centuries to scrub our existence from the world. Erasing our island from maps and records, changing navigational charts to warn of reefs and rocky outcroppings. We quietly told the world that New Scythia did not exist and worked even harder to tell sailors these waters were unwelcoming. Not that here monsters dwelled, but ruin, and emptiness.

But this man in irons had found a map. And on that map,

where on all others nothing existed, he found an island. Our island.

He was a man who sought to answer questions. That was what he was, above all else. A man who went seeking answers. And he wanted to know if our island existed.

"I just wanted to be able to say I saw it," he told me, later. After many nights demanding answers from him. After nights where I called him a liar and a thief. After nights when I'd stopped calling him those things, because I had seen beyond the dirty prisoner's garb, beyond the irons.

There's a strange thing, my son, that happens when you meet a good person. They make you see the flaws in yourself. Because we all, in the end, want to be good people.

I don't know that I was the only one who looked past his transgressions. Likely I was. Perhaps a guard or two might have seen that ending his life felt ridiculously wasteful or unnecessary. But I didn't just pity him. I was captain of castle security, and yet I found friendship in the company of a thief and a liar. I spoke with him every day, at first as enemies, and then as friends. We knew about the world outside, you must understand, but we never saw it. We never lived it. Here, on this beautiful island, among our wonderful sisters, we were perfect. But we never left this place. And he spoke about the outside world with such love. He was an explorer, this man, and he found wonder in every small corner of the world. That was what brought him to us. Not greed, but curiosity. He had found a sliver of this Earth he had never seen before, and he wanted to lay eyes on it, as he had so many other places.

Do you want me to say it? I'll say it. It's too late to lie now, after all, and it's better that you know the truth, because the truth is more beautiful than any lie I can spin. We had that in common, your father and me. We were called liars to our face, when neither of us had a taste for deception.

And so I will not lie. I loved this man in irons, this thief, this fool. This witty, brave idiot, who unwittingly forfeited his life by going to a place he found on a map and asked: What is this? What wonder does it hold?

Our partings changed over time. At first, I would matter-of-factly inform him his time would grow short. We'll have to kill you, you see. You've seen our island. And, at first, he would beg for his life, plead with us to understand his motivation to believe him.

And later, I would tell him his time was growing short, and that we would have to put him to death, for he had seen our island, but regret crept into my voice. Apology, even, as I knew, I knew in my heart, his intent, as stupid as it had been, was pure, was without malice. I'm sorry, I would say, near the end, but we cannot let you leave here alive, for you've seen our secret place.

He stopped pleading, eventually. His parting words would be only that he wished he had more time. That he wished things could be different.

I asked him once, near the end, if he regretted coming to New Scythia. If he wished he had not given in to his curiosity. If he'd left well enough alone.

But then we would never have met, he told me, and he smiled, and I knew, as I'd come to know him so well by then, that he was not lying. It wasn't some maudlin statement from a dying man. These were matter-of-fact words from someone with nothing left to lose. Perhaps you were the one last mystery I was meant to discover, he said, and I told him he was an idiot and that he'd die here no matter what he said to me.

But that night I went to the docks, and I found a small boat, recently repaired but out of service, and I brought it to a little cove, rarely used, and left it there. The next few nights I gathered supplies, a little at a time, food that would not perish, fresh water in skins that would go un-missed. I found fishing line and hooks, and clothing.

And a few days later I helped the man in irons escape.

I was captain of the guard, of course. I knew every route, every pathway. I knew by heart the schedules and patrols of my soldiers. Moving one ghost of a man a mile in this city might seem difficult, but I traveled the veins of the castle my whole life, and I walked unquestioned in any hall.

I brought this foolish man to that cove, to the little boat, laden with supplies, and I held his boney body in my arms, and I told him to run.

Come with me, he said. Come see the world. It's so much bigger than this place. New Scythia is a beautiful gem in the middle of the ocean, but you have so much more to see. Don't stay here.

This is my home, I told him. This is my responsibility. This is my place.

You'll be punished for letting me go, he said. I'll stay. Let them behead me, or hang me, or whatever fate awaits. I won't have you suffer for what I brought upon myself.

They'll throw you from the cliffs, I said. I'll throw you from the cliffs. I am captain of the guard. It will be my job to push you myself. I cannot ask one of my soldiers to do it. I will not have your death on their hands, and I will not force myself to look upon another whom I ordered to kill you for the rest of my life. It's the only way it will happen. If you stay, I will kill you.

We must have stood there for an hour, in each other's arms. I can still feel his heartbeat against my chest. The way the mustiness of the prison cell mixed with the cool ocean air. It sounds romantic, doesn't it? Star-crossed lovers. But there is nothing worse than star-crossed lovers. It is the cruelest of punishments, fit only for stories that romanticize the horror and pain and shame of it all. I wouldn't wish it on anyone else. Not my worst enemy. Not anyone.

That man, no longer in irons, stepped into the little boat and stared at me with eyes lost and alone. His breathing was shallow, as was mine. Tears fell hot down my cheeks. I knew I would go on. I knew I would return to my duties, and find some way of masking my role in his escape. Perhaps I would be punished. Demoted. Stripped of my rank. But that night I didn't care. Send me to the kitchens to work. I wanted nothing to do with upholding our cruel laws anymore. Not if they could lead to heartbreak like this.

Perhaps, in the end, I might have chosen differently if I'd

known about you, that night. It was too soon to tell. I had no idea. Not an inkling. But what choice did I have? He would have been sentenced to death even sooner if our affair had been uncovered. And then I truly would have never seen him again, never been allowed back to his cell, not even to say goodbye before the execution. No, it was for the better than neither of us knew. Especially with what happened next.

I watched him row the small boat out to sea, his eyes never leaving mine. I swear we would have locked eyes until the little craft carried him out into the fog. And that is why I saw the pain in his eyes before I heard the arrow hiss through the air, before I knew the thump I heard was the shaft piercing his heart. A perfect strike, a merciful killing blow.

The man slumped over in the boat, which the tide caught just then, pulling him slowly out to a watery grave.

I knew who made the shot before I saw her. Lampedo, then not yet queen but already one of our greatest warriors, walked quietly down from the rocky outcropping above to stand beside me, bow in hand. We said nothing for a long moment, only the waves and our breathing breaking the silence.

"I did this out of love for you, Orithyia," she said, finally. And after months of talking with the man who could not lie, I had become so very adept at discerning the truth when someone spoke. But I knew Lampedo, and I knew this was no lie. We'd been in love once ourselves, when we were young, before responsibility overtook us, and I knew always when she tried to deceive me.

"Why?" I asked. I didn't need an answer. I didn't want one. But what else do you say in a moment like that? What else do you do but ask why?

"Do you remember the first thing he said to us, when we found him?" Lampedo said. She'd been there that night. She was not part of the castle guard, but already being groomed to rule, and so she'd been there for the initial questioning. "He said, 'I just wanted to be able to say I saw it.' If he lived, others would come. No matter how innocent his intentions, his life would have meant destruction and war."

"Why let it go this far?" I asked. "Why here? Why not stop me at the castle?"

"You deserved your goodbye," she said. "And by all the gods, you deserved the blessing of not having him die by your hand. Let that blood be mine to carry so you don't have to."

I gritted my teeth and fought back grief. I thought, mistakenly, that my punishment would be less if I remained stoic and emotionless. It didn't matter, though.

"What happens next?" I said.

"Nothing," Lampedo said. "You will return to your duties. I will say that this man, this remarkable thief, had been planning his escape for months. So clever he was, he evaded our relentless castle guards, but was killed during the escape. I commend Captain Orithyia and her soldiers for their fine work."

"Why? Why do this?"

"I will be queen someday," Lampedo said. "And I will not let a mistake of the heart prevent me from appointing the woman I trust the most to lead my army."

"What if I don't want that?" I said.

"Then when I offer, you say no. Remain captain of the guard. Become a Keeper of Athena. You have free will, Orithyia. Gods know you've exercised it enough already. But I won't have you throw your life away tonight. Not for this. You can throw it away later."

Lampedo walked away, disappearing into the night. We never spoke of that conversation again. But you know the rest. She was true to her word.

I loved only one other being in all my life more than that man in irons, Artem. I gave that person away and sent him to the Island of Unwanted Things to keep him safe.

And for that, I will be sorry for all the rest of my days.

***

"One of the sitting queens of the Amazons killed my father. To keep a secret," Artem said.

Orithyia nodded.

"Why tell me this now?"

"I don't know," Orithyia said. "Because his memory deserved better. Because you shouldn't have to just be woven into a tapestry of secrets. Because I never thought I'd see you again and now you're here in front of me and I can't keep up the myth anymore. Because you never got to meet your father and sometimes that's a good thing, but other times, it's a tragedy, and I wanted you to know which."

"What am I supposed to do with this information?" Artem said. "I can't go avenge my father on Lampedo, right? Challenge her to a duel for my father's honor? Call her out for her lies to her entire people?"

"You could do all of those things," Orithyia said. "And you'll choose the right path, because I know who you've become. But I told you because I've withheld something that was your right to know for too long, and we're about to go to war together and I did not want either of us to die with secrets still untold."

Artem felt as though his skin were rippling with rage and disgust. He had always known there was something more to the story, that he never knew the whole truth.

"You loved my father," Artem said, the words difficult to form in his mouth.

"I did," Orithyia said.

"Why didn't you... You just went on with your life. You became their general. You led their armies. You never said anything, or did anything about it."

"Where else would I go?" Orithyia said.

Artem's mind flashed to the Island of Unwanted Things. Somehow, Orithyia read his thoughts.

"You see now why I sent you away," Orithyia said. "I stayed behind to maintain order, and to hold the walls from crumbling. I sent you away so you wouldn't be like me, trapped in a place you couldn't leave. I stayed to make sure you could leave."

"Unlike my father," Artem said.

"Yes," Orithyia said. "I stayed as a promise. To give you the freedom to leave."

"Do the others know?" Artem asked.

"As far as I know, only Lampedo and I know the whole story. Marpesia would have been furious with her sister. But she was content to leave your father locked in a cage for the rest of his life. For our safety. There was no right answer. Not for me."

Artem threw up his hands, frustrated and confused.

"I don't know what to do with any of this, mother," he said.

"Then do nothing," Orithyia said. "But you have it now. And it was unfair and unkind of me to keep it from you all this time. I'm sorry."

Mother and son locked eyes for a moment, neither sure of the other, both filled with dread and regret. Orithyia nodded and walked away, returning to the deck.

Artem sat in silence alone, reassessing his place in the universe, and what to do with all he'd learned.

Chapter 46: As old as time

The creature, plodding slowly and relentlessly across the floor of the Atlantic Ocean, had been called by many names. The Sleeper. The Hungerer. He Who Walks. The Great One. The Father of Monsters. The Change-Bringer. The Star-Child.

It had been important to a great many people, a great many societies. Cults that knew nothing of each other worshipped the creature as a god, as a devil, as a thing to scare children, as the bringer of the afterlife, or the end of the world. Madmen saw it in their dreams. Fishermen saw it in their nightmares. These things still happened, even now, despite that the creature, He Who Walks, the Great One, whatever name they chose for it, had not been seen by mortal eyes for millennia. The power of story was part of that immortality, the shared madness of folklore and whispered traditions. But it also emanated madness like sonar, pinging off weaker minds. It shared its dreams, to any who would listen, and those dreams were all the creature had to communicate. It had no words, after all, none that a mortal mind could hear, comprehend, and survive intact hearing.

And so mortals, as they are wont to do with things they do not and cannot understand, they projected their own desires onto the creature. Their hates, their fears, their dreams, their hopes. He became a symbol of absolute power, of destruction, of the end of the world, of the beginning of the next world.

Some of those worshippers followed the creature like lampreys, like parasites. They devolved from thinking, rational beings—or, at least, as rational and thinking as such unquestioning worshippers could be—into degenerate cannibals, more fish than human, hunched and bulbous, hungry and blind with rage. They were, perhaps, the truest of his followers, the closest to the truth of what the creature meant, what its purpose was.

In truth, no one would ever know what this great beast shuffled toward, what it wanted, what it needed. It ate if something was placed in front of it, but hungered for nothing. It walked toward where it was wanted, preternaturally sensing when the mad and the hungry called to it, whatever name they might have chosen to believe in, and that, perhaps, is why so many worshipped it as a god. For the simple reason that the monster came when called.

What few talk about, because few survive, is that the creature walks where it is called, and it eats what is put in front of it, and many of its would-be worshippers over the centuries had called this great beast down upon themselves, to their own ruin, and to the ruin of those around them.

And that, the dead soon learned, was what the creature wanted. To be called, to be loved, and to be fed.

Long ago, an immortal berserker, an Atlantean magician, an Amazon queen, and a child made of fire and sunlight drove the monster back into the sea. They harried it, burning its skin with magic and flame, and the waters ran black with the creature's hot, muddy blood. The fishlike followers hounded them, threw themselves onto the heroes' blades like sacrifices, until the trench that was Poseidon's Scar opened beneath them. With the Needle of the Moon and the Eye of Dreams, they weakened the creature, who was not, they knew, a god at all, but something else, something darker, something that could be driven off and stopped, if not destroyed.

The creature was mortally wounded, and descended into the

Scar, digging out a nest above the comforting warmth of elemental lava.

The heroes did not know, of course, that they'd driven the monster home. They couldn't. No one knew what went on within the inscrutable mind of this beast, where it came from, or why.

But there, in the darkness, the creature could dream. It could dream forever, its mind expanding through the cosmos, corrupting the thoughts of mortals for hundreds of years. It was never without followers, even when it had not been witnessed for generations upon generations, never without worshippers, and they gave it strength, gave it reason to dream. It slept within earshot of a tear in reality, and listened to the wail of mad gods across the planes existence. Its followers devolved further and further, living, eating, surviving in the darkness, passing into the veil beyond.

There they would have remained, until the end of the world, until the end of time itself. Until a weapon of war fell down upon the sleeping bulk of the monster, radiation and flame awakening it, sending out shockwaves through the psychic realm, becoming dreams in the minds of willing worshippers, ready to die for the monster.

Casual believers woke with fear in their hearts. The truly faithful knew their time had come. Madmen rose raving, and those who had not quite been mad found themselves falling rapidly over the edge of sanity. All across the world, eyes turned toward the ocean, looking out across the deep black seas, looking for the One Who Walks, the Hungerer, the Great One, the Father of Monsters, the Star-Child, the Change-Bringer.

Some had waited all their lives for this. Some had been brought up hearing stories of this day on their grandfather's knee. Some had found tell of this creature in a book and longed for the renewal his return would bring.

None doubted their conviction. None were afraid. Their time had come.

The people of Fogarty's Folly were not the monster's only worshippers, nor his most fervent, nor even the most plentiful.

They had the terrible misfortune of simply being the closest.

The creature, as old as time, strode on squat, bent legs across the Atlantic. It tore the guts from a transport ship loaded with new cars, which spilled into the ocean like playing cards. With an errant shoulder, it tipped over a cruise ship, sending a meal of thousands of people—some of whom woke the night before with the strangest dreams, of a many-eyed creature moving slowly toward them—to the waiting jaws of the creature's followers.

It left destruction in its wake, a mindless, sleepy, slovenly path.

But the closer it drew to Fogarty's Folly, the more its sleep-numbed mind began to wake. And the more it knew what it wanted, and what it was put here to do.

Chapter 47: Red water

I hope this never gets old, Yuri thought as he cut through the water like a knife.

He had grown more and more accustomed to his man-shark hybrid form, the transformation more natural, the massive bulk and strength it gave him less intimidating and awkward. But still, slicing through the ocean as if born to it gave him the same thrill it had the first time he'd done it without fear. He was growing to love these new powers, even if they made him a monster, even if they made him feel like an alien among the people he used to be just like.

Yuri darted forward, faster than the Amazon attack ship, tireless and strong, feeling more at home in the deep, lightless ocean than anywhere he'd been in a very long time.

Ever since he lost his father, Yuri had been intimidated by the sea. Not afraid, exactly. Maybe a little fearful, but it was a healthy respect, the sort of respect one learns through tragedy and loss. His mother had tried to make him truly afraid, and she had a good and honest reason for it. Yuri didn't hold it against her. She'd lost the love of her life to the ocean after all, and did not want to lose her son.

He wondered what his mother would think of him now, like

this. Horrified, certainly. He was her only baby, and now he transformed into a monster of teeth and muscle and fin, a nightmare on legs. But at the same time, he thought, I've become something the sea can't kill. Yes, there are bigger, more terrifying monsters than me in the ocean, but the sea itself welcomes me with open arms. It calls me home. I'm a part of it in a way no ordinary person can ever truly be.

He thought about the lessons Whitetip had taught him, the way being a were-shark had opened his senses in superhuman ways. He could sense the Amazon ship easily behind him, the way it sent ripples through the water, disturbing the surface. He heard whale calls, miles upon miles away. Somewhere in the distance, a creature splashed in the water, at play or hunting he couldn't tell, but he knew it was there, and he could feel its vibration, its heartbeat. It was a profoundly magical experience, Yuri knew, a way of being a part of a world that once threatened him. It felt almost spiritual. No, not nearly. It *is* spiritual. Nearly dying to the were-shark bite and surviving had become a spiritual experience. He felt like a part of something greater, and he sensed that his role in it was not that of a monster, but of a protector. This is my world now, and I must defend it. That's my job.

And I like my job.

He plunged ahead, in his element, arms at his side to allow his powerful shark tail to propel him forward. That had taken some getting used to, Yuri remembered, as hours in the water with Whitetip flashed through his mind. His human mind wanted to kick, or to paddle with his arms. I mean, I never had a tail before, right? How was I supposed to know?

But once he became accustomed to it, he wondered how he ever lived without a tail.

Yuri's reverie was broken when one of his superhuman senses picked up on something instantly recognizable: he smelled blood in the water.

He couldn't rely on sight much in this form—it was fine, but no better or worse than his human sight, which wasn't great to begin with. But his sense of smell was overpoweringly strong in this shape, especially in the water. And blood was something his nature wanted him to find. He slowed his pace, determining which direction the blood was coming from, and with more caution than before, he turned his path toward it.

It didn't take long to find what he was looking for.

The water ran dark with blood, an overlay of the vile tang of man-made chemicals and fuel in the water as well, turning Yuri's stomach even more than the gore. Bodies, in various states of destruction, littered the water, floating like ghosts in the darkness. He didn't have to get close to be able to tell what they looked like. Eaten, he knew. Torn apart. If I get close enough, Yuri thought, I'd see those needle teeth marks all over them. No question about it.

The whole scene created a macabre dance of corpses and debris. The ship—what looked to be a cruise liner, Yuri guessed, though he'd never been on a cruise in his life—hung in the background like a ghostly upside-down painting. Like every other time they'd encountered victims of the swarm of fish-men, Yuri found he was shockingly unconcerned about an attack—the creatures seemed to devour and run, never remaining to gorge themselves on their handiwork.

But they're close, Yuri knew. He could smell them in the water. A thick cloud of old meat and spastic motions, the sniveling, snarling sound of their alien language. Very close. Terrifyingly close.

He tried to take in the whole scene, the pale light filtering in from above, highlighting how red the water truly was, the faceless bodies, the overturned ship listing at the surface like so much thrown-away garbage.

I don't know how to stop them, he thought. They're worse than me, eating machines working their way across the ocean, piranhas on legs, a relentless cloud of murder. I might survive, but the others? How do we fight something like this?

Maybe this is how the world ends after all, he thought. And then he raced back to the Amazon ship.

He transformed back to human form seconds before arriving, knowing that his were-shark form made the Amazons anxious and preferring to not risk being stabbed as he climbed on board. Several of the warriors still stared, making Yuri self-conscious as he scrambled to find his shirt and glasses. Artem trotted up from below, clearly hearing the splash of Yuri's arrival.

"You don't look happy," Artem said.

"They murdered a cruise ship," Yuri said.

"An entire cruise ship," Artem said.

"Looks that way."

"This needs to end," Artem said. "This is obscene. The loss of life. We need to stop this."

"Not arguing there," Yuri said. "But if you have any suggestions about how to make that happen, I'm all ears, because dude, they ate a cruise ship."

"You said that."

"Usually cruise ships do the eating. This is some sort of horrific meta joke about human food consumption."

"You look a little frazzled, Yuri," Artem said. "Are you okay?"

"As okay as I can be considering I just swam through a sea of corpses," Yuri said. "Artem, I… what are you looking at?"

Artem had stopped paying attention and was looking just past Yuri's shoulder into the distance. Yuri turned to join him and released a string of swears.

"Tell me you see that," Artem said.

"Is that island moving?" Yuri said.

In the uncomfortably close distance, a mound jutted out of the water. It was somewhat round, like a dome, dark, like stone, and covered in a greenish moss.

But it wasn't an island. It was moving, steadily, away from them.

"That's its gods-damned head," Artem said.

"Pretend I'm clever enough to make a *Jaws* joke here," Yuri said. "I've got nothing."

"Its head is bigger than our ship," one of the Amazon warriors said.

"Yuri, do you see…" Artem said.

"I see them," Yuri said.

Artem drew both swords from his hips and shouted to the crew.

"Prepare to be boarded," he said, pointing across the bow. "We have incoming fish-men."

Orithyia joined them on the deck then as well, carrying a sword and buckler, wearing a lightweight armor. Yuri could tell by the way it was strapped on, much like the other Amazon warriors wore, that the armor could be cut lose if she fell into the water. Having seen what happened to the passengers of the cruise ship, Yuri had started to think that drowning might be a viable option to the other ways they could die today.

"Show no mercy, Amazons, for you shall be shown none," Orithyia said. "Fight for your lives this day."

She shot Yuri a shockingly warm smile, and then turned to her son.

"I'm proud we had the chance to fight side by side, at least once in this lifetime," Orithyia said.

"Whatever our differences, mother," Artem said, his eyes dark, his mouth a humorless line across his face. "I will fight today to make sure this is not our only battle together."

And just before Yuri gave into his were-shark rage, transforming into the beast that would let him fight like hell unleashed, he had a single thought:

Hey, they talked to each other while I was gone, Yuri thought. I did one good deed at the end of the world, right?

Chapter 48: A town gone mad

"What do you mean, he's indisposed?" Simon Yee hissed into his phone, resisting the urge to start yelling. "Sam Barren is never indisposed. I swear there's like three of him. How is he not available?"

"I can't reach him right now," the agent on the other end of the line, a guy named Rourke who Simon hadn't met face to face before, said apologetically. "Can I take a message?"

"You can take a message and pass it up the chain of command right now," Simon said.

"There's really no reason to be nasty about this, man," Rourke said.

"I'm in a town, alone, where we've now got a cult worshipping fish-people who I just watched eat one of their priests," Simon said. "I think that constitutes an emergency."

"That doesn't sound good," Rourke said.

"It isn't good. It's really not good. It's the opposite of good," Simon said. "So if you could find it in your heart to somehow get this information to Barren or anyone else who can mobilize some assistance from the Department ASAP, that would be wonderful."

"I'll do everything I can," Rourke said. "Just... stay safe, I guess?"

"That is the general plan," Simon said, knowing that to be both unlikely and untrue. He hung up.

Simon and Clarissa had made their way to the apartment building's rooftop to get a better view of what was happening in the town below. The bonfire had begun to burn with a new, greenish light, and the number of human-shaped shadows gathering there increased every few minutes. The town itself seemed mostly asleep, though, unaware of the growing danger.

"I swear all I wanted to do was not need to take a train to work in the morning," Clarissa said. "That's the only reason I volunteered to open a stupid chain coffee shop in this stupid town."

"I really thought this was going to be a quiet assignment," Simon said. He'd been crouching, trying to stay out of sight, but rose to his full height to get a better look at the town. What he saw turned his stomach.

"People are heading for the water," he said.

Clarissa, not quite willing to stand all the way up, knelt beside the waist-tall wall of the roof deck and followed Simon's gaze. Below, they could see people gathering, clustering in groups before walking downtown and continuing to the shore.

"They look like they're headed to a party," Clarissa said. She wasn't wrong. Simon could see people hugging each other, grasping hands excitedly, leaning in to talk. They look like they're on their way to Christmas Mass, he thought.

But they also knew they were up to something, he could tell. None of the people gathering carried flashlights or candles, any light source at all. They left their homes and businesses dark. Whatever they were doing, they didn't want any sign of their presence. He checked his watch. Three a.m. Most of the town remained asleep. He watched curiously as several police cruisers left the station near town hall and head toward the hilly main drag out of town, where they split up. Curious what they were up to, he picked one cruiser, its white paint job easy to spot even in the distance, and saw it turn and park perpendicular to the street leading up a main road to the highway.

"They're blocking the roads into town," Simon said.

"Or out of town. They're locking everyone in," Clarissa said. "We're going to be fish food. Literally fish food. Oh, man, Simon, I am a morbid person and I have thought a lot about how I don't want to die, and being eaten by fish-men didn't even cross my mind as one to put on the 'nope' list."

"I was going to tell you to take my car and get out of town, but…"

"Well, you missed that opportunity to be chivalrous," Clarissa said.

"There's got to be something we could do," Simon said.

"Run through the woods?"

"I mean save the people here who aren't volunteering to be worms on a hook."

"We could go banging on doors and try to get everyone up and out," Clarissa said. "I mean it's inefficient, but maybe if we cause enough of a panic, at least some people will escape."

"You really are morbid," Simon said.

"Thank you," Clarissa said.

Simon rubbed his forehead just above his eyebrows, trying to drive off the makings of a massive tension headache.

"The town does have that automated calling system, where they call every house in town that's signed up for alerts," he said.

"The ones for school closings and snow emergencies," Clarissa said. "I mean, that might not get everyone, but it could get to a lot."

"It'll also alert whoever is in the cult that we're onto them, but at this point, anything we can do to save people helps," Simon said. "It's worth the risk."

"Except," Clarissa said, pointing toward town hall.

Gathered in front of the tall, church-like structure, they could see a swarm of people, wearing what appeared to be the same style of cultist robes they'd seen on others in town. Maybe two dozen citizens, gathered in a semicircle, as if in prayer.

"Is that the town administrator standing on the steps?" Clarissa said.

Simon felt his heart sink. He'd met the town administrator and the man had seemed remarkably level-headed. Now he wore a robe and, as Simon watched, pulled on a cap or hood that looked like a poorly stitched squid.

"He's bought the funny farm too," Simon said. "Maybe if we..."

"Simon," Clarissa said, softly, her voice taking on a heavy tension far beyond the anxiety and fear it held before. She looked out over the water, past the bonfires, at the open ocean.

Simon trained his eyes to what Clarissa had seen and he felt his guts turn to hot acid.

"That can't be possible," he said.

But Simon had seen strange things in his role with the Department. He had a normal human's capacity for fear, but he was not inclined to hallucination or exaggeration. He tended, for better or for worse, to see things for what they were.

Rising out of the water was a head the size of a moving van, mounted on massive, sloping shoulders. Thirteen eyes blinked, never in unison, each a uniform glowing red and gold, but different sizes, like a child's drawing. Some sort of beard hung from its face, masking its features, everything a gleaming, wet green-black in the moonlight. It was impossible to judge the size of the thing, not from here, but Simon guessed its shoulders had to be the length of two city buses end to end.

And it was headed straight for Fogarty's Folly.

"Tell me you're seeing this, too," Clarissa said. "I need to know I haven't lost my mind."

"I see it," Simon said.

"What are we going to do, Simon?" Clarissa said.

Simon took a sharp breath and looked down at the town. He pulled his phone from his pocket, wondering if Sam Barren, head of the Department, was deploying help right now. The last piece of his Department training kicked in.

Don't die in a fight you can't win. You are the watcher. Escape if you can to warn the others. Don't let what you know die with you if you can.

"We're going to run for it," he said.

Chapter 49: Fight for your life

Artem danced across the deck of the ship, his blades never lacking a target.

The fish creatures—long limbs, sharp claws, infinite rows of teeth—were everywhere, and for each one he cut down, another climbed over the rails and onto the ship. Artem didn't bother with the niceties of civilized combat. Each swing of his words was meant to kill with maximum efficiency, his only goal to avoid hitting a friendly target.

The Amazons fought like hell as well, each with her weapon of choice, be it spear or sword, axe or bow. One Amazon had climbed the main mast and was, sniper-like, driving arrow after arrow through the skulls of the monsters, one shot, one kill, over and over again.

Another, spinning a spear like a baton, found her weapon trapped in the guts of one creature, and before she could draw the daggers at her hip another fish-man set upon her, sinking needle-like teeth into her shoulder. She cried out, more in anger than in pain, but Artem saw crimson blood splatter to the deck, brighter and thinner than the brackish sludge that poured from the creatures' bodies. He wove his way to her side, beheading the attacking monster while its jaws were still clamped on the

Amazon's shoulder, and Artem stood over her until she could climb to her feet. Her right arm hung useless at her side, but she slashed at onrushing beasts with her left, a dagger held in a reverse grip.

Another monster grabbed the wounded warrior from behind, but fell aside as a violent clang rang out. Artem's mother, a spray of fish blood across her face, bashed the monster back on its heels with her shield and ran it through.

"We need to get into formation," she said. "We can't keep fighting them from all sides."

Orithyia was right—the attack had happened so fast, and the ship was so narrow, that the Amazons had found themselves cut off from each other. With only a half-dozen warriors in addition to Orithyia and Artem, fighting off the ever-growing horde seemed impossible.

Then Artem heard a roar.

When the fish men first attacked, Yuri had disappeared, knocked from the deck by several charging creatures. That didn't last long, though. Now in full-on were-shark form, Yuri became a force of nature. He fought without discipline, without skill, without grace, but those long arms, tipped with dagger-like claws at the end of each hand, tore the fish men to ribbons effortlessly. No skill was needed, Artem thought, when you were an unstoppable killing machine. He watched half in horror and half in pride as the once-fearful, once jokester of a man grabbed a fish creature in his jaws, crunched down on it without a blink of hesitation, then threw the creature into the ocean, a flopping, limp carcass. Yuri's tail—so ridiculous here out of the water, became a battering ram, knocking a row of attackers off the deck with such force Artem heard bones snap like twigs.

Artem saw a particularly large fish-man climb on board just behind one of the other Amazons, a golden-haired fighter with a scar down one cheek whose name he never learned. He went to help her but knew even with his speed he'd never get there in time.

"Yuri!" Artem said, pointing to the creature with one of his swords. Yuri didn't hesitate for a second. The shark-man barreled through a dozen fish-men, stomping several to death just by striding on them, snapping another's neck with a backhand. The blonde Amazon cried out as the fish-man's claws raked down her back, but before the beast could strike a killing blow, his head went soaring into the ocean like a ball, skipping several times, as Yuri decapitated it with a swing of his mighty, clawed hand.

The Amazon, despite the pain of the injury, despite the battle going on around her, favored Yuri with a radiant smile, the sort of gleeful grin Artem only saw in combat. It was the grin of a survivor running on adrenaline.

The water churned pink with blood, and the deck was slick and slimy with it as well. Artem gutted a fish-man who ran at him with a quick slice of both swords like inverted scissors, and another he impaled through the heart. Yuri helped the injured Amazon join Artem and the others in the center of the deck, where they formed a protective circle. Someone, one of the Amazons Artem regretted, in the heat of battle, never learning the name of, handed her quiver of arrows up to her fellow fighter on the mast so she could continue to take out fish-men at a distance.

One of the Amazons cried out in surprise as she was yanked from her feet, landing on the deck with a bone-rattling bang. A wounded fish creature had her ankle and was trying, despite its own grievous wounds, to drag her into the ocean. Orithyia drove her sword through the creature's skull and helped her sister-in-arms to her feet. The fallen Amazon winced, her leg bent in a way that told Artem she'd injured it in the fall.

He felt something trickle down from his forehead and reached up to touch his skin. He'd apparently taken a blow to the head somewhere in the fight, and blood ran from his scalp down to his eyebrow. He smeared it away and readied himself. There'd be time for injuries later. Now, he knew, it was question of survival.

"We can't keep this up forever," Artem said.

"Then we die on this ship together," one of the Amazons said.

"I'd rather live to fight another day, thank you," Artem said.

Even as they spoke, Artem heard a rhythmic thumping from below deck. He could hear wood splintering and snapping. The bastards are trying to sink us, he realized. That's the sound of them battering the hull, trying to tear a hole in our ship.

Even as he said this, he felt the deck begin to tilt, just a bit, then more, the port side listing lower in the water. He rocked on his heels to keep his balance and watched as Yuri, with shocking gentleness, put a hand on an Amazon's shoulder who was about to tip over until she could regain her footing. One of the injured Amazons went to one knee, giving up any attempt at remaining standing, her face a mask of pain. It was the one who had been bitten, Artem saw. Her skin was pale and clammy, her eyes sunken. She's lost a lot of blood. We don't have much time.

"There's got to be a way to slow these things down," Artem said. Maybe we take the fight to them below the water, he thought. "How damned many are there?"

Artem shot a look to Yuri.

"Did you get a count when you were underwater?"

Yuri shrugged his massive, silvery-gray shoulders.

"Math? When I'm like this?" he said, his voice comically low and garbled by the transformation. Artem realized how disconcerting it was to hear Yuri speak while in shark-man form and made a mental note to never ask him to do so again. It was, even in the heat of battle, skin-crawling.

"Then we fight until they stop coming, or until the last of us falls," Artem said. He adjusted the grip on his swords as another wave of fish-men crawled aboard, hissing and showing their teeth.

The entire mass of fish-men exploded in a flash of blue electrical light, splattering Artem, Yuri, and several of the Amazons in gritty fish guts.

"Gods damn you, Barnabas," Artem said, but he couldn't help the rising joy in his heart as he saw the *Endless*, its bigger watercraft looking almost bulky compared to the Amazon attack ship, drift into view from the darkness. Barnabas stood on the deck, his ridiculous flintlock pistol magical focus held out dramatically, glittering with the aftereffects of his spell. The pistol-shaped wand flashed again, and for the second time, a row of fish-men were all but wiped from existence, a merciless magical energy tearing them apart.

Echo leapt from the deck of the *Endless* to the Amazon ship, now carrying a long, moon-white spear instead of her trident. She used it to end the lives of several fish creatures without missing a beat and then, with a strength that still shocked Artem despite having seen her do such things over and over again, pulled on a rope she'd tied to her belt, dragging the smaller ship closer to the *Endless*.

"We're sinking," Artem said.

"I noticed," Echo said, grinning. She turned to Orithyia. "Get your injured to our ship. I don't think we have the ability to stop this one from going under."

Orithyia wordlessly ordered her warriors to carry the wounded as she herself stood ready to defend their escape. Artem joined her, as did Echo, and Barnabas' magic flashed a third time, this time at the water, where the surface sprayed with an explosive force. Bodies of fish-men floated to the surface like the remnants of an uncared-for aquarium.

"Leave me," the severely wounded Amazon said as her peers tried to find a way to move her to the taller ship. The archer, perched above, provided cover for her sisters as they crawled across the rope Echo brought with her, picking off monstrous amphibian arms as they reached up from the deep to grab at them.

"No one is going to be left behind," Artem said. He barely had the words out of his mouth when Yuri scooped the wounded Amazon up like a baby in one arm and jumped with shocking, almost comedic, grace from one ship to the other. He gently laid her down on the deck and jumped back, his weight causing the attack ship to tilt even more.

Artem and Orithyia covered for the archer as she dropped down to the deck and made her way to the *Endless*. Finally, mother and son made their escape, with Echo—also capable of the same superhuman leap Yuri had made, but far more grace—the last to leave. They watched in horror as the fish-men began to tear the smaller ship to splinters, looking for prey that was no longer there.

"Now, Muireann," Barnabas said, and Artem felt something akin to a soft breeze blow through his hair. Everything around him took on a strange stillness, the sounds of battle distant and soft.

"What was that?" Artem said to Echo.

Before Echo could answer, Muireann, walking quickly down from the foredeck, spoke up.

"It's an invisibility spell," she said. "I can't hold it up forever, but it's strong enough to give us a chance to catch our breath."

Artem put a hand warmly on Barnabas' shoulder.

"She's a better magician than you are, isn't she?" Artem said, smirking.

"You're really going to make fun of the guy who just blew up two dozen man-eating monsters to save your handsome arse?" Barnabas said, holstering his flintlock.

"Tell me you were successful," Artem said. Beside him, Yuri let his shark-form drop, returning to his normal shape and size. Yuri spit on the deck.

"Tell *me* I didn't eat one of those things," Yuri said.

"You don't remember?" Artem asked.

"Everything's sort of a blur after I got knocked off the ship," he said.

"That's alarming," Echo said, holding out the spear in her hand to Artem. "The Needle of the Moon."

"So you have the Eye and the Needle," Orithyia said.

"Yeah, but what do we do with them?" Yuri said, asking the question on everyone's mind.

"I think... I think we have to kill that," Echo said. Artem turned to where Echo was looking.

In the distance, a massive form, a bald, green-black head atop slopping, humanoid shoulders, was rising higher and higher from the ocean. Water and seaweed poured from its skin, which even at this distance appeared wrinkled and thick, like an elephant's. Just beyond the giant form, Artem could see electric lights. A small seaside town, right in its path.

"Well, then," he said. "I think we need a plan."

Chapter 50: But how do they work?

Echo crouched down on the deck, holding the Needle of the Moon upright in her left hand. She looked over the disaster that was her crew, covered in gore, exhausted, but not afraid. Yuri had transformed back into his normal self, but clearly had lost his glasses along the away, and it threw Echo off a bit to see him without his specs.

"So you've got the two MacGuffins," Yuri said, tightening the strings on his pants as he tried to get comfortable in his own skin again. "But how do they work?"

"No idea," Echo said.

"Actually," Barnabas said, sitting down on the steps leading up to the foredeck. "I can shed some light on that."

"Really," Artem said, his tone teetering on droll. "And you're choosing to enlighten us now?"

"Why tell you until we had the gear?" Barnabas said. "Besides, if I told you, I'd have to admit how I got the information."

"Why am I afraid I'm not going to like how you got this?" Echo said, rubbing the bridge of her nose to stave off a headache.

Barnabas turned to Orithyia and gave her a sincerely apologetic look.

"I snuck into the Keepers' library," he said. "Sorry."

"If we weren't in the middle of the ocean fighting for our lives, I'd be angry with you," the general said, her voice strained. "But just this once, I'll let it go. Tell us what you know."

Barnabas drew the Eye of Dreams from inside his coat, the amber-colored sphere seeming to look at each person on the deck in turn.

"This is called the Eye of Dreams for a reason," Barnabas said. "It can be used, at a spellcaster's direction, to force a being of great power into a slumber without end. To become caught in the Eye of Dreams. Which is what happened the first time this creature was defeated."

"It's a prescription sleeping pill for evil gods," Yuri said. "I dig it."

"I feel like there's a 'but' in there somewhere," Artem said.

"Well, the creature in question can fight it," Barnabas said. "Which is why, in that first fight, the wizard didn't just, y'know, hocus pocus, zippity doo da, put a hex on that thing and knock him out for a thousand years."

"He needs to be distracted," Echo said.

"Yes," Barnabas said. He pointed at the Needle of the Moon. "Which is where that comes in."

"I'm going to poke him until he gives up?" Echo said.

Barnabas cocked his head curiously.

"Y'know, that's not entirely inaccurate," he said. "But that's a mythical weapon. It was made by hands not of this world. So, when you strike with that, particularly if you strike a creature of evil or dark intent, it causes all the more harm."

"Again, I think there's a 'but' you haven't said yet," Artem said. Barnabas nodded.

"Right. You can't just goose his rump with it. You're not going to like this part."

"Do I like any part?" Echo said. "There's an ocean full of man-eating fish-men a hundred yards from us and we're about to try to kill Squidzilla with a marble and a stick. There is no part of this I like, so you might as well pile on."

Barnabas winced.

"You're going to want to poke the creature in the brain with that," he said.

"I'm going to want to what it in the where?" Echo said. She whipped her head around to look at the monster, still stomping slowly toward the coast, rising taller and taller out of the water with each step.

"In the brain," Barnabas said. "Or at least that's what worked last time. The Eye demands the creature sleep; the creature, in turn, uses its psychic will to fight against the Eye. A hot poker to the brain is a really effective way to put him back on his heels during a psychic duel."

"He's enormous," Echo looked up at the creature's head, towering high above. "What's that, a two-hundred-foot climb?"

"Two hundred now," Artem said. "And rising."

"So we need to move quickly," Orithyia said.

Echo's mouth hung open, half in frustration, half with the mind-blown realization she was going to have to scale a titanic monster and stab him in the brain.

"Well, okay then?" Echo said questioningly. "I guess I'll start climbing?"

"What about the fish-men?" Yuri said. "Won't they try to stop us?"

"What's this 'us' you speak of," Echo said. "You're not going up there."

"Oh, yes I am," Yuri said. "First of all, I basically can't die. Second of all, while I was never much of a climber, I happen to think that because my hands grow what amounts to a pickaxe at the tip of each finger when I transform, so when you need to climb a mountain of meat, I might be pretty useful getting you up there."

"That is possibly the grossest thing you've ever said, and you are absolutely not wrong," Echo said.

"Did you just say a mountain of meat?" Barnabas said.

"I did," Yuri said.

"God, I missed you, you weird bastard," Barnabas said.

"I'll go as well," Artem said. When Echo started to protest, he cut her off. "I can climb better than any of you, I can fight with either hand, and I am really enjoying killing these fish-men. Let me be your rear guard, Echo. You need to focus on climbing, not fighting."

"I'll go as well, I..." Orithyia said, then let out a sharp gasp and clutched her side.

"General," one of the Amazons said, putting a hand quickly to Orithyia's abdomen. Her fingers came away bloody. "You're injured."

"It's fine," Orithyia said. It was only then that Echo saw the bags beneath her eyes like bruises. The dark stain to her armored pants she assumed before was just seawater.

Echo was shocked to hear Artem's voice. It was something she hadn't heard from him in a long time, soft and gentle, worried.

"Mom," he said. "When did this happen?"

"During the fight on the ship," she said. "Look at all of you. You're all bloodied as well. There are others in far worse..."

She let out a sharp cough then, and Echo could see from the way her body trembled that the general was masking a much worse injury than she let on.

"You'll never make it if you come with us," Artem said. He shot a look to Barnabas, who picked up on it instantly. My boys, Echo thought, the pride she felt in this ragtag group giving her a little bit of hope. They act like they hate each other, but the three of them have always looked out for the others.

"We need you here, general," Barnabas said.

"I can keep up this invisibility spell a little longer, but the moment our people disembark, we'll likely be spotted," Muireann said.

"Barnabas, bravado aside... without the three of us, can you repel an attack?" Echo said. "Don't give me your tough wizard routine. I see two Amazons too injured to fight, and you need to be able to cast whatever mojo you need to do with the Eye."

"We'll keep the ship safe," one of the Amazons said proudly

even as she wrapped a bandage around a nasty tear in her forearm.

"Echo, if the creatures come near the *Endless*, the ship will defend itself," Barnabas said. Something about his tone chilled Echo in a way she'd never experienced before.

"What do you mean, defend itself?" Echo said.

"This is a haunted ship, Echo. The spirits here are kind to us because we give them what they want. This ship is their only tether to the world they have departed from. If anything tries to hurt this ship, I pity the world of unearthly fury these restless spirits will inflict on them," Barnabas said.

"You sound like you're afraid of the ship," Artem said curiously.

"I'm terrified of this ship," Barnabas said. "Have you ever noticed how *nice* I am to it?"

"I have had more strange conversations since I met the group of you than I've had in total my entire life," Muireann said. "And I'm not even human."

"So, captain, what are your orders?" Barnabas said.

"I guess we bring the ship around and try not to die," Echo said.

"Good plan. Very inspirational. I can see why you're in charge," Yuri said.

Chapter 51: Punch Cthulhu in the face

The *Endless* sailed right up alongside the behemoth, seemingly undetected. Yuri had his doubts about that. He wondered if, somehow, those thirteen eyes they could see glowing hundreds of feet above them had seen the ship's approach and determined them to be a non-threat, just a bunch of lunatics in a wooden boat in a rush to die.

They were close enough to smell it now, the reek of rot, dead fish and vegetation, a musky, pungent animal stench that made his eyes water. It was the smell of something that bathed in death, that slept in filth, that was a part of the darkest of places. Yuri fought off a wave of nausea and studied the thick hide, now so close he could almost reach out and touch it. We really could climb it, he thought, looking at the uneven, wrinkled skin. There's no shortage of handholds. We'll be like bugs crawling up a human's leg.

"One upside," Yuri said. "That gut of his is pretty noticeable. We're not climbing a flat vertical surface. Good thing he doesn't work out."

"Your optimism is, as always, appreciated, if probably misplaced," Artem said. "Where do we even start?"

"I have an idea," Yuri said. He pulled off his shirt and began ripping it into strips.

285

"I'm almost afraid to ask where you're going with this," Echo said.

"Wrap these around your hands," Yuri said. "Make yourself gloves with the cloth."

"Oh," Echo said.

"Absolutely not," Artem said, instantly understanding. "Leave me my last shred of dignity, Yuri."

"I'll transform. The two of you hop on. I can at least get you part of the way up there," Yuri said. "Once we get over the ridge of his stomach, the ground will be flatter and you can climb without me, but this will at least get you a head start."

"This is a terrible idea," Artem said.

"But it'll work," Echo said. "You can carry us both?"

"I'm stupidly strong in shark form," Yuri said. He waited until both of his companions had wrapped their hands from wrist to fingertip. "Just be careful. My skin's like sandpaper when I transform."

"I figured that was what the hand wraps were for," Echo said. "We'll try not to get rug burn."

Yuri bowed his head and let the monster flow through him, feeling his muscles swell, his bones creak and pop, his jaw widen into a monstrous cavern. He doubled in size and weight, a hulking, beastly predator in his own right, tail casually swaying from side to side. He lowered his frame so that Echo and Artem could climb on his back, one on each side of his dorsal fin, and then, with a leap far easier than it should have been for a creature of his size, Yuri jumped from the edge of the ship to the side of the giant monster.

He landed with a disconcerting thud, but he was ready to react right away, claws on each hand spread wide to grab hold of the uneven, green-black flesh of the colossus. The flesh wobbled beneath him, but the creature itself did not seem to react to the intrusion, at least not immediately. Yuri dug the claws on his toes in as well, gaining better purchase, and he began to climb, only moderately encumbered by the weight of his friends.

Neither said a word. The stench of the creature was

overwhelming this close up; its blood was tacky, which, while uncomfortable, made the climb easier, letting Yuri get a better grip rather than slip.

Like an athlete climbing a rock wall in a gym, Yuri worked his way higher, trying not to think about what he was digging his hands into. Finally, the surface seemed to curve like a dome, becoming less vertical. He felt painfully far from the water, but dared not look down to see how far the plunge would be if he slipped.

"We've got company," Artem said.

"Don't let go yet," Echo said.

Finally, Yuri crested over the archway of the creature's stomach, providing his companions somewhere to put their feet. Strange, Yuri thought, that the creature hadn't done anything to stop them. Were they just insects to him? Were they nothing to bother with?

Or, Yuri realized, seeing a swarm of fish-men climb up over the creature's gut, he's going to let his parasites do the work for him.

"I've got this," Artem said, dropping from Yuri's back to stand on the creature's sloping gut. He drew both swords and assumed a fighting stance.

"Artem, don't," Echo said

"This is what I came along for the ride to do, Echo," Artem said. "Yuri, get her as high as you can. I'll buy you some time."

Yuri felt Echo grab hold of his shoulder tighter, but said nothing. Instead, Yuri continued this ascent, still shocked that the giant creature hadn't even looked at them. Below, he heard the sounds of Artem's blades whistling and striking true, but there was no looking back. Just climbing ever higher, one arm over the other. As a were-shark, Yuri felt almost tireless. At this height, carrying not one but two people, the lactic acid should have built up in his arms by now, his muscles should be aching, but no, he just kept going, as relentless as the predator he took his shape from.

It wasn't until they reached mid-chest that the creature finally turned its gaze on them.

That massive head swiveled around in what seemed like slow motion, long tendrils hanging from its chin and jaw, dripping seawater down in buckets. All thirteen eyes turned their focus on them, unblinking, staring for what felt like an eternity.

It lifted its right arm as if preparing to strike.

"Go!" Yuri said, his own voice sluggish and alien in this form, sounding nothing like himself. I sound like a monster when I look like this, he thought. But I can also fight like one.

Echo didn't wait: she hopped up onto Yuri's shoulder and sprang up higher, using the Needle for leverage, tossing herself even further up the creature's chest, where the skin faded from black-green to mucus yellow. She darted around a large curve of muscle and out of sight.

Now, Yuri thought, I can unleash the monster.

He opened his jaw wide and clamped down on the creature's skin, tearing a huge, bloody chunk from its stomach. Like a demon, he began clawing away, ripping and shredding. The giant being reached for him, but instead of punching, it grabbed hold, taking Yuri's oversized body in its grasp. He held on though, forcing the monstrosity to tear its own flesh as it peeled him away, sending a cloud of syrupy blood spraying out into the night sky. Its grip was immensely powerful, crushing Yuri's body beneath thick, bony fingers, but that just meant Yuri could turn his rage upon those fingers as well. With tooth and claw he tore into the creature's digits until he found yellow-white bone, covering himself in its blood, blood that smelled like seawater and death, blinding him as it got in his eyes.

It tried to change its grip, to crush him, to rip him in half, but Yuri could tell that the colossus could no longer properly move two of its fingers, the index finger—longer than Yuri was tall—down to the bone, the tendons torn to ribbons, leaving a useless digit barely hanging on. He kicked at its palm, feeling his clawed toes biting in, sending gouts of blood flowing like a fountain, and then, only then, did the creature finally make a sound. Yuri would carry that sound to his grave, a haunting, wordless bellow, the sound of madness and eternity, and he wondered if it would have driven him mad if he weren't half-insane already as the were-shark took over.

He acted on pure instinct now, slashing, tearing, brutalizing the immortal thing's entire hand. It occurred to Yuri in the distant space where his conscious mind hid while the shark rampaged that this was the hand of a god, that it had existed for millennia. And that he alone had scarred it, maimed it beyond recognition.

The air around him swirled with a powerful gust of wind, and Yuri could not understand what was happening at first. He expected to die, or to go unconscious or to plunge into the ocean, but where was this air coming from? What was happening?

The creature released its crushing, suffocating grip on Yuri and then he knew exactly what had happened.

He threw me, Yuri thought as he hurtled through the air like a cannonball. He couldn't kill me, so he threw me aside. I made an immortal monster panic and swat me like a bug.

He laughed silently as the world became a blur of stars and sea and ever approaching earth, and he laughed until the wind was knocked from his massive, indestructible body as it struck wood and dirt and stone.

And for a little while, everything went dark and silent.

Chapter 52: Holding the line

Artem watched his companions continue to scale the hide of the colossus and turned his attention to the gathering fish-men, scaling their master's skin like a defense system, like a disease. What were you, Artem thought, studying them in greater detail than ever before. Their bodies were more human than not, if you could look past their faces with those wide, impossible jaws. Their proportions were unnatural, large hands and feet made for swimming, long, lean limbs, but the musculature, the shape of them, they felt so familiar. And certainly, to his fighter's eye, they were vulnerable in all the ways humans were. He could see where his blade would pierce chest or skull easiest; creases where he knew pivotal tendons existed to maim or cripple them.

There were just shy of a dozen now, staring at him, hissing, but not moving forward. They weren't afraid, Artem sensed. No, they had a pack mentality, and they were looking for a way to surround him, hard to do with their monstrous god's sunken chest to Artem's back.

This is what life will always be like, he thought, loosening his arms, swinging his blades. This is the world we've been given. Stop a war, unleash a monster. Stop a monster and what then? Capture a thief, kill a father. Save a young woman in need of shelter, lose your lover to violence. Is this what a good life is? A cycle of punishments for doing the right thing?

I think Merrick knew that all along, he thought, remembering conversations with his husband before he fell. I wonder if that's why he never left the Island of Unwanted Things. He didn't want me to leave, either. Maybe he knew the world outside was nothing but cruelty to anyone who did the right thing. And still it found us. The world came to our door. And we did the right thing.

Artem assumed a battle stance and waited.

I wish I could stop myself from doing the right thing, he thought. But I can't.

"Come on!" he yelled at the fish-men, who startled at the sound of his voice, then charged at him, broad feet slapping against the fleshy surface beneath them.

Artem pushed all doubts out of his mind, as he always did in combat. He became nothing more than an instrument of his weapons, his eyes seeing every flaw in his opponents, blade striking home again and again. He opened one creature's throat with a flick of a sword, sending a spray of blood into the eyes of another. He used that distraction to take off its head with his other sword, spinning to plunge the first blade into the heart of a third monster.

They gathered closer around him, so Artem instinctually backed up toward the chest of the colossus. He kicked one fish-man in the knee, caving in its leg, and finishing it off with a sword to through the eye. With his off-hand he pierced yet another's torso, slicing upward as one would gut a fish. Feeling himself surrounded, he leveraged himself up and over, using the giant monster's wrinkled skin like steps, leaping behind the circle of white-gray fish-men.

He watched stoically as one of the living creatures began feasting on the remains of a dead one, but in the heat of battle, his repulsion was a distant thought in the back of his mind. Instead, he used the distraction to cave that creature's skull in from behind.

He slashed a sword across the back of one fish-man's legs, sending it to the ground; seeing it chomping and biting with its oversized mouth, Artem kicked it, sending the creature tumbling down the giant monster's belly and into the ocean below.

The fight began to blur then, becoming nothing more than the sound of sword through flesh until something racked across his back, between the facets of his armor, the pain shocking him into reality. He elbowed the attacker and felt needle teeth splinter against his arm. Something bit his forearm, but the bracers he wore took most of the impact. He used his free hand to stab the attacker through the eye, but the momentary grapple let yet another slash its claws across his thigh, white hot pain turning his vision bleary. He slammed the pommel of his sword down on that creature's hand, then removed that hand from its body with a flick of the wrist.

Artem stole a glance skyward, to see where his friends were. He watched, to his horror, as Yuri was snatched up by the car-sized hand of the great colossus, pulled away like a pest. Artem turned his attention back to his own attackers, who seemed to be increasing in number by the second. He saw red for a moment as something sharp pierced his shoulder, and then it began to rain, harder than before.

No, Artem realized, looking at the drops of moisture hitting his blades. Not rain. The black blood of the giant beast.

Above, he could see Yuri tearing the monstrous being's hand to shreds, sending down a storm of sticky blood. The fish-men looked up as well, as if shocked to see that their god could bleed. Some began to crawl up the monster's chest, pursuing Yuri, as if they could make the pain stop, as if they could save their deity.

And then the giant cried out in pain.

It pierced Artem's mind like a shard of glass, nearly causing him to drop his swords. Fighting it through pure discipline, he gritted his teeth and prepared to keep battling. But the fish-men, too, were not immune to the cry—they hunched and wailed, clutching vestigial ears as the maddening cry persisted.

Artem muscled his way out of the crowd. It didn't take long for the fish-men to begin to recover—as the cry subsided, they split their attention, half climbing higher, half still intent on killing Artem.

Artem backed up another step and felt the ground go out from under him. He slipped and fell, sliding down the monster's massive shelf of a gut, the surface oily and slick. He instinctually sheathed one sword and plunged the other into the great beast's hide to try to stop himself from falling, but something worse happened—with a grotesque ripping noise, the blade cut through the flesh, leaving a blood trail behind him as he slid.

Artem reached the point of no return, the curve where the monster's belly turned into a steep slide down into the ocean. Seeing the oncoming onslaught of fish-men headed his way, Artem did the only logical thing.

He let himself fall into the black waves of the ocean below.

Chapter 53: The ship will defend itself

"I don't know if you guys ever truly understand what I'm saying," Barnabas said to the ghosts all around him as they maneuvered the ship. "But if you can put a little distance between us and the giant walking garbage pile before Echo stabs him in the brain, that would be fantastic."

Barnabas had visions of capsizing as the enormous monster thrashed about, the Eye of Dreams rolling off the deck into the ocean. *If we can just get a few hundred feet at least, enough to give us some space in case Echo's brain surgery goes badly.*

He could barely make out what was happening, but remembered the spyglass he kept in his ridiculous pirate's coat and never used. He pulled the glass out and scanned the giant creature's body until he saw his friends making their ascent. They really did look like insects, he thought. *A caterpillar crawling up a pant leg or shirt. No wonder the creature is paying us no mind. We're insignificant.*

Then he saw the battle shift, watched as Echo—who he could barely make out by the gleam of the Needle of the Moon—darting off to one side, Yuri staying to do some damage and distract the creature. It wasn't until Yuri went to work the monster seemed to notice them at all, but when it did.

294

"Oh, no," Barnabas said.

Orithyia staying close and hugging her bleeding side, overheard him.

"What? What is it?" she asked.

"Yuri just got the big guy's attention."

Barnabas watched through the glass as Yuri—like a rabid animal in a trap—went to town on the massive hand that held him, blood and flesh flying away like confetti. He can't survive this, Barnabas thought. That thing's going to crush him, or eat him, or rip his arms and legs off like a psychopathic kid with a fly.

But then something happened. Barnabas couldn't make it out, exactly, but Yuri disappeared from view for a moment and then...

The cry was inhuman, deafening, piercing. It cut right through to the core of his mind. A deep roar, yet simultaneously a scream, equal parts rage and pain, coming from the colossus itself. It howled with a sound that transcended hearing, a psychic wave of agony. Barnabas watched helplessly as Yuri was flung away like garbage, tossed aside like scrap. He had no time to worry about his friend, though, nearly struck blind by the psychic backlash of the monster's screams, eyes watering as he looked to Muireann, who had dropped to her knees, clutching her ears at the sound.

Muireann, Barnabas thought. Oh, that's not good.

Barnabas drew his flintlock and put a hand on Orithyia's shoulder.

"We're going to be boarded. Ready your fighters," he said.

"How do you know?" the general said as Barnabas walked past her toward Muireann.

"Because that feedback we just heard scrambled our brains and I'm not sure Muireann's spell of invisibility is still doing any good," he said. He trotted to Muireann's side, who accepted his help getting back to her feet.

"It's not," she said, gulping loudly and wiping tears of pain from her eyes. "I'm sorry, I couldn't maintain it with that scream in my ears."

"No one could," Barnabas said. He drew the Eye of Dreams

from a satchel he wore at his side and looked up to the giant monster's shoulders, trying to spot Echo or Artem. "I wish I'd had time to teach you how to use this thing, in case I don't..."

"It's not the sort of magic I can use," Muireann said. "It takes a..."

"A scoundrel," Barnabas said, smirking at her.

"I was going to say a book-learned magician and not a natural, but if it makes you feel better, yes, I think it needs a scoundrel," she said, returning his smile. "I'll watch over you as best I can."

Barnabas caught sight of Echo, just a sliver of white in the darkness hundreds of feet above them.

"All of this might not matter if our fearless leader up there can't get in a good shot," he said.

Before he could say another word, he heard the scrambling of claws on wood and watched as the first of the fish-men climbed up over the rail. Barnabas took a shot with his pistol, a lesser spell than he'd used before, and a bolt of flame exploded against the fish-man and sent it falling backward into the sea.

"Here they come!" Barnabas said.

The Amazons sprang into action, evenly spread out across the deck to protect as much as they could. Their archer had taken up residence long before in the crow's nest with as many arrows as they could find, and was already picking off fish-men as their heads peered over the railing. But there were too many of them, of course, and no matter how many arrows she fired, no matter how many spells Barnabas sent exploding through the flintlock wand, it was only a matter of moments before the fish-men boarded.

Barnabas watched in horror as one of the Amazon warriors nearly had her throat ripped out, narrowly dodging a fatal blow and falling aside as Orithyia stepped in to defend her, standing over her fallen comrade. He himself picked off a fish-man who had begun trying to climb the main mast to reach the archer.

It's getting awfully crowded on this ship, Barnabas thought.

Then he felt a cool breeze drift past his cheek.

A second later one of the fish-men was thrown like a ragdoll into the ocean, soaring thirty feet in the air.

The ghosts of the *Endless* became very visible just then, and the battle began to turn. Barnabas could see one sailor, the pirate who had judged him earlier, choking a fish-man to death with a spectral chain. Another was run through by a ghost in a polo and khaki shorts, one of the racing sailors who inhabited the ghost ship. An old Navy man battered two of the creatures from the deck with a wooden hook. Other ghosts wrapped coils of ropes around the creatures' necks, stringing them up like Christmas decorations.

It was a horrific, violent, terrible sight, but Barnabas had never been so happy for the existence of vengeful spirits in his entire life.

"In any other circumstance, this would be the stuff of nightmares," Muireann said.

"Don't make the restless dead angry," Barnabas said, hacking down a fish creature that had made its way up the stern to the quarter deck. "I told you the ship would defend itself."

A Viking sailor—an old favorite of Barnabas', one of the first he saw on the ship when he first found it—ran past them, complete with a horned helm, a wild beard, a massive battle axe, charging into the fray like he had been waiting for centuries for this to happen. Perhaps he had.

"If we get through this, you're going to have to tell me how to thank them," Muireann said.

"Only one way," Barnabas said. "Never stop sailing."

Chapter 54: The Needle of the Moon

Echo went blind for a moment.

Not literally, she knew. Instinctually, she sensed her eyes still worked. But the pain in her head, a shattering scream through her synapses, turned the world dark, topsy-turvy, twisted her stomach into knots. She was close enough to feel the vibrations from the scream the giant beast uttered, the guttural roar in pain she knew, just knew, had to be Yuri's fault. As her vision returned, as the pain in her head turned to a dull ache, she smiled.

Only Yuri can make someone so mad their frustration strikes people blind.

It took a moment to get her bearings again. Somewhere on the shoulder, clinging for dear life to striated muscle. She hauled herself up, pushing away the sense of nausea and dull throbbing pain from the psychic attack she'd just weathered, and she felt her skin crawl as she realized exactly where she was.

She'd reached the creature's sloping, muscular shoulder. His trapezius muscle was ropy and powerful, but somehow lazy at the same time, a ski slope of a downward angle. From here, she could see the back of the creature's head. Bald, but with seaweed and old roots clinging to it, some even woven into the skin like piercings, attached over time, she imagined, while the creature slumbered for centuries. One large ear, more of a cavernous hole like a reptile's, stood out prominently, as well as thick veins like plumbing, pulsating with blood and stress.

She steadied herself with the gleaming white spear and prepared to charge. This is it, she thought. I'm like six billion feet above the water, and I'm going to stab some cheap Cthulhu knockoff in the skull with a magical spear and this is the stupidest thing I've ever done and man, I have done some stupid things in the past few months. I miss being normal. When do I get to be normal again?

She hefted the Needle of the Moon, tempted to throw it like she would her trident, but the idea of missing, or worse, having it not penetrate the skin and bone and bounce off, falling to the ocean below, terrified her. She made sure the chain Grimmin had given her was tethered to it, then bounced on her legs as if preparing to run a race, and took aim, intending to charge for the base of the creature's skull.

But then it turned and looked at her.

And Echo saw into oblivion.

Thirteen eyes stared at her, eyes that had seen millennia traverse in front of it, eyes that had watched the destruction of land masses, of entire cultures and species and people, eyes that had consumed knowledge and forgotten it. Eyes that had witnessed the world change a million times over and slept through half of it. Those thirteen eyes blinked at her, and Echo saw that this was no unthinking beast, no ravenous creature with no desire other than to consume and destroy, but was something else; something smarter, something far more dangerous and malevolent than she had ever given it credit for.

She saw a hellscape in those eyes, and she knew now why those creatures in the water below worshiped this monstrosity. There was eternity there, and immeasurable power, and something unexplainable, a calling that she felt in her core, in her soul. But it didn't want her, and she didn't want it either. The voice repulsed her, turned her stomach, and she sensed in those eyes that this was a being, not a creature but an entity, that wanted nothing more than to see the end of things. This was the end in every story, the dreams that never wake, the darkness we fear waits for us at the end of all things.

And it was looking right at her.

Echo didn't know why she did it, but she yelled just then, some incoherent challenge. She thought it was nonsense, that she was just stringing together syllables like a madwoman, but no, she realized, it was a language, the old Atlantean tongue.

Somehow, gazing into the abyss, the genetic memory she carried with her, spoke through her. The same things that let her breathe beneath the waves and fight with a ferocity that came from the past of her people and not the present of her training. The old souls that passed through all Atlanteans, she tapped into that, not deliberately. It gave her a courage she didn't know she had, didn't know she needed in this very moment. Something in that shared past had seen what this creature could do, the death it could bring, and it told her to strike. She heard a voice in her head, an old man's voice, and she knew, knew right then, it was the Atlantean wizard from the story of this creature's last defeat, offering his courage, telling her she was braver than he ever was.

The monster fully turned its attention to her now, red-gold eyes burning. The drooping beard covering its mouth came to life, not seaweed or hanging flesh as she suspected but grasping things, like thick vines, squid-like arms, whipping around with a flexibility that hid how powerful they were. Echo could hear the muscles in them stretch and groan like steel cables in the wind, creaking violently. As they lifted, she saw the monster's mouth, it's true mouth, a lamprey's circular maw with row after row after row of endless teeth, a meat grinder that stank of death and decay.

Again, Echo fought to maintain her consciousness, to keep herself sane, to stay focused. The tendrils around its mouth reached for her and she instinctually swatted them away with the Needle, its long, shining blade hacking those grasping arms from the root, sending them falling away like cut weeds.

She felt the creature shift again, its shoulder moving beneath her feet, and she saw, out of the corner of her eye, one massive hand—mangled beyond comprehension, but still useful, still a blunt weapon it could strike her down with, rising to smash down upon her head. The tendrils blocked her from getting any closer to the head itself, a wall of whirling arms. I'm not fast enough to get through this, she thought, I'm not agile, I need to fly...

Above her, the night sky broke, just a sliver of light in the black, black clouds. The moon filtered through, a crescent among the stars, perfect and bright, like a scythe. She felt the Needle come to life in her hand, warming at the touch of the moonlight, as if the weapon had waited for this for centuries.

The creature bowed its head down to look at her once more, closer, and she knew. She knew it was admiring her, a worthy adversary, another fool it would consume and dream about when it slept. Just another fool of a mortal who thought it could stop the wheels of eternity from spinning.

Echo unclipped the Needle from her chain and inhaled, focusing like an Olympic athlete, holding the Needle of the Moon like a javelin.

She reared back, and she threw.

The spear burst into a streak of white arcane energy, a splash of blinding brightness that obliterated the shadows all around them. She heard a sound, a hissing tear, as though the blade cut through more than just the air, as if sound and time and space suddenly meant nothing. A crescent followed it, an arcing silvery blade of light, reflecting everything and nothing at once, splitting the space between Echo and the creature's hungry eyes and mouth.

The Needle of the Moon struck true.

The blade pierced the creature's central eye, an explosion of red and black and white and gold, and the spear kept going, burying itself until the blade disappeared. It disappeared into the skull of the colossus, driving it back with a forceful blow, as if Echo's throw had been a punch from a fist the creature's own size. Its head snapped back, and once again Echo heard that terrible howl of pain, worse this time, not just pain but something deeper, a soul-crushing despair, a cry of defeat and surrender and rage. The monster's body twisted and wrenched, sending Echo tilting and falling. She dug her hands into the wrinkled skin, trying to regain her footing, but now the monstrosity, driven mad by pain and rage, flung its arms desperately about, trying to destroy an enemy it could not see.

Echo looked to the water below, hundreds of feet beneath her.

I hope that light show was enough for Barnabas to know it's his turn, she thought.

She saw that mangled hand once again searching for her and she knew there was nothing more she could do. Like a champion diver, she leapt from the great beast's shoulder and shot like an arrow to the ocean below, where darkness awaited her.

Chapter 55: The Eye of Dreams

The sky lit up like a phosphorous explosion and Barnabas decided that had to be the sign he was looking for.

He'd always been what he considered a combat magician, someone who could stay focused on his spells in terrible, distracting conditions, but the situation on the *Endless* was a bit above and beyond the ordinary. Ghosts howled and wailed as they defended the only home they had left in this world, and that alone, would be enough to throw off Barnabas' concentration. I've been on this bloody ship for years and they've never made a sound and now they decide to start crying like the stuff of nightmares? he thought. Thanks, guys. I appreciate your timing.

Add on top of that the screeching and growling of the fish-people, their incoherent babbling in anger and pain and hunger as they tried to destroy the ship and everyone on board, and then on top of that the battle cries—and, Barnabas noted with a knot in his gut, the stoic sounds of pain—from the Amazon warriors, and the entire ship became a cacophony of distractions.

Still, he thought, I have a job to do. I'm going to do it. If it kills me. Which, judging from the way the giant monster was thrashing about, is probably what it's going to do.

He held the Eye of Dreams up above him in both hands,

aiming it toward the colossus. The sphere was warm to the touch, almost comforting. It felt like a living thing, which was not as comforting. And most alarmingly, it spoke to him.

He caught only bits and pieces at first, the Eye of Dreams speaking at first in a language he didn't understand, then bits and pieces of languages he could recognize but not understand, and then a language he did understand: the spoken form of the words of magic.

Command, it told him.

I'm trying, he thought. What do I command it to do?

Sleep, it said.

Yeah, see, I'm trying that, he thought.

Before he could make another attempt to control the sphere, a fish-man charged at him on the quarterdeck. Holding onto the sphere with one hand carefully, Barnabas blasted the creature with his flintlock, sending it spiraling off the deck. He heard another thump as behind him, Muireann cast some sort of sleep spell on another fish creature, leaving it drooling and unconscious on the floor.

"Sorry," she said.

Barnabas shot her a weak smile and placed both hands back on the sphere. He looked up at the giant monster again, and found his eyes drawn to its face. The thirteen eyes. No, he realized. Twelve now. Echo did some damage up there, he knew. That must be where she pierced its skull. It's just waiting to be rocked to sleep, he thought, if I can just figure out what I need to do next. The monster swung its arms around blindly, like a boxer in the dark.

He winced as he heard one of the Amazons cry out in what sounded like mortal agony from the deck below.

"What's wrong?" Muireann called out.

Barnabas bit back a sarcastic comment about his own incompetence and shook his head at her.

"I don't know," he said. "I can hear it speaking to me but I can't focus on what it's saying."

"Well, then," Muireann said, and she threw both arms out to

her sides.

The world went deathly quiet.

In an instant, every sound was gone. The fight all around them continued, both sides bloody and battered, but here, in this moment, Barnabas felt instantly isolated, as if underwater. And with that, the Eye called to him.

He held the Eye to his forehead, and his body went numb. No, not numb, not exactly. Detached. As if it were no longer his. The sphere was a new color now, no longer amber, but a deep, pale gold, the color of first light, or last. Barnabas held the Eye tighter and spoke not to the sphere, but to the monster itself.

"Your time has come to a close," he said, not in his native tongue but the language of magic. "Go back to your slumber, Star-Child. This world is not ready for you, and you are not ready for it. Go home and rest, or you will know what true oblivion feels like. Sleep again, so you may rise again. You were awoken too early. The end of the world is not today, nor tomorrow, and you will need your rest if you are to see that day when it arrives."

He said the words, but they were not uttered with his voice, Barnabas thought. Someone else's thoughts had intruded on his own. But it worked; the massive monstrosity stopped thrashing and grew calm, arms falling to its sides. Its now-twelve eyes blinked lazily, slowly, their gold and red glow growing dimmer.

The creature turned, a complete reversal of direction, and began to plod back into the ocean. Its movements were zombielike, sluggish, unrushed. Barnabas found himself thinking of a toddler who had been ordered to bed and went without question.

The water hissed and bubbled as the colossus sunk lower and lower beneath the waves. It passed within meters of the *Endless*, and Barnabas watched in curious horror as the fish-men, no longer interested in fighting, dove desperately into the ocean, chasing after their sleepy god.

The Eye of Dreams pulsed in Barnabas' hands like a heartbeat. He felt himself being drawn in as well, the temptation of eternal rest, of dreams that never ended, of a sleep as long as time far beneath the waves.

Muireann's circle of silence dropped, and reality came rushing back into Barnabas' ears and mind. The cries of the wounded, the splash of fish creatures diving into the ocean in a panic. Somewhere in the distance a bell buoy rang incessantly.

Barnabas stared into the Eye of Dreams. It still glowed with a warm light, but faded rapidly, its job done. He cradled the glasslike ball in one arm and leaned heavily on the ship's wheel, shaking off the feeling he'd been drawn somewhere else, an eerie sense that the Eye had wanted him to join the colossus beneath the waves.

"Did it work?" Muireann said. Barnabas lifted his head up from the wheel to saw the ondine, a gash on one shoulder but mostly unharmed, rocking exhaustedly on her feet.

He pointed across the waves to where the enormous titan had once stood. Bubbles burst and glimmered in the dark water, but it showed no sign of returning. Even its sycophants and parasites, the fish-men, seemed to have turned and fled, whether because they knew the battle was lost or simply to remain close to their silent god, Barnabas did not know.

"I think it went where the Eye told it to go," Barnabas said.

"Are you sure?" Muireann said. She put a hand on his shoulder, as much to steady herself as to support him.

"I don't know," he said. "But I sure as hell wanted to go and it wasn't even speaking to me. Whatever this thing is, it's hard to ignore."

"What do we do now?" Muireann said.

"Hope that thing doesn't come back," Barnabas said.

Chapter 56: Sharks, just falling from the sky

Simon and Clarissa made their way down out of the apartment building and started a hair-raising jaunt between buildings and cutting through alleyways to avoid detection. Fortunately, it seemed, most of the cultists had gathered along the main thoroughfare through the downtown, so it only took a block or two to get away from the bulk of the robed believers.

They paused behind a gas station to catch their breath and watch as a set of hooded figures, whom Clarissa said she swore owned the local yarn shop, walked by, chatting about how pleasantly warm it was despite the hint of rain.

"This whole town has lost its damned mind," Clarissa said. "Any luck reaching your boss?"

Simon risked a glance at his phone, trying to cover the light the screen gave off in case anyone happened by.

"Nothing," he said. "I mean I got through to the Department. They may be sending people. Or..."

"Or we're on our own," Clarissa said.

The longer the march of cultists went on, the more lights from what Simon suspected were non-cultists started to click on throughout the downtown area. He could see lights in windows, and at one point watched a heavyset man he'd seen around town but never spoken to stick most of his body out his second-floor window and throw his arms up in the universal motion for "huh?"

"Simon, we can't leave all the regular people behind," Clarissa said. "I know the smart thing is to run, but... like I have people in town who work for me. Kids. I can't just leave them to be, you know, eaten by fish-people."

"I'm not feeling so great about our escape either," Simon said. "But honestly, we're two people. What can we do?"

"Get the rest of the town on our side? It's not all townies here. Half the people who live here are recent transplants."

"You think we can organize a militia in twenty minutes?" Simon said. "This is a fancy catalogue shopping town, Clarissa. I don't see a lot of people rising up with makeshift weapons to defend themselves."

"You never know," Clarissa said.

"Actually, I do," Simon said. "I once saw an uprising in a town that had a vampire problem."

"Wait, what?" Clarissa said. "Did you just say vampire problem?"

"Whole town got wiped out," Simon said. "Man, what a nightmare. But that's what you get when you send a bunch of regular people up against the supernatural."

"Can we at least try the phone thing again?" Clarissa said. "Look, there's that... thing walking this way, that gigantic thing, Simon. Maybe if we warn everyone they can head out of town. We only saw a few cruisers. They can't stop everyone, right? Overwhelming odds."

"The cops could start shooting."

"I see a giant monster about to step on the entire town, dude," Clarissa said. "I think a couple of bullet wounds is a fair trade to get out of Dodge."

"You... would make a really good Department agent, you know that?"

"I am unsure if that's an insult or a compliment, but I'll just say thank you and hope you listen to reason, Simon."

Simon turned back toward town hall. Maybe, just maybe, if the cultists started moving their way to the beach as a group, they could get into the hall. It was a small town, not one with a huge budget for technology, so he had to believe the phone system was relatively simple. Of course, the older the phone system, in his experience, the less logical sense it made to a modern user. But still.

"Okay fine. You're right. We'll—"

Before Simon could finish speaking, both he and Clarissa found themselves doubled over by a staggering pain, Simon involuntarily covering his ears against a sharp, inhuman scream.

"What the hell is that?" Clarissa said as the sound subsided, only to nearly jump out of her skin as something fell out of the sky and crushed a parked sedan across the street.

Simon and Clarissa let loose a string of curse words both of them had successfully held in check until now, including several composite swears so shockingly grotesque Simon found himself impressed and appalled.

"What the hell is *that*?" Clarissa repeated, pointing at the massive beast crawling its way off the car. Bleeding and battered, it was a shark, literally a shark, but with arms and legs like an oversized human. It staggered to its knees, looked at them with jet-black eyes while clutching a wicked gash in its side from the car, and then flopped down on all fours. "Sharks! Just falling out of the sky!"

"It's raining man-sharks," Simon said. "They left this part out of every prediction about the apocalypse ever written. How did no one predict raining man-sharks?"

Simon pulled the gun he'd kept tucked in the back of his waistband and held it out in front of him, ready to shoot.

"You have a gun?" Clarissa said, her voice uncomfortably loud in the otherwise empty street.

"I have a gun," Simon said.

"You had a gun this whole time and you're only letting me know now?"

"What good was it against a million cultists, fish-men, and a walking island?"

"What good is it against a man-shark?" Clarissa said, her voice cracking.

"Guys," a new voice said. Simon and Clarissa whipped around to see the man-shark had transformed into just a man, a very beat up, dark-haired man with a thick build, an unimpressive goatee, and an unexpectedly kind, round face.

"What. The. Hell," Clarissa said.

"Don't move," Simon said.

"Please don't shoot me, dude," the man said, dabbing his hand at the gash in his side. Simon's heart skipped a beat in horror as he watched the wound seal up as if in fast-forward. "I'm here to save the day."

"You're what?" Simon said.

"Hi," the man said, sitting down properly and waving. Clarissa waved back automatically. "I'm Yuri. I'm…"

He waved a hand around vaguely. I think he's concussed, Simon thought. Can man-sharks get concussions?

"I'm a superhero? Sort of?" he said.

"You're a man-shark," Clarissa said.

"Actually, we prefer the term were-shark. Like werewolf, but with shark at the end," Yuri said. "And me and my friends are, like, trying to stop that thing out there."

Yuri pointed at the walking island off the coast.

"Are your friends all were-sharks?" Simon said.

"Nah, I'm the only one of those on this squad," Yuri said.

"That implies there are other were-sharks," Clarissa said.

"Yeah, there's a bunch—man, I feel like garbage. I think he threw me a mile, dude."

"That thing threw you?" Simon said.

"Yeah, after I bit the crap out his hand," Yuri said, smiling proudly. Simon determined the were-shark was definitely concussed by the goofy expression on his face. "But I guess it's up to my friends to finish the job."

"Your friends, the superheroes," Simon said.

"Yup," Yuri said.

And that was when the sky lit up.

A white light streaked across the sky, a glittering slash that cast a glow all the way up to the clouds and sent shards of light across the surface of the ocean. Yuri started to say "Wow, that looks like something out of an anime," but was cut off when another scream echoed through the town, this one worse than before. Simon forced himself to flip the safety on his gun and holster it quickly before covering his ears again. When he put his palms against his ears, though, the left one came away with a trickle of blood.

The creature, the moving island, shrouded in night's darkness, thrashed and cried out, weaving drunkenly on legs that no longer seemed to want to support it. A warm golden light, falling like spores from the sky, danced around the monster's head and shoulders, and the beast waved its arms as if trying to drive it away.

And then everything went quiet.

Simon watched in disbelief as the creature turned its back on the mainland. He dared not hope for the best, but then the monster slowly, deliberately, began walking away, staggering as if half asleep, its massive, bulky body disappearing beneath the waves. And what waves, he thought, watching the surface of the water as it churned like something out of a wildlife video of a feeding frenzy. He heard animalistic cries of panic, of fear, far off in the water. And within seconds, the great shape had become fully submerged, dipping beneath the black waters of the Atlantic.

"Simon," Clarissa said. "The cultists?"

"Come on," Simon said. He helped Yuri to his feet, Clarissa slipping an arm under Yuri's shoulder to help him stand. Together, the trio awkwardly half-ran, half-stumbled back downtown.

The streets were littered with cultists. Many lay catatonic on the pavement, staring up at the sky. Some wept openly. A few cursed and complained, muttering things about disappointing showings or never again in their lifetimes, better get the grandkids ready. Some started to head home. One, whom Simon immediately recognized as the school superintendent, locked eyes with him, then looked away as if ashamed.

"Were these people… waiting for that thing to get here?" Yuri asked.

"That is what we believe, based on empirical evidence," Simon said.

"This town is off its rocker, kid," Clarissa said.

"Huh," Yuri said. "Reminds me of the place I grew up."

"I'm sorry to hear that," Clarissa said.

"So, um, thanks for the assist," Yuri said. "But I really need to get back to my friends. Make sure they're not dead and all."

"Ordinarily, I'd try to get you to stay," Simon said. "But at this point?"

Yuri patted him on the shoulder and pointed down the street.

"Easiest way to the water is this way?" he said.

"We'll help you," Clarissa said.

"On one condition," Simon said.

"Seriously, dude?" Yuri said.

"Just… come back and tell me what this was all about, huh?" Simon said. "I'm going to have to explain all this to my boss."

"Your boss?" Yuri said.

"I'm an agent of the Department of What," Simon said.

"The Department of What?" Yuri said.

"That's what I said," Simon said.

"That didn't answer my question," Yuri said.

"I kind of have the feeling this is the start of a beautiful friendship," Clarissa said.

Chapter 57: There is always a bond, wanted or not

Artem thought he was drowning, and compared to the alternative, he felt this would be a better way to die.

His fall from the belly of the beast had knocked the wind out of him, a sloppy drop when his sword's grip on the monster's gut came lose. The sword was gone, lost in the plunge, and now, turned around and blinded by saltwater in his eyes, Artem struggled to figure out which way was up.

But he'd also plummeted into a sea full of cannibalistic fish-men, whose god he had just assaulted, and so he fully expected to be fighting for his life in the brine any second.

He drew the other sword, the one he'd sheathed before he fell, and swam one armed to the surface, waiting for the first bite to tear into his flesh.

It never came.

Instead, he watched as light flashed through the sky, another brutal burst of psychic energy washed over him, and the towering colossus turned tail to walk away. The creature's departure caused the water around him to swirl turbulently, but also, he realized, all the fish-folk, every single one, began a panicked, spastic swim to stay with their master, following him like parasites afraid to lose the source of their survival. Several bumped into Artem as they swam, and there was a terrifying moment when a swarm of them darted so close Artem could feel their slippery skin against his, but it was as if he were nothing more than a minor obstacle between them and their true goal. The fish-people left him largely ignored, disappearing, with eerie, plaintive cries, almost childlike in their sadness, into the night, afraid to be left behind.

Artem carefully slid his one remaining sword back into its sheath and scanned the horizon until he saw the *Endless*, so close he almost cried. He began an exhausted, clumsy swim toward the ship, weighed down by the breastplate he wore. For a moment, he thought about cutting the straps, but despite what he'd learned about the Amazons, regardless of what had happened to his father, this armor was the only thing he had from that place that was his, and he would not let it sink to the bottom of the ocean.

He laughed at himself, suddenly remembering the earring he wore that let him breathe underwater, and had a ridiculous image of himself trapped at the bottom of the sea, too heavy to swim, unable to drown.

He reached the ship and looked for a handhold, but found none. He thumped a fist against the hull, noticing new scratch marks and splintered areas where the fish-folk had done damage. Barnabas would be furious, he thought, chuckling at the idea, then wondering if the magician had survived the encounter at all.

He felt himself tiring, his limbs aching, and called up to the ship for help, hoping anyone were alive to lend a hand.

One lean, strong arm reached over the rail and, unthinking, Artem reached up to grab it.

He looked into his mother's eyes. And she looked half-dead herself.

A second Amazon, her right eye gummed shut with blood, also appeared then, and together, the women pulled Artem aboard. He fell to the deck, limbs shaky from the swim, from the fight, from everything. Orithyia knelt down beside him, a hand on the nasty gash on her side. The other Amazon, the one with the wounded eye, ignored Artem to instead unbuckle Orithyia's armor and examine the wound.

"We need to get you stitched up, general," the Amazon said.

"We need to get everyone stitched up," she said. "I can wait."

Artem looked across the deck. They'd traveled with seven Amazons, Orithyia included. None were uninjured. Three walked around to the others, tending their wounds. Two were on their backs, and Artem couldn't tell if they lived or not.

Muireann helped tend the wounded. She seemed to have some sort of healing touch, Artem noticed, seeing the tips of her fingers glow blue as she touched the injured. *Maybe she's simply dulling their pain.* He didn't understand magic and didn't care to, really. It was good to see the ondine still lived, though.

And at the bow of the ship, Barnabas Coy stood watch, hands as always in his pockets, staring out at the sea. *He's looking for the others,* Artem knew. There was a haunted look to the magician, though, and Artem wondered what cost using the Eye of Dreams had demanded from him. Barnabas glanced back and noticed Artem, a bright smile crossing his face. He started toward him, but Artem held up a hand, mouthing the words "Not yet."

Artem turned his attention to his mother.

"I think we won this war," Artem said.

"We did," Orithyia said. "I know it sounds stupid, but I'm proud of you. Of what you've become."

"I want to say that means nothing," Artem said. "But dammit, after everything, Mother, it does mean something. I'm glad you're still here."

"I'm happy we got to fight at least once alongside each other," Orithyia said. "It's a ludicrous thing for a mother to say, but there it is."

"It's what we do. We fight. We do what we think is right."

"You deserve a better life than you were given, Artem," Orithyia said.

He studied his mother's face, pale from blood loss, shadows beneath her eyes. But he saw in her so much of himself, his features, his personality, the things he defined himself by. He saw someone who was flawed, like he was, and who was many things he did not wish to be, and many others he knew he'd always strive for.

Artem took his mother's hand and leaned his head back against the railing of the *Endless*.

"I have lived the life I was meant for," he said. "And you should feel no regret in that."

Orithyia, general of the forces of New Scythia, warrior of the Amazons, put her head on her son's shoulder.

And they said nothing for a long time, thinking of the past, and of the future.

Chapter 58: The exit music to *Jaws*

Echo drifted in the sea.

She could see the *Endless*, saw the lanterns lit against the darkness, saw Barnabas watching from the bow. She watched as Artem was hauled on board and breathed a sigh of relief. She could almost make out the ghosts now, returning to their duties, their ship safe, as was this town, as was the world, for a little while.

She leaned against a stray piece of driftwood, one she assumed came from the wreckage of the Amazon vessel. Or maybe it was something else. There'd been so much carnage, after all. So much death and destruction.

I used to be a surfer, she thought, recalling the Zen-like peace of mind she felt riding the waves. I used to be a simple person. I thought I was boring, and I thought I was ordinary, and now, every day, I know I'd give almost anything to get that back. But I can never go home again. I know that now.

Is this the life ahead of me? She thought. One horrific thing after another, one war, one monster, one apocalypse, over and over again? Is this what heroes do?

She worried about Yuri, the only one she hadn't seen since the titanic creature had submerged itself back beneath the sea. His life was ruined too. To be a good person, to be a hero, there is a cost. I know that now. And because of that, I know why people refuse to be heroes. It's easier to ignore what's going on in the world. It's simpler to turn a blind eye.

If you fight, you lose. You always lose. Even when you win.

And so Echo rested there in the cool New England water, letting the surf lull her into a peaceful, meditative state, until she noticed bubbles begin to gurgle up beside her. She watched them, curious but not afraid, certain nothing that came up from the depths could hurt her any more than she'd already been hurt.

Then she saw the dorsal fin, the great silvery back, the gill slits, the terrifyingly comic toothy grin of a were-shark staring at her. She laughed, and watched as Yuri let himself transform back into his human face, shirtless and more than a little beat up. He doggie-paddled over to rest on the same bit of driftwood Echo was holding onto and rested his chin on his arms.

"Hey," he said.

"Hey, you," she answered.

"Y'know, I came back to find you and we jumped right into saving the world," he said.

"I know. That sucked," she said. She looked at her friend, with his never-quite-right beard, looking especially baby-faced without his glasses. Her best friend. "I missed you, kid."

"I missed you too," Yuri said.

"Thanks for coming back," Echo said.

"Hey," he said, tapping the leather wrist cuff he wore. "This thing. It always points to you. It always will."

"Are you going to leave again, now that we've saved the world?"

"I'd rather not," he said. "I should go find Whitetip at some point. My teacher. And thank him. Make sure he's okay. But you should come with me. I'd like you to meet him."

"That'd be nice," Echo said. "I mean, I brought you to Atlantis. The least you can do is introduce me to a were-shark buddy or two."

"I'll set something up," Yuri said. "We'll have a potluck night."

They treaded water in silence for a few minutes, taking in the quiet, the strange stillness of the night, and more than anything, the way the ocean no longer scared them.

"So, this is our job now," Yuri said. "We're superheroes."

"I hate it," Echo said.

"I love it," Yuri said.

"Can I steal some of your enthusiasm?" Echo said.

"As much as you need," Yuri said. "Sidebar, I met a guy, he's an agent of something or other, might need to talk to him about what just happened.

"You were gone like five minutes. When did you have time to meet an agent?"

"You don't know me."

"I know you better than anyone, Yuri Rodriguez," Echo said.

"True," he said. "Should we paddle for the boat?"

"I guess," Echo said.

"Can I hum the exit music to *Jaws* while we do?" Yuri said.

"Whatever you need to do," Echo said. "I just want to go home."

Chapter 59: Balancing a scale

"We need to get the Amazons medical attention," Echo said, pulling Barnabas aside on the quarterdeck. The sun was just beginning to rise, turning the foggy skies pink and hazy. "How fast can we get them home to New Scythia using the faerie paths?"

"Fast enough," Barnabas said, reading doubt in Echo's expression. "Trust me. We'll get them home."

"We can't bring them to the mainland for help. If the authorities get even a whiff of what any of us are, they'll never let us go."

"A ship full of beings who aren't supposed to exist? I can't imagine why they'd stop us from leaving," Barnabas said. He called out a few orders to the ghosts around them, who, their home now safe from invasion, leapt into action, preparing the *Endless* to set sail.

"Guys," Yuri yelled, standing in some sort of oversized bathrobe he'd found in the hold and standing on the prow. "We have company."

Another vessel appeared out of the mists, one they'd seen before. It was battered and filthy now, with blackish grime marring its once pristine white hull, but Barnabas recognized it immediately.

"I hate necromancers," he said, rushing to the bow with Echo.

Muireann, seeing the new arrival as well, dashed to their side. "No," she said. "Not now."

Artem limped up to join them as well, leaving his mother resting under a blanket on the deck behind him with her warriors. "And here I thought the fight was over," he said.

"We can't fight him right now," Echo said. "We're a hot mess, and I don't know how much time some of the injured Amazons have left. We can't waste time in a fight with this idiot."

Something caught Barnabas' eye on the other ship's deck that caused a twist in his stomach.

"His crew is dead," Barnabas said.

"What?" Echo said.

"Oh gods," Muireann said. "They're all... he's raised his crew from the dead. Look."

"I can see them," Barnabas said, watching as different sailors shambled around, their bodies hunched and grotesque, an echo of the humanity they once possessed, shells of the living.

"They were alive when we left them," Echo said.

"I swear I didn't kill any of them when I jumped on his ship last time," Yuri said. "I just scared them a bit. Guys, those were not sailors who were used to fighting people like us."

"Looks like he wanted a ghost ship of his own," Artem said.

"And now he has one," Barnabas said.

Muireann put a hand on Barnabas' shoulder.

"Leave me," she said. "I'll deal with him. Just leave me and take these Amazons home. This is my mess. My problem. Let me handle the consequences."

"Let's see what he wants," Barnabas said. Muireann stared into his eyes, searching, as if she assumed he was up to something. Safe assumption, Barnabas thought. He stepped forward, in front of his crew, and called over.

"Hey there! Come to parlay?" Barnabas yelled.

Tessier stood on his own deck boldly, unarmed, surrounded by the walking dead that once was his crew. He looked worse for wear now, bags under his eyes, skin sallow. He looked angry, but also afraid. He's already sold that piece of himself, Barnabas knew. He's afraid of what happens when you fail to pay up in a deal like that. Which means either he's in no position to bargain, or he's willing to die to get what he wants. And necromancers are notoriously hard to kill.

Barnabas let the two ships get so close they no longer needed to yell. Close enough he could smell the decay on the yacht.

"Looks like you've seen better days," Tessier said.

"You too," Barnabas said. "Feeling okay?"

Tessier shrugged.

"I'm feeling rather immortal, actually," he said. "I see you have my little friend with you."

"Go to hell, Anson," Muireann said.

"Planning on setting up a summer home there," the necromancer said. "Care to join me?"

Muireann fumed beside Barnabas, but said nothing.

"Look, I can see you've got a boat full of wounded," Tessier said. "I'm not an ungenerous man. Just give me what belongs to me and I'll be on my way. Hell, you can keep the ondine. I just want what she stole from me."

"How bloody generous of you," Muireann said. "Like I'm something to be traded."

"We could see how you do in a fight against a ship full of warriors," Artem said.

Tessier laughed.

"Oh, I like you. One on one I wouldn't like my odds against you, whatever you are," Tessier said. "But you've done me a tremendous favor. I see corpses floating everywhere in these waters. I can't tell what those corpses are from, honestly—ugly little things, aren't they? But any corpse will do in my line of work. You won't just be fighting me. I'll raise every single one of these pale, bloated things to climb aboard your ship and do you immeasurable harm until I get what I want. I'm more than willing to go to war this very moment, my friends."

"Can he do that?" Echo said out of the corner of her mouth.

"Yes," both Barnabas and Muireann said simultaneously.

"I hate magic," Echo said.

"It's over," Muireann said, dejected. "I appreciate that you're willing to fight for me. I really do. But I can't ask you to save me after you just saved... everyone else. This isn't a fight you can win. It's okay. I know I brought this on myself."

"I have a better solution," Barnabas said, and he pulled the sphere containing Tessier's life force from his pocket.

"You bastard," Muireann said. "When did you steal that? Give it to me."

"Like I said, I have a better idea," Barnabas said, and with an underhanded lob, he tossed the sphere to Tessier, who lazily stretched out an arm and, with a simple spell, drew the sphere to him.

"No!" Muireann said. She grabbed Barnabas' arm with both hands, digging her nails into his skin hard enough he felt it through his coat. "That was not your choice to make! You've doomed me! Do you know what you've done?"

"I know exactly what I've done," Barnabas said.

"This better be some sleight of hand stuff, Barnabas, or I will throw you off this gods-damned boat myself," Artem said.

Tessier inspected the sphere, which went from pale white to a sickly green in his grasp. This seemed to satisfy the necromancer, who smiled, held the globe up like an apple in his fingers, and nodded politely to Barnabas.

"See, that wasn't so bad," Tessier said. "And here I'd heard that the infamous Barnabas Coy was a fool without honor. I'll tell tale of your fairness in the circles of magic, Coy."

"That thing wasn't worth the price she was going to pay for it anyway," Barnabas said. "You corrupted it long before you pulled that piece of you out of yourself."

"Power does corrupt," Tessier said. He pocketed the shard of himself, smirked a little, then laughed. "I honestly thought you were going to put up a fight."

"In another situation, we might have," Barnabas said. "But I had some time to figure out a better option."

"Barnabas, you knew I don't have much time left. I needed that life force. You've killed me," Muireann said. "You should have just let him do it. It would have been less cruel."

"Barnabas," Echo said. "What are you up to?"

Rather than answering, Barnabas reached into his pocket and felt for a cool, round object within. He withdrew the item and held it in his palm, presenting it to Muireann. It was smaller than the sphere he'd thrown to Tessier, but glowed with a similar light, though purplish blue rather than sickly green, brighter and warmer, with little flaws of lavender coursing through it like veins.

He handed it to Muireann, and felt his skin grow cold. He saw the flesh of his hand go pale, almost silvery, as the ondine accepted it, taking the globe in her thin fingers.

"What's wrong with your face?" Yuri said. "You just turned two shades paler. Are you going to throw up?"

Barnabas let out a little laugh, a bit breathless, but kept his eyes on Muireann as she studied the egg-sized sphere he'd handed her.

"Is this what I think it is?" she said.

"What did you do, Barnabas?" Echo said, an edge of fear in her tone.

"Nothing bad," he said. Muireann looked up from the sphere to study his face, and the magician smiled. "You need this, and I wasn't using it anyway. So… it's yours."

"This is a piece of your life," Muireann said, her voice barely audible over the sound of the sea crashing against the side of the ship.

"Just a piece. Freely given," Barnabas said. "I had time to learn a bit about this. You don't need as much if it's freely given. Because it means more. Magic is funny that way. All full of meaning."

"You didn't have to do this," Muireann said.

"And what, let you use a filthy sliver of soul from that guy to stay alive?" Barnabas said. He stole a quick glance at Tessier, who watched from his ship with an unexpected respectfulness. "I mean, my life isn't perfect, but it's better than that. I'm not all evil, after all. Just a little bit evil."

"Will that work?" Echo said. "I seriously, seriously hate magic. None of this makes any sense. Are you going to die instead now?"

Muireann shook her head.

"Just enough," she said. "What does this mean for you, though?"

"And why are you slightly blue?" Yuri said.

"I'm as much nereid as human," Barnabas said. "This is a bit of my humanity, to help keep you here, in the mortal realm. But our life force doesn't want to be empty. It abhors a vacuum. And so that other part of me just filled in the gaps."

"Like water," Muireann said.

"Funny how that works," Barnabas said.

"Did it hurt?" Muireann said.

"Like hell," Barnabas said. "But it's okay. Magic always has a cost. A little pain is nothing compared to fading away."

Muireann held the globe near her heart and looked to Barnabas, and then to the others, her face an explosion of emotions, terror and sadness, joy and relief.

"Go on," Barnabas said. "Given freely. Do what you need to do."

She nodded, almost shyly, then pressed the glass globe to her heart. It faded away, the light bleeding into her, her veins lighting from within. Barnabas wondered if the others had noticed it before—the way Muireann did not seem complete, the way there were cracks in the energy of her life, the fact that she was, slowly but relentlessly, coming apart at the seams. All of that went away now, the final stitching she needed, the last piece to cementing her stay here in our world, he thought.

As she absorbed the shard of soul, Barnabas felt a rending pain deep in his chest, a part of him gone, forever. Just a small piece. He'd never felt anything like it, but he said nothing.

Magic always has a cost. It's just a matter of whether you're willing to bear that cost or not.

"Every time I think I know you, you surprise me," Artem said, and Barnabas felt the Amazon slide an arm under his to steady him. *Of course Artem could sense I was about to fall over,* Barnabas thought. *The man reads body language like a psychic.* He was grateful for it, though, his legs wobbling beneath him. Muireann took his free hand in both of hers, saying nothing, just studying his face.

"Why?" she said.

"Balancing a scale," Barnabas said. "One foolish decision at a time."

"Well," Tessier shouted, his ship beginning to drift away. "This is charming and heartwarming, but I have a business transaction to make. Thank you for the entertainment, Coy. Enjoy your continued existence, Muireann. Maybe this means you'll stop stealing souls from people for a while, huh? Pinocchio is a real girl now or something. Ta."

Once the necromancer's ship was out of earshot, disappearing in the morning fog, Barnabas let himself lean more heavily on Artem.

"For the record," he said, his head spinning. "I'm going to kill that man if it's the last thing I do."

"I'm glad you said it first," Muireann said.

Barnabas and Echo made eye contact. She shook her head.

"If you ever start making sense to me, I'll know I've finally lost it," she said. "Now let's get these people home."

Chapter 60: Birthplace

The journey back to New Scythia was quiet and without incident. Barnabas guided them through faerie paths Echo didn't recognize, once passing through a strait lined with bright vegetation on either side, but mostly it was deep blue sea and iron gray skies. Speed was the priority, and Echo and her crew did their best to comfort the injured. Muireann knew an enchanted song that dulled pain, which she sang often. It sounded like an old Irish folk song Echo's grandmother used to play on a vinyl record until it skipped.

They were met at the docks by an honor guard of Amazon warriors, a cadre of Keepers of Athena, and both Marpesia and Lampedo. They seemed already aware of what had transpired—certainly they were aware of the *Endless* arriving in their waters, whether through scouts or magical means Echo couldn't tell, but in either case, medical care awaited on the docks as well. The injured warriors were carted off quickly, disappearing before Echo could thank them for their courage.

Artem's mother was last to leave, refusing, despite the brutal injury she did her best to mask. She grasped her son's hand tightly before leaving the ship. He seemed hesitant, almost ready to pull away, but Artem did something shocking—he leaned in and kissed Orithyia on the forehead before releasing her hand so Amazonian medics could take her away to be treated. Once the injured were cared for, Echo headed for the gangplank, watching to see if Artem would follow. He hung back, so she approached him.

"You coming with?" she said.

"I can never set foot on this island again," Artem said, his voice like stone.

"Is this because of something your mother told you?" Echo asked.

Artem said nothing, but a quickly raised eyebrow let her know the answer to that.

"What did she say?" Echo said. "Was it here? Just now?"

"Back on the other ship, before the final battle," Artem said. "She… she told me the worst thing you can tell anyone, Echo. She told me the truth. And she told me an origin story. Not the myth. The real one. And origin stories… well, you have one yourself. You know they are unkind things."

"But we come out better at the end," Echo said. "Heroes get origin stories."

"And villains," Artem said. He looked out across New Scythia, this place where he was born but never wanted him, and Echo was surprised to see his eyes well up with tears.

"It's a funny thing," he said, his voice soft, strangely tender. "I never thought I'd come back here. And when I was very small, when I first went to the Island of Unwanted Things, all I ever wanted was to come home. Because this was home. My mother was home, and the walls of that castle were home, and these docks, and the beautiful green fields behind the city they wouldn't let you see when we arrived. I wanted to come home and thought I never could."

Artem took a deep breath, as if he knew he was breathing in the last taste of his birthplace he'd ever experience.

"But then I got angry, and I decided I never wanted to come back," he said. "To hell with this place that didn't want me. I didn't want it either. I had no intention of ever returning, not once I was grown, not once I knew my worth. But I came back anyway. And they let me in, and those memories came flooding back, but now I know things and…"

Echo grabbed Artem's hand, half-expecting him to pull away. But he didn't, so she gripped that sword-roughened hand like he might float away.

"I can't come back here. It's too dangerous. That's what my mother did. She gave me a reason to know I can't ever return," he said. "I don't know if it was a warning or if it was just a trick to keep me away."

"I'm sorry I asked you to come back here," Echo said.

"Had to be done," Artem said, wiping his eyes irritably. "It's what we always do, right? The hard thing. We do what must be done. But you should go. Tell them what happened. Let them know who saved this world. And then we can sail away and never look back."

Echo nodded and made her way down to the docks, approaching the queens where they stood side by side, speaking with Clio, the Keeper of Athena. She sensed someone fall in line behind her. Barnabas, to her right. Yuri as well, but he hung back, his discomfort radiating off him like a fever.

"It's done then," Marpesia said, favoring Echo with a brilliant smile.

"It is," Echo said. "Your warriors fought bravely. I'm sorry for what they went through."

"That's what they were born to do," Lampedo said.

"And sorry about your ship," Echo said. "That was unavoidable."

Marpesia waved her off.

"There can always be more ships. You brought all of our daughters home," she said.

"You found the Needle and the Eye," Clio interrupted. "What will you do with them?"

"You're asking if we'll leave them here," Barnabas said. The Keeper shot the magician a wretched look of annoyance.

"Well, the Needle's gone," Echo said. "I left that embedded like

329

a railroad spike in the monster's skull. I don't know how we'd get that back."

"Probably where it belongs," Clio said. "The last champions who stopped this creature were unable to recover it as well. The Eye should be kept somewhere safe, though. No, I was not asking if you'd leave it here. I just want to make sure our records indicate where it can be found, should the need ever arise again."

"I really don't want to go back to the city of the yacuruna," Echo said. "I mean, they did a fine job keeping it safe, but it felt like a burden to them, and they've gone through so much."

"A new hiding place, then," Marpesia said.

"I have a suggestion," Barnabas said.

"In your possession is not an option," Clio said.

"I wasn't going to suggest that," Barnabas said. "Do you know the name Galatea?"

"The nymph," Clio said. "A soothsayer."

"Nereid," Barnabas said. "Who better to hold the Eye of Dreams than someone who is safely hidden away and can see the future?"

Clio nodded her head appreciatively, then frowned.

"We don't know where she's gone, though, or if she still exists."

"She exists," Barnabas said. "She's my mom."

"Oh," Clio said, clearly shocked.

Marpesia burst out laughing.

"You keep interesting company, Echo of Atlantis," the queen said. "I trust you'll get it to this nereid safely?"

"Of course," Echo said. "Thank you for your help in all this."

Marpesia looked to her sister, then bowed her head respectfully to Echo.

"I see Orithyia's son has not joined you," Marpesia said.

"He's not comfortable returning to the island. I'm sure there's a reason," Echo said.

Lampeto shook her head at her sister, but the elder queen ignored her, removing a sword from her belt, a short blade like a gladius. She handed it to Echo, sheath and all.

"Please give him this. From me," Marpesia said, again exchanging a strangely strained look with her sister. "And tell him thanks. We wish him well, wherever your journeys take you."

Echo accepted the sword and bowed her head in return.

"I will," she said, leaving this island to its mysteries and intrigues. She'd had enough of New Scythia and its secrets.

Chapter 61: Songs on the water

Muireann had never been there before, but she recognized the island they traveled to next immediately. She could hear the songs of mermaids in the distance. A hidden place full of hidden people. Perhaps, in another lifetime, she might have found herself taking shelter in a place like this herself.

But fate had handed her a different path. No, she thought, I walked right off my path. I demanded something different.

And look all the trouble that caused.

She had avoided Barnabas through most of the journey, a difficult thing on a small vessel. He seemed to understand, though, subtly moving out of her space when necessary, or staying in places easier to avoid when he could.

Once they arrived at the island, he casually asked if she'd like to go with him to see Galatea, his mother, to deliver the Eye of Dreams. Muireann politely declined. The idea of seeing other beings like her, nereids and nymphs, mermaids and sirens, hidden away in a paradise that was as much prison as home made her anxious and afraid. She didn't want to envision the life she might have otherwise had.

Barnabas and Echo went to the island together, leaving the rest behind. Artem wasn't much for conversation, but Yuri approached her on the deck as she watched mermaids splash in the distance.

"They almost killed me last time we were here," Yuri said, pointing at the mermaids.

"They have a tendency to do that," Muireann said. "That's the fate forced on them. Like how I was forced to steal souls. The gods have a terrible tendency to give women awful fates like that."

"I wasn't a were-shark then," Yuri said. "Just a dude, in a bad situation, trying not to get killed. And their songs lured me overboard. All things considered, it wouldn't have been a terrible way to go."

"Oh, it would have been a terrible way to go," Muireann said, but then smiled at Yuri. "Not many men can say they survived a mermaid's call."

"You're free now, right?" Yuri said. "From whatever horrible rules you were stuck with?"

"As free as anyone ever is," Muireann said.

"What will you do?"

Muireann shrugged. In the distance, she could see Echo and Barnabas rowing their way back, arguing over something.

"I don't know," Muireann said. "That's the funny thing about not being locked into a destiny, isn't it? You don't have anywhere you have to go anymore, so you just… keep moving."

"Better than being locked in a box, right?"

"Yeah," Muireann said.

"Well," Yuri said, brushing invisible dirt from his pants. "We're always moving. You could stick with us."

"Maybe I will," Muireann said. Yuri grinned at her and walked away, leaving her to her solitude.

She listened to the song of the mermaids on the water, echoing and rolling like waves. She joined in, knowing the words, the secret language of the sisters of the sea, and felt her heart break, just a little bit.

My heart breaks, because I am free, she thought. And for the first time, I don't know who I'm supposed to be.

Chapter 62: Atlantis

Echo didn't insist on her entire crew accompanying her home, but, whether it was out of boredom or solidarity, they did, even Artem, though the Amazon said little as they made their way through the streets of Atlantis to the royal castle. They met with Grimmin, of course, while Echo avoided her relatives with deliberate care. Her aunt she wanted nothing to do with, but her father she couldn't avoid entirely, and ended up with a stilted, if friendly, conversation with him in the hallway, too many people around for them to have an open discussion.

"I need a secret entrance," Echo told Grimmin when they were finally relatively alone so she could tell him how things went down.

"Princess, you are speaking to a veteran spymaster. If you want a secret entrance to the palace, you need only ask. We have several," Grimmin said.

"You're not joking," Echo said.

Grimmin shook his head.

"Shall I show you to one you can use?"

"Maybe next time," Echo said, though the idea certainly had appeal. She ran down the events at Fogarty's Folly, and before that, leaving out what she thought the Atlantean spymaster wouldn't need.

"Will you be staying?" Grimmin said. "I'm sure your aunt would love to chat with you over dinner."

"You missed a career in comedy," Echo said.

"That was my second choice," Grimmin said.

"But no, we should get back to the surface. It's been an adventure," Echo said

"Of course. Just let me know if you need any supplies for your vessel and you'll have them."

They parted company, and Echo stepped out into the halls of the palace, finding her friends scattered and taking in the sights. She located Barnabas near a large window overlooking the city, its gold and silver lights glimmering below like a sea of gems.

"So, what do you get out of giving a piece of your soul away?" Echo asked, smirking crookedly.

"Can't a good deed just be a good deed?" Barnabas asked, looking vaguely offended.

"It can, but that felt like a tremendous leap of faith, especially for you," Echo said.

"You wound me, Echo," Barnabas said.

"You are full of crap, wizard. Spill it."

Barnabas looked around to see if anyone else was listening, then rolled his eyes.

"I don't know if there's any benefit," he said. "Maybe there is. My mom's an immortal fairy creature, so who knows. But what I do know is that the world would've been poorer for not having Muireann in it, and all it cost me was a little bit of pain, so I did it."

"I still think you have an ulterior motive."

"And that's your prerogative."

"You earned this reputation."

"I know."

They stood side by side wordlessly for a few moments, watching the glittering city below.

"So where do we go from here?" Echo asked.

"I don't know," Barnabas said. "We do have a ship. We could go anywhere."

"I feel like that should be freeing," Echo said.

"Just sort of makes figuring things out harder, doesn't it?"

"Sure does."

"Could stay here a while," Barnabas offered. "Get you up to speed on Atlantean politics."

"To hell with that idea," Echo said. "I don't care we go, but we set sail right now."

Chapter 63: The Department of What, When, Where, Why, and Who

Simon Yee had to admit, having the were-shark make good on his word was a bit of a shock.

Sitting around a table at Ishmael's with that were-shark and four of his friends was a much larger shock. The fact that one of them could best be described as a bald Jack Sparrow cosplayer would have been the most shocking of all if Simon weren't well-aware of the fact that the friendly-faced kid across from him could transform into a giant man-shark.

"So, let me get this straight. You work for the Department of what?" Yuri said, sipping on a frozen coffee drink with whipped cream on top.

"The Department of What," Simon said for roughly the seventh time.

"That's what I said," Yuri said.

"That's its name. The Department of What," Simon said.

"You only handle what? What about when, where, why, and who?" Yuri said.

"We handle those too," Simon said. "I can see why you're in charge."

"He's not in charge," the girl who introduced herself as Echo said. They'd given him a thumbnail of their capabilities without giving much away, but she'd already piqued Simon's curiosity—an unsolved case involving a young woman about her age with the same unusual first name had caught his attention in the files from this area when he'd taken this assignment. Simon made a mental note to follow up on that.

"You are, clearly," Simon said. Just past Echo's shoulder, Simon caught Clarissa staring at him in horror, pointing frantically at the guy in the pirate costume.

"Sort of," Echo said. She'd related most clearly the events of the night of the attack, admirably vague about the cause and the resolution, but enough for Simon to work with. He'd have to write something up about this, and he told them as much.

"But you can leave us out of it, right?" Yuri said, hopefully

"Well as of right now, I only have two of your first names, and that guy hasn't even said anything to me," Simon said, pointing to the guy who looked like a cross between a mixed martial arts fighter and a supermodel. "But I'm telling you the truth. We track weird phenomena. The best thing you can do is give me some reason to believe it won't happen again."

Life in Fogarty's Folly had taken a bizarre turn for the normal after the night the giant monster appeared in the ocean. The cultists went back to their everyday lives, and Simon went into full-on investigator mode watching them for signs of another event. Mostly they seemed ashamed, disappointed, even depressed, but otherwise, exactly as they were just days ago. Mass hysteria, mass hallucination, mob mentality, whatever it was, it faded. There were some missing folks, of course, maybe a dozen in total who never went home that night. Some, Simon suspected, were eaten like the priest, but comically there were signs that at least two of them up and bailed on their entire lives in Fogarty's Folly, leaving with bags packed for less wacky climes. Simon couldn't blame them. Sometimes you get caught up with weirdos and the only thing you could do was hit the reset button.

And now here were these oddballs. They all bore battle scars, the sort of bruises and scratches that said they came by their injuries hard. The silent one and the other young woman—with long, jet-black hair that contrasted with Echo's sea-foam green undercut out of shear normalcy—studied the town curiously eyeing everyone who walked by, staring too long at cars as they idled. The pirate had his leg kicked out casually, Han Solo style, and feigned a boredom that masked the intensity with which he followed the conversation.

"Why this town?" Simon said. "That's what I'm wondering. The cultists, the monster… this is such an insular, boring town. I don't understand how this happened."

"I grew up in a town just like this," Yuri said. "Echo, too. Little towns, man. It's where the weirdest stuff happens. People get really strange in little towns."

"Maybe I should move," Simon said.

"Really? I was just thinking we could set up shop here," Yuri said.

"No," all his companions said in unison.

"Okay then, I can see I've been outvoted," he said.

"What will you say in your report, Agent Yee?" the pirate said.

"That there was a supernatural event, possibly impacted by an existing cult here in town," he answered. "A group of unique individuals intervened. The event was stopped. And things went back to normal."

That seemed to satisfy the costumed man, though he still watched Simon with disconcerting, half-closed eyes.

"Well, ah, listen," Simon said. "If you ever run into trouble here on the mainland? Just ask for me. I'll do what I can to help."

"We won't run into trouble," Echo said. "But I appreciate the offer."

"All we do is run into trouble," Yuri said.

"We're quitting trouble and going on vacation," Echo said.

"Like that will ever work," the silent man, finally speaking, said with a sharp laugh.

As if planned, they all stood up together as one—except Yuri, who struggled to jump to his feet alongside his friends. Echo gave Simon a polite nod.

"We're trying to keep a low profile," she said, looking dejectedly at several patrons staring at the pirate guy. "But if you run into trouble… we're around. It's unfortunately become our thing. Saving the world."

"Good to know," Simon said. They shook hands. "Take care, Echo."

"You too, Agent Yee," she said, and they walked away, heading for the docks.

Clarissa scooted up behind him, eyes wide.

"What. The hell. Was that?" she said.

"Something else I'm going to have to talk to my boss about," Simon said. "I have a feeling I'm going to be stationed here for a while."

"That's unfortunate," Clarissa said. "Want to open an Ishmael's Coffee rewards card?"

"No," Simon said.

"You get a free coffee every ten purchases," she said. "It's a bargain."

"Actually, I was wondering if you wanted a job," Simon said.

"I have a job. Managing this dump," she said.

"How would you like to come work for the Department?" Simon said.

Clarissa stared at him with a blank expression.

"What?" Simon said. "You handled yourself really well out there. You have a natural curiosity about the weird. I think you'd make a great agent."

"I'll think about it," she said.

"It's gotta beat this gig," Simon said.

"Don't knock it," Clarissa said. "Ishmael's has a great benefits package."

Simon finished his coffee, eyeing yet another town figure, a selectman, Simon knew he saw in a robe the other night. Yeah, he thought. This is going to get weirder before it gets better.

"Give it some thought," he said. "I have a bad feeling I'm going to need a lot of help."

Epilogue: The bargain

Anson Tessier arrived by private car at a small, private club in London. He wore a new suit, perfectly tailored, black with a shirt the color of blood. He'd recovered from his unnecessary time at sea, even had a chance to enjoy the results of it all. It had been a hassle, but he got what he went looking for, and, in the end, nothing had changed.

He had his bargaining chip, and now, he had a bargain to make.

The club had a door at street level, a heavy black door with eye slits that slammed open loudly. The bouncer on the other side of the door did not look remotely human, with green, pebbled skin and bright yellow eyes that peered out at Tessier as though assessing not just his worthiness to enter, but his worthiness to exist at all. The slot slammed shut again and the door opened, but when Tessier entered, the bouncer could not be seen.

Inside, he found a landing and stairs leading down. He began the descent. The stairs started off as black and white checkered linoleum, but as he reached a second landing, they turned to blackened stone, shining like onyx.

He descended further, where the stairs began to spiral rather than follow a straight line. Finally, perhaps two hundred steps later, he reached the bottom.

The building looked like an old mausoleum. Everything had a touch of Romanesque architecture to it, with beautiful columns and arches. But it had an alien feel as well, angles that didn't feel right, turns that twisted his stomach. He meandered, not seeing another being, living or otherwise, until the familiar sight of Lady Natasha Grey sat waiting for him in a red velvet chair.

"You're late," she said, rising to her feet. She wore an elegant dress of a material that evoked metal chainmail, her fair hair cut into a bob, her eyes, as always, devoid of irises and filled with flames.

"There was a complication," he said.

"I heard about your little complication," the Lady Grey said. She gestured for Tessier to follow. "I personally don't care, but your trading partner is on a schedule and does not like delays."

"Will this impact the terms of the agreement?" Tessier asked.

"You know it will," Natasha said. "I was able to buy you a little extra time, Tessier, but you know how exacting these beings are. They're all about rules and contracts. You did not live up to your end of the bargain. A week late? There are late fees for these things. They're right there in the contract."

Tessier clenched his fists, trying not to shake with rage.

"What are the exact costs?" he said.

The Lady Grey stopped in front of a featureless door of gray stone. She folded her arms across her chest and motioned to the door with her chin.

"I did you a favor, Tessier. Remember this," she said. "You'll have a chance to negotiate the terms of the contract in light of your missing the deadline. But as you were not here to broker the deal, I have simply set up a chance for you to sit down with the client face to face and figure out what that asking price should be."

"He's in there," Tessier said, his throat tightening. "Right now."

"Don't be afraid," Natasha said. "Actually, yes. Definitely be afraid. But don't let him see it. They sense fear and use it as a bargaining tool. One must put on a brave face."

"Of course," Tessier thought.

His mind darted to Muireann, and to Barnabas Coy, that smug charlatan, and the were-shark who terrified his crew and the rest of that band of fools who cost him so much. I will destroy them, he thought, placing a hand on the stone door, attempting to calm his nerves. So help me, if I live through this, I will make their lives hell.

Anson Tessier opened the stone door and was met by a soft gust of air, hot and stale with a hint of sulfur. He took a deep breath, stood tall, and entered, revenge replacing fear in his heart.

Also by Matthew Phillion

Novels in the Indestructibles Series – in print and e-book formats

The Indestructibles (Book 1)
The Indestructibles: Breakout (Book 2)
The Entropy of Everything (the Indestructibles Book 3)
Like a Comet (the Indestructibles Book 4)

Tales from the Indestructiverse

Echo and the Sea
Poseidon's Scar

The Indestructibles One-Shots (digital shorts)

The Soloist
Gifted
Blood & Bone
The Monsters We Make
Krampus in the City
Roll for Initiative (an Indestructibles Story) – also available in print

The Dungeon Crawlers Novella Series

The Player's Guide to Dungeon Crawling (The Dungeon Crawlers Book 1)
The Dungeoneer's Bestiary (The Dungeon Crawlers Book 2)
The Ghoul Slayer's Guidebook (The Dungeon Crawlers Book 3)

ABOUT THE AUTHOR

Matthew Phillion is a writer, actor, and film director based in Salem, Massachusetts. He is the author of the Indestructibles YA superhero novel series, the spinoff Echo and the Sea, and the Dungeon Crawlers series of novellas. A recovering journalist, Phillion has written about healthcare, cybersecurity, mental health, pop culture, and more. He can usually be found in the company of his sidekick, Watson the Wonder Dog, or acting as manservant to his belligerent cat Harley.